HEART OF CONSTANTINE

Barbara Monajem

Barbara Monajem

Text copyright © 2013 Barbara Monajem
All rights reserved.

Printed in the United States of America.

Published by Thomas & Mercer, Seattle

www.apub.com

ISBN-13: 9781477834770
ISBN-10: 147783477X

To all birds everywhere—even ostriches, of which there are none in this book. If I'd thought about it earlier, there would have been.

Spirit guide: An intangible life-form charged with guiding a human being. Guides may remain in spirit form or take temporary possession of living creatures—most commonly, birds. Spirit guides have their work cut out for them, as human beings are notoriously unwilling to listen to advice.

– D. Tull, *Encyclopedia of Not-So-Mythical Beings*

CHAPTER ONE

Constantine Dufray stood, brushing pine straw off his jeans, and told his pesky spirit guide to take a hike. The guide took possession of an owl and flapped away to a bald cypress by the bayou. Constantine sucked in the moist dawn air at the top of the Indian mound, where he'd spent the night trying to center himself. He doubted the spirit's choice of vehicle had anything to do with the last shreds of darkness. Being a bird of ill omen was just its damnable sense of humor. Although no one had died at Constantine's impromptu midnight concert, the night was not quite over.

Look on the bright side, the spirit said from its distant perch. *You didn't annihilate that fan. You didn't even snarl at him.*

Fine, but it didn't mean he'd succeeded in controlling the powers of his mind. After the tightly built, dark-haired youth at the front of the crowd had gawped at Constantine for a full hour, giving him a knot in the solar plexus and a tingling in his arms that made him long to strangle or punch or . . . Instead, he'd given the guy his guitar.

So what? Everybody gave away guitars. The ecstasy on the guy's face had made Constantine want to puke, which was annoying since he'd thought himself long past caring one way or the other about hero worship, but that wasn't the issue. Something about the young man's eyes, maybe, or his stance, had given Constantine a sensation of worms crawling through his gut, awakening the anger that always nested inside him.

But he'd mastered resisting the urge to smash through the worship with terrifying thoughts. If Constantine imagined the guy pulling a knife and stabbing himself, the guy might really do it. Instead, he'd channeled the anger into passionate treatment of his sappier songs and sent out terrifyingly *positive* thoughts: love, peace, harmony. It was a crock of shit, but . . .

Unlike the catastrophic concerts of several months earlier, there'd been no riot, no fights or knifings, no one carried away broken and bleeding or dead.

In other words, success. Right?

Someone's coming, the owl said.

Constantine cocked his head; the tree frogs and katydids had sung their last chorus before dawn, and all he heard were the morning's first birds. Dancing Dude again? The guy who sang and prayed on the mounds by night had idled his black van on the far side of the biggest mound earlier, but departed without performing one of his rituals.

No, it wasn't the familiar rumble of the van that greeted him now, but the soft thud of footsteps. That damned fan again! Constantine didn't have to see him clearly against the faintly pink sky to know. A worm pinged at his gut once more. He ignored it, stretching his hamstrings as the guy pounded across the grassy top of Baby Mound, the smallest of three built by prehistoric Indians. More by ear than sight, he sensed the guy's sure-footed leaps down the scrubby sides of the hill and his steady progress across the long field below and up the side of Mama Mound. Constantine blended with the tattered pine under which he had spent the last few hours and waited for the guy to be safely out of the way.

The youth thudded past him and down the other side toward Papa Mound. A huge live oak dominated one corner of the sixty-foot-high hill. Right outside the perimeter of the tree, a foot or two from the edge of the mound, something moved. A pale female form wavered on hands and knees, head hanging, long hair brushing the grass.

The guy reached the base of Papa Mound and started upward with all the finesse of a freight train. At Constantine's warning shout, the guy shot a glance behind, then pounded even faster toward the flat top of the mound. Too late, he hesitated, tripped, and dove over the girl, toppling her, and landed in a lopsided shoulder roll on the lawn.

∼

The dark van hurtled toward Marguerite McHugh, purring its deadly message. *I'm coming for you, you're next, you're next, you're—*

It slammed into her, and she burst from the dream she'd had almost nightly for the past two weeks. She took a few deep, shuddering breaths and tried to open her eyes. All she needed was to be calm. She was safely in bed, not dead on the road like Pauline, and in a few seconds she would wake properly, and everything would be fine.

"Marguerite?" She knew that voice. He sounded desperately frightened, but she had no idea why. Fingers fumbled at her wrist. "You can't be dead."

No, no, I'm not dead! Pauline is the dead one. But Marguerite's mouth refused to move.

"*Please* don't be dead!"

Zeb?

Marguerite felt her eyelids flutter, but she couldn't break the surface to reassure him. She heard Zeb say, "Thank God" and felt him let go of her wrist. She must be alive. Relief washed over her.

"What am I going to *do* with this shit?" Zeb said. "Oh, fuck, he's coming. I have to go, but he'll help you."

She heard Zeb hasten away, his footfalls pounding into the distance. Her mattress was too lumpy and the birds were too loud, and she couldn't figure out what Zeb had been doing in her bedroom, but her eyes still wouldn't open, and her brain felt like sludge. She drifted into an uneasy doze.

She woke again. Now . . . someone else was near.

She blinked away the fuzz in her eyes and her mind. She wasn't in her bed but outdoors, lying near a vast tree. Under her was a blanket, with blades of grass pricking through here and there. A crow cawed high above her. She hadn't been run over by the dark van of her dream.

She wasn't dead, like Pauline. *What time is it? Where am I?* Somewhere a car door slammed, followed by urgent voices. She sat up and looked around for Zeb but remembered his retreating footsteps. Then she saw the man. Her heart thumped dizzily against her chest. He stood a few feet away, silhouetted against the pink and gold of dawn. He wasn't looking at her but toward the voices. Blinking again, she followed his gaze but saw nothing but a vast field and, in the distance, the haphazard tops of a stand of pines. She was on a hill . . . She returned her eyes to the man. He was tall and wide-shouldered, with a long, dark ponytail hanging down his back.

What the hell is going on? How did I get here? She didn't remember a thing.

Then her sixth sense woke up, and she really saw him: a cacophony of colors, a spiked wheel of rage and despair. It hurt. God, it hurt. She clutched her hands to her head, gasping, and the rage withdrew, the spikes of the wheel turned inward, and the man shuddered as if he truly were impaled.

"Sorry," he said softly, his tone tight and flat.

The other voices neared. Two men, one with untidy blond curls and a darker guy carrying a camera, appeared over the brow of the hill and charged across the lawn. Fully alert now, Marguerite bristled with loathing. There were always a few paparazzi in town, and she recognized these two. They were obsessed with Constantine Dufray, and—*oh!*

God, he was beautiful. She had seen him before, of course—pictures aplenty and occasionally in person—but never this close. What presence the man had. It wasn't just the gorgeous high cheekbones and the copper skin of his half-Navajo heritage or his graceful build. He radiated power—intense, a little frightening, and fascinating at the same time.

"Got you!" cried the blond guy. "What could be better? Murder was bad enough, but now you're drugging and raping innocent women. You've had it, Dufray. Face it, you're dead."

"Sure am," said Constantine Dufray. Marguerite ignored the photographer capering about and stared up at the rock star, wondering if he recognized her. She'd seen him now and then at the Impractical Cat, the restaurant where he hung out, and she'd done her best to read his aura, but he'd become something of a recluse lately. He'd had the most awful bad luck at some of his concerts—even riots where people were killed. Sure, he was one of Bayou Gavotte's vigilantes, but would he try to murder his own fans? No way.

Go ahead, a voice said dully. Who'd said that? Not the reporter or his sidekick, and Constantine wasn't looking at her but up at the crow, which had fluttered down to a branch just above his head. The colors that surrounded him roiled and churned, fizzled and spat. His aura stretched and reached out toward her.

Accuse me. Get it over with.

Damn. She hadn't heard a voice in her head for years. It wasn't one of her favorite experiences. In fact, it ranked right up there with her worst. But this wasn't someone's secret wish sent out involuntarily. This was a voice that intended to be heard.

She found her tongue. "What did you say?"

The reporter bent down and shoved his recorder in her face. "Tell us about it, love. All the gory details."

Marguerite pushed his hand away. "I'm not talking to you." She'd known a few people who projected their thoughts, particularly when their auras were in turmoil, but nothing as clear and directed as this. It seemed that the rumors about Constantine Dufray's telepathic abilities were true.

Accuse me, the flat voice said again. *That's what you're here for, so just do it.* A maelstrom of bitterness and despair swirled around and above Constantine like a tight column of flame. The crow cawed loudly and skittered sideways along the branch. Marguerite knitted her brows, trying again to take it all in, and realized at last that she was on top of one of the Indian mounds, the only hills in Bayou Gavotte.

Oh. *Now* she remembered: Constantine's impromptu concert on the field below. His first public performance in months.

"Can't let him get away with it, love." The blond wasn't an Englishman, so the pseudo-Brit endearment only emphasized his obnoxiousness.

Marguerite frowned up at Constantine. "Get away . . . with what?"

Come on now, girl. Didn't he prep you better than that?

"Prep me? I don't understand."

Constantine rolled his eyes casually, indifferently, but his aura writhed toward her, flickered and shuddered, its message utterly contradicting his behavior and making her head hurt again. *Drugging and raping you, to be followed by ritual murder.* His aura withdrew, and the pain went with it. *It's all right, babe, you can play your role. I won't harm you, I swear.*

Constantine had *raped* her? A brief terror ran through her, but she shook it off and cleared her thoughts. Somebody must have drugged her—but Constantine? She didn't believe it. She fought away the last of the fog, blinking up at him and his aura. She sensed pain and anger and an overwhelming despair, but nothing of the predator in that whirlpool of emotions.

The reporter blathered in her face. "He's gotten away with brutal beatings, torture, and murder. You would have been next if we hadn't gotten here in time."

Marguerite dragged her eyes from Constantine and took a good look at the reporter and his smarmy grin. This was the kind of person whose aura she did her utmost not to see. Eagerness hissed and seethed in the reporter's aura, as if he relished this opportunity.

Maybe it wasn't an opportunity at all. *Prepped*, Constantine had said. *Play your role.* Maybe it was a setup . . . and he believed she was part of it.

Fury boiled up inside her—fury from years ago that would never go away. The media had destroyed her father. She hated reporters. She still wasn't sure what was going on, but she refused to give this one what he wanted.

She wiped the sleep from her eyes and smiled tentatively at the rock star. "Sorry, Constantine," she said. "Meditating's not my thing. I must have dropped off to sleep."

"Sleep?" the reporter shouted. "He drugged you! Don't you understand? He was going to rape you. He brought this bizarre paraphernalia up here." He waved a hand to where, several feet behind her, the photographer was taking shots of some firewood, a tin cup, and a copper mask. "God knows what horrors he had planned, but we've finally caught him at it. You'll be famous, your picture on the covers of magazines and all over the web: 'The Girl Who Brought Him Down.'"

How dare they? "What are you *talking* about?" she said.

The crow flapped away, and for the first time Constantine faced Marguerite. She tried to stand, but her head spun, and she swayed. Instantly he was there with a hand, warm and strong, pulling her up and setting her firmly on her feet. His eyes were cold, a disturbing contrast to the heat of his hand.

A blue jay screeched nearby, and another joined in. *Grab your moment of fame and run with it, babe.*

"Like hell I will," she said.

"Don't be afraid of him, love," the reporter said. "We'll get you away from here, keep you safe." The flash went off in her face.

She wasn't afraid. She was furious. "Damn!" she said, still shaky, but entirely sure of what she had to do. She put a hand on Constantine's arm and leaned into him. "Where were you?" she said, putting on a plaintive voice. "I meditated for ages, but I got bored waiting for you. That's why I fell asleep."

Constantine's cold eyes bored into her for a long moment. "Yeah, but on the wrong mound," he said, his aura suspicious even as he played along. "I said Mama Mound, not Papa."

The reporter huffed. This wasn't enough for him. He wanted a story, and if they didn't give him a good one, he would revert to the rape scenario.

"Whoops." Marguerite managed a giggle. "It's already morning, and we didn't even . . ." She paused. Through her fury, a sensible core suggested this was crazy and almost certainly stupid, but she knew the media, and nothing less would work. "We didn't even do it," she finished.

Constantine let out a long whoosh of breath. His lips curled in his famous grin, but his eyes remained cool and distant. The storm of color was quieter now, although still dense with pain. She was no telepath, and she didn't consider herself a reassuring sort of person anyway. The best she could manage was to squeeze his arm.

"Sorry, Nathan," he told the reporter. He took Marguerite's hand and swung it gently back and forth. "I guess there was a little too much meditating and not enough . . . doing."

She poked him in the chest. "You *owe* me. You can't promise a girl tantric sex and then not deliver. It's simply not fair."

9

~

Constantine put the question to himself and his spirit guide, which for the moment was occupying a crow: Why would this woman, who was participating in an attempt to destroy him, change her mind and protect him?

The most obvious answer: She'd decided sex with a rock star was worth more than whatever pittance Nathan Bone had offered to pay her. The next most obvious: She was working for someone else besides Nathan—most likely Constantine's elusive Enemy—and this apparent about-face was part of the plan. The third possibility: She was an innocent pawn.

It's because you're horny, the crow said in Constantine's head, which made no sense but was entirely true. Gingerly, Constantine put an arm around the woman. His rage was well under control—she wasn't cringing or clutching her temples—but since she'd mentioned tantric sex, it was all he could do to keep himself from wrapping his arms around her . . . breathing her in . . . consuming her.

Tantric sex? Hell, any kind of sex would do. Damn, she smelled good: sleep-tousled woman and the outdoors. The jays had gone about their business, and the crow taunted him from high in a pine. Lately, his guide had encouraged him to try having sex again—the last time had been eons ago, before the death of his wife—and the crow had been particularly persistent about this girl. Her name was Marguerite, and she'd done the faux finish on a few benches for the patio at the Impractical Cat. Constantine had made a point of avoiding her because her fresh beauty made him yearn. With his telepathic powers out of control, he couldn't afford anything so maudlin—and dangerous—as yearning.

He shouldn't be surprised she'd ended up selling herself for a media stunt. That was the way of the world. He suppressed a pang of disappointment. He must be getting soft.

No, just slow, the crow said. *You should have done her when I told you to.*

This was typically exasperating bird logic—advice so incomprehensible that Constantine couldn't bring himself to follow it. The last thing he needed was a turncoat girlfriend. When Marguerite's roommate, an older woman, had been found dead a few weeks earlier near his property on the bayou, he'd congratulated himself on ignoring the bird's pestering. Nathan had done his best to implicate him in the death—without the slightest justification, as the police had confirmed. Not that speculation about Constantine was unusual: He was a rock star and a vigilante, and even two years after the fact, some people still suspected him of poisoning his drug-addicted wife—but someone was systematically feeding Nathan with nasty accusations. Fortunately, it turned out that Marguerite's roommate had committed suicide with her own prescription meds. Someone had run over her when she was already dead—probably some poor fool driving too fast in the dark.

Nathan's take on the incident was that Constantine had planted the idea of suicide in the woman's head, reinforced it, and caused her to die only for his own amusement. He'd been accused of doing just that to a Baton Rouge police officer several years earlier, not for amusement but because he'd sworn revenge against the cop for beating up his friend Leopard. He'd been young, arrogant, and newly famous. If he'd listened to his spirit guide's advice, he wouldn't have boasted of supernatural powers but instead used them secretly. Either way, the cop would have died, which was all that mattered.

Now, and probably forever, he had to deal with the repercussions. Nathan would say—and his superstitious, trash-hungry public would relish believing—that he was thumbing his nose at the cops while he preyed on Marguerite. No matter how horny he might be, he could never risk sex with her now.

He ignored the bird's exasperated huff and smiled down at Marguerite, saying in his supposedly sexy rocker voice, "I'll make it up to you, darlin'. I promise."

"Fine," Nathan said, pouting. He'd been sending impatient glances in the direction from which he'd come. He must be expecting someone else to show. "I'll make it a nervous wreck story instead, just like his wife: 'Before and After Sleeping with Dufray.' Better make sure you get away before he kills you, too."

Marguerite rolled her eyes. "What is *wrong* with you? That stuff is all hype." She picked up the blanket she'd been lying on, shook off the bits of grass sticking to it, and folded it. "Constantine's a honey."

Now the crow was totally cracking up, cawing raucously both high in a pine tree and inside Constantine's head. "Don't ruin my image, girl," he said, grabbing the recorder and stomping on it, then going for the photographer, who froze midprotest and meekly handed over the camera.

"You know I'll tell the story anyway," Nathan whined. "If you don't erase the pics, I won't accuse you of destroying my property."

"Uh-huh." Constantine scrolled through the photos, deleting those of Marguerite, and telepathed a threatening message to both men to keep their cell phones in their pockets. "Who sent you up here this morning?"

"Wouldn't you like to know?" Nathan pulled out his phone anyway. He never did respond well to telepathic suggestions.

"Your source eluded you again, did he? Better tread carefully, Nathan."

Nathan grinned. "Is that a threat?"

"A friendly warning. Whoever this guy is, he doesn't want to be found out. He's using you to get at me, and if you learn too much about him in the process . . ." Constantine ran his index finger across his throat. "Let's start over, shall we?" Might as well get the inevitable pics over with; the girl wasn't playing befuddled or frightened anymore. Rather, she frowned from him to Nathan as if she disapproved of them both.

She wasn't playing, said the crow.

She is now, Constantine told the bird. *Calling me a honey, talking about tantric sex.* He returned the camera to the photographer and strolled over to the weird little spread on the lawn, which he'd just begun to examine when Nathan had shown up. A ring of stones enclosed four pieces of scrap lumber, two logs, and the broken leg of a chair. Underneath the wood lay a small pile of kindling and pine straw, and to the left were a mason jar three-quarters full of a dark liquid, a metal cup enameled with a red-and-yellow Celtic knot design, a white plastic bowl decorated with Chinese characters, and a tall copper mask in the shape of a bird of prey, with decorative feathers and turquoise ceramic beads strung along the sides and hanging from the bottom edge.

To the right a soft chamois cloth was spread on the grass. In the chamois was the clear imprint of a knife.

"I hate to admit it, Nathan, but I didn't do this." Constantine pulled his bowie knife from the sheath on his belt and knelt to compare it to the imprint. "Nope. Too bad, because it would have made great promo." He raised a brow at Marguerite, who was taking in the paraphernalia with a little scowl. *Come on,* he told the bird. *She must have been putting on an act.* For a woman who'd supposedly been drugged, who might have been raped, she was way too self-possessed.

What if playing it cool is her act? the crow said. Constantine experienced a second of foolish longing to go ahead and believe whatever the spirit guide suggested about Marguerite. Only a second, though; longings, like yearnings, were a no-no. "Any idea who this stuff belongs to, babe?"

Marguerite pursed her lips, reminding him of one of his profs from years ago. Not so strange, perhaps, since Marguerite taught linguistics part-time at Hellebore University. "No, it must have been put here while I was asleep."

A good answer, but he still didn't know whether to believe her. Two weeks ago, there had been nothing to connect him with the death of Marguerite's roommate. There was now.

"I'm not an anthropologist, but it's clear that whoever brought this stuff up here has confused his traditions," Marguerite said in a scholarly tone. "He chose several different kinds of wood for his fire. That broken chair leg is oak, for example, while the boards are ash and maple, and one of the logs is birch—all of which tie in with various sacred woods used by the eastern tribes."

Again—way too self-possessed, and, judging by Nathan's eager and genuine interest, this meant she wasn't working for him. Possibility number two yawned sickeningly. Constantine grinned at Nathan. "Isn't she something, dude?"

"The headdress is a reproduction of one in the museum here." Marguerite pointed to the building on the far side of the road below. "We don't know exactly what the original was like, because it's so corroded. I believe it came from someplace north of here. I'm no authority on this stuff, though. The museum won't be open this early in the morning, but—" Her eyes widened. "Oh, crap. What time is it? I have to go home."

"Six thirty-three," Nathan said, glancing toward the road again. "The day is young. Tell me more."

"There's not much more to say." She tucked a strand of long, honey-colored hair behind her ear; maybe she really was more unnerved than she let on. "It's obvious whoever set this up doesn't care about verisimilitude. He brought his black drink in a mason jar and was going to drink it from a Celtic cup."

"Black drink?" Nathan dove for the jar, but Constantine got there first. To Marguerite, he telepathed a message: *Get the cup and bowl.*

"An emetic, to induce vomiting for purification." Marguerite picked up the cup and bowl. Did she realize he'd told her to do so? Most people didn't even realize he was planting ideas in their heads, but her earlier questions had made him wonder if she did. "They used something with a lot of caffeine."

Constantine unscrewed the cap and sniffed. "Smells like coffee to me." He gave Nathan a whiff. "Want to try some?"

"Don't," Marguerite said. "He may have added ipecac if he wanted to be sure to vomit."

"Spoilsport." Constantine poured the contents onto the lawn and screwed the cap on again. He tossed the empty jar to Nathan, who might enjoy having the remnants analyzed, picked up the mask, and posed with it for the photographer.

Marguerite turned the bowl slowly in her fingers. "The Chinese characters on here have meanings like *peace* and *love*."

"You read Chinese?" Nathan asked.

"I wish. No, I recognized them from some candle holders I have at home, which is where I need to be right now." Marguerite frowned up at Constantine. "It's a drag, but we won't even have time for a quickie this morning."

"Sure we will." Constantine scooped up the chamois and the blanket and hurried her toward the stairs at the end of the mound. In his other hand he had the mask, and Marguerite still held the cup and bowl.

"And home would be where?" Nathan's voice pursued them. "What's your name, love?"

"Don't tell him." Constantine nudged her along. "You've already made it too easy. Make him work for the rest."

"What's he like in bed?" Nathan asked. "How many orgasms do you get from a quickie?"

Marguerite let out an annoyed "tsk" and started down the stairs.

Nathan called, "What do you suppose happened to the knife?"

CHAPTER TWO

Marguerite was pretty sure she knew the answer to Nathan's question, but hopefully Constantine didn't include mind reading in his unusual skills. She might be able to stop herself from blurting out Zeb's name, but it would be difficult not to think it. What was Zeb doing on the mounds at dawn? What was his part in all of this, and why had he taken the knife?

Another question: If Constantine hadn't drugged her and left her on the mound—and she couldn't bring herself to believe that after what his aura had told her—who had? She was reasonably certain she hadn't been raped; wouldn't one feel violated or, at the very least, sore? Not only that, if this was a setup to trap Constantine—which seemed likely, given the exchange between him and Nathan—raping her would make no sense. Still, it would be foolish not to get checked out. She needed to get to her car and see Lavonia right away. Lavonia would be able to examine her, maybe even do a test for semen. Although what they would do if it was positive . . .

It wouldn't be, and she should keep to easier questions for now. "Why isn't he following us?"

"He knows I'll hurt him if he does," Constantine said. "Nathan and I go way back. We had a profitable symbiotic relationship for a while."

"He got the cool stories and you got the bad-boy promo?"

Constantine's well-known grin appeared briefly. Close to him like this, walking along in conversation, her ordinary senses tended to take over, but he felt more or less safe to her in spite of the violence of his words.

"It sounds to me as if he'd be happy to destroy you," Marguerite said.

"That would be an even cooler story, but he'd have to be alive to tell it. Nathan should know by now that no good comes of tangling with me." A brief vision of another kind of tangling flashed into her mind and was gone.

She hadn't been thinking about sex just now, not at all. Generally, she didn't. She'd lost interest in sex years ago, almost before she'd tried it.

She'd been hoping to meet Constantine for ages, to decide for herself whether his telepathic abilities were real. One of the perks of taking a job in Bayou Gavotte was the increased likelihood of meeting him. She'd chosen to room with Pauline, whose property bordered his, for the same reason. But none of that had anything to do with sex.

Constantine wasn't the only reason she'd moved here, though. Bayou Gavotte, with its kinky clubs, was ideal for people with unusual abilities. It had probably started with hereditary vampires, who sprouted fangs at puberty and had a powerful sexual allure. The New Orleans area had been home to them for centuries. They still kept their identities more or less a secret—many people didn't even believe they existed—but they could mingle more freely in a town with vampire wannabes and various kinds of sex clubs. But some of the clubs had grown dangerous, recruiting underage or unwilling participants, and the underworld had come into being to keep the town safe in ways the police couldn't. Not that the entire populace approved, but most people accepted the situation because it profited them. Since the underworld had taken control of the dark side of town, tourist traffic had flourished, as had Hellebore University.

Marguerite hadn't told many people about her ability to read auras, because it generally caused more trouble than it was worth. Even so, the fact that many of her colleagues at Hellebore were deep into psychic studies made her feel at home. It was a good town for someone who didn't quite fit in the normal world.

"Did you see the guy who knocked you over?"

Surprise deprived her of speech. How much had Constantine seen? After a struggle, she managed, "Is that what happened? I was trying to wake up, but I was so out of it. I was still caught in a dream." Pause. "I heard a man cursing, but I couldn't get my eyes to open, and then he left."

"With the knife."

"I guess," Marguerite said. "Unless it was already gone."

"I saw him pick something up," Constantine said.

"Why would he take some random knife? He couldn't have known I was there or he wouldn't have bumped into me, so maybe he didn't know about the paraphernalia either."

"Interesting, isn't it?" Constantine's interest sounded deadly. Marguerite wouldn't want to be the focus of it. "There's a guy who comes to the mounds at night from time to time to sing and pray, which makes me wonder if this stuff is his, but what does the kid have to do with it?"

"Kid?" Her voice wavered.

"The guy who took the knife is young—in high school, maybe, or a freshman in college. He ran right past me on Mama Mound, and I recognized him from last night's concert. He took off, and by the time I got there, Nathan had arrived. I'll find the kid soon enough. He'll tell me what he knows."

At the implacable note in his voice, a panicky little chill struck Marguerite. Thank God she hadn't told him Zeb's name. "What if he doesn't want to? He must be hiding something."

"He'll tell me," Constantine said. "I won't give him a choice."

"You'll *hurt* him?"

"I'll do whatever it takes."

"That's awful!" Marguerite cried. Not surprising, considering his reputation, but she hadn't expected his attitude to make her feel ill.

"It works," Constantine said. "The kid's a runner."

How much more did he know? She hurried ahead down the last few stairs, needing to get away. Maybe if she found Zeb first, she could ask the questions, and Zeb wouldn't get hurt. Zeb was six feet tall, in good shape, and not afraid of a fight, but against Constantine and the vigilantes of the Bayou Gavotte underworld—headed by Constantine's drummer, Leopard—he didn't stand much of a chance.

"Here come Nathan's reinforcements," Constantine said at the sound of another vehicle. He hustled her willy-nilly across the field.

"My car's in the far parking lot," Marguerite said.

"Through the woods, then." They changed course, and shouts pursued them as they made it to the trees.

At one strident female voice, Marguerite shot a glance over her shoulder. "That's Myra, one of the museum's curators."

"Looks like Nathan planned on having her there this morning as a witness to the twisted story he hoped to tell," Constantine said. "She tried to stop us from having a concert here last night. She was spitting mad, and the cops had to all but carry her away."

"I saw that, poor thing."

"You were at the concert." Almost like an accusation.

"Purely by luck," Marguerite said, feeling defensive, which made no sense. Why shouldn't she be excited—no, overjoyed—that he was singing again? "I heard about it at the coffee shop and came right over. I couldn't resist. You haven't performed in months."

He didn't reply, and for a while they continued in silence, their footsteps soft on the pine straw. He brushed hanging vines away to let her pass. A squirrel scampered along a fallen ironwood, and a medley of crows called from above.

"Myra was just being protective of the mounds." Marguerite felt obliged to explain further. "She didn't want people climbing up the sides to get a better view because that leads to erosion. And she was afraid they would leave trash everywhere. Under the cover of darkness, nobody bothers with the rules. But your people seemed to have everything under control."

"Apparently not, if someone drugged you." At the same instant, he shot her a telepathic message infused with warning: *Did someone really drug you?*

What? "Of course someone drugged me! Do you think I willingly participated in that crappy scene up there?"

21

He shrugged. "Why not, if you needed the money? Let's say you didn't, then. Were you by yourself at the concert?"

For a hero, he sure was acting like a jerk. "Yes, I was by myself, more or less. I met a few of my students and saw a couple of other people I know, but I spread my blanket at the back so I could leave before the rush." Pause. "I'll have to think about it, try to remember who was nearby, which song I heard last . . ."

"You must have had a drink with you."

"A bottle of water," she said. "I always carry water in the car. God, I'm so thirsty."

He had a water bottle clipped to his belt. He uncapped it and offered it to her.

She hesitated, suddenly unnerved. His colors swirled alarmingly, and a flush of shame washed over her. He wasn't a rapist. He didn't go around drugging women. As a Bayou Gavotte vigilante, he saved the endangered and protected the innocent. She knew all this, and she'd never believed the horrible stories about him, but he was beginning to frighten her. This whole morning scared her. She thanked him, took a sip, and handed the bottle back to him.

Sharp little flares daggered his aura. He took a huge swig, and shame crawled through her again. Why? He was the one behaving like a jerk. With a chilly twist of the lips, he offered it to her a second time. "Want some more?"

Damn it, what right had he to be offended? He'd assumed the worst of her at first, he didn't believe what she said now, and regardless, *some* jerk had drugged her. She glared at him and took a substantial swallow. "Thanks."

His mouth twitched, and for once his aura and physical body were in sync. He downed the remaining water, the masculine column of his throat glorious in the morning light.

As he clipped the bottle to his belt, the amusement in his aura faded, and his voice was cool. "Do you think someone could have switched bottles while you were watching the concert?"

"No. I know people who've been date-raped. I never set the bottle down. I was holding it the entire time."

"Maybe you were so absorbed in the music you didn't notice." He sounded as if getting carried away by the music was stupid and disgusting. What was wrong with him?

"No," she said, "I would have noticed when I picked it up again." She could see he still didn't believe her. More and more rattled by the second, she picked up her pace, and they came out into the open. "There's my car. I really have to get home." A tiny tremor in her voice betrayed her. She thought she'd grown accustomed to disbelief, but evidently not.

Her little Honda sat forlornly alone in the parking lot. She dug her keys from the pocket of her shorts and tossed the cup and bowl into the trunk.

"This is your blanket?" The mask still dangled from his hand.

She nodded, spread the blanket in the trunk, and took the mask and laid it carefully inside. She'd expected him to object, to insist on keeping it—or perhaps keeping everything. She was pretty sure he'd telepathically ordered her to pick up the cup and bowl. It was not as clear as those self-destructive suggestions he'd made earlier, but definitely a different timbre from her own thoughts. If he wanted the items, why let her take them?

Surprise made her blurt, "Do you need a ride into town?"

He shook his head. "I'm fine."

He didn't look fine. She needed to get away before he asked anything more about Zeb. She cared about Zeb Bonnard; he was a troubled teen and one of the few people to whom she'd revealed that she could see auras. She'd had no choice when faced with Zeb's astonishing ability to control his own aura and his desperate need for someone to confide in about it. She couldn't leave him at the mercy of a vigilante, hero or not. She had to get some answers of her own first.

"What are you planning to do with that stuff?" Constantine's voice held a hint of laughter. She tried to read his colors, but whatever they revealed, it wasn't amusement.

"Find out who put it there," she said.

"You don't know?" Supercilious on the surface, intensely focused underneath. *Tell me the truth, girl.*

"Of course I don't know! Somebody drugged me, remember?" She shut the trunk. "I mean to find out who did it."

"No," he said sharply. "No."

"No what?"

"If you really don't know, don't try to find out. You'll put yourself in danger."

She scowled. "Then why did you tell me to pick up the cup and bowl?"

"Did I?" he asked, all innocence.

She didn't try to hide her annoyance. "That's not the only telepathic message you sent me, and we both know it."

"Most people can't tell that a telepathic message isn't one of their own thoughts."

24

She shrugged, not wanting to get into this discussion. "I repeat: Why did you tell me to take the stuff?"

"Because I couldn't carry it all myself. Don't have a vehicle with me either. I'll pick it up later, and I'll find out who put it here. You need to stay out of this."

"It's a bit late for that," she said.

"No, it's not." His tone made her shiver. She followed his eyes and the tilt of his chin to where the nose of a low-slung car poked out from behind a hedge bordering the parking lot. "You can back out of this mess right now. Pretend we've had words." A crow dove from the trees, its caws raucous and insistent. "Tell me to go to hell."

"After all I just implied about you to save your sorry butt?" The crow fluttered sharply onto the gravel, narrowly missing Constantine. He didn't seem to notice. His eyes flickered, dark eyes with flecks of copper, sparks of heat. "Last chance, babe." A BMW with Nathan at the wheel slithered toward them like a malevolent white rat. The snout of a camera followed their every move from the rear window. "Come on. Slap me across the face." He leaned toward her, offered his cheek.

More pissed off by the second, she took a step back. "Why would I do that?"

"To dissociate yourself from me. It's for your own safety. He may find out who you are and harass you a little, but once he realizes there's nothing between us, he'll leave you alone."

She glanced at the white car and back at Constantine.

"Hit me, and I'll distract him. Maybe you'll manage to escape him completely."

God, what a temptation. The last thing she needed was a reporter following her around. If he found out who she was . . . She shut that thought away. He might find out anyway. Regardless, she couldn't just quit.

"I'll have one of my bodyguards pick up that paraphernalia, and whoever set up that scenario will leave you alone, too," Constantine said.

"I can't dissociate myself from you yet," she said. "That would make people believe his allegations. I have to finish what I started up there." She felt a flush crawl up her neck. "I didn't mean that. I just meant—"

"Don't worry," Constantine said dryly. "I don't plan to take you up on your delightful suggestion. It was clever, but it won't keep Nathan away for long. He'll want more and more, and if you associate with me, it will only get worse."

She knew that, but she couldn't support him one minute and abandon him the next. It went against everything she'd been taught, everything she'd learned by her father's example.

And, she had to admit, that wasn't all that held her. The closer Constantine came, the more he was aroused. His words urged her to leave, while his aura pulled her closer. She didn't need a sixth sense to melt under the heat of his sensuality, but it sure came in handy. He could have been made of stone for all the interest he showed, but he was extremely turned on, and she knew it.

Miraculously, it turned her on, too.

She breathed him in. He smelled *fabulous*. Her lips yearned for the smooth bronze of his skin.

"Hit me hard, get into that car, and drive the hell away."

"Not on your life," she said, and swiftly kissed his cheek.

~

With a growl of despair, he gave in and pulled her hard against him, kissing her properly, while the crow cackled, *She wants you, wants you, wants you.* He sent it a halfhearted *They all do,* and let himself explore her.

But she's not afraid, the bird said as it flew away.

That didn't mean she was safe with him, but she was hot and sweet, and it had been too damned long. If he were a good guy, he'd just shoot her one of the one-touch orgasms he'd perfected during his long period of celibacy and send her away to become another of the chicks who raved about him.

But he wasn't a good guy, and she melted against him and kissed him back, and before he knew it, he was hard as a tree, gripping her ass, and grinding himself against her.

He was used to the incessant click of cameras, but she wasn't and pulled away first.

"Welcome to the tabloids," he said, as Nathan whooped and tore out of the parking lot. "By noon, we'll be all over the web."

She'd gone pale as ice, but she composed herself. "I'd better run while he's out of the way." She got into the car and buckled herself in. She rolled down the window and frowned up at Constantine, lips parted, as if she wanted to say something.

He shouldn't let himself look at her lips. He couldn't risk a relationship. He couldn't even risk a quick fuck.

"Good-bye, then," she said, eyes widening. Slowly, she drove away. He sent a kiss on the wind as her car disappeared from sight.

~

"Are you out of your mind?" Lavonia said. Her wild black curls quivered against her creamy brown skin. Even just out of bed, her voluptuous figure wrapped in a tattered pink robe and about to deliver a rant, Lavonia was drop-dead gorgeous.

Marguerite folded her arms against her chest, rubbing the goose bumps away. Lavonia always kept her air conditioning too cold, and by the time Marguerite had finished explaining what had happened at the mound—a little too incoherently for her own self-respect—she was frozen from top to toe. "Maybe. I don't know. Regardless, I can't call the cops." She got up from her chair by the kitchen table and paced to keep herself warm.

Or maybe to keep herself from freaking out.

Lavonia was her closest friend in Bayou Gavotte. Not that Marguerite considered any of her friends close, apart from Zeb; her aura-reading ability made that difficult. Still, Lavonia's was the shoulder she'd cried on after Pauline's suicide, and was Marguerite's support through the funeral and all the attendant business. She was also a witch, a psychology student, and a former nurse, and she had listened in growing disbelief to Marguerite's story. "You were drugged and maybe raped. You have to go to the police. You have to be examined at the hospital."

"I can't," Marguerite said wearily. "I already said, in public and for the whole world to know, that I fell asleep waiting for Constantine Dufray to have tantric sex with me."

"And you can now report to the same world that you were befuddled by a date rape drug. That when you woke and saw him, you couldn't think of anything but how sexy he was. That you temporarily lost your mind and said the first thing that popped into it."

"I can't possibly say anything so stupid!"

"You already said something stupid."

"I know that," Marguerite said in a small voice. "But it would have been worse to agree with what that foul reporter said."

"You could have told the truth." Lavonia tightened her dressing gown around herself and banged cupboards and drawers as she got the coffee going.

No, because the truth included what she'd read in Constantine's aura, and no one would have believed her. She'd stopped talking about auras long ago, because she'd had enough of not being believed or, alternatively, of being shunned. She hadn't told Lavonia about being able to read auras for fear that it would ruin their friendship the way it had ruined several of Marguerite's friendships in the past. Those who believed her felt she was invading their privacy by seeing the emotions they wanted to hide. She didn't *want* to see all those chaotic feelings, but all too often, she had no choice.

"No, I couldn't. The reporter would have put a spin on it to suit his purposes." The press had hounded her father for telling the truth, twisting it into something evil. A shudder ran through her. If Nathan found out whose daughter she was and raked up all that garbage again . . . But maybe he wouldn't. "Anyway, sounding confused and wasted would only have supported the reporter's horrible theories. I had to distract him with something his readers would like."

"You didn't have to. You wanted to." Lavonia glowered as she scooped coffee beans and turned on the coffeemaker. The noise of the grinder postponed her tirade for a second or two, but the instant it stopped, she burst out, "He's a dangerous man! He's not only a vigilante, but from what I've heard, he abused his wife and then poisoned her, whether you and the rest of his crazy fans want to believe it or not."

"We're not crazy. The abuse stories were the ravings of a woman addled by drugs, and he was hours away in Mississippi when she died."

"So he contracted with someone to kill her. You can't simply let this go."

"I'm not letting it go. I'm just not taking the usual route." She sat down again, shivering even more. Reaction, she supposed. She'd controlled herself fine up on the mound, just as she'd remained externally calm after Pauline's death, only letting go when safely alone. Not that she'd been particularly close to Pauline, but the suicide had been such a shock. Pauline's aura had shown that she'd been healing, getting over her horrific past, and then, completely out of the blue . . . she was dead.

Marguerite slumped in the chair. It hit her now, as it had several times on the drive over, that she was lucky not to be dead herself. Lavonia's cat, a sleek calico that had recently had a litter of kittens, rubbed against Marguerite's legs. She picked up the cat and caressed it, taking comfort in its warmth and its contented purr. "How are the kittens doing? Have you found homes for any of them?"

"They're fine. Yes, I've found homes for two, and don't try to change the subject," Lavonia said. "Are you afraid of Constantine? Because if you are, we'll do something about it. We'll get the police involved. We'll put you in hiding if necessary. I'll even get the coven to try a protection spell, although I'm still not sure we've got it right." She stormed into the living room, came back with a fuzzy lavender throw, and wrapped it around Marguerite. The cat jumped down and stalked away. "See? You're shaking all over. You *are* afraid."

"No, I'm freezing." She didn't need protection against Constantine Dufray, but saying so wouldn't encourage Lavonia to give her a quick checkup, here and now. "I'm not really afraid of him. He was actually quite considerate." When he wasn't trying to scare her away or kissing the hell out of her.

If anything, she was afraid *for* him. His life had been a series of catastrophes for the past two years, and yet he'd encouraged her to offer him up to the hostile world on a platter. Why? It would mean total ruin of his already disastrous career. Suspected murder might be titillating, vigilante brutality might seem justified, but rape? Nobody but pervs would go for that.

It hit her then: He didn't care about his career. *You're dead*, the reporter had said, and Constantine had agreed. The reporter had meant career-dead, but had Constantine meant . . . *dead* dead?

It made sense. Several months ago, he had appeared to attempt suicide, although afterward he'd told the media it was just a joke. Today, his aura had clearly revealed his emotional anguish, a ghastly mixture of bitterness, anger, and pain. He expected betrayal. How would it be to live like that? Maybe he really did want to die.

She couldn't let him. "I will not throw him to the jackals," she said. "It's too late for that anyway, even if I wanted to, which I don't. They believe I'm sleeping with him."

"Only because you said you were." Because she'd kissed him, too, but she hadn't mentioned that to Lavonia. She still didn't know what to think of it herself.

Oh, *God*, what a kiss. She'd never felt hunger like that before, never been so enmeshed in another's aura. Never *participated* like that, never felt such a sensation of enjoying and being enjoyed.

If he was so eager to get rid of her, why kiss her like that? Any woman with enough breath to run would hurry back for more. As for the image of their naked bodies writhing together that had surged into her head just before she drove away . . .

"What got into you?" Lavonia said. "It's one thing to like his music, but you're acting like a silly little fan-girl."

"So because I'm a fan, I shouldn't help him?" Marguerite huddled inside the throw. "He needed rescuing from that jerk of a reporter. I had no choice."

Lavonia rolled her eyes. "Maybe the rumors about his telepathic abilities are true. Maybe he planted that idea in your head. Tantric sex, my foot!"

"It was a great idea, and the credit is all mine." It was also completely uncharacteristic; she'd pretty much given up on sex ages ago, both thinking and doing.

On the other hand, if she thought about having sex with Constantine, she might finally warm up to the idea.

"I've always wondered if the rumors were true," Marguerite said. "It's one of the reasons I came to Bayou Gavotte— because I wanted to see him in person. Not that I expected meeting him to prove anything, but because, in a way, I owe him."

"Owe him? For what?"

Marguerite heaved a sigh. Lavonia probably wouldn't go for this either. "You know the story of how he supposedly sent telepathic messages to a corrupt cop, scaring him into killing himself?"

"Yes, I know the story. That cop was a jerk who deserved to die, but I don't know whether I believe Constantine had anything to do with it."

"I don't know either. But—and don't tell anyone this, please—that cop was my uncle, and he wasn't just a corrupt, violent police officer. He was also a pedophile. Don't tell me how I know—it's a long story—but I was afraid he would get to my little sister. So if Constantine did cause his death, then he saved my sister, and I owe him."

Lavonia huffed. "Even if the story is true, Constantine did it for vengeance. It had nothing to do with saving your sister."

"Not directly, but it prevented my uncle from hurting anyone else, and I can't help but be grateful."

"*That's* why you made a fool of yourself this morning?"

Oh, hell, she didn't know. Her mind was such a muddle.

Fortunately, Lavonia didn't need an answer. "Did they get pictures of you together? You'll be all over the tabloids."

Marguerite hunched a shoulder, while her stomach tied itself into knots like the ones on the Celtic cup. "I'll survive. It'll only be for a couple of days, and then some new gossip will take over. Anyway, people do scandalous stuff in Bayou Gavotte all the time. That's another reason I moved here— because for the most part, it's an easygoing town."

"Next you'll be saying it's your civic duty. That you're contributing to the twisted reputation of Bayou Gavotte."

Marguerite cut off a laugh. "Too bad there's nothing twisted about tantric sex. Now, listen. If they find out I came straight to you, you have to tell them it was for the calendar." Lavonia was designing a witches' calendar, and Marguerite helped with the illustrations.

"At seven on a Saturday morning?"

Marguerite waved the objection away. "I'm just glad you were awake."

"I have a meeting with Eaton Wilson this morning." Lavonia took two mugs out of the cupboard. "He wants to measure brain activity while people are having visions. He says they need to learn to induce visions by meditating in a sacred space before they can reproduce them in the lab. I think he wants someone to bounce ideas off who won't act like he's a nutcase."

"Kind of you." Eaton was borderline crazy, but so was Lavonia. In fact, much of Bayou Gavotte was on the cutting edge of weird, but the university community had to walk a fine line, in touch as it was with the ordinary scientific world. Marguerite added cream to her coffee. "If any reporters find out I was here, just tell them I rushed over first thing because I knew you'd be with Eaton all day."

"I'd better not be stuck with Eaton all day," Lavonia said dourly. "I do have a life."

Marguerite grinned. "You have plans with Bon-Bon?"

Lavonia visibly suppressed an answering grin with the mention of Al Bonnard, the handsome professor she was dating. "Don't change the subject."

Marguerite blew out a breath. "I will do my best to find out who did this to me, but methodically and in private, with no suspicion falling on Constantine."

"Unless he did it."

"Right," Marguerite said, and then the caffeine finally hit her brain. "But I don't see how he could have. I don't even remember the end of the concert, so I must have been drugged at the back of the crowd while he was at the front, singing."

"He could have paid someone to do it, just like he paid someone to poison his wife."

Marguerite threw up her hands. "Right, he beckoned to one of his roadies and said, 'Drug some random chick and drag her on top of the mound. I want to do an unconscious woman tonight.' Even if he were that perverted, he's definitely not that stupid. I tell you, I know he didn't do it."

Lavonia fumed silently, which meant she was gathering ammunition. Marguerite breathed in the warmth of coffee and life. "Mmm. Thank you."

"You're welcome, but you're taking an unscientific approach," Lavonia said. "If you're too attached to your hypothesis, you'll interpret the results to support what you already believe."

Marguerite nodded and took a bracing swallow of coffee. "You're perfectly correct, but you're doing exactly the same thing, and you know it. Please do me this favor, Lavonia. Either you examine me, or no one does. It's that simple."

Lavonia threw up her hands and motioned Marguerite into the bedroom. "When was the last time you had sex?"

"Well over a year ago, and you know that, too."

Ten minutes later, Lavonia had her conclusion. "No. It's unlikely you were raped. No residue, no bruising or chafing, no sign of forced entry or trauma to your cervix."

Marguerite let out a long breath and sat up. "That's a relief."

"Still, it's not proof positive. If you would let me send a sample to the lab—"

"No," Marguerite said.

"This doesn't prove he didn't drug you or have you drugged, and it doesn't prove he didn't intend to rape you. Or murder you. *Sacrifice* you." Lavonia's nostrils flared. "Are you *listening*, Marguerite?"

"It was almost dawn," Marguerite said. "If he wanted to kill me, he had plenty of opportunity during the night. In fact, maybe it was Constantine's presence on the mounds that stopped whoever really did want to light that fire from doing whatever . . . he had planned."

Lavonia pounced on the catch in Marguerite's voice. "You *are* scared."

"Of course I'm scared, but not of Constantine!" Not really.

Her friend glowered. "What happened to all the paraphernalia you described? I suppose, in your dippy fan-girl state of mind, you let him take it away."

"He didn't have a vehicle with him," Marguerite said. "It's in my car."

The dense warmth of a Louisiana summer morning greeted them outdoors. Marguerite shed the throw and sipped her coffee, and the shaking subsided to the merest quiver in her gut. Lavonia gave the strange loot a once-over. "The cup looks vaguely familiar, but for all I know, they sell them at Walmart. The bowl, not at all." She took out the bird mask, stroking the shining copper and the feathers. The beads winked in the sunshine. "It's beautiful, but sort of scary. Look at that cruel curved beak! Where have I seen one like this? At the mound museum?"

"It may have been modeled on an artifact on display there," Marguerite said. "There's also a book with paintings of what they think the original masks looked like, but no reconstructions, as far as I know."

Lavonia laid the mask in the trunk. "You said something about a knife. Where is it?"

"It wasn't there." Marguerite described the imprint on the chamois as she shut the trunk.

Lavonia huffed. "Constantine must have hidden it because it would incriminate him. I bet there's a cover of *Rolling Stone* where he's brandishing that very knife. Why aren't you terrified?"

Marguerite hesitated. *Because he kissed me?* That wouldn't cut it with Lavonia; it would only make matters worse. *Because he seems headed toward self-destruction, and I can't bear that?* Lavonia would reply that if Constantine's guilt was destroying him, it was exactly what he deserved.

"That's it." Lavonia swiveled and made for the house again. "I'm calling the cops."

"I'll deny everything you say." Marguerite hurried after her, slopping coffee onto the paving stones.

"Why?" Lavonia cried. "Even if Constantine didn't do it, someone did."

"Right, so I want to find out where all the paraphernalia came from, especially the mask. I thought you might have some ideas."

Lavonia put her hands on her hips. "The only idea in my mind at the moment is that you barely escaped grave danger, and now you're putting yourself right back in."

"It might be someone at Hellebore U," Marguerite persisted. "At least half the people at that concert were students. Quite a few profs were there."

"Sure, but you should leave the investigation to the cops."

Must she be so stubborn? "Also, there's another reason I don't want anyone else involved."

"And what might that be?"

Again, Marguerite hesitated. For obvious reasons, she couldn't mention Zeb. If she did, Lavonia would go straight to his father, Al Bonnard. Zeb would feel betrayed, and any hope of getting information from him would be gone.

"There's nothing, is there? Stop trying to stall me." Lavonia marched indoors.

"I'm not stalling." Marguerite followed her and shut the door, trying to sort things out in her mind. If some lunatic really had planned a rape or human sacrifice, how had Nathan found out? If it was just a setup to discredit Constantine, had they seriously expected Marguerite to back up their ugly story? Regardless, what did Zeb have to do with it all?

Meanwhile, Lavonia's expression would make a cactus wither. She wouldn't just let this go. She picked up her phone.

"We'll both look ridiculous if you call the cops," Marguerite said. "There really is something else, but I'll look even more ridiculous if I mention it to anyone except you." She'd been meaning to anyway. Maybe. "But you have to promise not to tell anyone."

"That depends on what it is," Lavonia said.

"And you're not allowed to put my dreams in your journal."

Lavonia's eyes widened, her nostrils flared, and she put down the phone. "You've had another prophetic dream?" Such dreams were one of Lavonia's favorite areas of study, and finding people with verifiable prophetic dreams wasn't easy.

Marguerite grimaced. Being bombarded by auras was plenty bad enough, and she sure didn't want this dream to come true. "I didn't think dreaming Pauline would kill herself was prophetic, because she had tried it before. Although I believed she was recovering, underneath I was afraid for her, so it came out in my dreams. But then she *did* die."

"And now you believe the dreams were genuinely prophetic?"

"I hope they weren't. I'm having new nightmares, but in these I'm the one who's going to die."

Lavonia plumped herself down on the couch. Tears welled in her eyes. "I don't want you to have *that* kind of prophetic dream!" Then, furiously: "Wasn't tonight warning enough?"

"In the dream, I don't get stabbed on top of a mound." Marguerite sat next to her. The cat jumped onto Marguerite's lap, waving its tail in her face and purring. She caressed it while deciding what to say; no need to describe the terror her dream evoked. "I get run over by a van. But the cops won't take me seriously if I tell them about it. Even

I don't take myself seriously. I'm sure it's only a jumble of stuff my subconscious is churning through."

Lavonia put an arm around Marguerite. "Just because you dreamed it doesn't mean it's going to happen. We always have the power to change our fate." She glowered at Marguerite. "All right, I won't go to the cops just yet. Let's have breakfast, and then I have to run and meet Eaton. We'll get together later and try to figure this thing out."

Marguerite drove first to the supermarket. Lawless, the little black-and-white sheepdog mix who had belonged to Pauline, would be all right a while longer because he had a doggy door, but she had run out of dog food—and people food, too. Pauline had been a difficult roommate, but she'd done most of the shopping and cooking. She hadn't been such a great cook, but her aura had so plainly said she needed to control whatever she could that Marguerite had acquiesced.

She swerved into the Chicken Bin drive-through for a breakfast sandwich—not for herself but for Lawless. He loved Chicken Bin, but people food for dogs had been against Pauline's rules. She sent up a silent apology to Pauline's spirit, hoping that maybe in the next life, whatever and wherever that was, there was no need for all those rules. Marguerite didn't have an affinity for dogs, and she didn't know much about how to take care of one, but she did know they liked company. Maybe a treat would make up for being gone all night.

"Hey, Miss Marguerite." The kid at the window, she remembered suddenly, was a friend of Zeb's.

"Hey, Jimmy. Is Zeb still working here?"

Jimmy grinned. "Nope. Fired for cussing out the boss."

This was how Zeb lost almost every job. "Where does he work now?"

"No idea," Jimmy said so glibly that it had to be a lie. She paid for the sandwich and left, wishing it weren't so obvious where Zeb must be working. Some of the clubs in town weren't all that picky about checking the ID of underage workers, and although Zeb was only seventeen, he looked eighteen or older. If he didn't want to be recognized, he would sign up to be one of the painted messenger boys who set up sexual contracts between patrons in the sex clubs. With his physique, they'd hire him in a snap.

The last thing she wanted was to cruise the sex clubs, and she didn't even have entrée to some. Not that a pretty, scantily dressed girl couldn't get in if she chose—but at a potentially horrendous cost.

She and Pauline had hired Zeb for heavy chores before. If he had no work, he might be available to mow her lawn—hopefully today—so she could question him about what he'd been doing on the mound and why he'd taken the knife.

On the way home, she stopped at the bookstore for a cappuccino. A display at the front of the store featured the most recent Constantine Dufray biography. She resisted temptation and went to look at the romance shelves. After spending fifteen minutes not making up her mind, she gave in, picked up a copy of the biography, and sat at one of the tables in the cafe. The author claimed to have dated Constantine in college. Hopefully her memories weren't entirely accurate, particularly not the bit about his thirteen-inch penis.

Not that it mattered to Marguerite one way or the other. Despite that kiss, she wasn't really involved with the rock star, and she wasn't going to be.

"Good God, Marguerite," said an irritable male voice behind her. "Tell me it's not true."

CHAPTER THREE

Constantine wrapped his arms around the huge branch on which he sat and laid his cheek against the roughness of the resurrection fern that covered its upper surface. From his vantage point high up in the live oak at the top of Papa Mound, he could see all three mounds and the museum. Over by Mama Mound, his people were clearing what little trash remained from last night's concert. He'd had them remove the firewood and kindling from Papa Mound first. The disgruntled Myra, after bitching at them for a few minutes, had retreated to the museum.

His guide, still in the form of a crow, perched twenty feet away at the end of the branch. It didn't say much; it didn't need to. The damned crow radiated self-satisfaction. One would think, judging by its glee, that it and not Constantine had kissed Marguerite.

It had also convinced itself that a torrid affair would soon ensue. *You may even marry her*, it said.

He refused to rise to that bait. Another marriage was even more impossible than casual sex. He had to get his mind under control first. The only way to avoid hurting the woman was, quite simply, to avoid her altogether.

For the umpteenth time, he wished he could get rid of the damned bird. Far too often, its advice was cryptic and contrary to logic and common sense. During his worst periods, he'd taken potshots at the current manifestation, but the guide always showed up again, patient, persistent, and, in retrospect, usually correct.

Always, the crow said.

He refused to get into that argument either. The guide wasn't infallible, but it saw patterns that Constantine couldn't, and its timing wasn't always right. Now and then, they managed to work in sync. The guide had pestered him to hold that impromptu concert at the Indian mounds, and everything had gone well enough, or so he'd thought . . . until this morning, when it became all too obvious it hadn't.

It was a step in the right direction, the crow said.

Toward controlling the powers of his mind, yes. Toward identifying his Enemy, maybe.

Toward getting laid, the crow added predictably.

He tried to address the bird with logic. He didn't trust Marguerite. Well, he didn't really trust anyone—but he couldn't let her come to harm. "If I don't get involved with her, she'll have a better chance of survival. I'll head out west, disappear into the mountains, and become a hermit. If I'm not around to be accused of anything, the Enemy will leave her alone."

Silence. The crow gazed into the distance.

"It's not a cowardly approach," Constantine insisted.

The bird ruffled its glossy black wings.

"I'm trying to protect her, damn it all."

The crow picked at its breast feathers.

Once again, Constantine wondered what he had done to merit the persecution of such a persnickety creature. "He won't risk harming her if it doesn't affect me."

The bird didn't reply. A squirrel scolded, and Constantine snapped at it, driving it away to the tip of a branch, where it chittered rudely before leaping to another branch below. The crow stared coolly for a moment or two, flapped its wings, and sailed off. Back in the day when Constantine had deliberately ignored his guide for months and ended up in that catastrophic marriage, it had first hammered at him until he had almost gone insane and then left him completely alone and bereft. Now they had a better working arrangement. Once the bird had made its point, Constantine wished it away, and it went. When it had something useful to say, it returned.

Constantine took out his cell phone and made a call.

"Yo," came the sleepy voice of Detective Gideon O'Toole, followed by a jaw-cracking yawn. Gideon was a good friend and the closest thing to a liaison between the police and the Bayou Gavotte underworld.

"Kid keeping you up nights, sport?" Constantine said.

"I would have done fine last night," Gideon retorted, "if you'd gone home after the concert. The curator woke me up not ten minutes ago to pick up where she left off at midnight. Said you'd been on the mound all night, which is against park regulations."

"That's all? What about the rape and human sacrifice?"

"Jesus, Constantine. Where did that come from? Even you wouldn't encourage that sort of story."

"Someone else kindly did it for me." Constantine recounted the morning's events, omitting mention of the guy who'd taken the knife.

"Marguerite McHugh," Gideon mused. "If there wasn't a connection between you and her roommate's death before, there sure is now." He blew out a long breath. "There was no reason to believe Pauline's death was anything but suicide, but it didn't feel right. Not that she went outdoors— she loved her garden—but that she wandered into the street and just happened to get run over. It seemed a little too macabre to be real. Nice to know my instincts are working." Pause. "Not so nice to know it might have been a murder." Another pause. "I suppose I shouldn't be glad that this almost certainly means your 'Enemy' is real."

"Finally beginning to believe me?" Constantine rasped. He'd had to suppress all his instincts to force himself to discuss his Enemy with Gideon. He didn't usually get along with cops, and he preferred to work alone.

But someone had been trying to destroy him for over two years now, starting with the poisoning of his estranged wife. Sheer luck had taken Constantine out of town the same night she was killed, or he would have been the prime suspect. The media, led mostly by Nathan Bone, had refused to let go, and unsolved crimes—and even some solved ones—were attributed to Constantine in the tabloids, and the methods described were all too possible for one of Constantine's abilities.

Those very abilities were the big issue. Nathan didn't know enough to understand what Constantine really could and couldn't do. Someone else did, though, and Constantine had squeezed a confession from Nathan that he had an unidentified source. That had led to suspecting every other vigilante, every bodyguard and roadie and friend—anyone who might have figured out more—but the search had led nowhere.

Constantine's fury and frustration had come out in his songs and then in his concerts. He'd lost control of his telepathy, blasting violence and hatred, death and destruction, and fans had been killed. Then the long hiatus, when he couldn't bring himself to perform. He'd meditated and prayed. He'd done sweat lodges and healing ceremonies with the bird's help. Gradually, he had seemed to improve.

Last night's concert had gone well—almost perfectly. Followed immediately by near catastrophe this morning on the mound.

"I always wanted to believe you," Gideon said, "but I'm a cop. I prefer solid proof." There was a brief silence. "What aren't you telling me?"

"If I told you, it wouldn't be what I'm not telling you anymore."

"If you really want my help, you might consider being more cooperative," Gideon said. "It's damned difficult working with you."

"Virtually impossible," Constantine replied.

Gideon sighed. "You think Marguerite was raped?"

"Probably not. Why would someone risk leaving his own DNA behind if the idea was to frame me?"

"If she calls us or shows up at the hospital, I'll let you know," Gideon said. "I wonder why she supported you in such a dramatic way. It seems way out of character. She struck me as scholarly and reserved." Pause. "She's a pretty girl, though. Smart, too. And—"

"Gotta go." Constantine ended the call before Gideon, who did anything his wife demanded like the love slave he was, started in on how badly Constantine needed a wife, too.

There. Duty done, responsibility discharged. From now on, he would stay out of Marguerite's way. If Gideon thought the girl needed protection, he would take care of it. Mentally, Constantine brushed her out of his life.

The crackpot bird said nothing. It should have at this point, but Constantine brushed away his consequent uneasiness as well.

His phone rang: Ophelia, Gideon's wife. She was a hereditary vampire, one of those rare human beings born with a gene that, with the onset of puberty, resulted in fangs, powerful sexual allure, and useful attributes such as excellent hearing, night vision, and physical strength. She was also a landscaper and one of Constantine's staunchest friends. "You don't know who Marguerite is, do you?"

He hated not knowing stuff, especially stuff that mattered. "Apparently not."

"Neither did Gideon," Ophelia said in a satisfied tone. "Her father was a filmmaker. He made some of the first great porn for women. I know exactly how great, because I watched a lot of it during my dry years." Before her marriage, Ophelia had gone celibate for a while, and she'd tried everything to keep her desires under control. "It's really gorgeous as porn goes, but there was a huge scandal when he was caught using a sixteen-year-old actress who had gotten hired with a fake ID. If he'd been an ordinary porn king, it might not have mattered so much, but he preached his own version of women's rights, which got a lot of influential people riled. The press ran with the concept that he was a pedophile."

"Sucks," Constantine said, "but so what?"

"Well, for one thing, it wasn't true. The guilty party was a male vampire who wanted the girl to be his leading lady in one of the films."

"And you know this how?"

"Tony told me." Tony was an older vampire who owned a restaurant in town. "McHugh's dead now, but there was a lot of respect for him in the vampire community because he didn't out them to save his own skin. But keep this to yourself, because Tony says Marguerite doesn't want her background generally known."

Good luck to her. Ninety-nine to one, Nathan would dig it up. Why had she taken such a risk with her story about tantric sex? Maybe it wasn't to protect Constantine at all but to protect herself from a rape story instead. Absurdly, a vague disappointment pricked at him.

At a tremulous wail in the distance, Ophelia said, "Talk to you later," then added smugly, "I just thought you and Gideon should be in the know."

Fine, but Marguerite's past didn't make any difference to him. With any luck, he wouldn't have to see her again.

He laid his head down again and resigned himself to a long wait. During a short reconnoiter when he'd returned to the mound, right after Marguerite left, he'd learned a little about the Enemy: a reasonably agile man of medium weight with around size eleven boots. Couldn't get much more average than that. The dude had done a hell of a lot more damage slogging up the mound, carrying Marguerite, than Constantine had in months of running. More interesting was last night's guitar. The kid had wrapped it in a sweatshirt and stowed it in some brambles on the back slope of the mound. When? Constantine wondered. Why hadn't he taken it home?

With luck, he'd be back for it soon, and Constantine would get all the answers he needed.

He dozed for a while in the dappled shade of the tree. A crow—possibly the same one—flapped onto a higher branch and alerted him, then soared away again. Now there were people in the park—four of them, headed slowly toward his mound. Two white men, one fortyish and balding and the other younger and taller, with a wavy bush of yellow hair. A woman in her thirties, with a voluptuous figure, smooth café au lait skin, and a faint frown. And Myra again, red-faced and angular with an impatient stride.

Constantine shifted against the great branch and visualized himself as one with the tree. With a little concentration, he could alter people's perceptions. He could make them feel ecstasy or pain; he could make them see things that weren't there. He'd done it regularly at concerts, sending visions into the minds of the audience. It felt like a combination of telepathy and some kind of aura manipulation—similar to giving one-touch orgasms but with mental rather than physical touch.

Which had been all very well until he'd lost control of his mind and sent his own angry, destructive thoughts into the audience, causing fights and riots—and even some deaths.

At least he hadn't lost the ability to conceal himself. Now, with the tree to help him—because the tree was what people expected to see—no one would notice him unless he wanted them to.

As the visitors toiled up the stairs of the mound, snatches of an insistent voice drifted up to him. "Deep-seated hatred . . . remnants of reservation upbringing . . . crowd control . . . dramatically increase the tendency to violence . . ." That was the yellow-headed dude.

"That's all very well," the balding man said, "but you can't base a study on just one individual. Even anecdotal evidence requires—"

"I'm not an idiot," the younger man said, and behind him the voluptuous woman rolled her eyes. "I just need Dufray to tell me *how* he controls people. He can sway whole crowds, making them deliriously happy or turning them to violence. Once I understand how, I can set up an experiment where others emulate him." He made a rude noise. "It's a lot more likely to produce useful results than your dumb visions."

"My visions," the older dude retorted, "are an effort to find ways to promote world peace."

The other guy snorted. "Yeah, like your drum circles and prayers. What a crock. Control is the only way."

Constantine contemplated the drawbacks of controlling one's tendency to violence. The younger dude's name was Roy Lutsky, but the crew called him the Loony Pontificator. It had started with letters and phone calls, after which the Pontificator haunted concert venues and the fan club office, yammering on and on, begging and pleading for interviews in the Sacred Cause of Psychology. Security had hustled him out more than once. Lately, the Pontificator had taken to sending abusive emails, pissing off the people who ran the fan club. Constantine could think of a number of methods of getting rid of the Pontificator for good, but none seemed worth the effort, and in any case, the bird would natter at him for weeks afterward about going against its advice. Last night, it had given him grief about his plan to punish a pervert who was harassing underage girls. The bird had decided it wasn't Constantine's job.

Fine, Constantine told it now. *That fits right in with my plans to go out west.*

You'd be a lousy-ass hermit, retorted the crow.

The little group crossed the mound in the increasing heat of the morning. The balding man appeared to have given up on both talking and listening. Myra looked as if she was being dragged against her will, while the voluptuous woman seemed to be thinking of something else entirely.

"They wouldn't let me within a hundred yards of the concert last night, but there was a sighting here this morning," the Pontificator concluded. He wore a mustardy-khaki safari costume today. Constantine gave thought to a temporary appellation of Monotone Yellow. Or Turkey Turd Man.

The voluptuous woman emerged from her reverie. "A what?"

The older man took a few steps onto the mound, gazing across the wide, grassy surface. "A sighting?" he asked. "Of aliens?"

"Of Constantine Dufray, of course." The Pontificator dug into his pocket for a little box of jelly beans and popped one into his mouth. "He's been impossible to find lately."

Constantine considered dropping out of the tree and scaring the Loony right out of the Pontificator.

"He seems to have been here all night," Myra said indignantly. "He has no respect for the rules."

"He's a rock star and a vigilante," the other woman said. "What else do you expect?"

"It's true, then!" the Pontificator cried. "He was here, but whoever called to let me know purposely waited until it was too late." He ate another jelly bean. "What did I do to deserve this?"

"He pops up way too often for my taste," Myra said. "Filling the park with noisy fans and having sex on the mound with his groupies."

The other woman wrinkled her nose. Not one of his fans, it seemed. "Do they party up here often?" Not too disapproving to be curious, though.

"How should I know?" Myra said. "I don't patrol the mounds at night, but we haven't had a lot of complaints lately. I'm irritated because he had a woman with him this morning, as well as a reporter babbling about date-rape drugs and human sacrifices. By the time I got up here, everyone was gone, leaving a bunch of debris behind. Dufray's people cleared it up, but he shouldn't have been here in the first place. If you ask me, it was just another publicity stunt."

"Why wasn't I told?" the Pontificator said. "He talks to tawdry reporters. Why not me?" He popped another jelly bean into his mouth, pulled out his cell phone, and stalked away.

Myra turned brusquely to the balding man. "What's your proposal, Professor Wilson?"

The older man went on at length about methods of inducing dreams and visions. Meanwhile, the Pontificator tore at his shaggy yellow mane and ranted and raved his way across the mound, covering all four corners and slopes and staring angrily across the deserted park at the other two mounds. He returned to the little group, which now stood in the shade at the outer reaches of the live oak tree. The squirrel chattered fiercely at this fresh invasion.

"I think it's a workable idea, Eaton," said the voluptuous woman to Professor Wilson. Shoe size: ten or eleven, fairly wide. The Turd's: a little narrower, eleven, maybe eleven and a half.

"Do you really, Lavonia?" Eaton ran his fingers distractedly through the remnants of his hair. "Just imagine: midnight under the full moon. A group of dedicated students meditating in this sacred spot . . . I'm sure we'll come up with at least a few good visions. It's a pity we can't bring the equipment here, but once they know how to induce a vision, hopefully they'll be able to reproduce the experience in the lab." He cocked his head anxiously at Myra.

"I don't suppose it will do any harm," Myra conceded, turning to the other woman. "Or any good, but that's not my problem. Lavonia, I want you present as the voice of reason."

"People see visions at Dufray's concerts," said the Pontificating Turd, messing with his cell phone. It looked like he was surfing the Internet. "The question is, how does he do it?"

"Clever lighting and a lot of people on drugs," said Lavonia. "You'll have to make sure no one comes to your meetings stoned, Eaton. That would skew your data."

"You have to ask Dufray to attend!" The Turd's tone had grown feverish. "You could have him explain how it works. They're not all on drugs. I've interviewed hundreds of fans. It might have to do with mass hypnosis, but my personal feeling is that he manipulates his aura."

"You'll have to time your meetings for right after they spray for mosquitoes," Myra said. "We'll get a spraying schedule from the city. Just make sure there's no drinking, no drugs, no littering, no sex, no running up and down the mounds. I'll hold you fully responsible for any damage."

"Once you've got Dufray here and he's done his thing, I'll interview him," said the Pontificator. "He won't be able to refuse when it's under the aegis of the university."

"That didn't work for you before," Lavonia said. "Maybe Constantine's not interested in your study."

Constantine gave her a thumbs-up and picked a baby acorn. The squirrel objected loudly. "Hush," Constantine said, crawling slowly along the branch toward the perimeter of the tree's vast spread. A red-shouldered hawk circled lazily overhead, and Constantine felt it laughing. His spirit guide must have gotten tired of inhabiting a crow.

"How can he not be interested?" demanded the Pontificator. "He'll be reported in all the parapsychology journals and maybe some of the less prejudiced scientific ones. He'll be invited to conferences, give demonstrations, get the respect and admiration—no, the adulation—of thousands. How can he not want that?"

"He already has that," said Eaton. "Much as I'd like to consult him about Native American rituals, I can't have him here. He would distract the participants, and if he really is telepathic, like they say, he'd skew my study as much as drugs would—maybe more." He wandered out from under the tree, gazing into the distance and humming to himself.

Constantine gave Eaton a thumbs-up, too.

"You just don't care, do you?" the Pontificator bellowed. "You don't give a shit about truly important work."

Constantine leaned over and dropped the acorn directly onto the monochrome yellow head.

"Ouch!"

The squirrel scolded Constantine again and scurried to
the tip of its branch.

"It must have been that squirrel," said Lavonia.

Another thumbs-up. Constantine selected another
acorn and bided his time.

"I'll get an interview out of him if it's the last thing I do.
It's criminal, the way he's thwarting the cause of science,
and you're just as bad, Wilson. As for the people who call
and deliberately mislead me—" The Pontificator gaped at
the screen on his cell phone. "What the hell? This is Marguerite!" With a shaking hand, he shoved the display toward
Lavonia. "*She's* the woman who was here with Dufray?" He
got right in her face. "You knew, didn't you? She's going out
with him, and you didn't tell me! Everybody's against me,
and you're as bad as all the rest."

Lavonia put up her hands. "Calm down, Roy. She's not
going out with him. She got caught in a publicity stunt and
went along with it. What else would you expect? She's a major fan."

"But she *knows* him now. Finally, a breakthrough! She'll
be able to get me an interview!" He pumped a fist. "Yes!"

"I doubt it," Lavonia said. "She's not planning to pursue
the acquaintance. She's a sensible girl, and she knows he's a
dangerous man."

Her words fell on deaf ears, judging by the way the Pontificator was capering about. Constantine stifled a twinge of
dismay. *Not afraid of me, huh?*

The hawk wasn't fazed. *You give up way too easily.* There was nothing to give up on, seeing as he wasn't after Marguerite, but the bird just laughed. Sailing up there on the air currents, life must be peachy keen.

Maybe it was right, though. Not only had Marguerite shown very little fear, but she wasn't the least bit sensible. She had stood up for him this morning, most likely on impulse. *See,* he told the bird, *I'm trying to take her at face value. I'm trying not to be suspicious.*

Good for you, it replied blandly. Constantine felt the blood darken his cheeks. Christ, why must it make him feel like a little kid asking for praise? He shook the guide's presence away and went on with his own thought process.

In spite of his warnings, Marguerite had kissed him. Again, not sensible at all. Not only that, her roommate had possibly been murdered—and maybe merely letting Gideon know about it wasn't enough. He took out his phone and sent Jabez, his bodyguard and fellow vigilante, to make sure she'd gotten home okay. There. He'd discharged his responsibility. Again. Damned if he would beg for more snarky approval from the bird.

The instant the Pontificator stood still, Constantine dropped another acorn.

"Damned squirrels!" cried the Pontificator, rubbing his head. "They should all be shot. I'm getting out of here." He took off with long, frustrated strides. Constantine stood up, leaned perilously out through the branches, and lobbed one straight shot directly at the back of his head.

"What the hell?" The Pontificator whirled. "Did you throw that at me? Did you?"

"Throw what?" Lavonia frowned. "Eaton, did you throw something?"

But Eaton was yards away and oblivious, humming under his breath while consulting a compass and a scrap of paper. "Sunrise . . . five something . . . a little bit southeast, I suppose, right around where the chicken house is." He squinted across the park in the direction of Hellebore University's agricultural complex and began humming again, this time one of Constantine's more peaceful songs, albeit somewhat off-key.

We've heard that before, the hawk said. Then, *Look who's on his way to the mound.*

"There must be somebody up that tree!" stormed the Ridiculous Pontificator.

"Only a squirrel." Myra gave an exasperated wag of the head.

"And a hawk! Look at that gorgeous hawk!" cried Lavonia, eyes on the sky. "Come on, Eaton. It's getting way too hot to be outdoors." They headed for the stairs.

Constantine swung easily downward. He had just landed on a huge limb twelve feet above the ground, when the fan from this morning crashed out of a path in the woods and thundered up the side of the mound. With a delicious slow-motion anticipation of the enfoldment of doom, Constantine waited for the conflagration. The guy bounded onto the surface of the mound, the others turned, and all hell broke loose.

"Zeb Bonnard!" Myra hollered, her ruddy complexion turning to flame. "I'll wring your neck!"

Something pinged in Constantine's gut, like last night but not quite, and then was gone. What *was* that? And why?

This kid matters, the bird said, whatever that was supposed to mean.

The Idiot Pontificator joined in. "You damned hoodlum—you're the one who made that crank call, sending me up here when it was too late!"

"Roy, that's uncalled for!" Lavonia cried. "You have no proof Zeb did anything."

"Zeb, Zeb," said Eaton, "think of your poor father. Think how your mother would have felt."

The four of them surged toward the kid. He danced back, fists clenched. The Furious Pontificator let out a howl of rage and lunged.

Constantine joined in the fun. One moment Zeb and the Pontificator were locked together in a death grip. Then the Pontificator was on his hands and knees on the grass, and Zeb was scrambling up, panting and heaving. Constantine nodded at Myra, winked at Lavonia, and said to Eaton, "We should talk some time, Professor Wilson."

The Pontificator got hurriedly to his feet. "Dufray! Finally, we meet! Your bodyguards don't understand the importance of my work, but I'm certain you—"

Zeb's fist slammed into the Pontificator's blathering face. "Fuck your work, you stinking bastard! Die, you scumsucking sonofabitch!" He drew back his fist for more.

"That's enough, Zeb," Constantine said.

Zeb subsided immediately, his mask of hatred dissolving in a flurry of other emotions: resentment, shame, fear.

Constantine motioned with his chin. "Get your guitar, and don't leave it outdoors again. Let's go."

∼

Could it get much more embarrassing? The acting head of the Chemistry Department had crept up behind her while she was reading about the thirteen-inch penis. Her face hot, Marguerite clapped the paperback shut.

"But if you're really going out with that sleazy rock star," Al Bonnard said, "why would you need to read that trash?" Since she'd never heard Al express an opinion about Constantine before, his choice of epithet came as a surprise. So did the mild sparking of his aura. He had a sharp tongue, but usually his aura was only marginally more emotional than a mannequin's.

She pulled herself together. "Damn it, did Lavonia already call and tell you everything? I thought she was somewhere with Eaton Wilson."

"Of course she called me, but I would have found out anyway." Al sighed, setting down his espresso and pulling up a chair. He tossed a couple of the chocolate-cherry bonbons from which he got his nickname onto the table. "Eaton's got some harebrained scheme about inducing visions. Even in Bayou Gavotte, science has to toe the line. He'll never get funding for it, and no one will publish his results, so I don't know why he wastes his time." Pause. "Or Lavonia's." He took out his phone and ran a finger across the screen. "You seriously don't know, do you? Marguerite, you're all over the web."

She cringed. "Already?"

"You're not really having tantric sex with that fellow, are you?"

"I'm not having tantric sex with anyone," Marguerite said repressively.

"It sure looks like you're having some kind of sex with him." Images popped up on the screen. Crumpled clothes, tousled hair, and a mildly annoyed expression. It wasn't what she would have chosen for public view, but . . .

The next picture appeared. Marguerite's entire body heated at the sight of herself in a passionate clinch with Constantine Dufray. She covered her eyes with her hands. "Oh. My. God." She got ahold of herself, externally at least. The Celtic knot that had taken up residence in her gut this morning was trying new and original twists, but she didn't need to show it. She sighed and lowered her hands. It was just a kiss. No big deal—as long as they didn't link her with her father. If and when they did, she would deal with it. Somehow.

"What the hell got into you?" Al said.

Constantine's tongue? "I was caught unawares," she retorted. "Somebody drugged me while I was at that impromptu concert last night at the mounds. I woke up to find myself in the middle of a publicity stunt cooked up between Constantine Dufray and a reporter."

"Even Dufray wouldn't cook up this crap," Al said. "A bunch of drivel about drugs, rape, and human sacrifice can't possibly help his career, if anything can at this point. Did you call the cops?"

Jeez. "No, because I'd already told the reporter I was up there waiting for Constantine. I don't want to look like a complete idiot." She unwrapped a foil-covered bonbon.

"It didn't occur to you that saying you were sleeping with Dufray was idiotic?"

"All that occurred to me was that the reporter was trying to make me say horrible things without any proof at all.

When it comes to reporters, I have a knee-jerk reaction at the best of times." She fumed silently for a minute, slowly consuming the candy. She scrunched up the foil wrapper and dropped it into her pocket. "Please don't tell anyone about it. I had Lavonia check me, and I wasn't raped, so it's okay."

"It's not okay." Al frowned at her, then put up his hands in a typical male gesture. "However, what you do about it is your business. The one small mercy is that the media don't have your name. So far you're just his mysterious new love—though why they insist on calling the unfortunate participant in every celebrity's latest sexual exploit their 'love' is beyond me—but somebody's sure to recognize you and let them know."

Marguerite shuddered. "But when they realize I'm not having a relationship with him, it'll blow over." She hoped.

"I'm glad to hear that," Al said. "Even though we're in Bayou Gavotte, it doesn't exactly enhance the dignity of Hellebore University." He made a face as she handed the book to the cashier. "You're actually *buying* that trash?"

She bristled. "Why not? Now that I've met him, I'd like to learn more about him." She exchanged grins with the cashier.

"What a waste of money," Al tsked. "Be a fan if you must, but don't forget that the man's not safe."

"Don't be a mother hen, Al. I get enough of that from Lavonia." Time to change the subject. "Does Zeb have a job at the moment? I need someone to mow my lawn."

"No, he lost his last job and failed a drug test at the next place he applied," Al said, his tone morphing from concern to exasperation. "His grades last year were terrible, and his

French is so abysmal that I had to hire that little goth girl, Juma, to tutor him. To top it off, I just got a call from Myra at the mounds. She caught him running there this morning, for which I would ground him if there was the least likelihood he would obey me. He got into a bar brawl a few days ago. With my luck, he'll get caught in one of the clubs next. He's completely out of control." He closed his eyes and squeezed the bridge of his nose. "At least his poor mother isn't here to see it."

"At heart, he's a good kid," Marguerite said. "I know it's hard being a single parent, but he'll turn out fine. You'll see."

"I wish I could be so sure." Al shook his head wearily.

"He won't come to harm mowing my lawn." Marguerite signed the charge slip and picked up the book and her coffee. "I'd be happy to pay him to weed the garden and trim the hedges, too. Pauline used to do all that."

"I'll mention it to him, but I can't promise anything." They made their way toward the door. "From what Myra said, he went berserk and attacked Roy Lutsky right in front of her, Lavonia, Eaton Wilson, and Dufray." He blew out an exasperated sigh. "Lavonia told me much the same story, but she says Lutsky started it. Typically softhearted of her to stick up for Zeb, but I'll be fortunate if Lutsky doesn't charge him with assault." Another sigh—this one even more irate than the last. "And if that wasn't bad enough, next he went waltzing off with Dufray."

A chill shimmied down her spine. "Zeb went someplace with *Constantine*? Why?" Now Al's annoyance made more sense.

"Because Dufray crooked his little finger," Al said explosively. "I don't know what to do about that boy, Marguerite. He's developed a violent temper since his mother died. If he gets under the influence of a vigilante like Dufray, anything could happen."

Right. Anything at all.

CHAPTER FOUR

You didn't argue with Constantine Dufray, Zeb told himself. If he hadn't been so mad at Lutsky, he would have laughed at the others: Myra glaring but throwing up her hands, Professor Wilson dithering and apologizing to everyone on Zeb's behalf, and Lavonia gawping at Constantine—for once at a loss for words.

Zeb avoided looking at Lutsky, who was still struggling to stand, because he would only want to deck him again. Instead, he obeyed orders and retrieved the guitar. No way was he going to apologize to Lutsky or to anyone else. Fortunately, Constantine didn't seem to expect him to. He motioned Zeb forward with a flick of the chin and jogged ahead of him toward the stairs and on down. Zeb tried to explain about the guitar, saying he'd left it on the mound because his dad would confiscate it if he brought it home, so he had to find a friend to take care of it for him—which was true. Dad would say a guitar would distract him from his schoolwork, which was bullshit. He didn't do his schoolwork now, so what difference would it make?

He'd meant to retrieve the guitar while on his morning run, and instead he'd bumped into Marguerite and all that shit up on the mound. Finding that had been pure luck—something he was short on lately—and he'd gotten away with the knife, the only thing that really mattered.

Constantine not only didn't respond to his explanation about the guitar, but he didn't speak the whole way into downtown. No, you didn't argue with him, but what about lying? Once the questions started coming, Zeb would have no choice. He needed to fold his aura tight and get into the safety of what he called the Zone, because there nothing fazed him. No matter how bad things were, once in the Zone he could make himself sound polite and cooperative and with luck be uninteresting enough that he could slip away.

Zeb followed Constantine through a wrought iron gate into the courtyard behind the Impractical Cat and suffered a pang at the sight of the concrete benches beside the fountain. Marguerite had done the faux finish, and Zeb had delivered them himself a few weeks earlier, when his father had finally let him get his driver's permit.

Zeb liked Marguerite. She never tried to tell him what to do. Never tried to make him talk about his mom. Not only that, she understood stuff about him that no one else did. He'd never even realized he was manipulating his aura until she explained it to him. But asking if she was okay was tantamount to admitting he'd been up there on the mound, and if Constantine had seen him take the knife . . . Life was hell, and it was getting worse by the minute.

They were greeted by soft Caribbean music and two wilted and sulky girls sitting on the only bench still shaded by the wall of the neighboring building. The girls straightened, widening their eyes and giggling at the sight of Constantine.

"Here for the waitress jobs?" He sounded bored.

They nodded and giggled again, and he unlocked the back door and motioned them through. "Help yourselves at the soda fountain. Sooner or later somebody will show up to interview you."

The girls cast longing glances at Constantine as he led Zeb into the kitchen. Leopard—drummer, restaurateur, and head of the underworld that kept the clubs in Bayou Gavotte safe—glanced up blearily from his coffee, grunted at Constantine's brief intro, and flicked a hand toward the coffee urn.

Constantine filled two glasses with ice water and passed one to Zeb. "Drink Lep's pigwash if you like," he said, "or have one of my cappuccinos."

Zeb flicked a glance from Constantine to the indifferent Leopard. "Um . . . both?"

Expressionless, Constantine shoved a coffee mug toward him. Zeb set the guitar against the wall, served himself, added sugar from a bowl on the table, and huddled around the mug.

He wasn't a kid anymore. He'd gotten away with decking a pervert in a bar a few days earlier because the guy couldn't risk bringing himself to the attention of the cops, but Lutsky might well charge him with assault. Dad would already be plenty pissed off when Myra called to rant about him running on the mounds. Zeb didn't much like Lavonia, who thought fucking the old man gave her the right to act like she was Zeb's mom, but she would probably tell Dad that Lutsky had gotten physical first. For what it was worth.

He tried to get into the Zone, but it didn't work. He'd let himself get too riled, and not knowing what to expect next didn't help one bit. He'd gotten reasonably good at dealing with his dad, but he couldn't predict Constantine's behavior, and the rock star was every bit as intimidating as people said.

In silence, Constantine made him a very dry cappuccino. In more silence, he fired up the grill and produced two huge plates of eggs, tomatoes, home fries, and toast. He set one in front of Zeb and dug in.

"Shit, man," said Leopard, who had for several minutes been staring out the window with a glazed expression, "here are a couple new ones. Did you let those other chicks inside?"

"Too early in the morning for eye candy?" Constantine speared some home fries and proffered the fork to his friend.

Leopard batted the fork away. "Those chicks don't qualify as any kind of candy."

"Poor jaded Lep." Constantine nodded toward Zeb. "My friend here beat on the Pontificator this morning."

Zeb sputtered. Pontificator? Dad would love that one.

Leopard brightened and reached across to high-five Zeb. "Well done, my man!" He made a face out the window. "Let 'em suffer a bit longer."

Constantine went on eating, and Zeb tried to gauge how soon he could leave. The longer he stayed, the more uneasy he became, and the more he felt like he needed the Zone, the more it eluded him. In any other circumstance, he would have been dying to talk to Constantine, like any other fan. As it was, the best he could hope for was to get the hell away.

"So tell me, Zeb," said Constantine.

Zeb's hope evaporated.

"What's your grudge against Professor Lutsky?"

Relief surged up, resentment in its wake. "It's no big deal. I can't stand him, and I lost it." The lack of sleep lately wasn't helping his self-control either.

"I can't stand him either, but I haven't beaten him up. What's the story?"

Zeb sliced at his eggs and said nothing. Constantine waited. Zeb raised his fork to his lips, glanced at Constantine, and threw it down. "Oh, for fuck's sake. If you really must know." He seethed a few seconds more, struggled, and spat it out. "The bastard killed my mother."

"Say what?" Leopard grimaced at Constantine. "Shit, man, I told you we should have done him."

Constantine showed nothing but mild interest. "He didn't literally kill her, I assume. Indirectly, though?"

"Maybe, but it was his fault, the stupid jerk." Zeb took a deep breath. "He hit on my mother, and she told him where to go, but I guess you know what he's like. Once he gets an idea in his big, fat, stupid head, he never lets go. He kept pestering and pestering her, trying to get her to run away with him. Anyway, they were at the same conference in New Orleans. She got a ride home with him, and their car went off the road. It hit a tree, and my mom died, and that bastard only got a few bruises."

"He's the one who should have died," said Leopard.

Grateful, Zeb nodded. "I freaked out, and I wanted to kill him, and I tried, too." He shrugged. "I was, like, only twelve. I didn't stand a chance. Now, though, I might be able to do some damage." He shoveled a mouthful of egg and potato. "I'm going to be in such deep shit over this. And for running up and down the mounds," he added glumly, spreading strawberry jam on his toast.

"Training for the Classic?" Constantine's eyes were almost sympathetic. "I ran it a couple of times."

"Cool," Zeb said, surprised.

"Running's a good way to burn off rage," Constantine said.

Bullshit. What was this, a frigging therapy session? The only alternative to rage was the Zone. If he folded his aura, rage couldn't get at him—not his own rage, not anyone else's. If he folded it tightly enough, *nothing* could get at him. He stayed in the Zone most of the time, because once there, he could avoid thinking—about his father and his dead mother, about decisions, about life and death—and just do what had to be done.

But his aura wasn't doing what he wanted, so he let resentment take hold again. People usually got that just fine. "Better than anger management classes, that's for sure. Lutsky says I should go through forgiveness therapy so I won't hate him anymore. Not that my dad gives a flying fuck about Lutsky or Myra and the stupid mounds, but he plays all the standard hypocrisy games like everyone else, so he'll make me go."

"Lutsky kills your mom and then gripes at your dad 'cause you don't like him?" Leopard rocked with laughter. He shuffled toward the coffee urn to the gentle reggae beat, dreads bobbing.

Zeb decided Lep was okay. "Well, it wasn't *his* fault, of course. It was just an unfortunate *accident.* And *everyone* was in love with my mother because she was a vampire." Not that he usually let this information slip, but the underworld knew all about vampires, so it didn't matter. "You know what people are like with vampires. Can't help themselves, although with a little discipline and self-control, it's not that big a deal."

He was getting off track. He was probably even trying, deep down, to impress Leopard and Constantine, which was mortifying. "What with Dr. Wilson worshipping her and a zillion other assholes wanting to sleep with her, who could blame poor, *poor* Dr. Lutsky for going off the deep end? And he was so *devastated* afterward. So terribly *sorry.* What a *tragedy.* Shit!" He banged his fist furiously against the palm of his other hand.

"Jesus, a freaking soap opera," Constantine said. "You had four witnesses this morning that Lutsky attacked you first. If none of the others support you, feel free to call on me, for what it's worth."

"Um, thanks." This would have been an incredibly cool offer under any other circumstances, but Zeb knew all about bargaining with the devil. "Lavonia will probably stick up for me, but it won't do any good. My dad will just say I need to learn self-control." He stood. "Well, thanks for breakfast. And for the guitar. I gotta go face the music."

"Sure, Zeb," Constantine said. "But first, why did you take the knife?"

~

"Knife?" Zeb's voice cracked.

Constantine didn't want to feel sympathy for the kid. He would far prefer last night's instinctive dislike, but to some extent, that had dissipated. His spirit guide said it had something to do with the kid mattering, but, as usual, it made no sense.

Regardless, he needed information. "Who are you protecting, Zeb?"

Silence.

"Somebody drugged a woman and left her on the mound."

More silence. A shrug.

"He may have raped her."

"No." Zeb shook his head rapidly and then went still again.

"You know he didn't rape her?" Silence again. "You don't think he did? You just hope he didn't? Which is it?" More silence; a stubborn kid. "It looked like he was planning to sacrifice her. Why wouldn't he make use of her first?"

Zeb went green, but shook his head again. "Look, is Mar—is she okay?"

Ah. So Zeb did know Marguerite, and Marguerite knew Zeb, and she'd kept that to herself on purpose. Didn't want him to question the kid. Again, the suspicion surfaced that she knew more than she would let on. That her motives weren't what they seemed.

Inside his head, the spirit guide bristled with annoyance. Before it started making a nuisance of itself, Constantine acknowledged what Marguerite's behavior more likely meant: that she just didn't want him to hurt Zeb. "Marguerite seemed fine when I last saw her, driving away from the mounds. That doesn't mean she wasn't raped. It doesn't mean she's not in danger now. If she's a target, it's your responsibility to protect her, not the man who's threatening her."

"She's not a target," Zeb choked out. "He likes—I mean, *everybody* likes her."

Ignoring Zeb's slip of the tongue, Constantine said, "You know and like Marguerite, and you know who did this, and yet you're protecting him." Pause. "Why would you want to protect someone like that?"

Silence again.

"You don't feel any sense of responsibility here? Not concerned about Marguerite? Not about some other girl getting kidnapped, maybe mutilated or murdered?" Pause. "No shame in you at all?"

Zeb flushed darkly under his tan but maintained his silence.

Constantine leaned back. "Okay, so we've established that you're too much of a lowlife to go for guilt, so how about bribery? Would front-row tickets do it? Backstage passes for you and all your scummy friends? Your pick of the groupies?" He watched chagrin cross Zeb's face, chased and replaced by fury. "Not enough, evidently. How about cold, hard cash?"

Zeb clenched both his fists and his teeth.

"No." Insulted, was he?

"Threats, then. I'm a dangerous man to cross." Constantine resisted the temptation to demonstrate immediately what he meant. Instead, he just said, "I can make your life hell."

Zeb's voice and eyes were bleak. "My life is already hell."

"I can make it worse," Constantine said, and then wished he hadn't. The kid's shrug wasn't one of bravado, or even of indifference.

Desperation. How familiar.

A chicken stalked past the window. It fluttered awkwardly onto the fountain and glared at Constantine with an unfriendly red eye.

A *chicken?*

"Whoa," Leopard said, opening his laptop. "This is serious business, kid. You don't want Constantine pissed off at you. Better give him the answers. Way too much of the bad shit you hear about him is true."

"Thank you," Zeb said. "I appreciate your advice. It's very kind of you to warn me." He turned to Constantine. "Fuck off."

The fool had no idea who he was dealing with. Constantine leaned forward, hands clasped. "Zeb, I don't want to hurt you," he said, meaning it but preparing himself all the same.

He'd always done what he had to, and this was no different. Marguerite didn't know any better and couldn't possibly be expected to understand. As for the bird in its many forms, all annoying, it could go to hell and wait for him there. "I don't want to hurt you," he repeated, "but I will."

The kid didn't respond, so Constantine released a brief twinge of pain. Nothing much, just enough to show him.

Zeb's eyes widened, but he showed no other sign that he'd felt the pain. "You can still fuck off." He stood. "I thought you *protected* innocent people."

Stupid, pigheaded kid. Outside, a whole host of birds were making a god-awful clamor. It sounded a lot like cheering.

"Which reminds me," Lep said into the charged silence that followed, "looks like someone got to that perv before you, bro." He clicked a few keys. "Some young guy beat the crap out of him in a bar the other day."

If Constantine hadn't been frowning at Zeb, trying to figure him out, he wouldn't have seen that betraying flicker. "You're that guy."

Zeb jutted his chin in response. "He's been hitting on a friend of mine. She's only fourteen."

Constantine blew out a long, slow sigh. Why couldn't that aggravating bird have given him this useful info earlier? But that was always its way—incomprehensible commands or veiled hints. "Go away, Zeb. I'll give you a while to think about it. Don't kid yourself—you *will* give me the information I need. You'd be a lot smarter to do it before someone else gets hurt."

Zeb went out, leaving the guitar behind. The chicken dropped from the fountain and out of sight. Good riddance.

Then it reappeared inside his head, clucking madly.

Lep eyed Constantine over the laptop screen. "That was unusually merciful of you. What's going on?"

"Shut up!" Constantine shook his head violently. "Get the hell out!"

"Who are you telling to shut up? I'm a dangerous man, too." He slid off his stool, let fly a few playful punches, danced away, and then leapt onto Constantine from behind.

"It's this frigging bird," Constantine said with a grunt. He stood and shoved his arms apart, sending Leopard and the stool flying. "Flapping around in my head like some manic chicken, talking absolute bullshit." He thudded his forehead with the heel of his hand and retrieved the fallen stool.

"Sure you don't mean chicken shit, bro?" Lep chuckled and went over to the espresso machine. "Glad I'm not a fucking Indian, stuck with a spirit guide. Enough shit going through my head without birds crapping in there, too."

"The bird says," grumbled Constantine, "I should stop being an asshole."

"No doubt about that." Lep tamped coffee into the portafilter.

"That hurting this kid will backfire on me. That's supposed to be news? I know how karma works."

Lep grunted, positioning the shot glasses.

"It says this kid is a gift from the gods," Constantine said.

Lep glanced at him. "Say what?"

"It says I might be able to redeem myself by way of this kid."

"Redemption." Leopard's voice was contemplative; espresso dripped slowly into the shot glasses. "We could all use some of that."

Constantine rested his head in his hands, listening to the coffee and the comforting hiss of milk being steamed. The spirit guide also said Marguerite was a treasure from the heavens, but he wasn't about to admit he'd even heard that one. Sure, it sounded good, but what was he supposed to do with her? Say he got up his nerve and slept with her. Even if, by some miracle, that didn't turn out to be a catastrophe, his Enemy was still out there. What if Marguerite got hurt through association with him? Why couldn't the bird tell him something useful about his Enemy instead?

On that issue, it was utterly silent.

Now that the bird had spoken its mind, it was taking its sweet time pecking its way across the patio and out of his head.

Lep set a double espresso on the table before Constantine and returned to his laptop. "Your bird might be right. I don't know what's going on with the kid, but he looks exactly like you used to: glowering over a cup of coffee before you did something."

"Great. So what's my role here? Mentor? Moral preceptor? I don't think so." Constantine noticed himself glowering and downed some espresso.

"You know what I think?" asked Leopard innocently.

They'd been over this countless times. "Your solution to everything is not the same as mine."

"Life is simple when you don't have a chicken messing with your mind, saying 'Do this, don't do that.' Maybe if you got laid now and then, you'd be able to think straight."

A bird cackled from some distant height. Not a chicken, though. Small mercies.

"Nathan Bone says you're making it with a hot babe. That news actually woke me up for a moment or two. Tantric sex, no less." He eyed Constantine and sighed. "I had hopes that for once it might be true."

"Shut up, Lep. I need to protect the girl, not destroy her." He paused. "I need you to do me a favor. Two favors."

"Sure, as long as you do yourself a favor, too, and start thinking seriously about getting laid."

"Believe me, I'm thinking about it way too much." He shook his head. "See what you can find out about Zeb—where he lives, some history on his parents, who he hangs

out with. Also, get me whatever you can on a prof at Hellebore named Eaton Wilson."

"Will do." Lep's cell phone chimed, and he read the display. "It's Jabez. He's at the babe's place. Says you sent him
there to scope the place out."

Constantine's heartbeat ramped up. "What's wrong?"

Lep hooted. "You *do* want to screw her! There's hope for
you yet." He relented. "She's not home yet, but something
went down last night. Jabez says you need to get over there
right now."

~

With a vague hope that he might recognize something, Marguerite led Al to her car to see the paraphernalia in her
trunk.

"Quite an impressive mask," he said. "The photos on the
Internet don't do it justice. Now, where have I seen one like
it?"

"There's a drawing of something similar in the mound
museum," Marguerite said.

"That must be why it seems familiar. For what it's worth,
the beads look homemade. The cup and bowl don't ring a
bell."

She thanked him and had just shut the trunk again,
when Janie, one of Lavonia's witch friends, waltzed up with
Roy Lutsky, whose aura was churning even more than usual
today. Marguerite groaned. Usually, bumping into acquaintances was one of the pleasures of small-town life. Not today.

She'd forgotten about Roy. Lutsky had been a pain
in the butt when he was errand boy for her father in his

college days, and he hadn't improved with time or a PhD in psychology. Unfortunately, thanks to her father, Lutsky knew she could see auras. He'd also gotten her the interview that had landed her the job at Hellebore University, so she owed him.

Damn.

"Why didn't you tell me you're going out with Constantine Dufray?" Lutsky demanded. "You were supposed to call me if you so much as met him!"

Marguerite cursed under her breath. Ages ago, Lutsky had asked her to read Constantine's aura if she got the chance—and she'd reluctantly agreed. Trust Lutsky to bring it up in public. The man had no tact or sense of time and place. Next he'd be blurting out questions about what she'd seen in the rock star's aura. "I'm not going out with him," she said in a hurry. "I only met him a few hours ago. Give me a break!"

"You've definitely been kissing him," Janie said. "Did you know your picture is all over the Internet?" Her eyes slid flirtatiously to Al. "Hi, Bon-Bon."

"Don't call me that," Al snapped, and Janie giggled. Marguerite didn't blame him. He was a distinguished-looking man in his late forties, and Bon-Bon was a juvenile sort of name. On the other hand, as long as he handed out candies, the nickname wouldn't go away.

"Finally, someone who is seeing him socially," Lutsky said. "The fan club people, except for Janie here, won't give me the time of day." His gaze bored into Marguerite. "What's he like up close?"

Fortunately, neither of the others knew what he was getting at. Janie said, "Yummy," and Al rolled his eyes.

"The same as at a distance," Marguerite said repressively. "Gorgeous and scary."

"You can get me an interview." That was Lutsky: a statement, not a request.

"No," Marguerite said. "I can't."

"Don't harass her," Al said. "She got caught in a publicity stunt, but she's not the sort of woman to date a rock star."

That rankled, but before Marguerite could retort, Janie said, "Oh, come on, Bon-Bon. What woman wouldn't want to date him?"

"A woman of discernment," Al said. "Which you clearly aren't."

She chuckled. "Marguerite didn't look all that discerning in the pic we saw." She grinned. "Is he a good kisser?"

"Yes," Marguerite said irritably.

"I bet," said Janie, dreamy-eyed.

Lutsky paced up and down behind the car. "According to the tabloids, his wife, Jonetta, said sex with him gave her nightmares."

"Such edifying reading material," Al murmured.

"Tabloids provide a useful societal function." Lutsky's brows drew together. "The sexual aspect of Dufray's abilities is not what I wanted to tackle, but it'll do for a start."

"Not by way of me, it won't," Marguerite snapped.

"Testy, aren't we?" Al gave her a wry smile. "Go home. Bathe. Put on some clean clothes. Then you'll feel better."

"No, she won't," Janie said. "There's only one cure for sexual frustration. She wants that hunk to finish what he started."

"You'll be making a significant contribution to academic knowledge every time you sleep with Dufray," Lutsky said eagerly. "If you tell me all about it, that is."

"Don't be an idiot. She's not really taking up with that freak," Al said.

Again, Marguerite had to suppress a retort. She could take up with Constantine if she damned well pleased.

"You didn't call him a freak when you asked me to get free tickets," Janie said.

"Those were for Zeb," Al retorted, "and a major tactical error on my part. If anything, attending those concerts increased Zeb's tendency to violence. I'm lucky he wasn't trampled to death. It's hardly a suitable environment for a scholar like Marguerite."

"Even scholars have sex drives," Janie said. Now it was her turn to roll her eyes. "Oh, come on, guys. Jonetta was on drugs. She was hallucinating. According to what I've heard from quite a few adoring fans, he can give a woman an orgasm with just one touch."

"Now that does sound like a hallucination," Al said dryly.

"Or even without touching her at all," Janie added.

"Where's the fun in that?" Al huffed. "What a bunch of baloney." As a chemistry prof—a garden-variety scientist—he tended to pooh-pooh anything the least bit woo-woo.

Lutsky stopped pacing and frowned at Marguerite. "There may be some risks. His wife also said being in the same room with him was sometimes so painful that she'd pass out—but those hardly matter in the pursuit of scientific knowledge."

Marguerite got ahold of herself. "I'm tired and dying for a shower. Nice to see you all, but I really must get going."

"I need to interview you first," Lutsky said, motioning toward the bookstore. "I'll buy you another coffee."

Marguerite gritted her teeth. "Thanks for your generous offer, but I have to go."

Janie said, "Come on, Marguerite. Dish."

Marguerite managed not to snap again. "No."

"No what?" grinned Janie. "The one-touch orgasm? The tantric sex?"

"The hysteria-induced pain and the fainting spells?" murmured Al. "The tabloids probably paid his wife for that one."

"Even if you're not sleeping with him," Lutsky said, "you damned well *will* tell me your impressions from this morning."

"Later," she said to the lot of them and drove home. She would have to tell Lutsky something, but she needed to plan exactly what to say. Sure, she owed him, but she probably owed Constantine far, far more. Not that she was ever likely to tell him so, because she had no idea how to go about it, given the chance. *Did you really induce my scumbag uncle to kill himself? Because, if so, thanks very much!*

Not the sort of thing one said aloud, even if one had good reason to mean it.

If he hurt Zeb, she might not feel so grateful anymore. But maybe Zeb would tell Constantine why he'd taken the knife, and everything would work out all right. With luck, in a day or two, she would thankfully crawl back out of the limelight to her calm, peaceful, private life, and Lutsky would have no reason to pump her for more information. Sighing, she turned the corner into the quiet cul-de-sac, where until a few weeks ago she had shared a house with Pauline and shared it now only with Pauline's dog.

Two vehicles were parked in front of her house: a big blue pickup truck and a familiar white BMW. People gawked from behind windows. A few kids hovered by the curb. And on her front porch, sitting in the wicker chairs and chatting like the best of friends, were Nathan the reporter and Constantine Dufray.

CHAPTER FIVE

She'd done this before; she could do it again. This was no phalanx of reporters, merely one slimy pseudo-Brit, and if he had a camera, it was small and not in your face like that horde of photographers with their flashes when she was a terrified child.

Regardless, she intended to go right past these two publicity freaks into the house, lock the door, and take that much-needed shower.

She got out of the car. On the porch, Lawless thumped his tail in greeting but didn't move from where he was lying next to Constantine on the side away from Nathan. This was surprising and yet not. If she had a choice, she would sit as far away from Nathan as possible, too; on the other hand, Lawless didn't like strangers. Even if he'd escaped the backyard and been wandering—which he did all too often—he wouldn't treat someone he didn't know as a friend.

She smiled politely at the hovering kids. She opened the trunk to remove the dog food and other purchases, and suddenly Constantine was right there. Lawless stayed put, shaggy head on his paws, watching.

She glared at the rock star. "What are you doing here?"

"Waiting for you, sweetheart." She couldn't read the expression in his cold eyes, nor could she stop him from dropping a swift kiss on her lips. A dizzying kiss—he smelled dark and good. He'd taken a shower and changed into clean clothes, and his aura was almost peaceful, except for little wisps of desire. Had his dead wife once felt like Marguerite did now? She didn't want to deal with desire, his or hers.

He reached for the dog food, but she grabbed him by the T-shirt and pulled him toward her again. "What did you do to Zeb?" she hissed.

Annoyance fizzled in his vibes. "Nothing much." Pause. "Yet."

She got right in his face. "Where. Is. He?"

His mouth hovered just above hers. "How should I know? 'Going home to face the music,' I think he said." His tongue flicked out to brush her lip, but he withdrew abruptly and hefted the bag of dog food.

So Zeb was okay, at least temporarily. "Get rid of that reporter," she muttered, grabbing the grocery bags and slamming the trunk shut, the mound paraphernalia still inside. She shot a murderous look at Nathan as he ambled forward, grinning.

"Hello, hello, Marguerite McHugh," the reporter said.

"Fuck off," she said before she could stop herself, and then realized she didn't have to. When the ten-year-old Marguerite had said the same to the reporters, it had only strengthened the case against her dad; now she could curse as much as she pleased. She stormed up the walk.

Don't go inside the house, Constantine said in her head.

She slowed, turning to stare at him, then away. "I'm busy today. I have to get my groceries in the fridge and leave again." She hurried up the steps.

I said, don't go inside.

He had such gall! She set the grocery bags on the porch, unwrapped the breakfast sandwich, and gave it to Lawless, who gulped it down and sank his head onto his paws again. "Constantine, I don't know why you're here," she said, fumbling through her keys. "I told you I'm busy. Later, I may be free, but—"

Constantine plucked the keys from her grasp. "For our quickie, of course." *Wait until Nathan's gone.* "I promise you, darlin', I'm so hot for you that we'll both be exploding in a flash." His aura simmered now, desire in its maroon, red, and gold hues flickering, arousing her in spite of herself.

Oh, no. Surely he didn't really mean what he was saying. No way. Yes, he was a masterful kisser, but she hardly knew him, and only a few hours ago he'd been trying to drive her away. And yet this chemistry and the images that streaked through her head enticed her. She wasn't used to finding sex alluring. Growing up in the shadow of a sex scandal had pretty much removed whatever luster sex might have had to start with.

Behind them, Nathan snickered, and she whirled. "Go away, Nathan. You're not invited." Neither was Constantine, but unfortunately she couldn't telepath that right back at him.

"Aw, come on now, love," Nathan said. "The daughter of Porno McHugh must have a comment to make."

"I already made it," she said. "If you read up, you'll find it's exactly what I said to the reporters all those years ago." It had been a disastrous mistake, but bad language didn't reflect on her father anymore. "Go away, or I will call the cops and have you removed."

"But that scene up on the mound makes so much sense now," Nathan whined. "It was a great promo move on Constantine's part."

She had to get into the house before she blew. "Give me my keys," she growled at Constantine.

"Go away, Nathan." Constantine's aura flickered dangerously, but his demeanor remained completely calm.

Nathan gave a gusty, obnoxious sigh. "You're so bloody cold. Poor Marguerite didn't realize having sex with you meant her daddy's sins would be dredged up all over again."

"Why should I care? He's dead, and it's old news," Marguerite said, proud that her voice didn't tremble one bit, but her fingers shook as she stuck the key in the lock. She shouldn't be this upset. This was exactly what she'd expected. Lawless crowded up next to her, getting in the way.

"If I were you, I wouldn't even let this dude into your house," Nathan said. "He's not what he seems."

"Since *you* are exactly what you seem," Marguerite said, "I know better than to heed anything you say. Besides, I know precisely what Constantine is—he's *fabulous*." And if he touched her, she had no idea what she would do.

Nathan tsked. "Such a pretty girl you are, and so bright and well educated, and yet you're completely under Constantine's thumb. I quite like you, Marguerite. I'd much rather report your safe escape than your unfortunate demise at the hands of this murderer."

"Last chance, babe," Constantine said, amusement in his tone. *You can still change your mind*, said his voice in her head, not laughing at all. Aloud, he added cheerfully, "Better run while you can."

Oh, no, you don't, thought Marguerite. This was a danger-ous game, but anger trumped all. "I'd much rather let you catch me," she said coyly and felt like throwing up.

"Ooh," Nathan said, eyes wide, big grin. She took a deep breath. She would *not* allow him to get to her.

Constantine put a warm hand on her shoulder. "Come on, babe. Let's go shower and have some fun."

An image of herself and Constantine, wet and naked, slid into her mind, and Marguerite shivered in spite of her-self. Had that image come from him, or was it her own? His image, she thought, but it fit naturally, perfectly in her mind. She had never been so receptive to sexual suggestion before.

"Beat it, Nathan," Constantine said. "Or else."

"Yikes!" Nathan took off down the sidewalk. "When Con-stantine says, 'or else,' it pays to obey." The kids and neigh-bors continued to gawk. Nathan got into his pricey little car and zoomed away.

Finally, Marguerite got the blasted door open.

≈

Constantine pushed her gently inside. Lawless shoved in after her and slumped to the floor again. Constantine re-moved the key from the lock and shut the door. He rested the bag of dog food against the wall.

"Oh, no!" Marguerite said, barely above a whisper. A boom box stood to one side of the door, and the DVD player had been unhooked and half pulled off its shelf. Books and CDs were all over the floor. She set the grocery bags down.

"There's no one in here," Constantine said. "I already checked." Seeing all those music CDs strewn around hurt just as much now as a half hour earlier when he'd checked out the house. He would replace anything that was damaged—if she let him. She wouldn't have let him in the house if he'd given her a choice. He got out his cell and texted Gideon O'Toole.

"Oh my God." She picked her way through the debris on the floor.

"Sorry about delaying you, but Nathan didn't need to see this. The kitchen is a mess."

She headed straight there without a word and gaped at the smashed canister and flour all over the floor. "What could someone possibly want to steal from the kitchen?"

"Nothing," Constantine said. "I think your dog came indoors and surprised whoever it was, and the intruder threw the canister at him. He has one humdinger of a headache this morning."

"Oh, poor baby! You've already had enough trauma in your life." Marguerite went down on her knees beside the dog.

"Below his ear," Constantine said. "I cleaned him up."

She separated the shaggy hair to examine the abrasion. "Thank you! He must have been outdoors, probably outside the fence, when the house was broken into. Since Pauline died—she was my roommate—he's worse than ever about digging his way out and wandering in the woods." Her voice choked up a little, but she swallowed it down. "You came in through the doggie door and surprised the bad guy, huh?" Lawless licked her hand, and she wiped it on her shorts as she stood. "He was Pauline's dog, and they'd really bonded, and then she died. I wish I knew more about taking care of dogs."

I wish I knew more about taking care of women, Constantine thought. Looked like he was stuck taking care of this one whether she liked it or not—until he defeated the Enemy. But now, at last, he had a witness who knew something. Zeb *had* to talk. There was no other way.

He had to keep Marguerite close and safe and also maintain his distance. He had to make her trust him, but he couldn't risk trusting her, even though surprisingly—stupidly— he kept wishing he could. Not that it would accomplish anything. He couldn't have sex with her if he trusted her because he couldn't risk hurting her, and he couldn't have sex with her if she was untrustworthy because—

Because you might really hurt her. You're going to confuse yourself to death and save the Enemy the trouble, said some cheerful, self-satisfied, and wisely distant bird.

He followed as she glanced into all three bedrooms. "They don't seem to have touched what little jewelry I have. Pauline had even less. Why waste their time burgling such an unpromising house?" She turned and bumped into Constantine, who had been wondering much the same thing.

As well as inhaling the scent of Marguerite and her bedroom. He'd known immediately which one was hers when he'd gone through the house earlier, and not just because one of the other bedrooms was an office and the third had no sheets on the bed. Now her scent assailed his nostrils, and his prick rose rapidly to attention. Damn. Usually, he had complete control over his libido. Maybe Lep was right, and it had been just too un-fucking long.

"Get out of my way," she said, her voice quivering.

"Don't be afraid. I won't hurt you."

"I'm not afraid of you," she said, shoving at him. "Stop looking at my bed. What I said out there on the porch is irrelevant. The answer is no."

What? "I didn't mean what I said out there either. That was for Nathan's benefit."

"Maybe, but you meant it all the same. You may not intend to do anything about it, but you want it. I can tell, and it's really getting on my nerves." Pause. "And not in a good way!"

"What do you mean, you can tell?" He was certain his cold demeanor was as secure as always. He was keeping his thoughts corralled inside his head. He looked down at his jeans. Sure, there was a bit of a bulge, but . . .

She looked down as well, and a beautiful blush rose up her throat. "Move!"

He backed away down the hall, hands raised. "Sure, you're an attractive woman, but I didn't come on to you. I kissed you this morning because it was a good way to get rid of Nathan."

"No," Marguerite said. "You kissed me because you wanted to. You were pretending you weren't interested, but . . ." She shook her head. "You are just plain weird, and you're creeping me out."

Not enough, evidently; she was way more pissed off than scared. "How could you possibly know whether I wanted to kiss you? I gave no sign. I didn't give one now either, until you gave me the once-over." Women were always giving him the once-over, but he never responded in such an alarming way. He'd learned to be totally Zen about sex. It wasn't a need, just a drive, and one could sublimate one's drives if it mattered enough. In his case, it mattered way too much.

"I just know," she said gruffly.

Huh. So she was affected, too, more than she cared to admit.

Grumpily, she added, "You're so horny it hurts, and it's making me extremely uncomfortable. You need to leave. I appreciate your checking out my house, but I need to call the cops and get a police report." Her eyes widened. "Hey! How did you know about this mess?" She drove him ahead of her into the living room. "What were you doing in my house earlier, and how did you get in?"

"I picked the lock," he said. "I've already informed Gideon O'Toole, a friend of mine in the police force. He'll be over shortly. I asked him not to come until I got rid of Nathan."

"Gideon O'Toole," she said. "He's the one I spoke to when my roommate died a couple of weeks ago. He was sweet." Pause. "He's a friend of yours?"

"Why not?" Constantine was used to incredulity—how could a vigilante be cozy with a cop?—but in her, the surprise annoyed him enough that he added, "His wife has been one of my closest friends for years."

She stared at him, brow wrinkled, as if trying to read him. He resisted the temptation to smooth that worried brow. She had a lovely face, thoughtful and determined, with warm hazel eyes and kissable lips that tempted him every time he looked at her.

"Even murderous vigilantes have friends," he added.

She nibbled her lip, blinking. He wished he were the one doing the nibbling.

"I can produce references," he added plaintively.

"Are you suggesting we should be just friends?" She huffed. "I don't think so."

"Since you seem determined to support my sorry ass, we'll have to be just something for at least a day or two," he said. Why was she so sure he lusted after her? "I told Gideon about what happened this morning on the mounds, by the way. Wanted him to hear it from me first."

"Fine, but why did you decide to check out my house?"

Evading the question, he said, "Either the guy was skilled at picking locks or he had a key. I saw no sign of forced entry anywhere." The thoughts ticking through her mind showed clearly across her face—chagrin, worry, anger, a touch of fear. "I'll replace the lock for you," he said.

"That's not necessary," she said immediately. "Where was Lawless when you arrived?"

"The dog? He was hiding under the house."

"He doesn't usually like strangers," she said, picking up a few CDs, shuffling them, dropping them again.

Constantine winced; he believed in treating CDs with respect. "Animals like me." He didn't care much about what most people thought of him, but he had to stifle a wish that Marguerite . . .

No. He squatted, gathering the CDs, gently sorting them and restoring them to their cases. Marguerite's eclectic taste included all of his own CDs. He probably shouldn't find that encouraging, but . . .

He shouldn't want to be encouraged, period. Next he would be rationalizing, telling himself it would be different this time. Then he would come on to her, and when she succumbed to his advances, all hell would break loose.

One of his own early CDs had been broken in two. He would definitely replace that one whether she wanted him to or not.

"You don't need to tidy my stuff," she said. He ignored her, and she added, "Why did you decide to check out my house? How did you even know where I live?"

"I've seen you at the Impractical Cat a couple of times. I wondered who you were, so I found out. You teach linguistics part-time at Hellebore and do faux finishes to supplement your income." He flashed his rock star smile. "Gorgeous honey-colored hair and hazel eyes aren't exactly a dime a dozen."

"That's mighty close to coming on to me," she shot back. "Now answer my question."

"I walk along the bayou quite a bit. That's why your dog knows me. I've been watching you on and off for a while."

"Really."

"Yes, really." Why didn't she seem rattled?

She just looked at him. "If you wanted to attack me, you've had plenty of opportunity. And if you only want to look, well, looking's free. Stop trying to freak me out like you're some wacko stalker, because I don't believe it, and you still haven't told me why you checked out my house."

"You'd be a lot safer if you did get freaked out." He should just telepath her some really scary shit and get it over with. He waited for the bird to lambaste him. It said nothing.

He sighed. "I was concerned about you after what happened on the mound. I sent Jabez, my bodyguard, over to snoop around and make sure you weren't endangered here, too. He realized something was wrong and let me know."

"Why would my being drugged on the mound suggest that my house had been burgled? That makes no sense at all."

"But your house *was* burgled," Constantine said. "Maybe it didn't make sense then, but it sure does now."

Marguerite watched Constantine put the cushions back on the couch and processed his remark. "But *you* thought it made sense then. And you've been watching me, and not for sex."

That wasn't entirely true. She was good to look at, and looking was all he'd ever get to do—that and using his imagination—so why not? The bird must have gotten tired of contradicting him, but he knew better than to think it might have changed its mind. It would simply wait until proven right. Which, in hindsight, it often was.

He just couldn't take the risk that it wasn't, especially not now.

At a low growl from Lawless, Marguerite went to the window. "Detective O'Toole knows something about this, too, doesn't he?" She opened the door for Gideon. Constantine put a hand on Lawless, and he subsided, closing his eyes.

The cop came in, gave a silent whistle, and asked the obvious question: "Is anything missing?"

"I don't know." Marguerite led him through the kitchen and then into the hall. "I haven't had time to go through anything, but there was very little of value. At first glance, the other rooms look fine, but some of Pauline's stuff looks as if it may have been disturbed. I've been going through it over the past week, and I'd put it all in tidy piles." Her voice faded down the hall, and Constantine stayed where he was, finishing with the CDs and going for the bags of groceries. In the kitchen, he put the perishables in the fridge and freezer, neither of which held any unpleasant surprises. The last bag was from the bookstore; on a whim he peeked inside.

Jesus Christ. Why was she reading that tripe? On the other hand, it did show interest, right?

Shit.

Some damned bird or other cackled in the distance.

He left the book in its bag on the kitchen counter and returned to the living room just as Marguerite and Gideon finished their tour. "I put your perishables away," he said.

"Oh. Thanks." Clearly, her mind was elsewhere. Definitely not on him, or that he was trying to be helpful, or even . . . *fuck.* She looked tired, and worried, and all he could think about was kissing her, about whether maybe she could like him, even a little bit. *You're pathetic,* he told himself.

A soft flutter of wings descended into his mind. *No, you're cool,* said the bird. *You're fine.* It hardly ever did that anymore. When he'd been a screwed-up kid, the bird's reassurances had kept him sane.

Which just went to show how close to the edge he was now.

"But why would he dig through the piles of Pauline's stuff?" Marguerite asked, sinking onto the couch. "It's mostly paper. Why leave the boom box by the door and the DVD player half-unplugged?"

"He must think we're idiots." Gideon gave Constantine an exasperated look. "Not that I blame him. The chief has decreed that what happened on the mound was a publicity stunt, so that's what I'm stuck going with."

"It's better that way," Constantine said. "This is my deal anyway."

Marguerite's perplexed frown went from one to the other of them.

"This is a search masquerading as a burglary," Gideon explained. "If the dog hadn't surprised him, you probably wouldn't have known anyone had been here at all."

"Okay," Marguerite said slowly. "But if so, what was he after?"

"Even more important," Constantine said, "did he find it?"

"How are we supposed to know that, if we don't even know what it is?" Marguerite demanded. "Pauline had nothing of value, and neither do I."

"Do you have an office at Hellebore?" Gideon asked. "Did Pauline?"

"I have a small room," Marguerite said. "We cleaned out Pauline's office last week."

"We being who?" Gideon asked.

"A lot of people," Marguerite replied. "We left it unlocked so people could go in at their convenience and take anything that was theirs or that they could use. There's a lot of loaning of books and so on that goes on, and I didn't need any of her office supplies." Her eyes widened. "You think this ransacking has something to do with Pauline?"

"Since hers is the only room that shows signs of really having been searched, it seems likely."

"But why? She was just an ordinary person—a fiftysomething literature prof."

Gideon blew out a breath. "That's what we have to find out. Make out a list of everyone you either know or think went into her office to go through her things and email me a copy." He handed her his business card. "If you find anything missing from the house, let me know, and I'll add it to my report."

But she wasn't listening. Her eyes gazed at nothing, her thoughts clearly in the past. "I knew it," she said. "I knew it when you spoke to me about Pauline the day you found her."

"Knew what?" Gideon asked, ever the cautious cop.

"You thought it might not be a suicide," she said. "I told you I didn't believe it, and I insisted that she was better. You came up with a lot of standard platitudes, but you were uneasy the entire time."

"You're right," Gideon said. "I don't know how you could tell, but I was."

"You think Pauline was murdered," Marguerite said.

∼

Zeb closed the French text with relief. How could he be expected to concentrate on reflexive verbs? He was still surprised that Constantine had not only let him go home but hadn't had him followed. Maybe when you could torture by telepathy, you didn't need to know your victim's address. He was pretty sure the rock star had sent him a twinge of pain back there in the Impractical Cat. He'd finally been in the Zone by then, somewhat protected by his folded aura, but he couldn't keep it wrapped tightly around himself day and night.

"That sure was a waste of time," Juma said.

Zeb liked Juma. She was the super-studious type, taking high school and college courses at the same time. She hired herself out to tutor almost anything, but she didn't expect anyone else to care about the stuff she liked. While Zeb struggled with French verbs, she'd curled up with her laptop, translating love poetry from Old Provençal. She was also into goth, but it suited her raven hair, pale skin, and major attitude.

"Before you do the lawn-mowing thingy, let's go to PJ's for coffee," she said. "Zelda just texted me, and she'll be there, too."

"Okay," Zeb said, relieved to postpone going to Marguerite's. She might just want her lawn mowed, but on the other hand, even if she'd been unconscious when he bumped into her on the mound, she might know by now that he'd been there. An article on Yahoo! News said she was going out with Constantine Dufray, but Dad had told him and Juma that Marguerite had been caught in the middle of a publicity stunt. Which was bullshit, whether Marguerite knew it or not. Regardless, she might have questions, not only about the knife but about why he hadn't stayed to help her—questions he couldn't answer. His life was beginning to feel like a game of Whack-a-Mole. No matter how much he tried to protect people, some other crap popped up.

They took their time walking through the swelter of the day to PJ's Coffee Shop. Zelda was already there, grumpy because every guy in the place had his eye on her. She seemed to grow more gorgeous every day, although if you analyzed her attributes separately—red hair, bright-blue eyes, a cute nose sprinkled with freckles, small breasts, no hips, and a truly lovely smile—she shouldn't be any more attractive than any number of fourteen-year-olds. Not only was she underage, but she was also way, way younger than most of the guys who hit on her. She had explained it to him one day when he'd intervened between her and a jerk who was trying to convince her to sleep with him. Actually, she'd showed Zeb her fangs, surprising the hell out of him for a second or two. "They make me irresistible," she said glumly.

And how. She already gave off massive amounts of allure. She was trying to learn to control it, but the perv he'd beaten up in the bar the other day was only one of the many guys she had to fend off on a daily basis.

He knew how that worked; his mom had been a hereditary vampire, too. Eaton Wilson still worshipped her even after she'd been dead almost five years, but Zeb didn't resent him too much, because although he was a pussy and a bit crazy, he meant well. Oh, and he wasn't responsible for her death. Every time Zeb thought about Lutsky, he burned up inside. Dad seemed to think playing practical jokes on Lutsky should satisfy Zeb's urge to beat the dude to a bloody mess. He even encouraged the jokes and showed some appreciation afterward, but it wasn't enough. "Get over it," Dad had said. "I know you hate Lutsky, but nothing will bring her back."

He'd almost punched his father out over that one, only controlling himself because his mom would have wanted him to. She'd told him time and again that Dad needed lots of love and understanding. Not that it had done a lick of good; Zeb was still controlling himself, but just barely.

Zelda scooted them right back out of PJ's, carrying a cup holder with their iced coffees. "Let's go to the park so we can have some privacy."

This made no sense to Zeb—it was hot as hell outdoors and cool in PJ's, and he was more than able to protect her from other guys—but he walked the block to the park with the girls, who seemed in a jolly sort of mood. They settled themselves on a bench under a live oak near the playground, which was almost empty. Not surprising, at 90-plus degrees and 100 percent humidity.

He slouched between them and stretched out his legs. "Why are we out here again?" Sweat was making his back itch. Why had Constantine let him leave? He'd finally gotten himself into the Zone, ready to take whatever came his way, and then Dufray had let him go.

Regardless, Zeb couldn't help but be glad of the reprieve. He had too much to take care of as it was. He couldn't afford to waste his energy anticipating telepathic pain from Constantine Dufray.

"Well," Juma said and giggled.

He stared. Juma never giggled. She wasn't the type.

"Well," Zelda said. "The thing is, Zeb, we both like you a lot."

"I like you, too," Zeb replied impatiently. He didn't want to be here. He wanted to get some sleep. He wanted to figure out what to do next and then do it. Oh, hell, he wanted everything to be done. Over with.

"So," Juma said, "Zelda and I have come to an agreement. We've decided we want you for our first."

"Both of us," Zelda said, as if that clarified something. "We both want you for our first."

"First what?" He was dealing with matters of life or death. What if Marguerite had overdosed on that drug she'd been given? What other innocent person might be next? He didn't have time for women acting all mysterious. "What are you talking about?"

Across him, the girls exchanged glances. "You tell him," Juma said.

"No, you," Zelda said. "You're older."

"And you're a vampire," Juma said. "It's your specialty, right?"

Zelda scowled. "I'm only fourteen!" she whispered. "I shouldn't even be *thinking* about this!"

"Oh, all right," Juma said. "Zeb, we want you for sex."

"Both of us," Zelda said again, with her dazzling vampire grin.

What the hell? He sat up. His sweat-soaked shirt made a sucking sound as he pulled away from the bench. "Are you nuts?"

Juma giggled again. "Not both at once, silly, although by what I've heard, most guys would go for that."

Zelda rolled her eyes. "Guys can't help being twisted."

"Thanks," Zeb said, trying unsuccessfully not to imagine being in bed with both of these crazy girls.

"Even if we wanted that, which we don't, the timing is all wrong," Juma said. "I need to have my first sexual experience soon, and Zelda has to wait a couple more years."

"Almost three," Zelda said, "unless we go to Mississippi to do the deed. The statutory age there is sixteen."

"Ideally, it would be the other way around," Juma said. "Zelda first and then me, because I'm not interested in sex at all."

"And I'm already getting way too interested," Zelda said. "I get horny a lot, but Mom said that's only to be expected in a vampire."

Zeb tried pulling his head together. Reluctantly—lately he'd had little or no sex drive—his dick was reacting. "Um . . . why me?"

"Mom said my first guy has to be someone stable," Zelda said. "Someone who won't get all obsessed with me. A guy I can trust."

The last thing Zeb felt these days was stable, but he let that pass. "And you?" he asked Juma. "Seeing as you're not interested in sex, why bother?"

"I'm seventeen, so I'm legal. I have to get it over with sometime, and Zelda's mom agrees you're safe."

Just what a guy wanted to hear—how goddamned safe he was.

Jesus. If they only knew.

"Safe for women, we mean," Juma added. "If I were a guy, I wouldn't want to tangle with you, but you're a good friend for a girl."

"Sort of like Constantine," Zelda said.

Like *Constantine?* Zeb leapt up off the bench. Zelda and Juma knew Constantine Dufray, of course, what with Zelda's mom being a club owner and Constantine a vigilante, but . . . He glared down at the two girls. "In what way could I possibly be like him?"

"He's a great friend for a woman," Zelda said. "Scares all the other guys away, but he's totally safe. He was my Aunt Ophelia's best friend when she'd given up guys and was super horny, and he never, ever hit on her."

Yesterday, Zeb would have been flattered at this comparison. Today, not so much.

"Also, you're really cute, so it won't be too much of a hardship," Juma said.

"Good to know," Zeb said sourly. He glowered at them over his plastic cup and sucked up the rest of his coffee. At any other time, he might have considered getting Juma interested in sex a worthwhile challenge, and although at the moment Zelda felt sort of like a little sister, in a few years that might change. He'd definitely go for the experience of sex with a vampire.

Except that he might not have a few years. Vampire sex was only one of the many, many life experiences he might just have to do without. Too many people needed protecting, and he was taking so many risks lately that he had begun to fear for his own life. Along with that came the big question: if it came right down to a life-or-death situation, would he kill or be killed? He didn't want to think about that. Not yet.

"Well?" Juma said. "Will you do it? Me, sometime soon; Zelda, when she's old enough."

"Unless you fall in love with Juma or someone else in the meantime," Zelda said. "I won't hold you to it if you already have a woman. That would be contemptible and totally unworthy of a vampire."

Zeb took the top off his cup and drained what was left. "Tell you what. I'll think about it, and you think about it too, and—"

"We've already thought about it," they said in unison. "We want you."

"We'll discuss it again, if and when I'm available." He tossed his cup into a nearby trash can and walked away, adding under his breath, "And if I'm alive."

CHAPTER SIX

Constantine watched the dawning of both understanding and indignation in Marguerite's eyes. "If you suspected it wasn't a suicide, you should have told me," she said.

"I don't like to jump too far ahead in my thinking," Gideon said. "There was every reason to believe it was suicide, and yet . . . it didn't feel right."

"Of course it didn't! She *was* better. She *was* doing fine." Marguerite jumped up. "Why didn't you *tell* me?"

"Feelings aren't evidence," he said. "Why voice something that upsets people and leads nowhere?"

"But . . . but why would someone kill poor Pauline?" Her gaze sought inspiration in the untidy room. "What could someone have wanted that was worth killing her for?"

"At the moment, your guess is as good as mine." Gideon shrugged. "Probably better."

"Right now, I have no clue, but it's a relief that she may have been murdered."

Constantine let out a whoop of laughter.

She colored, eyes wide. "I didn't mean it like that. It's just that I have to be able to trust my, uh . . . instincts."

"The same instincts that refuse to accept that I'm a wacko stalker?"

"Yeah, those ones." Pointedly, she turned to Gideon, who was watching them with ill-concealed amusement. "Fine, but how did he do it? She overdosed herself with her own prescription meds. There was no sign that she'd been attacked, restrained, or anything of the sort. Right?"

"None," Gideon said. "The only physical damage occurred when somebody ran over her after she was dead. No surprise if someone didn't want to report that."

"Especially if the killer did it just to make good and sure," Constantine said. Marguerite shuddered, but he couldn't even congratulate himself on finally freaking her out because it was the Enemy who'd done that. All he got credit for was putting what might have happened into words. He began picking up the books and sorting through them.

Marguerite made an agitated turn through the relatively small clear area in the middle of the room. "It makes no sense at all." She threw up her hands. "She had nothing of value." She made another turn. "No enemies." Back again. "Well, she hated . . ." She rounded on Constantine again, who stepped back. "You don't need to do that. In fact, shouldn't Detective O'Toole be dusting for fingerprints?"

"Not for a burglary without the chief's approval," Gideon said. "Yes, I know it's not really a burglary, but we can't tell the chief that."

"Why not?" Marguerite demanded.

"Long story, but the chief won't accept our murder theory without real evidence. He has already decided the episode on the mound this morning was a publicity stunt." He shrugged. "We're not likely to find any prints, Ms. McHugh. This guy is no slouch."

Marguerite grimaced. "Maybe, but—"

Constantine interrupted. "She hated . . . ?"

Marguerite glared at the two of them. "Men," she said baldly. "Absolutely loathed them."

"Doubtless with good reason," Constantine said. "We're not a pleasant gender."

"Speak for yourself," Gideon said. "Why did she hate men?"

"An abusive father followed by an abusive husband, and no, neither of them could have killed her or done this because they're both dead. Her dislike of men made for quite a bit of constraint with her male colleagues at Hellebore, but she'd learned to keep it to herself. In any case, none of them had reason to kill her or ransack her house. Would you please stop cleaning up?"

Just standing there would drive Constantine crazy. He had to *do* something. "It's that or play the cello." She blinked, and he added with a tilt of the chin, "The one in Pauline's bedroom."

Gideon, damn him, was shaking with suppressed laughter. "Constantine has a lot of nervous energy," he said. "He's also compulsively tidy, and it does him good to be useful."

With great difficulty, Constantine roped and hog-tied his annoyance. He didn't need the help of this well-meaning cop. He didn't need anyone's help.

"That's all very well," Marguerite said, "but this is police business. I don't see why Constantine can't just leave." She winced.

Oh, fuck, oh *fuck.* He hadn't corralled his emotions well enough. He'd *hurt* her again, just as he had on the mound. He snarled at the distant bird. *See? I* don't *have control.*

Marguerite gazed at him wide-eyed, a flurry of emotions traversing her face, but he had no difficulty recognizing one of them.

How dare she feel sorry for him?

～

Marguerite knew by Constantine's aura that she had hurt his feelings. He was quiet as stone, but he wasn't made of it. Well, of course not. Nobody likes rejection.

She fumbled for the right words. "I would chalk it up to stress," she said, "but that's no excuse. It's just that I hate being in the public eye, and the more I associate with you, the more I will be. I don't know how you stand it, day in and day out." Not only that, his horniness would drive her crazy, but no way was she getting into that discussion with Gideon here. "If you want to put the books away, that would be great." That wasn't entirely sincere, but she meant it when she added, "Although I'm sure we'd love to hear you play the cello."

"No, we wouldn't," Gideon said, apparently unaffected by the emotions roiling around the room. "We're working on a murder case. We need to be able to think."

Constantine's grin would have convinced anyone else. "I think better when I'm making music."

"Well, *I'd* like to hear you play it," Marguerite said. His aura calmed slightly; evidently, he believed her.

"I'll leave in a couple of minutes," Gideon said, "and then you can do all the playing and thinking you like. How do you want me to handle this, man?"

"Leave it to me for now."

"But . . ." With something akin to panic, Marguerite blurted, "I don't mean to be rude again, but what does Constantine have to do with this?" She turned to Constantine, desperate to explain without hurting his feelings again. "I really appreciate your going through the house first to make sure I would be safe, but you're not a police officer." To Gideon again: "Constantine can't investigate Pauline's murder—which you can't just ignore, regardless of what your chief thinks—and besides that, Constantine and I aren't really involved with each other. I was unlucky—at the wrong place at the wrong time—and just happened to be drugged and left on the mound."

It didn't just happen, Constantine said in her mind. Judging by the expression on Gideon's face, he agreed.

Oh, God.

The connections tumbled through her brain like vowel shifts across the centuries. She started pacing again. "It's a sort of daisy chain—a link between Pauline's death and this ransacking." A turn. "The ransacking and my drugging." Back again. "My drugging and . . ." She gazed into Constantine's dark, cold eyes. "Nathan and his informant. The one who told him to come to the mounds this morning."

"Yep," Constantine said.

"His informant and the murderer," Marguerite said, and sat plump down on the sofa.

Gideon sighed. "Told you she was smart."

Constantine's mouth quirked up. "So you did."

Whoa. Gideon had spoken to Constantine about her? When?

Constantine's smile disappeared as quickly as it had come. What a pity, because it had been a genuine smile.

She marshaled her thoughts and took a deep breath. "So you don't think I was a random choice for drugging last night."

"It kept you out of your house for a good long time," Gideon said, "and it provided a victim for the scenario on the mound."

"Thereby killing two birds with one stone," Constantine said.

"But he couldn't have known I would be at the concert. I was driving home from the coffee shop, and some kids yelled to me from their car. They'd just heard about it and were telling everyone they passed."

"Maybe it was a spur-of-the-moment decision," Constantine said, "like the concert. We were jamming in the Cat and just decided to go for it."

Gideon stood, turning to Constantine. "Anything else you want me to do?"

After a distinct pause, Constantine told him, "I'll text you."

"About what?" she demanded, glaring from Constantine to Gideon. "Detective O'Toole, if Constantine is planning to beat up . . . some innocent person to get information, you need to know right now that Pauline wouldn't have approved any more than I do, even if she *was* murdered."

"Ms. McHugh," Gideon replied placidly, "if you would kindly show me the paraphernalia from the mound, I'll be on my way. You can pick up the police report on the burglary tomorrow."

Unbelievable. "How can you just leave a murder investigation in Constantine's hands?"

"This is Bayou Gavotte," Gideon said. "The police deal with some crimes, while the vigilantes handle the others. If Constantine can find the murderer and dispose of him without anyone the wiser, you'll be safe, he'll be safe, and the rest of our fair town will be ignorant but safe."

"And what if Constantine—or any other vigilante—disposes of the wrong person?"

"I won't," Constantine said.

She turned on him. "But what if you do? How will you reconcile it with your conscience?"

"How kind of you to assume I have one," Constantine said. "As far as I know, I haven't screwed up yet."

"And you're okay with this?" she demanded of Gideon.

"Not really," he admitted, "but it's efficient, and I'm prepared to live with it until we come up with something that works better. We have a better record than the justice system, if that's any consolation." He went out the door, and Marguerite followed.

Lawless squeezed past her and into the street to greet Zeb, who was deep in conversation with a group of kids. She shook her head and flicked a hand at him. *Go! Go!* He gave her an unreadable look, detached himself from the group, and loped away down the street just as Constantine emerged onto the porch.

~

Judging by the defiant glance Marguerite shot at Constantine, she seriously expected him to take off down the street after Zeb. Seemingly, she also thought she could prevent him from doing whatever he needed to do to the kid, whenever he decided to do it.

God, she was such a turn-on.

Constantine strolled into the street, made nice with the kids hovering there, and signed the CDs they were clutching, while Gideon drove away in his old Mercedes and Marguerite retreated indoors, taking the dog with her. He called Lep to get the background on Zeb.

"He's been suspended from school once or twice for fighting," Lep said, "and he failed a couple of drug tests when applying for jobs. Tested positive for both weed and opiates." This surprised Constantine; he wouldn't have pegged Zeb as a druggie. "His mom was a vampire—which we already knew—and his dad's acting head of Chemistry at Hellebore. Several years ago, he won the Sexiest Professor Award."

Constantine did a mental eye roll.

"Seems to be at his wits' end about the kid, who went down the tubes after his mom died," Lep went on. "Zeb's a bit of a loner, but he's reasonably well liked by the other kids at school. No girlfriend at the moment, but he's pals with that goth chick Juma who tutors him in French."

This might seem like a strange pairing, but along with her dedication to schoolwork, Juma had major attitude—a result, Constantine assumed, of her difficult upbringing. He didn't know her well, but she seemed like a good kid. He couldn't see himself leaning on her for info about her friend.

"And the girl he beat up that perv over? It was Zelda Dupree."

Even worse—Zelda was like a daughter to Constantine.

"As for Eaton Wilson, he's a bit of an eccentric, but students like him. He's been in the running for Master Teacher a couple of times."

Constantine thanked Lep and texted Gideon with a request for more information, about which he intended to say nothing to Marguerite. He didn't need any more guilt trips just now.

Surprisingly, she'd left her front door unlocked. He found her manically sweeping the kitchen. "I can't believe he just *left* me with you," she said.

"If you didn't want me to come back inside, you could have locked the door."

"You pick locks." Her grip on the broom slackened, and her expression softened. He could have sworn she sensed his inner turbulence, which was impossible. He had himself latched down so securely that he hardly noticed it himself.

Calmly, coolly, displaying no feelings whatsoever, he said, "But I wouldn't have." Not that he didn't want to. He wanted to pick all her locks, break down all her barriers, and *invade* her.

She would like that, the bird said. *The invasion part, that is.*

Her fingers tightened around the broom again. Sweep. Sweep. "I realize that due to my stupid attempt to protect you from Nathan, I have to play a role for a day or two."

This was so ass-backward. He was supposed to do the protecting. No one ever protected him.

It occurred to him suddenly that he had taken her words at face value. He was trusting her in spite of himself.

"But the fact remains that you can't stay here." She put up a hand. "It's not that I don't like you." One brush-off after another. "I'm sure you're trying to help, but . . ."

Clearly, his spirit guide had gone out of its mind. Unfortunately, it was still in possession of his. He took the broom out of her clasp. Her bosom rose and fell, her nipples showing hard through the thin T-shirt. *Nothing to do with sex,* he told the bird. *She's just riled.* He looked away and set to work with the broom, but it did no good at all. He wanted to pull the T-shirt over her head, peel the bra away from those quivering breasts, and feast on her.

"Gideon says I need your protection, and I don't see why. The guy seems to have gone through Pauline's stuff, and I already know there's nothing worth anything there. He has no reason to come back."

"We don't know what his reasons are for anything he's doing, except to get at me."

"I understand your need for self-preservation—"

"You understand nothing about me. I refuse to be responsible for any murders I don't commit myself. Therefore, I need to protect you." He stilled the broom. "Go ahead and take your shower while I clean up." No big deal; he wouldn't imagine her naked and wet only a few feet away. He'd think about that new riff he'd been working on the other night. It was one hell of a sexy riff; he'd written it just after watching Marguerite and her dog from the safety of the bayou. He'd been thinking about toppling her into the water and taking her then and there.

Oops, said the bird.

Marguerite was looking at him as if he'd gone out of his mind. "You want me to take a shower." Pause. "While you're in the kitchen." She threw up her hands. "Thinking about me wet and naked!"

"I'm not—that is, I won't be—" Christ. He was babbling. What had happened to being Zen about sex? She was just another woman, and being horny shouldn't reduce him from total control to incoherence. "I didn't telepath anything. What are you, a mind reader?"

"No, of course not." She averted her eyes. "I just *know*."

He pounced on that. "*How* do you know?"

"I just do."

Well. This was interesting, and it put him at a tiny bit less of a disadvantage. It might be fun to find out what went on in that honey-blond head, behind those hazel eyes. "It doesn't matter what I'm thinking. I'm attracted to a lot of women, but I don't act on the attraction. You're a fan, and in your imagination you've painted me as something entirely different from what I actually am. You have a skewed idea of me."

"No," Marguerite said, "you *are* skewed."

He couldn't help but grin at that. "True, but you can go take your shower. I swear upon my honor and all that's holy, I will not come on to you."

"I believe you," she said. "But has it never occurred to you that I might come on to you?"

~

"No." Anxiety tore into the arousal in Constantine's aura, shattering, scattering the sensual vibe. He put up a warning hand, set the broom against the fridge, and fended off Marguerite with the other hand, too, as if she really were attacking him. "Don't even *think* about coming on to me."

Now, *this* was genuinely bizarre. "Ordinarily, I wouldn't be thinking about it," Marguerite said. "Believe it or not, devastatingly attractive as you are, I would prefer not to think about it. I do without sex most of the time. It's just not interesting, but as long as you are aroused, I will be aroused as well."

"No," he said again. "It's too dangerous."

"Why? Are you HIV positive?"

"No, and I don't have any other STDs that I'm aware of. I'm just not safe."

Oh, *God*, he pissed her off. But it didn't matter, since she had no intention of coming on to him, now or ever.

"What are you going to do to Zeb?"

"Whatever it takes," Constantine said. "Why didn't you tell me you knew him this morning?"

"Because I planned to talk to him myself. I arranged for him to mow my lawn, but that's a bust now. He's a troubled kid and doesn't get on well at school or with his dad, but he gets on fine with me. He would have talked to me."

"A friendly conversation won't cut it," Constantine said. "You know what Zeb let slip? That the guy who drugged you knows you and likes you, too."

Nausea rose into her gorge.

"Scary, isn't it? Makes you sick, doesn't it?" His aura twisted and stretched, and a vision of a monstrous glistening snake flashed into her mind.

"You're so *horrible*," she said, her voice shaking. "I feel so sorry for you."

Constantine's aura burst into flames. He laughed—a short, harsh bark. "Me?"

"Yes—you." Marguerite's head hurt, and her stomach heaved, but she stood her ground. "You're so unhappy and filled with . . . with pain and misery, and you hurt people instead of talking to them, and—"

"Don't jump to conclusions," Constantine said icily. "I fed Zeb breakfast. I talked to him plenty. I offered him tickets and the pick of my groupies. I even offered cash, but he wouldn't tell me what's going on. If I have to hurt him, I will. And since you don't want me here, I'll send one of my bodyguards to protect you."

"I don't want your damned bodyguard," she said. "If and when I decide I need one, I'll get my own. Get out of my house. I'm going to lock the door. Kindly refrain from breaking in again."

∾

Constantine barely got in a few words about keeping the dog and her phone beside her at all times before she slammed the door behind him. His cell phone rang. He wasn't in the mood to talk to anyone, but he never ignored Zelda. "Hey, kid. Can I call you back?"

"No," said the vampire. "I need your help. I think my friend Zeb wants to kill himself, and I don't know what to do."

Constantine went slowly down the steps and stopped on the walkway, listening to Zelda blurt out her fears for Zeb and to the absolute silence in the back of his mind, which meant the bird knew full well it didn't need to add a word.

"He's your hugest fan in the world," Zelda said. "If he'll listen to anybody, it's you."

Constantine got rid of Zelda, offering meaningless comfort and help that he knew might have had a slim chance of acceptance yesterday but would now be refused. For all he knew, his threats had pushed the kid closer to the brink.

A blue jay fluttered past and landed on a crepe myrtle, looking ever so perky and pretty among the leaves. *How about a truce?*

Very funny. We tried that, remember?

Not with me, dummy. The jay cocked its head to one side. *With the chick.*

Constantine turned and considered knocking, considered trying Marguerite's door, but . . . what was the point?

You'd get laid, said the bird.

And then everything will be hunky-dory, right? It'll all fall into place.

Yes! the jay screeched, and Constantine got into his glossy blue pickup truck and glowered all the way to downtown Bayou Gavotte, wishing he had the guts to believe it.

CHAPTER SEVEN

"That's one heck of a long penis." Lavonia stared at the charcoal-pencil sketch Marguerite had just finished of the most intense sex dream of her entire life.

She supposed it shouldn't be a surprise; she wasn't prone to sex dreams as a rule, but awareness of Constantine's desire for her was well-nigh impossible to shake off. For a long moment after shutting the door behind Constantine, she'd just stood there, resting her forehead against the cool wood with her eyes closed. She listened to his footsteps and to his voice, low and indistinguishable, as he answered his cell.

Done. Finished. Gone.

Violence was a lousy way to get information. She had to find Zeb before Constantine hurt him. Since he didn't have a job elsewhere, he might have signed on at one of the sex clubs. Some of them didn't care about the rules and hired any minor foolish or desperate enough to work there. They didn't openly flaunt their infractions for fear of the underworld, but as a painted messenger boy, Zeb wouldn't be easily recognized—by most people.

Because most people couldn't read auras. Most people couldn't control them well either. Zeb did, and because of this, Marguerite had a good chance of spotting him.

She locked the door, went straight for her phone, and called Tony Karaplis. If there was one man in town who could protect her and also stand up to Constantine, it was Tony. He also had entrée to every sex club in Bayou Gavotte.

"Love to go clubbing with you, baby," came Tony's deep voice, "but won't that piss off Constantine Dufray?"

Cripes. "Please don't tell me you're afraid of him."

Tony chuckled. "Nah, but I hear you're his woman now."

"I am not his woman," she snapped, "and he can piss himself dry and shrivel up for all I care."

"That bad, huh?" Tony said. "All right, then. What time should I come by?"

That settled, she showered, shut herself in the bedroom with Lawless and the cell phone, and conked out. She slept the sleep of the justified until the phone woke her just before the climax of the dream.

It was about Constantine, of course, and filled with symbolism that was far too easy to interpret. Constantine's penis encircled her twice, binding her arms to her sides, before looping between her spread legs and poising itself at the opening of her vagina. Grumpily, she'd tried to reassure Lavonia that she was doing fine, but her friend insisted on coming over anyway. When she got there, she exclaimed about the break-in, fussed over Lawless, and commended Marguerite on having the sense to call the cops. "Which you should have done about being drugged on the mound," she added predictably.

"Constantine told them," Marguerite said. "*Before* I called about the break-in."

"He wanted to get his version of the story in there right from the start," Lavonia said cynically and told Marguerite about the rock star breaking up the fight between Roy Lutsky and Zeb on the mound. "I'm pretty sure he was throwing acorns at Roy, although how he managed to keep out of sight in the live oak is beyond me. He winked at me," she added. "I wish he hadn't, because it made me sort of like him, and I don't think I should. He sure is a hunk. What in God's name is this?" She picked up the sketch pad from the couch where Marguerite had left it.

"I had a sex dream about him. It must be because I was reading this stupid book." Marguerite tossed the biography to her friend. "It says he has a thirteen-inch penis."

"The one you've drawn looks more like thirteen feet," Lavonia said, holding the sketch at arm's length and turning it this way and that.

"At least," agreed Marguerite. "He insists that I need protection. He made me promise to keep Lawless and the cell phone with me at all times." Which was why she'd been awakened just before what would probably have been the most astonishing orgasm of her entire life.

"That doesn't look like protection to me," Lavonia said. "It looks more like bondage."

It felt like bondage, too, but of an emotional kind. Could he really send dreams? Supposedly, he'd sent the nightmares that had caused her uncle to kill himself. Had he sent her this dream today? If so, why? It made no sense, seeing as he'd warned her away.

"Constantine looks incredibly sexy and powerful, with those gorgeous muscles and wild hair, and you look like you're enjoying it," Lavonia said. "In fact, you look completely abandoned to pleasure." She hesitated—not something Lavonia was wont to do—and Marguerite knew what was coming. "Why didn't you tell me your father made pornographic movies?"

Marguerite made a show of nonchalance. "Why would I? It's not that big a deal."

"Maybe not to you, but it sure is unusual."

Marguerite shrugged, purposely ignoring the avid interest in her friend's eyes. "I didn't know much about what he did until there was a scandal. He was just a regular father like anyone else."

"Al said you'd be embarrassed about it," Lavonia said, narrowing her eyes, "and he was right."

"I'm not embarrassed," Marguerite retorted. "My father was a wonderful man and a great filmmaker. I just don't get off on explaining over and over again that he was not a pedophile and getting pitying or disgusted looks in return, because no one ever believes me." Familiar fury simmered within her. "See? You're doing it right now."

"You were just a kid, so how could you know? It wouldn't be surprising if a man in his forties wanted to have sex with a sixteen-year-old girl."

"No, it wouldn't, but he didn't." Enough of that subject. She'd alienated people before by insisting on what she knew and couldn't prove. She'd learned the hard way to shut up and keep her distance.

Which she hadn't managed to do with Constantine. Maybe being bombarded with his images of ripping off her clothes had stripped away her customary restraint as well. Enough of that, too. "And no, my dream wasn't prophetic. I'm not going to sleep with Constantine. One thing's for sure, though. I'd much rather dream about sex than about being run over by a humongous van."

After that, Lavonia tried to persuade her to spend the rest of the day making positive affirmations about a long life stretching into the future, with or without sex, but instead Marguerite went through Pauline's entire room and grew more and more frustrated. Even if something was missing, how would she know? These weren't her belongings. Not only that, half her mind was taken up with thinking about Constantine, so it was with great relief that she finally opened the door for Tony Karaplis.

She'd first met Tony soon after moving to Bayou Gavotte. She'd gone with a date to Blood and Velvet, the premier vampire club in town. Clubs like this usually had a few real vampires in attendance, but mostly it was random partiers and vampire wannabees, many of them in costumes. The idiot with whom she had gone out that night—not that she'd realized what a dummy he was at first, because he'd been a reputedly brilliant graduate student in chemical engineering, introduced to her by Al Bonnard—had been okay for the first part of the evening, not coming on too strong. The luscious costumes made her long for a sketch pad, but since she was carrying only a teeny black purse on a string, she settled for soaking in and memorizing the costumes and scribbling on a couple of napkins. Her date accepted a hit of Ecstasy from one of a group of ravers and became far too happy and hot to trot. She put up with it, fending him off as best she could, until he stuck in some fake fangs and tried to bite her.

She slugged him and was eyeing the crying, cowering result of her handiwork without the slightest sympathy, when Tony appeared through a doorway at the back. The crowd parted to accommodate his approach. He was fiftyish and not exactly good-looking, with his battered ex-bruiser's face and substantial mustache. "Tony Karaplis," he said, offering a large hand and a stunner of a grin. He shoved the remains of her date into the arms of a gothed-up partier and slid onto the stool opposite Marguerite.

"Are you the owner of this place?" she asked him dubiously. What a hellish struggle not to respond to that grin, but she knew a hereditary vampire when she saw one. Her dad had always had one or more in his movies. They were ideal for porn, because they had amazing libidos and were immune to STDs, which made it safer for all concerned. Responding to a vampire's smile might get her very quickly into a situation like the one she'd just tried to avoid. Well, not quite. Sex with a real vampire was likely to be physically satisfying, but that didn't make it worthwhile.

Tony shook with laughter. "Not a chance. I run a pizza parlor, Tony's Greek and Italian." She'd seen the place, not far from the Impractical Cat, but she'd never eaten there.

She introduced herself. "Nice to meet you," she added politely, "but you may as well know right now that I'm not interested in being bitten, even by a real vampire. Been there, done that, not my thing."

"McHugh," Tony mused. "Any relation to—?"

She laughed at his pause. Most people in the vampire community had known her dad as Porno McHugh and had no idea of his first name. "He was my father."

"Well, well," Tony said. "What can I do for the great man's daughter?" He had the most endearing twinkle.

"Get me some paper to sketch the costumes on?"

"Your wish is my command," Tony said grandly and ordered her a fresh iced tea and paper and pencil. The waiter showed up with a clipboard and eraser as well. "Sketch to your heart's content, and when you're done I'll take you home or someplace with even better costumes. Nobody'll bother you while you're with me."

She spent a good hour sketching and watching in amusement as Tony received one indecent proposal after another. Women slithered up to the table in a continuous stream, sometimes in pairs and even one threesome, young girls and middle-aged partiers, and even one much older lady who turned out to be a writer doing research. One and all made it clear what they needed—desperately—from Tony, and one and all he turned away with a smile, kind words, sometimes a caress. He gently directed the sidetracked writer to another club called the Oubliette, where more serious vampire types could be found. A select few were invited to drop by his restaurant.

"I'm good," Tony said during an all-too-brief lull, "but I can't fuck them all." Since that night, he and Marguerite had gone clubbing now and then, when she wanted to sketch and he wanted to dance with a woman who didn't crawl all over him.

Now, she'd just finished showering and hadn't tidied the living room, so the sketch pad still lay on the couch. He sauntered in, looking tough, cool, and sexy in a typical vampire way. He gave her a hug and took possession of the couch and the remote before noticing the sketch pad. He broke into whoops and guffaws. "What have you done to Constantine? That's quite some dick."

She snatched the drawing away, clutching it to her chest. She didn't need this kind of embarrassment. When he stopped laughing enough to listen, Marguerite asked, "Do you know Constantine personally?"

"Known him since he was eight years old. I was a sort of father figure to him when he and his mom moved to New Orleans."

"What about his own father?"

"Died when he was a kid, back in Arizona. Or New Mexico, maybe." Gently, he removed the sketch pad from her clasp. "What made you give him a dick like that?"

"I drew it from a sex dream I had this afternoon." After a second's hesitation, she risked saying, "I think Constantine sent the dream to me." At the worst, Tony would scoff, and she could hardly blame him.

"Could be," Tony said, as if sending dreams were an everyday occurrence. Perhaps vampires accepted the unusual as a matter of course because they were unusual themselves. He scratched Lawless's spine. "He's certainly hot for you and extremely possessive."

"You spoke to him about me? Why?"

"I wanted the other side of the tabloid story." Tony chuckled. "Had a bit of fun, too. He's one jealous guy."

"About me? No way. We're not *really* in a relationship." Tony rolled his eyes, and she added, "He's crazy. I want nothing to do with him."

"Uh-huh," Tony said. "That explains why you're recording your sex dreams about him." Lawless flopped onto the floor, exposing his belly for Tony's caress. "Move out of the way. I can't see the TV."

"I had to get it out of my system somehow." She paced back and forth. "Sure, I find him attractive, but I wasn't even looking for a boyfriend. I do much better without one. I'm not the one going around totally horny and pretending to be cool." She stopped, hands on hips, breathing irritably down her nose. "What is the *matter* with him?"

Tony shifted to see around her. "The way I figure it, this dream is his attempt to compensate for not fucking you."

"Oh, how charming." Marguerite began pacing again. "I don't hop into bed with a guy the day we meet, and usually not at all. I was having a nice, peaceful life until he came along. Well, apart from my roommate dying, and me being drugged and left on the mound, but that seems to be connected with him, too."

"If I recall correctly from what I read on the Internet," Tony said, "you're the one who announced you were having sex with him." He kicked off his loafers and stuck his feet under Lawless's warm belly.

"To protect him from the reporter," she said.

Tony guffawed. "No ulterior motive, baby?"

"None! You're as bad as he is. It drives me *nuts* not to be believed when I'm telling the simple truth." Thanks to being able to read auras, this was the story of her life. She should be used to it by now, but apparently she never would be. "This morning, he tried to freak me out by saying he's been watching me from the bayou."

"He's been stalking you? That's a new twist. Do you mind?"

She felt herself blushing. "No, not really."

"So everything's cool. He wants you, and you want him." When she glared, he added, "It's not that he doesn't want to screw you, baby. He hasn't had sex for quite a while, and as far as I could tell between threats and growls, this is the first time it's really mattered to him."

Marguerite halted, frowning, then moved aside to get out of Tony's line of sight.

The vampire flipped channels. "He's always been particular, except when it came to Jonetta. Nobody who knows him understands why he married her." He shrugged. "I haven't seen him with a woman for a good long time. Don't ask me why, because I don't know."

"When I got pissed off and threatened to come on to him," Marguerite said, "he acted as if I really were attacking him."

Tony made an incredulous face. "That boy is so screwed up."

"He said it would be dangerous for us to have sex."

Tony considered. "And yet he wants to keep you. Hence the long lasso of a prick that can haul you in, bind you, and fuck you all at once."

Marguerite felt herself flush from head to toe.

"But only in your dreams, unless he sorts himself out." He decided on a channel and set down the remote. "Go put on some clothes, baby. I promised him I wouldn't come on to you, but visualizing you naked under that robe isn't helping."

Marguerite went away to get dressed. He was watching soccer on ESPN when she came out of the bedroom fifteen minutes later in a skimpy red number that matched a new pair of garnet earrings. He turned off the TV and stood.

"Very sexy," he said contentedly, licking his fangs. "Color of blood. Constantine will be jealous as hell."

Oh, crap. "He's not going to follow us around, is he? Or send one of his bodyguards to shadow us? I have private business to take care of."

"Looking for that young dude he wants to talk to, you mean? No problem. He says you're wasting your time, but he'll give you till tomorrow morning."

"He has so much gall!" Worse than that, he'd guessed exactly what she was planning. He would do exactly as he pleased, whenever he chose. She was no match for him, none at all. She *had* to find Zeb tonight.

On the way out, she grabbed her backpack, which contained a smaller sketch pad. "It'll give me an excuse for scrutinizing people. Let's try the Chamber first. They have decent food." They drove the few miles into downtown Bayou Gavotte, and after a quick meal and no sign of Zeb, they toured several other clubs. Marguerite took her time, focusing, peering across rooms and into dark corners.

"Why are we taking so long?" Tony griped. "Either you see him or you don't. He's not invisible."

"No, but if he's painted, he might be difficult to identify, and if he's hiding . . ." She shrugged. She wasn't about to explain this to anyone, but Zeb was good at making himself inconspicuous. If he didn't want to talk to her, he might well succeed.

At last there were only two more likely possibilities. One was the Threshold, which had the worst reputation in town for violent sexual activities and breaking the rules about minors.

"We're not going there," Tony said. "Constantine's handling that one."

"What?" She gritted her teeth. She hated the Threshold, but Zeb was the sort of attractive, well-built kid who could get hired there. "What if he finds Zeb there?"

"Didn't I tell you he's giving you till tomorrow?" Tony sounded as offended as if she'd dissed him personally. "He's going there to check into rule infractions, maybe punish someone who needs it. If he finds Zeb, he'll just get him the hell out."

So they went to the Merkin, with its baroque decor and focus on historical debauchery. It was owned by several professors at Hellebore University, and the obscene poetry and murals probably provided more of an education than a semester's worth of lectures. Inside, they found Nathan Bone holding forth from a gilded chaise in the bar, the focus of a group of avid listeners, one of whom was Janie. The witch waggled her fingers and grinned.

Nathan did a nasty little double take and sprang up, whipping out a camera. "Rocker's girl steps out with playboy restaurateur. Does Constantine know who you're with tonight, love?"

"Of course he knows, you walking, talking cesspool." She clutched Tony's arm and grimaced for the camera. She should have expected this, but she'd been too caught up with worrying about Zeb.

"Sticks and stones may break my bones," said Nathan. "Constantine's going to look like such a loser when pics of you and this dude are all over the Internet."

"Who *is* this asshole?" Tony pried Marguerite's clutching fingers off his forearm. He jabbed a large fist at Nathan's chest, jabbed again, backing him up to the bar. "Want me to take him down?"

Yes! "No, if Constantine wants him punished, he'll take care of it himself." She slipped her hand through the vampire's arm again. "Cool it, Tony darling. We came here to dance, remember?"

Nathan smirked, clicking more pictures. "Why aren't you worried, Marguerite? Nobody believed me when I first reported it, but now it's obvious. Your roommate's death wasn't suicide. Constantine sent her nightmares. He induced her to kill herself, just like that cop in Baton Rouge. Next he'll do it to you."

Tony growled low in his throat and moved in to do some serious damage.

"Wait." Marguerite crammed her disgust back down her craw. She raised her voice, which might with luck be overheard above the music. "Nathan, the only dreams I've had since meeting Constantine are about sex, and believe me, they're very, very good ones."

This evinced a number of giggles and oohs from the women in Nathan's audience.

"That's only for starters," Nathan retorted. "Look what happened to his wife."

Marguerite rolled her eyes. Maybe without Constantine around, she could get some useful information. She lowered her voice again. "Nathan, who's feeding you this garbage?"

"Someone who knows how dangerous Constantine is," Nathan said dramatically. "Someone who knows he has to be stopped before someone else dies."

"What a load of bull," Tony said. "Come on, baby. If you don't want me to deck him, let's go."

"Tell me who!" Marguerite repeated, and then the flickers in Nathan's aura told her. "You don't even know who your informant is, do you? Then what in God's name makes you think you can believe him?"

"I'll find out who he is soon enough," Nathan said. "Work a story from all angles, and the whole truth will come out."

Not necessarily, thought Marguerite, reminded of her father and the vampire actors whose secret he hadn't betrayed, regardless of the cost to him. She recalled something Constantine had said up on the mound, and her stomach gave a nauseating little flip. "Be careful, Nathan. Maybe your informant doesn't want to be found out, especially since he's not telling the truth at all."

Nathan shook his head mournfully. "Nah, he's just scared of Constantine, and who can blame him? Don't say I didn't try to warn you, but I'm still on your side, Marguerite. Smile for the camera again!"

They left him at the bar and made a slow circuit of the club, but again there was no sign of Zeb. In the dance hall, where entirely modern music clashed with seventeenth century decor, Marguerite burned off some of her frustration with vigorous exercise. Unfortunately, Nathan didn't choose to reappear until later, when she was plastered against Tony in a slow dance. She tried to put a bit of distance between them, but Tony held her tight. "Ignore him," he said. "If you want to be with Constantine, you'll have to get used to it."

"The whole world will think I'm a slut," she muttered, although given her parentage, they'd probably already passed judgment on that one. "Anyway, who said I want to be with Constantine?" And then, "Damn it, Tony. You have a hard-on!"

"Why not? It's fun being turned on." Tony moved a big hand down to cup one of her ass cheeks. Nathan snapped another picture. "Maybe these pics will convince Constantine to get his act together."

Marguerite slapped his hand away. "Stop fondling my butt. Let's go sit down."

But the instant Tony sat still, women flocked around him. Marguerite sketched the costumes, some of which were fabulous, but her heart wasn't in it. Nathan stopped by to take another photo of Marguerite (as he put it) pouting.

And then, at last, at last, she saw what she'd been waiting for all evening. She mightn't have recognized Zeb except for the tight, uneasy aura that was his trademark. That he didn't try masking it told her what she needed. She gave Tony's shoulder a brief, meaningful squeeze. "I'll be right back."

Zeb was waiting for her just past the restrooms in an alcove that held a neglected-looking pay phone. He'd chosen a good spot; music from the dance hall penetrated, but they could speak together in low tones. Black and white greasepaint sectioned Zeb's face into four equal parts; she supposed, by the powdered wig, that he was meant to be eighteenth century. His shirt hung partway open to reveal a well-muscled chest and a silver chain from which hung a heavy cross studded with purple stones; he also sported a matching ring and an ankle chain. His knee breeches were as revealing as a ballet dancer's tights.

"Good God," she said faintly.

"Dressed for success," he said with a crooked grin, but fatigue and anxiety pervaded his aura. His dark eyes searched her, as if assessing her motives.

"Sorry about this afternoon," Marguerite said. "Constantine wasn't supposed to be there, but my house got burgled, and he's friends with the cop who came to do the police report."

He frowned. "Someone broke into your place? What did they take?"

"Nothing, as far as I can tell, but I think Lawless surprised them into leaving in a rush."

"Huh," he said. "Well, I don't suppose it has anything to do with anything, and I don't think you're in danger, but maybe you should leave town for a while just in case."

"I can't go anywhere right now. Classes start next week, and I'm teaching two this semester." She paused. "Constantine believes I *am* in danger."

Zeb's aura bristled. "Constantine needs to butt out of my business."

"Why not enlist him as an ally?" she said. "I don't know what you've got yourself mixed up in, but he's used to handling dangerous people and situations."

"He's used to hurting people, you mean." His aura sparked, and he glanced warily in the direction of the dance floor.

"He's not here," Marguerite said. "I told him I needed to talk to you alone."

"And he agreed?" He sounded incredulous. "I still don't get why he let me go."

"Just for tonight," she admitted. "He thinks I'm wasting my time." When he said nothing, she plowed forward. "What's going on? Is there anything I can do to help?"

Zeb's face twisted. Zigs and zags of agitation spat like fireworks around his form. He swallowed. "No. If Constantine hadn't shown up this morning, everything would have been fine. It was just a stupid practical joke. I would have handled it."

"I'm sorry, Zeb, but for me getting drugged and dumped unconscious up there is a lot more than a practical joke." She hated to ask this, but . . . "Did you drug me? I find that hard to believe."

His aura quivered and wept. "Of course not!"

"But you know who did."

Now his aura surged with flames of misery. "Yes, but I'm sure it wasn't meant to harm you."

"Constantine said you told him the person who did it knows and likes me."

"That's why I know he didn't mean you any harm. It has nothing to do with Constantine, and if he'd just stay out of the frigging way and leave me alone—"

"Constantine says it does have to do with him, and I agree. Otherwise how would a reporter have known about that little scenario and shown up just in time?"

Zeb shrugged. "It's just a coincidence. Everybody knows the mounds are one of the places he hangs when he wants to be alone."

This was true. For a while last year, fans had haunted the mounds day and night, but they'd never found Constantine and had finally given up.

But this morning wasn't a coincidence. Someone had sent Nathan there.

"Just believe me, will you?" Zeb said. "The scenario had nothing to do with Constantine. Nothing at all."

CHAPTER EIGHT

There was a long silence. Marguerite knew Zeb was wrong, but she also knew he meant every word. To confirm it, she said, "You're certain of that, aren't you?"

"Positive," he said. "I swear. Will you please tell Constantine?"

"Yes, but it's not that simple." She hesitated, and his eyes widened, each eye contrasting oddly against the two colors of paint.

He lowered his voice even more, but it bit all the same. "You're going to tell him I can control my aura."

"What? Of course not," she whispered indignantly. "And I trust you not to tell anyone I can see auras either. The problem is that Constantine may not believe what you're telling me. If it was a practical joke that had nothing to do with him, who was it aimed at?"

Stubbornness descended like a cloud. "I can't tell you that."

"Okay," she said, unsurprised. That would have been too easy. "How about the knife you took? Would it have implicated the person the joke was aimed at?"

He made a dismissive gesture, his ring winking in the light as a restroom door opened and closed. "Yeah, but don't bother asking where it is. I separated the blade from the handle and threw them away in different places. Nobody's going to find them. It's over."

"It's not over," Marguerite said. "You don't believe that either."

His eyes evaded hers. "I've got to get back to work."

This totally sucked. He'd trusted her once upon a time. Maybe if she confided in him, he would consider trusting her again. "Listen, Zeb. I'm going to tell you something else, but you have to keep it to yourself."

"What?" His voice was impatient; his eyes flicked down the corridor. "I'm working. I can't just hang here."

"The police don't think Pauline's death was really a suicide," she said.

"Huh?" The paint cut his frown in two, black wrinkles and white. "I thought she overdosed on her own meds. That's what Lavonia told my dad."

"Yes, but they suspect someone forced her to take them."

"Wouldn't there have been signs of a struggle?" Suspicion descended again on his brow. "I don't believe it."

Marguerite took a deep breath. "I don't know how it was done, Zeb, and neither do the cops or Constantine, but I *do* believe them. Pauline was doing fine up until the day she died. She was reasonably happy, and she was definitely not suicidal."

"How can you be so sure?" Pause. "Oh. Her aura, I suppose. Still, why would anybody want to kill Pauline?" Finally, his aura flickered a little: uncertainty.

"I have no idea." She tried again. "Zeb, you know something, something that matters, something that might mean the difference between life and death. I can't believe you'd willingly endanger anyone."

Zeb sagged, definitely rattled now, but all he said was, "Sorry. I have to get back to work."

"Listen to me!" she hissed. "If she really was murdered, and you're keeping back something that might identify the murderer, it makes you an accessory!"

"I don't know who did it," he said, but his aura wavered again.

He might not know for sure, she thought, but he could probably make a good guess. "Zeb, please—"

"Oh, fuck," he said softly. "My dad's here." *Relief*, she thought, in spite of his curse. Being chewed out by his father had the merit of being familiar and relatively safe.

"Where?" Marguerite began, and then she heard Al, too.

"I got a call that he was here," Zeb's father said loudly over the music. "He looks older, but he's underage, and if you don't find him and give him to me, I'll make big trouble."

Zeb's aura folded tidily into tolerate-the-parent mode. He turned toward the wall, dug into the pocket of his knee breeches, and took out a roll of bills. "Keep this for me."

Apparently he still trusted her in some ways. She took the money at the same instant a camera flashed behind her. "Gotcha!"

"Hell," she muttered and stuffed the roll down her bra. Could it get any worse?

"Oh, Marguerite," Nathan said gleefully as she turned. "Propositioning babies now? Your daddy would be proud."

She rolled her eyes and went past him down the hall. "I don't know why Constantine puts up with you."

"I'm not a baby," Zeb said plaintively behind her. "I'm legal for sex, just not for being in the club. Unfortunately, in spite of her gorgeous tits, all she wants is for me to mow her lawn."

Nathan hooted. "That's one way to put it," he said, as Al Bonnard came around the corner, looking pained.

"Marguerite, call me when the lawn mower's fixed," Zeb said helpfully, "and I'll be right over. Okay, okay," he said to his father. "I'm coming."

Tony appeared behind Al. "Now do I get to deck the asshole?"

"No," Marguerite said, flapping what she hoped look like an indifferent hand. She would play along and act cool and sophisticated if it killed her. She slipped her hand into the crook of Tony's arm. "Let's have a couple more dances and then move on. The night is young, and we haven't hit *all* the clubs yet."

They escaped shortly afterward. The dense, damp night enveloped them like the maw of a fearsome, panting beast. The heat made her itch. Tears stung behind her eyes as she visualized the headlines. *Rocker's Girl Robs the Cradle.* Next they'd be calling her Nympho McHugh. She just wouldn't turn on her computer in the morning. Wouldn't surf the Internet. Wouldn't open her emails. If she didn't know what they were saying, it wouldn't hurt her. She took a deep breath. Soon this would be over, and she'd never have to be stuck in the limelight again.

"Get anywhere with the kid?" Tony asked.

"No." She scowled into the darkness. "Sort of. He wouldn't tell me who he's protecting, but he insists the scenario on the mound had nothing to do with Constantine."

She scratched one itchy palm and then the other. "I'm sure he meant what he said." Now her cleavage was itching, too. "But I'm equally sure Constantine won't believe him. Tony, he'll hurt Zeb! What am I going to do?"

But Tony had no answer for that, merely informing her, after checking out her entire house, that Constantine would have someone keeping watch in her neighborhood all night. "Do you have his number? He says to call him if you need him."

"For what?" she cried. "I wished I'd never—wish he'd—" She didn't know what she wished.

Tony grabbed her cell phone and programmed in Constantine's number. "Calm down, baby. He's only doing what he has to. He's a good guy at heart."

"A good guy wouldn't have to hurt Zeb," she said.

Tony gave her a hug and left. She showered off the sweat to get rid of the itching, but even clean and cool, she lay awake far too long. Either the scenario was meant for Constantine or it wasn't. Either Zeb was lying or Constantine was deluded. As for whoever had killed Pauline, that was just another complication in what already made no sense. Regardless, Constantine was going to go after Zeb, and she couldn't stop him. She resolved to call Gideon O'Toole in the morning and tell him what Zeb had said. Maybe he could talk some sense into Constantine or go talk to Zeb himself.

On that faint hope, she fell asleep.

She shot toward wakefulness a couple of hours later, as the dark van of her nightmares visited her again, enormous and evil and more appalling than ever before. *I'm coming for you. You're next!* It slammed into her, and she woke choking on a sob. After the first few heart-thundering moments, she slumped back on her pillow.

And immediately sat up again. No way would she let herself fall back into that stupid nightmare. If she were going to end up right back in dreamland, she'd far prefer Constantine's variety.

Oh, God. Was she already in the nightmare again? She could still hear the deadly, inexorable rumble of the van.

She heaved herself off the bed and listened hard. This was no dream. The sound came from a real engine, close by outside. Then another sound penetrated—a low growl from Lawless.

She found him crouched in the kitchen by the doggie door, bristles up, growling, whimpering, growling again. The well-lit porch contrasted with the intense darkness of the yard, and she hurried to the front to see only the empty road stretching away under the streetlights. Then, out of the corner of her eye, she saw what she was looking for: a dark mass under an oak tree just past the edge of the woods next door. A van like the one in her nightmare.

She got out her phone and dialed without a second thought. Constantine didn't answer. She left a message: "There's a van idling outside my house. There's no time to explain, but I've been having nightmares about this van. Hurry, or it'll too late."

She turned the phone over and over in her hand. She couldn't just wait and hope he would call. He might be asleep. He might be miles away, and she didn't know which bodyguard he'd sent or where to find him. Lawless's growl rose to a crescendo. She scurried into the kitchen again, pulled him close, and muffled him. "Shush. Hush. Don't bark. *Please* don't bark." She locked the doggie door so he couldn't get out the back. What good would it be if Lawless scared away the intruder before Constantine arrived?

Hurriedly, she dressed in jeans, a dark T-shirt, and running shoes. She could call 911, but she didn't want another kerfuffle, not with all the other crap going on. *Cradle Robber Scared of the Dark.* Maybe she should call Gideon O'Toole. She dug into her wallet for his card but didn't find it, and she couldn't risk turning on a light to search properly.

Meanwhile, Lawless moved to the front door, still growling. Marguerite peeked through a crack in the curtains. A light came on inside the van. A few seconds later, the car door slammed shut and the engine slipped into gear.

Too late! He was leaving. She had to at least get the tag number of the van. If they could identify it, and therefore its owner, Constantine might leave Zeb alone. Shutting Lawless firmly indoors, she crept out into the back garden. Lawless's frantic howls pursued her. She reached the corner of the house just as the van purred slowly down the street in the still, heavy air. Marguerite pushed her bike through to the street and followed.

$\sim$

Constantine Dufray had hoped to talk with Eaton Wilson, but according to discreet inquiries made by one of Lep's people, the professor had gone to visit some mounds in Mississippi and wouldn't be back till past midnight. Gideon had reported that two vehicles were registered in his name—a Volvo and a black van—but neither was parked at his house. Constantine set someone to watch for the return of Wilson and either or both vehicles. Another of Lep's people con-firmed that Zeb had left the Merkin with his father and gone home, so he at least was accounted for.

Constantine had spent most of the evening in the roof garden of the Impractical Cat working on some songs, but now, hanging out by the bayou with no distractions, he couldn't stop thinking about Marguerite. For once, he didn't feel like playing his guitar, and his guide had gone to roost in a tree down the bayou and was utterly silent. Af-ter Tony had dropped Marguerite at home, he'd called to tell Constantine about the sex dream she'd had that after-noon. "Not saying you shouldn't send her more, kid, but it's not polite to get a woman stirred up and then not follow through."

He hadn't meant to send that dream—more proof that he'd lost control of his mind. If he didn't rein in his thoughts, he would send her another one, which she didn't want. It wasn't fair to either of them to feed an attraction that could never go anywhere. The best he could do for now was cool himself down.

He stripped and made a polite request of the water-dwelling creatures to excuse the intrusion, with a particu-larly respectful nod to any water moccasins that might be lurking under the bank. In all his unworthiness, the animal world hadn't deserted him so far. He dove in and swam.

The animals might tolerate him, but the fates were laugh-ing at him tonight. He swam across the bayou and lazed in the water's caress for a couple of minutes, and then, from the pocket of his jeans on the far bank, his cell phone rang. Cursing, he struck out across the bayou, but the call had gone to message before he got to the other side. He hauled himself up by a convenient root and glanced at the display: Honey and Eyes. He dried off in a hurry and scrambled into his clothes and shoes. As he took off running through the woods, all hell broke loose: the screech of a hawk, the urgent swoop of a bat, and the distant sound of Lawless, howling fit to bust.

Within two minutes he was on Marguerite's back porch. He banged on the back door, calling her name, and Lawless whimpered in response. Using the spare key he'd abstracted from a kitchen drawer that morning while putting away her groceries, he went inside, but Marguerite was nowhere to be found. Her little Honda stood in the driveway. The chain was on the front door, so she must have gone out the back. But where? And why?

Lawless scrabbled frantically at the locked doggie door. Constantine's phone vibrated. He dialed voice mail and listened in growing dismay. If she'd been kidnapped . . . at gunpoint, maybe, so she'd been forced outdoors without the dog. Or maybe she'd just gone to investigate, crazy fool! The dog might show him. He opened the door and called desperately on his guide for help. Lawless tore around the side of the house, sniffing at the fence where this morning Marguerite's bike had been stashed, and lunged through the gate. He snuffled across the front yard and bounded away down the road.

She'd followed the van on her *bike?*

Relief and hope stirred in him. With luck she wouldn't get far before the van sped up and she lost it. But no reassurance came from his guide, only urgent cries for haste. He went inside for her keys, started up the little Honda, and took off after the dog.

~

After the first burst of speed down the street and around the corner, Marguerite kept up easily with the van, which rolled contemplatively through the neighborhood from one stop sign to another. She left her headlight off and coasted directly behind the vehicle, out of view of both side mirrors. The driver might still see her in the center mirror, but that was a risk she had to take. Hopefully he would have no reason to check behind him until they reached a major artery, by which time she should have his license plate number and be on her way back home.

But the license plate proved damnably hard to read. Mud plastered the sides and rear of the van, obscuring much of the plate, and one of its little sidelights had burned out. At the fourth unsuccessful attempt to get close enough to read the plate, it dawned on Marguerite that the van was trundling along far too slowly. Slowly enough, she realized, to make it easy for her to keep up.

A dreadful coldness crept into the pit of her stomach. She hung back a little, telling herself not to be silly. There was no reason to think he had seen her, or that he even knew of her existence. He might even be some random person looking for an address, but she had to make sure. The van might be headed for a nearby gas station or an all-night supermarket; it might be going only as far as the next street or miles into the country. As long as the driver didn't know she was following him, she would be okay.

Actually, she felt downright stupid following a dream. It was one thing to believe that Constantine could send her dreams and another entirely to believe that a recurring nightmare had anything to do with real life or with a real van that happened to idle at the side of a road at night.

Ahead of her the van approached a corner, veered a little to the right, and stopped. If Marguerite had been squinting at the license plate instead of pondering her next move, she would have collided with him. She skidded to a stop, heart skittering in her breast. The driver's door opened, and a figure began slowly to emerge.

His aura flared, its message clear. The man in the black van intended to kill her.

Faster than thought, Marguerite flew around the passenger side of the van, teetering along the edge of the ditch, where there was scarcely room to pass, in terror that he would run around the front of the van and grab her.

But no . . . He was supposed to run her down, wasn't he, according to the dream? He had left just enough room for her to pass, and he climbed leisurely back into the driver's seat and put the van into gear.

Marguerite tore off down the street, thoughts racing. The closest well-lit area was several blocks away. He could catch up and hit her at any time. She shifted up onto the sidewalk, where the curb and the trees lining the road offered a little protection, and whipped around a corner. The van driver hung behind, not driving dangerously, just keeping up, waiting for his chance.

Marguerite rounded another corner, and the sidewalk ended abruptly at a drainage ditch. In this old quarter of town, trees had uprooted the sidewalks, and there were new ones under construction everywhere. She skirted the ditch and crossed the street before the van reappeared. A new sidewalk had been completed on the other side, which took her for another two blocks. But twisting and turning, running out of breath, Marguerite knew she couldn't keep it up for long enough. Following this erratic course, it would take two, three times as long to get to the main drag. Straight ahead of her, maybe five more blocks . . .

But of course the driver of the van knew this, too. The engine picked up speed and roared behind her. Again the sidewalk came to an end. She fought the onslaught of panic, slipped, and an oak tree loomed out of nowhere. She skidded sideways and crashed, landing hard in a mess of weeds and grass.

∾

Constantine caught up with Lawless, who followed a fairly straight course for several blocks and then a progressively more twisted one. He covered the same street twice and plunged forward again, nose to the ground, around another corner.

And stopped, nosing in the ditch, whimpering. Half in the ditch, its wheel bent against a huge oak tree, lay Marguerite's bike.

Constantine jumped out of the car. "Marguerite?" he called, and then again louder, but his answer came from the dog, who bounded into a vacant lot. He raised his hands, invoking the creatures of the sky to his aid. *Find her,* he pleaded. *Save her.* A bat wheeled and dipped in an erratic course ahead of the dog. An owl beat past on frantic wings. Constantine took off in pursuit.

∾

In a haze of fear, Marguerite scrambled up, abandoned the ruined bike, and plunged past a fence too high to climb into a vacant lot. She dodged around trees and stumbled through the remains of a demolished house, bruising her knees and scraping her hands on old bricks and concrete supports. *He's supposed to kill me with the van,* she kept telling herself. *That's what happens in the dream.* But it was just a dream, and she didn't know anymore what was real and what wasn't.

Finally she had to stop. She heaved her lungs full again and again, gradually quieting her breath, and listened. The night was noisy with tree frogs and katydids, but even so, a vast silence and emptiness seemed to surround her, and for a while she heard no foreign sounds. She should call the cops, but she had no idea where she was. She crept through another vacant lot and more woods to the huge open parking lot of a church. Which church? She didn't know, but if she crept around to the front, she would be all too visible in the ghastly light of the moon. She retreated to the edge of the woods and got out her cell phone.

And froze. The engine purred its threat, and the van drifted around the corner toward the front of the church, quietly, patiently, without headlights. The moon lit up the driver's head, smooth and horrifyingly featureless but for the eyes staring her way. Had he seen her? His aura roiled, flared, lunged with murderous intent. The church—dark, empty, and doubtless locked—offered no sanctuary. She dashed back across the corner of the vacant lot. There were houses on that side, but a six-foot fence surrounded the first yard. The van stopped in front of the church, and she heard, clearly as a shot, the sinister click of the closing of the driver's door.

Once again terror took over. She heaved herself at the fence, scrabbling and sobbing, and fell back. Much too high. Back through the vacant lot or along the fence? *Quick, quick, decide!* No sound but her own breathing and the thundering of her heart. Then a crow, its slumber disturbed, cawed loudly overhead, and around the side of the church came a flurry of bats, swooping and diving. Marguerite fled before them along the fence. One bat flickered close enough to touch her, and then another, and she shied violently aside and fell through an unlocked gate at the far end of a yard.

Marguerite scrambled up and with shaking hands locked the gate behind her. The bats wheeled back toward the churchyard. She crept through the dark, quiet yard, out the front gate, and across the deserted street into a garden. Yet another fence, a low one, and a bevy of barking dogs a few doors down. She slipped around the back of an empty house damaged by a fallen tree, forced herself across a tangle of wire fence and creepers, and turned into the next road in the opposite direction from the dogs. Under a tree in another yard, she caught her breath again and listened for the sounds of pursuit. Silence, except for the insect chorus and a few lagging yips from the dogs. She got out her phone, trying to figure out where she was so she could tell the cops.

Then the engine purred its approach, and the van rolled around the corner toward her.

Marguerite took off again through a maze of yards. A screech owl flitted from tree to tree ahead of her, calling tremulously. If she made a ruckus knocking on a door and calling for help, would anyone wake or come in time? What if she endangered someone? No, she had to go on, find someplace bright and public. And safe.

Finally, *finally* lights showed in the distance, and the thin sound of voices raised in an eerie chant. Marguerite heaved herself over another fence into a wooded area without much underbrush. Maybe it was another abandoned lot; there were so many since the hurricanes. She threaded her way through the trees, fending off low branches, leaping fallen logs. Her pursuer scrambled over the fence behind her, breathing heavily but not desperately, bursts of sound like tiny chokes of laughter issuing nastily from his throat. Possessed of a demon, she thought stupidly as she ran. *Almost there, almost there* . . .

Before her chanted a circle of people in flickering robes, surrounded by a shimmering dome of light. His breathing rasped close behind her. He touched her, grabbed at her shirt. Bats swarmed and dove, and the man grunted in rage. The owl screeched, the circle widened toward her, and Marguerite took one last desperate leap. She burst through the dome of light with a crack loud enough to rend the sky and blacked out before she hit the grass.

CHAPTER NINE

Zeb ran through the streets of Bayou Gavotte, searching for the black van. It felt as if he hadn't slept in days. After playing suitably contrite while his dad ranted the whole drive home, he'd cleaned off the greasepaint and collapsed into bed, setting his cell for an hour later. These days and nights, nastiness was afoot, and he was the only one who could stop it. When he woke, he dressed, checked his dad's room, and pocketed his ring of copied keys. It was getting pretty heavy, seeing as he'd copied any key he could get ahold of, but he never knew which vehicle or building he would need to open. A quick reconnoiter showed that the van wasn't in Eaton Wilson's driveway where it belonged. He set off to find out what tonight's mischief would be.

It looked like more than mischief, though. If anyone but Marguerite had fed him that story, he wouldn't have even considered believing it. But Marguerite was safer than most people, and when she'd told him, months ago, that he didn't need to keep his aura folded with her, he'd been blown away. It was like having an angel sent by his mom, which was about as hokey as you could get, but it sure felt good to let go.

Only a few months ago, he would never have believed he could be thankful his mom was dead. Her heart would break over what faced him now. He'd been juggling for weeks, playing ugly games that were getting uglier by the day. What if Marguerite was right and Pauline had indeed been murdered?

Too bad he couldn't consult Constantine. Zelda'd been texting all evening, which was a goddamned nuisance at the club. *U OK?* she'd ask. What was he supposed to reply? *Hunky-dory, girl—pimping's my dream job.* If he even hinted at what he was doing, she'd tell her mom, who was a freak about club rules. And Zelda wouldn't take *Busy L8R* for an answer. She'd decided he needed life advice and was bent on getting him to talk to Dufray. If he didn't know her better—Zelda was a straight shooter—he'd think she was in cahoots with the rock star. If he agreed, she might let up, but not if she knew why.

He wasn't about to ask Dufray for help, because the rock star would take matters into his own hands, and Zeb wasn't ready for that. He had to make up his own mind about what needed to be done.

He wished he didn't have to go it alone, but for now there was no other way. He wished he could ask Constantine questions he really needed answered—such as how did a vigilante decide when murder was justified? When it was the only answer? How did Constantine steel himself to kill someone? He'd made inflicting pain look sickeningly easy.

Zeb could have sworn Marguerite was safe, that she'd just been in the wrong place at the wrong time last night, but with each block he grew less and less certain, and without really intending to, he found himself approaching her house. Dark and quiet. Only the songs of a zillion bugs and frogs filled the night. If Lawless were here, he would come to the door to check Zeb out. And the car wasn't there, which seemed strange. Was she spending the night with the old dude she'd been with at the Merkin? If she was dating Constantine, why would she go dancing with someone else? The guy looked like an old mobster. A bodyguard?

Zeb circled Marguerite's place, but Lawless didn't bark, didn't whine, didn't come to say hello. More than a little uneasy, Zeb left her street and wove through the nearby neighborhoods, eyes peeled for any sign of the black van. Instead he found Marguerite's car, empty and unlocked, by a crumpled bike in a ditch.

~

"Marguerite." A harsh voice battered her. "Wake up!"

Marguerite surfaced in a paroxysm of terror and lashed out, sobbing, at the arms that imprisoned her.

"It's okay, Marguerite. You're safe, babe. It's okay."

She forced her lids open and met Constantine's dark eyes. "Oh," she sighed, sinking gratefully back into his embrace. "Thank God you're here." Then the whole thing slammed in on her, and sobs rushed up, unstoppable. She threw her face against his chest and shook with their force.

His arms tightened, and he cradled her, rocking gently. A babble of voices broke through. Female voices. Lavonia, taking charge: "Bring her inside the house." Lawless's wet nose shoving at her, his worried whimper, and Constantine's arm drawing away to comfort the dog and then cradling her again. Stray words: "Couch. Coffee. Doctor? Police? Can she walk? Better carry her."

"Leave us alone for a minute," said Constantine. "Go make coffee, but no doctors. I've texted a friend who's a cop. No, she's fine. I'll carry her in."

The voices faded, and Marguerite lifted her face, shuddering breaths slowing now. She sniffled and dug in her pocket for a tissue to wipe her nose. "Where are we? Did you catch him?"

"Unfortunately no. I got here too late."

They were on a garden bench in someone's backyard, and she was curled on his lap. She felt comfortable there, and safe, but she wasn't a baby to be carried, so she resisted the urge to lay her head on his chest again. "Let me get up."

"Marguerite," said Constantine into her ear, "I can't have sex with you, but allow me the pleasure of holding you." He paused. "Before I ask you what the hell you thought you were doing."

She struggled out of his clasp and sat beside him. "You didn't answer your phone. He was driving away. I needed to get information any way I could." She blinked, brushing the hair out of her eyes. Lights shone from the house, and Lavonia watched them from behind a set of sliding doors. She wore a long, dark, flowing robe. A meeting of her coven?

"That's no reason to risk your life." Constantine spoke gruffly, his aura like the limp dangling of wilted leaves. "Let me handle this mess. I may be a brutal sort of guy, but I don't want the deaths of innocents added to my fuckup account."

"You were going to find Zeb and beat the truth out of him. I *had* to follow that van."

He didn't reply, and the cacophony of bugs singing love songs in the night only deepened the silence between them.

Lawless panted at their feet, and the moon hung low in the sky.

What had she expected? He wasn't the sort of man to concede or change his ways. "It was an old Ford van, but I didn't even get the plate number," she said, dashing away more tears before they even had a chance to emerge. "It was half-covered with mud, and so were the lights around it, and I couldn't use my headlight, and I didn't have a flashlight . . . There was an 8J in the middle, but that's all I'm sure of. Do you think Gideon can get somewhere with that?"

"Maybe." He took out his phone and sent a text message. "In the meantime, what am I supposed to do with you? You *do* need protection, girl."

"So does Zeb," she shot back. Lavonia still hovered behind the French doors.

His cell phone rang. "Jabez, I need you to pick up a little red Honda and bring it to me." He gave an address Marguerite didn't recognize.

Marguerite gaped. "My car?"

"Quickest way to follow you. I was in the bayou when you called." He told Jabez where to find the car. "The keys are in the ignition. Say what? Okay, man—thanks." He hung up. "If it's been stolen, I'll get you a new car, babe."

"Not necessary. *In* the bayou?" She shuddered. "What about snakes? You could have been bitten!"

"I'm an Indian, babe. At one with nature. Snakes, birds, bats . . . we have a special rapport."

"Right." Marguerite's tone might be sarcastic, but recollection stirred at the back of her mind. Bats? She couldn't even *think* about that right now. Then his thigh brushed hers, mildly invasive, definitely sensual. Sighing, she said, "We have to talk."

His aura flickering with frustration, he moved a fraction of an inch away, ran his hands through his hair, and braided it swiftly behind his head. The curls of his desire tightened like ferns going back in time, fiddleheads doing their best to contract and disappear. She felt an urge to hug him, to swear that everything would be okay. How could sex with him be dangerous when he had such control over himself? He'd never shown her any physical violence. He'd tried to scare her away, but without much conviction. What was he afraid of?

Because afraid he was, although she doubted he would ever admit it.

He said, "Tony told me you saw Zeb but didn't get anywhere."

"It was weird. He's absolutely convinced the scenario on the mound was not directed at you."

Constantine gave an obnoxious little snort. He shouldn't be so beautiful, not when she couldn't move him, couldn't change his mind.

But she still had to try. "He said it was a practical joke, and he meant it. I'm sure of it." With a sigh: "I *know* he did."

His aura sprang like a pouncing cat. "How do you know?" His mouth twisted. "You just know. Right?"

She nodded. Swallowed. Waited. She didn't want to discuss this.

"I'm going to worm it out of you, babe, sooner or later." His teeth flashed white in the darkness.

"If I explain myself, will you promise not to hurt Zeb?"

He considered a moment. "Nope."

She let out a breath of relief. "It's all for the best, then, because you wouldn't believe me, and even if you did, you wouldn't like it."

"Why not? You believe I sent you a dream this afternoon, and you liked it."

True, but why was he mentioning it if he didn't hope something more physical would come of it? "Did you send it?"

He shrugged. "Maybe. I don't seem to have much control over my thoughts." The fiddleheads of desire had reappeared briefly, but now they tightened hard. "Your friend Lavonia was babbling something about prophetic dreams."

"Don't worry. A thirteen-foot penis would be waaaay too daunting."

"Thirteen feet? No, no, babe. Didn't you read the book? It's only thirteen inches."

"Where else was I supposed to get information about you?" She gaped. "Not really!"

Now he laughed. "No, of course not. And we shouldn't be talking about this, because it's not going to go anywhere."

Wrong, she thought, with absolutely no justification except that she wanted it to go somewhere.

Wow. She actually wanted to have sex. She couldn't just—just *ignore* being turned on for the first time in she didn't remember how long. "I had dreams that Pauline was going to die, and she did. Then I had dreams that a big black van would run me over."

"And you still went after it." His aura simmered; his eyes bored into her.

"I didn't believe the dreams were prophetic. I'm still not sure whether I do. Maybe they were just telling me something about what was going on. Putting information together in my dreams because I couldn't do it in my conscious mind." Pause. "Besides, I had no choice."

And he could look as pissed off as he liked. She wasn't about to back down. "I believe Zeb."

"And therefore I'm just a paranoid rock star vigilante who thinks the world is out to get me."

"I didn't say that," Marguerite said. "I believe *both* of you."

~

Zeb found the black van parked in a row of vehicles belonging to Buildings and Grounds at Hellebore U. There were now magnetic signs on the sides identifying it as university property. He forced himself to unlock it and look inside; no one. He locked it again, resting his forehead against the cool metal of the door. He didn't know why he was so relieved; he'd already been sure—hadn't he?—that Marguerite wouldn't be, couldn't be in there. He opened the hood, disconnected the battery, and pulled out a couple of spark plug wires. He'd done what he could, and if there was something else to do, he was too tired to think of it.

He had no idea where Marguerite might be. A minute after he'd found her Honda, a cop car had come by, shining its headlights on the vehicle; now, on the way home, he jogged past the same spot. The bike remained, but the car was gone. He detoured tiredly past her house—still dark and silent.

He jogged home, hid the spark plug wires in the neighbor's shed, and climbed in his bedroom window. His father was asleep. Thankful for that mercy at least, he shucked his clothes and got into bed. He was just dropping off when his cell phone chimed.

Zelda was texting him. Again. *U up?*

At frigging 4:00 A.M.? The girl was nuts. *No.*

Don't B down. We luv U!

Not down. Why did she keep thinking he was down? She didn't know he was contemplating murder. *Asleep. C U tomorrow.*

Promise?

Sure. What was with the girl? Was Juma angling for a definite date? If so, she'd text him herself. Juma wasn't shy.

Whatever. Right now, all he wanted was a few hours of oblivion.

He turned off the phone, wondering if Juma's goth philosophy extended only to dress or if she would relish telling the world she'd slept with a killer. He'd thought lack of sleep was doing it to him, but contemplating murder was sheer hell on the libido.

∼

She believed both of them. *Crazy girl*, thought Constantine.

Across the lawn, the sliding doors opened. "Come inside," Lavonia called. "The coffee's ready."

Constantine stood and offered Marguerite a hand. Just as well that they had to go indoors, seeing as they'd reached an impasse. However, there were other possible avenues of approach. Not only that, he now had another, far more interesting mystery to solve.

A nightjar called nearby: *And once you solve that, things will start falling into place.* According to his spirit guide, everything falling perfectly into place was the inevitable result if only Constantine would cater to its every whim, obey its every command. It would be a damn sight easier to do that if its commands made sense.

They'd managed to cooperate this evening out of sheer necessity. Marguerite was alive. She'd clung to him. He'd rocked her while she wept. *Isn't that good enough for now?*

The nightjar called again, plaintive and noncommittal.

"Zeb is as convinced as you are," she said, "or he was until I told him Pauline didn't commit suicide. Then his—he, uh, wavered. I could tell."

"Of course you could," Constantine replied cordially. "His what?"

"It doesn't matter," she retorted. "I could tell he was surprised, and that the idea that Pauline might have been murdered really affected him."

Not that what she was describing couldn't be discerned by observation alone, but it seemed Marguerite had some unusual ability. Her secrecy didn't surprise him. His vampire friends kept their fangs as secret as possible. Other friends with unusual abilities did, too, and although he spread plenty of rumors about himself, very few people knew what he really could and couldn't do. Close friends, though . . .

But she didn't see him as a friend, only as an inconveniently sexy rock star who wanted to hurt a guy she cared about. "If you tell me what wavered and how you know so much about people, I might be more likely to believe you."

She rounded on him, practically snarling. "Forget it. I'm sick and tired of begging people to believe me." She hurried ahead of him into the house.

Well. This was interesting. What had sparked that outburst? If she didn't tell him, he'd find out anyway. Contentment seeped into his veins.

No. He couldn't afford contentment. He couldn't allow himself to enjoy her too much or to want her too badly. He needed to know more about Marguerite as a step toward finding his Enemy, but that was that.

Lavonia ushered them into a small sitting room with one pink ceramic lamp, gauze-curtained windows all around, and a multitude of plants in badly painted pots. The three other witches had changed out of their costumes. Janie, who worked at the fan club and was perpetually hot-to-trot, waggled her fingers at him. The other two eyed him with wary interest.

"Where are we?" Marguerite asked. She sat at one end of a couch. Constantine sent Lawless over to flop beside her and lounged in the doorway, being picturesque. Women always noticed him, always took stock, and in place of indifference, he sent them zings of appreciation in return. As for the few he cared about . . .

He was going to lose both Marguerite and Zelda if he hurt Zeb.

"This is Janie's place," Lavonia said.

"Janie and I are acquainted." He grinned at her avid eyes. "Don't waste your time, darlin'. You should know by now that I'm immune to love spells."

Janie gasped and looked embarrassed for all of a millisecond.

The other ladies laughed. "Trust Janie," said an older lady with a kindly face.

Janie smirked.

"No sex spells either," Constantine said. "They'll bounce right off me, and you'll be stuck with whoever—or whatever—they land on." The others laughed, the older one said something about frogs that definitely weren't princes, and Janie's smirk dissolved into a pout.

Lavonia introduced the others to him: Joan (the older lady, who emanated good humor) and Glennis (thirtyish, freckled, and knitting nervously). Apparently, Marguerite already knew them all.

"I called a special wee-hours Circle tonight." Lavonia rounded on Marguerite. "What did you think you were doing? You had been warned, and you went out at night alone without even the dog!"

"It seemed like the only option at the time," Marguerite said. "And for what it's worth, I didn't get run over."

"No thanks to you," Lavonia retorted. "How did you end up here? Have some coffee."

Marguerite accepted a mug. Constantine declined. Joan yawned and sipped her coffee. Nervous Glennis hadn't touched hers. She caught Constantine's eye, shied away, and knitted even faster.

Marguerite blew on the steam and said, "Those lights I saw—like a dome. And the voices, chanting. Were they from your circle?"

"You saw lights? And heard us?" Lavonia gaped. "We were in complete darkness except for the moon, and we were chanting very low, because we didn't want to disturb the neighbors."

Everyone stared at Marguerite, except Horny Janie, who was giving Constantine a long, slow once-over.

"You have some kind of Sight, Marguerite," Lavonia said.

Marguerite flushed. "Don't be ridiculous. I must have been hallucinating." She set down her cup and picked up a pillow cross-stitched with pictures of herbs. She smoothed out the lace edging. "I'm sure it was because I'd been running forever, terrified out of my mind and gasping for breath. I thought I was going to die, and then there was this horrendous noise that felt like my head cracked in two."

"That's when the guy who was chasing you hit the Circle," Lavonia said. "It stopped him in his tracks."

"It was amazing," said Joan, the older lady. "Never in all my years in the Craft have I seen anything like it."

Marguerite's color slowly faded toward normal. Constantine only had ordinary sight, but it was enough to tell how much Lavonia's suggestion had discomposed her. Now she was hugging the cushion to her chest.

"We met tonight to do a protection spell," said Lavonia. "I was worried about you." Her eyes flicked to Constantine and back. "We were envisioning a dome to cover you and keep you safe. And it worked! Not the way we imagined, but it protected you amazingly well!"

This was true. His guide could only do so much. At the moment it was silent, bent out of shape from the work of stirring up hordes of bats and blaming him for the necessity of doing so.

"You have no idea," Joan said. "We work at magic for years and years, and there are plenty of personal rewards, but for something to really work like this did . . . it's such a confirmation!"

The others nodded their agreement, except Glennis, who was in the grip of knitting fever. Lavonia went on, "You ran right into the Circle without breaking it, which is astonishing in itself. Usually only animals and children can do that. Then there was a sound like the loudest crack of thunder you ever heard, and he was thrown away from the Circle! It was incredible. He flew back maybe thirty feet, and after a couple of seconds, he got up and ran away."

"Did you recognize him?" Marguerite said. "Or anything about him?"

They all shook their heads. "We went through this with Constantine while you were unconscious," Lavonia said. "He was medium to tall, medium build, wearing a stocking mask." She shuddered. "You didn't see him properly either?"

Marguerite shook her head. "The only time I saw his face he was quite a ways away, staring at me. And yeah, he didn't seem to have hair or real features, so a stocking mask sounds right." Her voice quivered. "Really creepy."

Rage roiled up inside Constantine. He squashed it right back down before he gave her a headache on top of everything else. Right emotion, wrong time and place. Instead, he watched her hand run over each of the cross-stitched herbs in turn. The flowers were all pink, even the lavender and borage. Not impossible, but definitely boring. Boredom was a fair antidote for rage.

"There's nothing more sinister," Lavonia said. "I suppose we should have tried to catch him, but he was gone before we even realized what had happened—"

"No." Constantine put up a hand. "I'll find him, and I'll take care of him."

For a long moment, no one said anything. They all seemed suitably impressed. Too bad he couldn't impress himself so easily.

Marguerite, he realized, had homed in on Nervous Glennis, watching those flying fingers with a telltale little frown, raising her eyes to assess the entire woman, then deliberately letting her gaze wander. She'd be hopeless at poker.

He telepathed a question. *Is she usually so tense?*

Marguerite's eyes flew to his in a glance compounded of wariness and concern. Well, well. Progress on two fronts at once. Glennis might just be unnerved because of his rep, of course, but . . . Marguerite grabbed another cushion, Pepto-pink corduroy this time. A tiny white quill poked through the fabric. She pulled out the feather and smoothed it between her fingers.

Constantine let his gaze wander from one woman to the next until he'd done them all and then settled on Horny Janie again. Judging by her catlike expression, she was as usual trying to figure out how to seduce him. He gave her a tiny jolt of encouragement. She lit up instantly, and across the room, Marguerite went very still.

Of course. As usual, she just knew.

"There's got to be a clue someplace," Janie said with a blatantly fake innocence that reminded him of Jonetta. His dead wife had been a lousy actress, too. He'd always known that, but he'd thought she was a reasonable woman and had been blindsided by her obsessiveness and spite.

Janie batted her eyelashes at him. "Like, uh, maybe in that stuff that was on the mound this morning. I mean, it's all got to be connected, right?"

"Clever of you to think of that, Janie." He sent her another hot little jolt, followed by buzzes of approval to each of the other witches in turn, wondering if it would bother Marguerite. "Have you ladies seen the photos on the Internet?"

There was a chorus of assent and commentary from the others, and for the first time, Glennis spoke. Blurted, to be accurate. "I really must be going. I have work tomorrow." She bunched up her knitting.

Janie smirked. With short, sharp movements, Marguerite plucked out a couple more feathers.

"Work?" Lavonia said. "On Sunday?"

"Oh," Glennis quavered. "Right. I don't have to work."

"Did anything in the photos ring a bell?" Constantine gave Janie a hint of a smile and plenty of sexual pull. Marguerite's nose twitched as if at an unpleasant smell. Was his deliberate response to Janie pissing her off? Not a way he'd envisaged getting rid of her, but it might do the trick. Whatever worked, right?

The bird grumbled sleepily. *Would you bloody stop lying to yourself?*

Glennis stuffed the knitting into a tote bag. "This has nothing to do with me, and it's awfully late, so—" She rose.

"Wait, Glennis. Where are your beads?" Janie sounded positively gleeful. Constantine resisted the urge to look at Marguerite. The faintest sign that he was interested in other women—without even a suggestion of sex—had driven Jonetta into violent rages. She'd hated his fans. She'd even attacked a few.

Either Marguerite saw what he was doing or she didn't. Either she could handle it or she couldn't, and he didn't know which he wanted anyway. *And that's not a lie.*

Joan said, "That's true, Glennis. You had a string of beads on before Circle."

Glennis threw a look of sheer loathing at Janie. "So what? I'm going home." Reluctantly, Constantine sent a tad of paralyzing fear Glennis's way. Apart from the panicked flickering of her eyes, she didn't move.

"Now that I think about it, those beads were something like the ones on the mask," Lavonia said. "Not the same color, and it's not so obvious from the photos, but Marguerite showed me the real thing."

Constantine telepathed: *Did you show Janie, too?*

Marguerite gave the slightest shake of the head. She must have noticed what he had done to Glennis—how, damn it?—for he read disapproval in her eyes, and her voice was gentle when she said, "Please let us have a look at them, Glennis. We need any help we can get."

Glennis was near to tears. "They have nothing to do with anything, and I have to go now."

Janie tittered. "What's the matter, Glennis? Not so sanctimonious about right and wrong anymore?"

Lavonia shot a glare at Janie, grabbed the bag from Glennis, and dug around inside. She pulled out a long leather thong twined with copper filament and decorated with jasper and glazed green ceramic beads. "Yes! They're very much alike. Where did you get this, Glennis?"

"I don't remember. It was ages ago."

"No, it wasn't!" Janie scoffed. "It was last month. We were manning the Magical Oils booth in the town square, and you kept going on and on about how Eaton Wilson gave it to you."

"You must be mistaken." Glennis pressed her lips together, martyr-like.

Janie smirked. "No, I remember wondering how you could possibly want to sleep with such a dork."

"He's not a dork!" Glennis cried. "He's a gentleman, and you're disgusting. You never think of anything but sex. Such spells are an improper use of magic. They'll come back to bite you, and you'll be sorry!"

"Hey, if that sex spell I'm sending Constantine bounces onto a vampire, I'll be *very* happy." Janie grinned. "If it lands on Eaton, I'll barf."

"Your spell wouldn't affect him anyway," Glennis said passionately. "He's too *good.*"

"What if it turns out he's not so angelic after all? What'll you do then?" Janie cast a coy glance Constantine's way as she taunted the other witch. Without the slightest hesitation, he responded with more sexual pull. If Marguerite didn't like it, she could lump it.

She was watching him, but as far as he could tell, she didn't react at all.

"We'll ask Eaton," Lavonia said firmly, looking as if she couldn't decide which of the players in this dumb drama pissed her off more. Constantine sent her a little buzz just for the fun of it.

Lavonia's eyes grew wide, and Marguerite bit her lip on what he was sure was a smile. *Yes!* A peacock pranced through his head in full display.

Lavonia cleared her throat. "He'll remember if he gave her the necklace, and if so, he'll know where he got it, and that might lead us to the source of the beads."

Janie wasn't about to leave her spot in the limelight. She put her hands on her hips. "Maybe we don't need to ask Eaton. What color was the van that chased you, Marguerite? What make?"

"A Ford, black as far as I could tell, or maybe a very dark blue or green. Why?"

"Cha-ching!" Janie spread her hands. "Eaton Wilson has an old black Ford van."

CHAPTER TEN

It wasn't Eaton," Marguerite said flatly, but Glennis let out a yowl of fury and lunged. She got in one resounding slap at Janie's face before Constantine slid smoothly in to separate them with a lot of aura force and scarcely a touch.

Marguerite sprang up to take Glennis back to the couch. Janie took advantage of Constantine's proximity to cling to him; his aura shot her a hot, sensual pulse before he peeled her away and handed her off to Joan. He wasn't turned on by Janie at all, just playing her.

"Janie, you should be ashamed of yourself." Marguerite put an arm around Glennis. "Eaton's completely harmless, and you know it."

Janie responded with a malicious little smile. Marguerite let out a breath. Things would not be pretty when Janie figured out she was a pawn in Constantine's game.

Whatever that was. He hadn't seemed surprised at Janie's revelation, but he leapt on Marguerite's immediate defense of Eaton. "Are you saying there was something about the man who chased you that definitely marks him as 'not Eaton'"?

Unfortunately, there wasn't anything physical, but she hadn't had much of a look. She couldn't explain that Eaton simply couldn't have had her attacker's aura. "No, but Eaton wouldn't do something like that. He's a good person, as Glennis said. And if he has a black van, I've certainly never seen it. He usually drives a Volvo."

Constantine surveyed Lavonia and Joan, nudging them with his aura. Did they have any sense of what he was doing?

Lavonia sighed. "It's true about the van. He doesn't use it much, though, except for carrying lumber or furniture or whatever. He loaned it to me to pick up a dresser I bought not long ago, which is how I know. But I can't picture him stalking and chasing somebody."

"He's been auditing an anthropology course," Joan admitted—she was the secretary of that department at Hellebore U—"but that doesn't prove a thing." She passed a box of tissues to Glennis.

"He's a gentle soul," Lavonia said. "A New Age hippie, totally into peace and love." She put up her chin at Constantine. "You were on the mound this morning up in that oak tree. I have no idea how you managed to stay out of sight, but you must have heard what Eaton said. He's the one who wants to experiment with visions on the mound."

Janie had been pouting again, but she pounced on this. "See what I mean? He's nuts. He used to pester us about Celtic myths and Wiccan rites. Before that, it was Hindu goddesses. Now he's into Native American religions. Who knows? Maybe he's having visions ordering him to kill people."

"You bitch!" Glennis sobbed. "How can you say such awful things?"

"Just trying to get to the truth," Janie said. "Right, Constantine?"

"Yes," he said, "the truth." His aura flared, and Janie backed right into the sofa and plopped down. "Easy enough to ask Eaton," he added coolly.

Janie bounced up again. "You can't trust him to give a straight answer. He's got some weird-ass shit going on right now. I know, because I went to Alabama with him a while ago."

Glennis raised her eyes from a clump of soggy tissues. "You *what?*"

Janie's shrug could only be called insolent. "Seeing as it was my first time casting a sex spell, I figured I'd try it on Eaton, because a hard-up, dorky sort of dude should be easy, right? And he sure was. Fell like a tree and asked me to spend the weekend with him."

Glennis paled. Something shot out from Constantine's aura and tapped Janie upside the head.

"The whole truth," Janie said, almost as if she were talking to herself. "I wish I'd bespelled him earlier, because he'd already made his plans and wouldn't budge. We went to these dumb Indian mounds and walked and walked and walked, and he tried to convince me to talk to Constantine about his research on visions. He took measurements and drew maps, and went on and on about performing sacred ceremonies to cleanse the earth, which he figured Constantine would relate to. Ritual fires and purifying drinks and a bunch of other crap."

"Knives?" Constantine smiled at her.

"N-no." Janie gazed back, all adoration. "Not that I remember. But that doesn't mean he's not crazy."

"How about songs or prayers?"

"Yes!" Janie arched her back, thrusting her breasts forward, eyes half-closed. "He even tried one of your songs, but he can't sing worth a flip. But the weirdest of all was that he's still madly in love with Veronica Bonnard."

A shiver traversed Constantine's aura, dark and swift, and hung there. "Bonnard. A relation of Zeb's?"

"She was his mother," Lavonia said, "but she's been dead for several years."

He shrugged, and the shiver dissolved and was gone.

Janie came to herself and realized she wasn't the center of attention anymore. "I mean, how boring would it be, screwing a guy who can't stop talking about a dead woman? So I didn't bother with him in the end."

Glennis straightened, pale with dignity and blotchy with tears. "No, he turned you down." As if she'd been let off a leash, she grabbed the string of beads and stuffed it into her bag. "And I'm leaving!"

"Going to warn Eaton that Constantine is after him?" mocked Janie with a triumphant glance at the rock star, but Glennis was already out the door.

Constantine motioned with his chin to Marguerite. "Thanks again, ladies. Come on, gorgeous. Let's get you back to bed."

The expression on Janie's face would have been priceless if it hadn't been so enraged. Marguerite downed the rest of her coffee and thanked them all again. Outdoors, they watched Glennis zoom away.

Marguerite's car was parked across the street. Jabez must have dropped it off while they were inside. She opened the rear door for Lawless. "I'm going to follow her."

"Why? You don't believe Eaton did it."

"I want to see what happens when she tells him what's going on." She got into the driver's seat and started the car. "You can come if you promise not to hurt him." Which was an entirely ridiculous thing to say, and she knew it.

"If he's innocent, he's safe. I won't condemn him on the say-so of some dumb chick trying to impress me."

Marguerite took off after Glennis. "It was creepy how you played her. How you played all of them."

His voice went hard, his aura prickly. "For a second or two there, I thought you were enjoying it."

"Oh, it was definitely cool. But it's still creepy, and Janie will refuse to talk to me for months." She added ruefully, "On the other hand, your adoring female fans must love it."

"That's the whole point, isn't it?" Those bitter little prickles shot in all directions. "Songs, visions, feel-good vibes, even orgasms for the luckiest ones, and the result is lots and lots of sales. It's just hunky-dory, babe, but sometimes it backfires."

"You mean obsessive fans? Or women who realize you've just been playing with them and that you don't really want them at all?"

"You do see a lot, don't you, Marguerite? I bet you could do a mighty fine job of playing me, if you wanted to."

"I'm just trying to understand you. I don't want to play anyone!"

"I'm not sure I know how to do anything else," he said. "It's how I've survived."

"Right." Might as well jump in. "As a matter of interest, did you kill anybody at the Threshold tonight?"

His aura flared. "Tony's been blabbing. What else did he tell you?"

"Nothing I hadn't figured out for myself, such as that killing people isn't good for you."

"It so happens I didn't kill anyone. I just watched from the shadows. Nobody saw me, but club management must have gotten word that the underworld was going to send a spy, because nobody even came near breaking the rules. Nobody was underage, all the participants seemed willing, and the guy we were particularly interested in didn't even take out a knife." They turned onto Eaton's street. Constantine's voice was a chill wind in the hot, dense chorus of the Louisiana summer night. "The scumbag could use a good fright, but what kind of nightmares should I send someone who likes cutting games? He may get off on being the victim if it's just a dream, or the fear may excite him even more. Don't want to encourage the asshole." She felt him shrug in the darkness. "It's an entertaining creative exercise."

"Some of your songs," she said. "They're dreams you've sent people, aren't they?" Specifically, the one he'd sent her uncle, but she couldn't discuss that. "Not your way of thinking, but your take on others or on what would frighten them." She sighed. "That explains it, I guess. Your love songs are so beautiful, and some of your stuff is unbelievably spiritual. It didn't seem to fit together, but now it does."

"Don't get too comfy about me, babe." He was right. She should be cautious; she should make a point of staying unnerved. Even if he hadn't beaten or killed anyone tonight, he'd done it before and would do it again. She shouldn't want to be with him at all.

Instead, desire crawled all over her, powerful and intense. This must be some dumb reverse psychology at work, she thought irritably. What she couldn't have, she wanted even more.

But . . . were these her own feelings, or was he now playing her? She glanced at him. Arousal glowed in his aura. He caught her eye, and his aura reached out and danced with hers. His aura confirmed the source of her feelings. Auras were often less vivid in the dark, but arousal tended to show regardless.

"Damn it," she said. "You're thinking about sex again."

"Always, when I'm with you, darlin'."

"Control yourself, for God's sake." Which was unfair of her, because she was pretty sure a good part of that arousal had been her own. Mutual chemistry, each of them feeding upon the other's desire . . .

Dragging her focus back where it belonged, she pulled up behind Glennis's car in front of Eaton's old two-story clapboard. The porch light was on, along with a low light in the front room.

Constantine was out before she'd turned off the car, and Lawless bounced up, eager to join the party. "I forgot about Eaton's dog," Marguerite said. "She's a yappy little thing, and she might be in the yard. Lawless likes her."

"Sorry, boy. Not this time." Constantine's aura gentled briefly. "Go to sleep. We'll be back."

Lawless yawned, circled a couple of times, curled up on the back seat, and closed his eyes. Warmth and sadness swept over Marguerite. This was a Constantine she liked.

"Go ahead and try the front windows while I check for the dog," he said. She tiptoed up the front steps, watching as he slipped around the side, his aura stretching ahead of him toward the back garden. Eaton's dog yipped once, then subsided completely.

Marguerite peered through the blinds, but the front room was empty. She hurried around the side of the house. Constantine had braced himself between a drainpipe and a crepe myrtle to peek in the kitchen window. "Too bad neither of us has vampire hearing, although so far it's pretty obvious. He's making coffee and looking bewildered while she waxes hysterical."

"I don't think he's much of an actor," Marguerite said. "Come down and give me a boost. If I can just see him, I'll feel more comfortable about leaving."

"Take my word for it, all he's doing right now is trying to wake up."

Why was Constantine stalling? "Come on," she said, "I want to see him."

"Want to? Or need to?"

"Fine. I'll go onto the deck and peek through the back door."

"Not a good idea," Constantine said. "The dog's there. I'm having a hell of a time keeping it from yapping as is."

"Then pick me up so I can see in the window!"

"That's an even worse idea," he said, jumping down. He lifted her, one firm hand on her hip and the other curled around her thigh. Pleasure raked down her with merciless teeth. She gasped, arched back, and slumped against him. "Told you," he said.

She straightened furiously. Embarrassment took over, anger on its tail, while her core throbbed anxiously, demanding more. "What is the *matter* with you? If you don't want it, stop thinking about it!" She got ahold of herself and peered in the window. Glennis was getting mugs from the cupboard while Eaton, dressed in a T-shirt and boxers, tipped maple cookies onto a plate. What hair he had stuck out in all directions.

"See? Nothing interesting. You could have just believed me," Constantine said. "Or did you *need* to see him?"

"Yes, I needed to," she said. "And you need to keep your desires locked up inside you where they belong. He's coming toward the window. Let me down."

He did—so quickly she almost fell.

Above them, the kitchen window slid up. "I don't know about the van, Glennis," Eaton was saying. "I left it at the mechanic's for a tune-up before I went out of town this morning. That's better. There's a nice breeze tonight." His voice and footsteps receded.

"Did you 'suggest' that he open the window?" Marguerite whispered.

"We want to hear them, don't we?" His murmur tickled her ear, kindling tiny fires down below.

Mentally, she doused the fires with ice-cold Coke. "He's innocent. I'm sure of it. But in the interest of not playing stupid games, I don't think Janie was lying either—just putting her spin on things."

"Uh-huh." Constantine blew on her ear. "Mostly, she confirmed what I already knew."

"Stop that!" Marguerite hissed and backed into a holly bush with a muffled yelp. "What do you mean, already knew?"

"Tsk." He put his fingers to his lips. "We can't have an open window with you making all that noise."

"It's your damned fault—" She shushed herself just in time.

"The open window makes me nervous." That was Glennis. She pushed it sharply shut.

Obviously enjoying himself, Constantine climbed back to his former perch. "The cops haven't found the vehicle yet, but Gideon told me this afternoon that Wilson owns a black van."

"That's why you weren't surprised about it," Marguerite said, and immediately wished she hadn't.

He chuckled. "The secret of your Sight is safe with me, babe, but it would be even safer if I knew what it was." He let that sit, but she waited him out. After a while, he said, "Some guy with a dark van—I call him Dancing Dude—comes to the mounds to sing and pray at night from time to time. Weak voice, off-key. Wilson was humming one of my songs this morning on the mounds. That, coupled with his interest in rituals . . ." She felt him shrug in the night. "He was out all day in the Volvo and returned shortly after the black van showed up at your place."

It hit her like a slap. "You already believed him innocent. You were playing me, too, first by agreeing to come to Eaton's place, and then by messing with my defenses!"

He jumped down. "Just trying to understand you. Are you pissed off yet?"

"Always, when I'm with you." she said irritably. *"Darlin'."*

"So why insist on associating yourself with me? By what Tony tells me, Nathan got a whole new load of shit tonight to put out there on the Internet."

"Yep," she said, suddenly glum. "He'll say I'm screwing you, Tony, and Zeb, and he'll imply there are dozens of others as well. He'll say that's what comes of being brought up surrounded by porn stars, when actually it made me completely lose interest in sex."

"Completely?" His mouth was mere inches from hers, his aura a devilish sizzle in the hot night.

"Almost completely." She turned away. "Please don't do this to me if you don't intend to follow through." Now that he was out of the way, she pulled herself up by the drainpipe and braced herself against the window. "Eaton's properly awake and frowning. Standing there with a mug dangling from his hand, just like the one we found on the mound. Looking incredulous. Glennis is opening her laptop, chattering like a squirrel the whole time. I bet she's going to show him the story about you and me on the mound. Eaton's pretty oblivious, so he may not have heard about it, or if he did, he may not have given it a second thought."

Constantine's voice was calm, his aura as aroused as ever. "A vehicle that I think was the same van stopped at the mounds briefly an hour or so after the concert the other night. I was meditating on Mama Mound, but I heard it pass on the road, idle for a while, and then pass the other way a while later."

If he could do cool and indifferent, so could she. "You think that's when I was brought there?"

"You or the paraphernalia, or both. If it wasn't Eaton, then someone borrowed his van—probably the same someone as tonight." He stood close below her, too close. "I might have been playing you a little, babe, but mostly I wanted to verify what Janie said. Those pics on the Internet didn't include a close-up of the mask. Can you picture her zooming in and studying the mask so carefully that she would recognize beads that were something like some other beads she'd seen a month ago?"

"Not likely," Marguerite whispered, thinking furiously. Had someone described the beads to Janie? "She was hanging out with a crowd around Nathan in the Merkin earlier tonight. I suppose he might have shown people pictures of the mask, and she might have remembered Glennis's necklace, but it seems far-fetched." She paused. "And I can't see her accusing Eaton to a reporter or to the cops. She can be malicious at times, but she's not that bad."

"My *beads*?" Eaton Wilson made for the back door and flung it open. Constantine took Marguerite by the waist and lowered her slowly, trapping her between a Leyland cypress and the fence. The heady aromas of tree and aroused hunk circled her like a lasso. Or a thirteen-foot penis. She wrapped her arms around herself, put her eyes to a crack in the fence, and tried to pay attention to what was happening in the yard.

Eaton stormed across the back porch and down the steps. The dog, which had been panting quietly until then, bounded up to him, almost tripping Glennis in the process. Eaton strode across the lawn to a shed. He flung open the door and flicked on a light. "This is where I do my pottery. They were right here, in this tin. Twenty, twenty-one or so, and they're all gone!" He whirled in the doorway and bumped into the dithering Glennis. "You said Marguerite has the mask? Thank God some of my beads are in good hands. I don't care about the cup, but I worked hard on those beads, and I want them back."

"What about the mask? Isn't it yours?"

"No! What use would it be to prance around wearing a mask? Rituals can be cathartic, but spirituality is an internal phenomenon." He set the tin down inside the shed, switched off the light, and closed the door. "I'll call Marguerite tomorrow."

"Unless Constantine has it now," Glennis said. "I don't like that man one bit."

"He's written some beautiful songs," Eaton said, whistling for the dog, but instead of following him, it decided to bark.

"He kills people!" Glennis retorted. Her aura wobbled in tune with her voice.

Eaton put an arm around her. "Hey there, Glennis. Don't cry." He whistled again and called the dog. "I'll contact the police in the morning. The beads, maybe the van . . . I wonder if anything else has been taken."

"But what if they come and arrest you?" Glennis said. "They might say you're the one who chased Marguerite. Do you have an alibi?"

"Of course not. I didn't get home till well after midnight, and after that I was in bed asleep."

"I wish I could give you an alibi," Glennis said, "but too many people know I wasn't here." Her aura flushed, and Marguerite stifled a giggle.

Eaton said, "I wouldn't want you to lie to protect me." He moved Glennis gently toward the house, his hand at the small of her back. "Not that I'd have any problem with you spending the night."

Glennis's aura blossomed, a bouquet of bright, fresh colors, shimmering with delight. How lovely for her, thought

Marguerite wistfully. She had a feeling her own lovelife would never be that simple and sweet.

The dog barked at Marguerite through the fence. She'd been doing pretty well at ignoring the rock star pressed close beside her, but now she whispered, "Can't you stop it?" The dog barked louder.

"I don't want to," Constantine murmured. "It thinks it's protecting Eaton." The dog barked some more.

"What is it, Nellie girl? A possum?" Eaton said. "Don't you worry about me, Glennis. Dufray doesn't harm innocent people." If his attitude didn't prove he wasn't guilty or even afraid, nothing would—unless Eaton was unbelievably devious and also spectacularly good at concealing his aura, which he wasn't.

"He and the vigilantes have done a lot of good for Bayou Gavotte," Eaton said. "The clubs are safer, and the tourist trade is flourishing. Apparently, he wants to talk to me. He said so on the mound this morning, right in front of Roy Lutsky." He ushered her up the steps to the deck.

"Poor Roy. But you're not going to go talk to Constantine, are you?" Glennis bleated.

No time like the present, Constantine telepathed. He took Marguerite's hand and moved quietly toward the front of the house.

"What if it's just a ruse to get ahold of you?" Glennis cried. "Oh my God, what if Constantine followed me over here?"

Her voice faded as they reached the front yard. Constantine went up to the porch and rang the doorbell. Marguerite let Lawless out of the car and followed. Maybe a doggie playdate would make their errand seem a little less hostile to Glennis.

"So that's why Nellie was barking," Eaton said, when he opened the door. "Come on in."

It took a good while, but cookies and coffee later, they had a few more pertinent facts: first, that Eaton not only didn't intend any ritual involving knives, but (when prompted to look) he was missing a carving knife with his initials on the handle. His aura showed him to be appropriately distressed. "Why would anyone try to implicate me in something so terrible?" he said. He swore he hadn't been near the mound the previous night, and if his van had been stolen, it had also been returned before he woke the next morning. When Constantine went to the car to bring in the mask so Eaton could have a close look (and be reassured as to the condition and safety of his beads), he asked, "Are you all right, Marguerite? I'm relieved to see you in such good hands."

"I'm fine," she said, thinking about Constantine's good hands and wishing she really were in them, then wishing she didn't wish that at all. What was it about him that moved her so strongly? It couldn't be just sex. Sex was inadequate and disappointing, considering all the hype. Even a spectacular orgasm left a gaping void behind.

She'd thought about it enough to realize the void was due to a lack of true intimacy. Not that she hadn't wanted emotional closeness—and not that she hadn't tried—but guys didn't like girls who could read their every emotion. If Constantine figured her out, he would back off like all the others. So why did she so idiotically want to have sex with him?

"Aren't you scared of him?" Glennis whispered.

"No," Marguerite said. "Under all those frightening vibes, he's mush. Just a sweet, cuddly teddy bear."

The door opened, an owl hooted twice, and a vision of a slavering grizzly bear prowled through her head. She stifled a giggle, and the owl hooted again. Constantine came back in with the mask, his aura carefully neutral. Longing poured over her. His longing or hers? He was trying to conceal his feelings, so she couldn't quite tell. Both?

Then why not just do it? At least that would get it over with and the disappointment started, so she could move on.

Eaton examined and identified his beads. "I use them for jewelry," he said, "but they look very good on here." He examined the mask front and back and sighed.

He knows more, doesn't he? Constantine telepathed.

Marguerite hesitated, then nodded ever so slightly. The rocker's aura shivered, but his voice was free of guile when he asked, "Any idea who might have made it?"

Eaton ran his fingers over the copper sheeting, stopping at a half-inch nick along the otherwise perfect edge, then moving on. "No idea."

Constantine stood and thanked Eaton. He took the mask, and they collected Lawless, who'd been cavorting with his playdate in the yard. When Constantine held out a hand for the car keys, Marguerite gave them to him without objecting. She let Lawless into the back and got into the passenger seat. "He was lying. That's not like Eaton at all. And yes, I just knew, but you could tell, too. His body language is so blatant."

"Wise of you not to try to deny it," he said coolly.

"I'm not trying to prevent you from figuring out who did this," she said, weary now. "I just don't want anyone to get hurt."

He started the car and pulled away from the curb. "Who do you suppose he's protecting?"

"The same person as Zeb, I guess. When you consider how upset he was about the beads going missing, it's strange he didn't let on that he knew where the mask came from. But by then, he wasn't angry anymore, just bewildered and a little sad . . ." Damn. She wished she could openly explain how she knew. She was so tired of hiding what she was.

Halfway to her place, he said, "Believe me, I understand. There's plenty of stuff I don't want to explain about myself either."

No, duh. She sat in silence while he drove her home, thinking hard, worrying about Zeb. As he pulled into her driveway, her practical brain started working again. "Shouldn't I be dropping *you* someplace?"

"I'm not leaving you alone, babe." He got out and opened the back door for Lawless.

She opened hers. "That's kind of you, but—"

"No buts," Constantine said, and in spite of herself Marguerite let out a long breath of relief. Lawless growled low in his throat and took off toward the house, nose to the ground. Constantine stood, head cocked. A nightjar called close by. "Let's go inside."

She took the keys and unlocked the front door. Lawless squirmed past her. Inside, it was entirely dark, but it shouldn't have been. "When you let Lawless out, did you turn off the back porch light? Because I didn't. It was on when I left on my bike."

"Maybe it burned out," Constantine said doubtfully, but it hadn't. They switched on all the lights and went from room to room. Nothing seemed to be missing; nothing had been disturbed.

She shivered. "This is really creeping me out."

He pulled her close, took out his cell to send a text message, and then another. "I let Gideon know. Jabez will come in a while to keep watch."

"Poor Jabez. When does he get to sleep?"

"He doesn't sleep much, but he'll have all day if he wants it." Pause. "Off to bed, babe. I'll get the guitar I left down by the bayou and be right back."

"I'm not staying here alone for even two minutes," she said.

Pleasure suffused his aura, so beautiful it twisted her heart. He *wanted* to protect her. Then anxiety tore into the pleasure. Why? What was he afraid of?

"Come with me, then," he said. They made their way through the dark, warm garden. The intoxicating scent of night-blooming jasmine teased her as she followed him through the back gate. Frogs chorused cheerfully. Lawless scampered down the trail to the bayou.

His aura glowed with arousal. The darkness was pitchy hot. No, maybe they were both hot. Or maybe she just wanted someone to cling to. She wondered if maybe he wanted that, too, regardless of his fears.

The guitar in its case was cached near a vast water oak. Marguerite stroked the rough bark, trying to focus on the practical. "If Eaton recognized the mask, someone else will sooner or later."

Out of the darkness came his voice, cool and faintly amused. "So why did Zeb remove the evidence that implicated Eaton but not what implicated someone else?"

She hadn't thought of that. "It was a lot easier to conceal the knife, I guess."

"But he could have taken both. Or maybe he doesn't share Eaton's opinion about whoever stole the beads and made the mask."

"What I want to know is, who was the setup meant to harm? Eaton and maybe someone else? Or you, Constantine?" That was the crux of it . . .

His aura loomed and swayed in the charged darkness. She couldn't see her own aura, but felt his mingle and tangle with her space. How could they not touch each other? Why should they not join in every possible way? All her questions hung suspended in the dense night air.

After a while, he asked, "Do I have to choose?"

And just like that, everything clicked. "The scenario was aimed at more than one person!" She let that sit for a moment. "It seems awfully far-fetched."

"It's the most attractive option. I'm not delusional, and Zeb truly believes it's aimed at whoever he's protecting. My Enemy—evidently a malicious sort of dude—is simply killing two or more birds with one stone."

"And we are no longer in opposition." She leaned against the oak and spread her arms wide. "If only for that, I love this idea."

Delight and desire thrust up together, flames and sweetness, and suddenly he was hard against her, ravenous and strong. Oh, *God*, she got off on kissing this man. The merciless pleasure took up where it had left off at Eaton's. Their tongues licked and fenced in heavy, eloquent silence. Heat unbounded crashed along every limb, curling her toes, twining her fingers into his hair, sending a desperate throbbing to her core. His erection pressed against her with delicious promise. His aura clung to hers.

Then subtly, something changed. He withdrew a hair's breadth. She moaned and pulled him closer, nipping at his lips, seeking his tongue again. She grabbed his buttocks and ground herself against him. She wanted this. Wanted *him*.

He growled. A hot hand covered her breast. She arched into his hand, groaning with anticipation and longing. She pulsed and ached with desire. Abruptly, he buried his face in her neck. An orgasm tore through her, sending her high, high over the moon.

He pulled away. Their auras ripped apart. She cried out and fell to her knees, curling into a ball.

CHAPTER ELEVEN

Oh, fuck. What had he done? He dropped to the ground beside her, fighting down his own pain, while Lawless whined in distress. "Did I hurt you?" He rested his hand gingerly on her arm. "Marguerite?"

She slapped him away, uncurling as she did, and scrambled to her feet. "Don't you *ever* do that again." She stormed away, Lawless close behind.

Bewilderment rolled over him on waves of unendurable chagrin. He knew he had problems controlling his emotions—particularly his anger and frustration—during sex. He'd learned that with Jonetta, causing her unbearable pain, and every time he'd considered having sex since then, all those negative emotions had roiled up, stopping him in his tracks.

Then the anger had spilled over into his concerts . . . but he'd conquered that, or at least come close. Logically, sex should be the next step, as the bird kept insisting.

Except that at the last moment, he'd . . . Might as well admit it. He'd chickened out and given her a one-touch.

Which hadn't worked. He'd hurt her. Hurt himself, too, but he was used to that.

If he couldn't even give a woman an orgasm anymore, he might as well throw himself into the bayou and drown.

Too bloody bad he could swim. Anyway, with his luck, the nutria would band together and shove him up onto the bank. He grabbed the guitar and took up the rear.

"What was that supposed to be?" she ranted. "One of your famous one-touch orgasms?"

"Uh . . . yeah. Something must have gone wrong." Ahead, more lights were on in Marguerite's house. Much as he valued Jabez's friendship, he didn't want to look like a complete ass in front of him, or at least not more than he already did. "Jabez is here." Silently, he asked Lawless to accept the bodyguard as a friend.

"Just when I was beginning to think sex might be interesting," she said, and her voice broke on a sob. "That it might be worth the risk, on the off chance it would be enjoyable and—and worthwhile, and you ruin everything." She marched furiously up the path.

Could we discuss this later? Great—now he was telepathing to her without even meaning to, and it was too late anyway for Jabez not to have heard what she'd said.

"Swept the house," said a deep voice. He was under the golden rain tree at the edge of Marguerite's yard. Lawless had already gone ahead. "No bugs. Hey." He smiled approvingly at Marguerite. Every goddamn guy in his band and entourage wanted him to get laid.

Never going to happen.

It has to happen, lamented the nightjar his guide was possessing at the moment. *There's no other way.*

Constantine shut it out of his head, turning his attention to real life.

If it doesn't happen, nothing *will fall into place,* the bird said.

Shut up. Constantine gritted his teeth and waded through the unfriendly darkness toward the house.

The bird wasn't about to let go. It pursued him in the form of a barn owl, flapping past on urgent, desperate wings. *Until it's too late! Too late! Too late!*

It was already too goddamn late, and he should have kept his distance right from the start. Even if he wasn't a total catastrophe as a lover, Marguerite didn't want a celebrity boyfriend. She would never put up with the horrors of fame.

When had his thoughts started traveling *that* road? He couldn't afford to want her as a real girlfriend. She wasn't even going to be a one-night stand.

Oh, *God*, he wanted her.

In the light from the living room window, her expression was aghast. "You had to check for *bugs?*"

"Seeing as we don't know why someone broke in again..." Constantine shrugged. "Any trouble from Nathan and the rest?"

Jabez chuckled. "We sent out warnings. So far the neighborhood's clear. One dude tried approaching by way of the bayou, so I stuck a snake in his boat. Nathan posted pics of your lady here dancing with Tony." He paused as if he wanted to say more but changed his mind. It must be bad. "I put someone on to watch him. If you want me to run him out of town, just say the word."

"Thanks, man. Keep an eye out till dawn, and then go get some sleep." Jabez disappeared silently into the night, and they went into the house. Marguerite sank onto the couch, hugged her knees to her chest, and closed her eyes. Constantine took the guitar from its case, sat at the far end of the couch, and tuned it, watching her. Dark eyelashes showed stark against her pale skin. A tear welled up and rolled down her cheek.

"Hey, babe, don't cry." He set the guitar down but didn't dare touch her. "Just ignore Nathan and the rest. This'll all blow over soon."

She shrugged and swiped at the tear.

"I can leave now, and you can say you dumped me. The problem is, they'll assume I dumped you because you went out with Tony. The alternative is to give me another day or two and then dump me. Whatever you like, babe. I didn't mean to hurt you. I swear I won't touch you again."

The spirit guide huffed in Constantine's mind. *Idiot! She wants you to touch her.*

Yada yada yada, fall into place, Constantine told it. *I heard you the first time. And the second time. Go away.*

"You didn't hurt me much," she said. "You hurt yourself. A lot."

This was true, but how did she know? "I didn't hurt you much?" he repeated, wanting to believe her, not sure he dared.

"All I got was some fallout from the pain you were suffering and a huge dose of frustration." She stood. "You decide. You drop me, I drop you, I don't care which or when, as long as this is over with." She went into her bedroom and closed the door.

He blew out a long, slow breath. So . . . he needn't have given her the one-touch. He needn't have pulled away at all.

Then she opened it again. "Alternatively, you could just tell me why you're afraid to sleep with me."

For a horrified moment, he stood stunned, appalled at her insight, mortified beyond endurance, closing himself up tight, tight . . . He was *not* a coward, damn it. He'd been afraid before, and he'd handled it. He never gave up or gave in. He always found a way to fight back.

This isn't a fight, you muddleheaded twit.

But before he mustered a response to either the bird or the girl, she closed the door. This time it stayed shut.

∼

Zeb woke to the sound of his father bitching downstairs. "Sorry, but we're right out of ink and almost out of paper. Zeb's been wasteful as usual. He can damn well replace them himself."

This was total bullshit. He hadn't used the printer in weeks. A female voice answered his dad too softly for Zeb to recognize it. He dragged himself out of bed and headed for a cold shower in the hope it would wake him up. This crap had to end soon. A guy needed to sleep now and then.

Bathed, dressed, and more or less functional, he folded his aura, arming himself in a light version of the Zone. The female turned out to be Juma. "Jesus God, not more French verbs."

"And a cheerful good morning to you, too." Juma leaned against the kitchen counter, sipping iced tea—looked like strawberry-mango—from PJ's. "It's my mission in life—at least this week—to make sure you get the pluperfect right before school starts." The corner of her eye flickered briefly.

Whatever the pluperfect was, he didn't need it now or ever. What was that sketch of a wink supposed to convey?

Crap. She'd better not be ready for the great deflowering. Not happening—at least not now. Once this mess was over and done with . . . If he came through it alive . . .

He had to come through it alive. He wouldn't be able to protect anyone if he was dead.

"Once I wake up, I'll blow the pluperfect all to hell." He dumped coffee beans in the grinder and switched it on. The noise never failed to irritate Dad. Since he had so few opportunities to get his own back, Zeb made the most of it. Not that he could make more than halfway-decent coffee with these beans or this coffeemaker. One of these days he would get himself an espresso machine like the one Constantine had used at the Impractical Cat.

Unbelievable that after yesterday he was still idolizing Constantine Dufray. Although face it—after last night he didn't blame Dufray one bit for wanting to torture the truth out of him.

"I deactivated your phone," said his father. "I may consider reactivating it if you behave yourself. After the French lesson, which will have to be done without the printout Juma wants because you wasted all the ink, go get a ream of paper and a new set of printer cartridges."

Zeb had never thought of phone deactivation as a positive before, but at least Zelda wouldn't text him at all hours of the day and night. He threw a glance at his father. "Sure, no problem, but it wasn't me. I only use the printer during school." Come to think of it, there was one advantage of death—it didn't include school.

"I suppose you're not the one who's been surfing porn either," his dad said, pouring himself a glass of milk.

"Nope." What with all the running around protecting idiots, he didn't have time to surf anything.

Juma snorted, and his father rolled his eyes. "If it's not you, and it's definitely not me, then who do you suppose it is? The cat?"

Zeb poured the coffee grounds into the filter and started the brew. "Maybe we have a poltergeist."

"That reminds me," Dad said. "I need you to sweep out my lab, too." He'd turned the spare bedroom into a home chemistry lab. More than once he'd asked Juma the super-student if she would consider going into chemistry instead of literature. "Two of my best beakers *somehow* fell on the floor and broke."

Lately, everything was Zeb's fault, whether he was responsible or not. "Maybe another possum got in and couldn't find a way out. Or a raccoon."

"If that was the case, we would have another dead animal stinking up the room," Dad grumbled. "Don't try to distract me, Zeb. We all know you surfed the goddamn porn."

Zeb remained in the Zone and took a mug off the shelf.

"Maybe it was a demon," Juma said. "A sex demon." She took a peppermint candy from the dish on the table and popped it into her mouth.

Or a murderer, Zeb thought wearily, wondering how long he would be stuck with Juma this morning. Much as he liked her, he had stuff to do.

"Why would a sex demon need porn? Doesn't get enough of the real thing?" Dad had being cool with cute young chicks down pat. Mercifully, he didn't sleep with them, because it would blemish his perfect reputation. Oh, and get him fired, too.

Juma sipped her tea, flirting from under her black eyelashes. "The only sex demon I know has to fight women off. Porn is safer. There's nobody to get rid of when you're done."

Dad shook his head in mock dismay. "Young women are so cold-blooded these days." He downed the glass of milk, lifted his keys from the nail by the back door, and crammed a folder stuffed with papers into his briefcase. "I'll be having brunch with Lavonia later. If you can't get Marguerite's lawn mower working, trim her hedges or weed her garden. Do something useful and legal, for God's sake."

"What's with him?" Juma asked, once Zeb's father was safely out of the way.

"He caught me working at the Merkin last night." When she made a disgusted noise, he said, "No, I wasn't prostituting myself. I was just playing messenger boy."

"That place is totally historically inaccurate. I'm surprised your dad didn't ground you."

"He doesn't believe in grounding," Zeb said. "He very conveniently decided that after I ran away from home years ago. He knows it won't work, so he plays the victimized parent instead."

"You ran away from home? Why?"

This he wasn't about to get into. "Life sucked after my mom died. As my shrink puts it, my father and I had different ways of grieving."

"Such as?"

Trust a girl to want some emotional detail. "He buried himself in his chemistry lab. I got into a lot of fights at school and then ran away."

"Huh." Juma eyed him from under her lashes.

He guzzled some milk from the carton, then poured himself a cup of coffee and splashed more milk into it. If he fucked up and died, his corpse would have strong bones. "The answer's no. Not today."

"It's a good thing I have a thick skin," Juma said, "or I'd take that for a major brush-off." She chucked her empty tea container into the trash. "Anyway, what makes you think—?"

"When a girl gets that look in her eye, it only means one thing. Not that I really mind being sized up like a piece of meat, but I'm not in the mood."

"Guys are supposed to always be in the mood."

"Come on, Juma. If anybody should know better than to believe all the usual myths, it's you." Juma was the weirdest girl he'd ever met—goth front and major attitude combined with an insatiable hunger for learning. "All the other freaks in the running for valedictorian just do it for the grades, but you actually *like* learning all this junk."

Juma grinned. She had a good smile. "Sure do." Her face hardened again. "Okay, then. When?"

"When I'm not preoccupied with other crap."

"But you *will* do it."

If I'm still alive. If I'm still sane. If my libido returns after I commit murder. So many ifs. "Seems likely." Not.

"Cool. I think." Unaccustomed nervousness quivered across her face. She was an interesting-looking girl, dark tousled hair, firm features, plenty of leg and boob. He could do without the black lipstick.

"But there are conditions," he said. *You wash off the lipstick, for one.* On second thought, maybe he'd do it for her. There were plenty of ways to get a girl turned on, and this girl would certainly require work.

She crossed her arms over her breasts. "What conditions?" She was putting on attitude to defend herself; she didn't really want to have sex. She might even be a little frightened. Maybe he could change that. He might not get to finish what he'd started, but what the hell.

"For one thing," Zeb said, "we're going to do it more than once. In fact, several times."

Juma's eyes widened for a second before she managed to roll them. "Trust a guy." She got a mug from the shelf.

"Believe it or not, this is for your benefit," Zeb said. At her huff, he added, "Mine, too. I mean, let's face it, 'getting it over with' isn't much of a turn-on. You have a lousy attitude about sex."

Juma poured herself some coffee. "This is true."

"My mother told me there are two reasons for sex. One is—"

"Your mother discussed sex with you? How old were you? She's been dead for ages, right?"

Zeb winced, as he often did when people spoke of his mother's death. "I was twelve. I asked and she answered. It was just before she was killed."

"Well," Juma said, "since one of them is to procreate, which I have no intention of ever, ever doing—"

"She wasn't giving me the birds and bees, Juma. She was talking mind and emotions. Procreation is physical, but sex is all in your head. Surely the super-student knows that." He almost burst out laughing. He'd actually gotten her looking uneasy.

"I've read that, of course," she said. "I'm not so sure I like the idea. Or that I even agree."

"You will," Zeb said, grinning affectionately at her. "Now hold onto your rampaging emotions and don't freak out. The first reason is to express love."

Juma made mock gagging sounds. Definitely unnerved.

"To reinforce the bond between a couple with a deep emotional commitment," he added. "Fortunately for you, that's not us."

"Whew," Juma said, taking refuge in her coffee.

"The second reason is to have fun. That's what we're going to do."

Her eyes widened even more, but then her cell phone chimed. She looked relieved. "It's Zelda. I promised I'd text her as soon as I saw you. I didn't come here to discuss sex, although I'm glad we did, because it proves she's nuts." Entirely herself again, she punched in a message. "She sent me to make sure you're okay."

"What is it with that girl? She texted me five times yesterday. The last one was—" He glanced at the kitchen clock. "Less than four hours ago, asking if I was down. And she keeps saying if I need life advice, I should talk to Constantine Dufray. What is *up* with her?"

"She thinks you're depressed and maybe suicidal. Since Constantine acted suicidal for a while several months ago and then got over it, she thinks he might be able to help you. She says you're a lot alike."

"She's nuts if she thinks that. Whatever gave her the idea that I want to kill myself? Oh. That damn vampire hearing will get you every time. She read into something I said. It's nothing."

"Uh-huh." She eyed him appraisingly. "Well, something's going on. You definitely could use some beauty sleep, and you're too preoccupied to want sex."

"I'm not suicidal." A ghastly thought hit him. "You didn't tell my dad, did you?"

"Now you *have* hurt my feelings." She did look quite peeved. "My skin's not that thick."

He didn't have the energy for apologies. "Give me a break, Juma. I know you wouldn't rat on me, but I'm tired, I'm stressed, and I'm in deep shit." He paused at her expression. "No, I'm not dealing drugs, and I'm not planning on killing myself. Tell Zelda to butt out. No, that would hurt her feelings. Tell her my dad deactivated my phone. Tell her I already talked to Dufray, and we didn't get along."

"You didn't get on with Constantine? I thought you were his biggest fan."

"I like his music," Zeb said. "That doesn't mean I have to like *him*."

She eyed Zeb again. "Now I understand what Zelda means. For a second back there, you reminded me of him."

"You're as bad as Zelda. I'm nothing like him." Although once he'd committed murder, he might well be.

Juma kept on talking. "She said you were safe like him, but I'm beginning to think you're not safe. Like him."

"Good." He took her coffee and set it down. Fortunately, she'd drunk away most of the lipstick. He kissed her once, and then, when she smiled, he kissed her again, thoroughly. She seemed to like kissing, which was an excellent start. "You're right. I'm not safe at all."

He'd meant to tease her, but something in his eyes seemed to worry her instead. "Zeb, what's going on? If you're up to your neck in something dangerous, you *should* talk to Constantine again. It doesn't matter whether you like him or not. Zelda and I want you alive and safe."

Me, too. "Tell Zelda that before I do anything desperate, I'll talk to Dufray." An even better idea surfaced. "In fact, tell her to tell Dufray that." With luck, that might even keep the rock star off his back for another day or two.

After that, if he hadn't got up the guts to take care of things himself, he'd *have* to go to Dufray.

～

Marguerite woke in broad daylight but lay still on her back, eyes closed. The house was quiet except for the click of Lawless's claws on the wood floor. Her eyelids felt glued together. She rolled over to go back to sleep.

She heard Lawless slump to the floor with a doggie sigh.

Which meant her door was open. She'd fallen asleep with it closed and Lawless on the other side.

She opened her eyes. Lawless lay in the doorway, head on paws, in not-really-patient dog mode. Maybe he wanted breakfast, but no way could he have opened that door.

Where was Constantine? If there were an intruder in the house, Lawless wouldn't just lie there. But why would Constantine open her door? To see if she was awake? To just watch her? But she didn't see him anywhere . . .

She blinked, wiped the sleep from her eyes, and surveyed the room. Everything was as it should be . . . dresser, laundry basket, bookshelf, and her towel and robe hanging on the closet door, clothes in the closet . . . back to the towel and robe.

They'd never had an aura before. She sat up. If she really, really looked, the towel wasn't quite the right shape, and . . .

"Gotcha!" Suddenly, not just the aura but the rest of Constantine was visible. Why hadn't she seen him before? "You found me right away. What do you see that other people don't?"

"How dare you trick me like that?" She got out of bed, grabbed the robe and towel, and stomped to the shower. She didn't know what pissed her off more, being watched (not really), being tricked (clever of him), or being outed and therefore obliged to explain (yeah, that was it).

Served him right if he didn't like what he was about to hear. Too bad the prospect of unveiling herself made her feel ill. In the shower, she considered how to vanilla-coat her invasive ability. To make it as uninteresting as possible.

It was her own fault, of course. She should never have let on that she'd seen his fear, but she'd been exhausted and scared and disappointed and furious, none of which were conducive to self-control. She'd humiliated him, so why should he hesitate to do the same to her?

She emerged and dressed to the aroma of coffee and the hiss of steaming milk. She went into the kitchen armed with a pot of deep-pink nail polish.

Constantine had raided the fridge for mushrooms, peppers, and tomatoes, which he was chopping into neat little piles. "Cappuccino?" he asked.

"Uh, sure," she said. "Where did that espresso machine come from?"

"Lep brought it over. He wanted to meet you, but you were still asleep. Gideon confirmed that Eaton Wilson's van was stolen from the mechanic's parking lot, but so far it hasn't been found." He set shot glasses under the machine. Espresso dripped through while he steamed the milk. She'd expected an angry vibe, but although his aura was more guarded than yesterday, it was tinged with excited little fizzles, like a kid expecting a present. He set before her an absolutely gorgeous cappuccino with a swirl in the froth and sprinkles of cinnamon. "Fair's fair. I let you in on one of my secrets. Now you tell me how you read me so well."

Fine, but it wasn't going to be a present, not for either of them. He was so beautiful and completely impossible, and she would absolutely die if he shunned her. How could he do anything else? It must be bad enough to be under constant scrutiny. He wouldn't want a lover—or even a friend—who saw right through him all the time, who humiliated him by her very existence. She sat on a kitchen chair and tried to paint the little toe on her left foot, but her hand shook. "Damn."

He left the room and came back a few seconds later with the nail polish remover. He sat cross-legged on the floor in front of her. "Spit it out, babe. It can't be that bad." He cleaned up the mess on her toe and set to work.

"It is." She took a breath and blurted, "I see auras."

"I figured it was something like that. Excellently cool."

Oh, crap, he was one of those. She hadn't told all that many people, but those she had fell into two categories: enthusiastic, curious, and often jealous, or frankly appalled. Usually the first group merged with the second in the end, once they realized what the auras told her.

"So what's the big deal?"

That was a different response, but since he had so many weird abilities, hers probably didn't come as a surprise. "I can tell a lot about people by their auras," she said.

"Yeah, obviously," he said. "So what's the problem? It seems like a useful tool."

"Right, like camouflaging yourself against a towel and watching someone. Useful and completely nosy and obnoxious."

"Come on now," he said. "You don't really mind me watching you."

She felt herself blushing. Cripes, she wasn't sixteen anymore.

"I assumed tricking you a little would get the confession over with faster," he said.

"How did you do it? Is that why Lavonia didn't see you in the tree?"

A smile twitched at the corner of his mouth. He had a great mouth and astonishing kisses. "It's just illusion," he said. "I can telepath images as well as thoughts, to make people see what I want them to. In that instance, the image blended my shape with the tree's, so they didn't notice me." He paused, carefully painting her little toe. "A friend of mine is a true chameleon. He genuinely blends into the background. It would be interesting to know if you can see his aura when he's in total camouflage."

Marguerite sipped her cappuccino and said nothing. Maybe if she let him talk, he wouldn't ask any more questions.

He finished one foot and started on the other. For a guy, he did a mighty good job of painting toenails. "So what do auras look like? It's got to be more than colors, like I've read about in books."

"It's complicated," she said with a sigh. "Yes, it's partly colors, but nothing simple like red being anger and green being envy. Auras manifest themselves in varying combinations of colors, shapes, and sizes, and they move constantly, sort of like electronic waves with irregular cycles. Some people have very, uh, talkative auras, while others are calmer and more restrained. Some people—maybe your friend is one of them—can hide their auras almost completely. It's a lot like reading body language, only there's another dimension, which makes it easier to recognize the nuances of feelings people are trying to hide, like anger, jealousy, fear." She paused; this was his chance to explain what had happened last night—what had made him so afraid.

He didn't. Evidently, he didn't want to discuss it. She didn't blame him; a vigilante wouldn't willingly admit to being scared. He was putting a good face on it, pretending last night's humiliation didn't matter, and she should respect what little privacy he still possessed.

But not about what he'd shown her of his own volition. "These illusions you produce. Is that why people say they see visions at your concerts? Like snakes and eagles and spiders? Like the bear that prowled through my head at Eaton's?"

"Yeah, except that rather than trying to blend, I expand my aura—at least I assume that's what it is—and send telepathic images. It's fun to do, and fans like it." He capped the bottle of nail polish and set it aside.

He hadn't freaked out about her aura-reading ability. He'd seemed merely . . . interested. That practically qualified as a miracle.

Maybe he was so used to people prying into his private life that he just didn't care. Marguerite's mother had certainly found it unbearable. Dad had been harder to read, except when the scandal broke and he'd been hurt, but everyone knew that, and he'd welcomed her childish sympathy. Marguerite had been dropped by a couple of boyfriends and had dropped a few as well because of her stupid ability. As for her uncle . . . oh, how that jerk had hated her for seeing in his aura that he had lustful feelings for her. She'd only been a kid, but she'd threatened to scream bloody murder if he so much as touched her, and he'd backed off.

A useful tool, Constantine put it. Well, it *had* saved her from the sexual molestation her uncle had envisioned. And she'd been insane with worry when, after her father's death, her mother had decided to move to Baton Rouge with Marguerite's timid little sister, because he might try it with her, and he might succeed. Mom had refused to believe a word against him. Marguerite would have had to make a huge stink. Another media freak-out, a slander suit from her uncle— it had all spread out before her in a ghastly array. She'd had no proof, and she'd never been able to find any. She just *knew*.

And then Uncle Dan had beaten up Leopard, Constantine had publicly sworn vengeance, and soon afterward, her uncle had shot himself.

She didn't agree with physical or psychic violence. It didn't feel right to thank him for causing her uncle's death—to approve of causing anyone's death—but in this case she sure wanted to. She wanted—

CHAPTER TWELVE

The doorbell rang. Thankful for the reprieve, Constantine sprang up to answer it. He might not be able to read auras, but she'd clearly been thinking about asking him something, probably something personal. He'd told her how he produced illusions to *avoid* any personal questions. There were so many rumors about his psychic abilities that it didn't matter whether she blabbed about it or not. He listened for the chicken in his head, but there was only silence.

Which didn't mean he wasn't a coward. It meant he already knew he was.

Leopard walked in and figured him out right away. "Jeez, man. You didn't get laid yet? Jabez says she's a hottie." He was carrying a mug of his usual execrable coffee.

When they arrived in the kitchen, Marguerite smiled at Lep and put out a hand. "Nice to meet you."

Lep shook her hand. "Looking good. You holding out on him, girl?" Typical Lep, getting straight to the point.

"I don't think so," Marguerite said seriously, "but I haven't had the opportunity to find out for sure."

"If you'd just take him to bed and get it over with, we'd all appreciate it very much."

Constantine's guide had ignored him so far this morning, but now he felt it rolling its eyes. *Amen*, it said.

"I'll be sure to take your wishes into consideration." Marguerite smiled.

Yearning slammed Constantine. He wanted her in his bed, in his life, smiling at him every damn day, making love every night.

Making love. Not the way he usually thought of it. Hadn't thought about it like that for too many years, if ever. Love . . . just wasn't an emotion he allowed himself to feel.

So, he asked the guide, *if I have sex with her, the next step is love?*

Afraid so. The guide sounded amused. Constantine returned to chopping veggies for omelets.

"Jabez is doing such a good job of keeping Nathan away from you that he's stalking me now." Lep scrolled down the screen of his phone. "And I quote: 'For your safety as well as C's, talk to me.' He's such a drama queen. I'll have to get a new email address."

"This is a different spin," Constantine said. "Yesterday he was worried about the safety of everyone else in town."

"It sounds to me," Marguerite grumped, "as if he'll take any twisted idea and run with it."

"Pretty much," Constantine said. Compared to love, Nathan's crap was easy to handle. "Might as well see what he has to say, Lep. After what happened last night, we have to follow every avenue."

Constantine turned to Marguerite. "I'm giving an interview today at the Cat. You want to come, babe?"

Marguerite glared. "Of course not."

So much for the prospect of love. His spirit guide might love him—it must, to stick to him through thick and thin—but he wasn't a lovable guy, and Marguerite hated the media. "It's *Rolling Stone*," he cajoled. "I know the guy. As interviews go, it won't be too bad." She showed no sign of weakening, so he added, "Better than staying here. They've already started showing up, and it'll just get worse."

"Who, they?" she asked, but immediately realization crossed her face. "There are reporters out there?"

"Some," he said. "Jabez comes by from time to time to disperse them, but they're a persistent bunch."

"They're crazy. I have nothing to say to them. Won't they just follow you?" She didn't seem to need an answer. She swallowed and paced a bit. "No, because I'm easier prey. Even after we make it clear we're not together, they'll harass me for a while." She threw up her hands. "I have to go to work. Yes, I know it's Sunday, but I have to pick up some stuff to prepare for classes. I'm teaching a new course this term."

"Then you'll take Jabez with you," Constantine said, and when she bristled, he added, "I insist."

"I understand that I need a bodyguard," she said irritably, "but Jabez needs his beauty sleep."

"Give her Reuben," Lep said, alight with mischief.

Let Lep have his fun, although Reuben had better not. "Sure," he said, and, annoyingly, she agreed.

Lep left after breakfast, and ten minutes later, Reuben arrived. "Your bodyguard's coming up the walk," Constantine said, wondering if his aura was giving off jealousy vibes. Since he couldn't do anything about it, he decided he didn't care. "I've gotta go. Later, babe."

Those hazel eyes that saw so much shone with sadness, acknowledging that what little they'd had together was done. "I'm going to miss kissing you," she said.

Shaken, he opened the door and left.

~

Feeling like a wimp, Marguerite drove over to Hellebore University accompanied by a gorgeous blond bodybuilder and Lawless. No way she was leaving him at home alone because for all she knew the intruder would come back *again*.

It was true that she had work to do this morning, but she shouldn't be so cowardly when it came to the media. Compared to what Constantine went through day in and day out, a little bit of harassment was nothing. Quite frankly, she needed to grow up.

Thanks to Reuben and Jabez, she'd made it to the car unmolested. A cop at the end of the street ushered them through the crush of cars and reporters and gave them a good head start. Once they were well away, she peered across at him. "Have I seen you on the cover of a romance novel?"

"One or two," Reuben said nonchalantly. Then he grinned. Sounding much more like a normal guy, he added, "Actually, you haven't seen them yet. I got my first contract a few months ago, so the books won't be out for a while. One of these days, I'll be voted Mr. Romance. Just you wait and see."

"I can believe that," Marguerite said. "I'll be looking for those covers for sure."

Encouraged, he gave her his card with his website and Facebook addresses. "I'll be posting them there, too." Then he asked, "Have you slept with Constantine yet?"

Cripes. "You guys are like a bunch of gossipy girls! What business is it of yours or Lep's, or anyone else's for that matter?"

"Whoa," Reuben said, holding up his hands. "Don't get all bent out of shape. We like the dude. It does him good to get laid."

"Sure, but sex isn't necessary. It's his business if he does without." She frowned. "Besides, how can you tell?"

Reuben laughed without much humor. "Believe me, we can tell. Do us all a favor and seduce him."

"That's more or less what Lep said." She pondered how to probe without revealing what little she knew. She'd had to appeal to Constantine's sense of fair play to get him to admit anything at all. "It's not like he'd have a hard time finding a willing woman. Maybe he prefers being celibate."

Reuben snorted. All right, so she already knew that wasn't the case. "Let's assume he wants it. Why does he do without?"

"Beats me," Reuben said.

"Okay, then, how long has he done without?"

"Can't say for sure," Reuben said. "He's only become unbearable in the last six months or so."

"Has he had any girlfriends since his wife died?"

Reuben considered. "Nothing that lasted long. Can't say I blame him for being turned off a bit after Jonetta, but the other chicks were okay."

At least she now knew how to direct her prodding. They were approaching the road that ran in front of the

Humanities Building. "Are you supposed to dog my every footstep?" she asked.

"'Fraid so."

"I don't think anything bad is likely to happen to me in here," she said. "Especially since I have a real dog with me. And people who don't have keys can't get in on weekends."

"Maybe, but something bad will happen to me if I don't stick with you," Reuben said. "Simple as that."

"Let's go get a coffee then," she said. "This is going to take a while." She turned right instead of left into the parking lot of a restaurant that made tolerable lattes. She parked under a tree, leaving the window down for Lawless, and they went inside. On Sunday mornings it was invariably packed for brunch. Almost immediately, they ran into Al Bonnard, Lavonia, Janie, and Roy Lutsky, an ill-assorted crew if ever she'd seen one. The AC wasn't on particularly high—nothing like Lavonia's house—and Lavonia's hands were clasped around a mug of steaming coffee, but she was shivering. So was her aura. She gave Marguerite a wan little smile.

"I hear you had quite a night last night," Al said. "Have a bonbon." He held out a bag to her. Janie had one scrunched-up wrapper in front of her, but Lutsky had a pile. Chocolate-freak Lavonia seemed to have lost her appetite.

"Thanks." Marguerite took two and offered one to Reuben, who shook his head. She dropped the other candy in her backpack. Chocolate always came in handy sooner or later.

Lutsky glowered. "As usual, I missed everything. Anywhere Dufray is, I'm not. Marguerite, you *have* to get me an interview with him."

Behind her, Reuben made a rude noise. Lutsky scowled at the bodyguard and swore under his breath. Janie, needless to say, was assessing Reuben's charms. "Jeez, Marguerite. There are pics on the Internet this morning of that middle-aged playboy fondling your butt. That's how many hot guys in two days? Four? Five?

"Only three," Marguerite said. "This is Reuben, my bodyguard for the morning. Tony was last night. Reuben, would you mind ordering takeout for us? I'd like a latte."

Reuben sauntered over to the counter, followed by Janie's hungry eyes and Lutsky's angry ones. Marguerite unwrapped her bonbon and savored it.

"For someone who just had a near-death experience, you look mighty cheerful," Al said.

"I'd be cheerful, too, if I had three hot guys in a twenty-four-hour period, one of them a rock star," Janie said bitterly. "Actually, Reuben's better looking than Constantine."

"Reuben is a romance novel cover model," Marguerite said. "He doesn't seem to be anywhere near as violent as Constantine."

"Don't be so sure of that," muttered Lutsky, while Janie took off to scope out Reuben up close. "Have you had sex with Dufray yet?"

Before Marguerite had a chance to gather herself to retort, Al cast his eyes heavenward. "Are there no sane people left in Bayou Gavotte? Either they're violent, obsessed with sex, or just plain obsessed. Even my stable, practical Lavonia, who only dabbles in witchcraft, isn't immune. She's a basket case this morning."

"I had nightmares after I got home to bed," Lavonia said. "Really horrible ones."

"Maybe you're coming down with something," Marguerite said, ignoring Lutsky's glare, hoping he would realize he was way out of line. "Sometimes fever will bring on nightmares, and you don't look at all well."

"I don't have a fever." Lavonia opened her mouth as if to say more, then shut it again, but it didn't take special sight to see she was deathly afraid. Of what?

Oh, hell. Now Lavonia thought *she* was having prophetic dreams? "Call me when you get home," Marguerite said. "I'll make you chicken soup or something. I'll have to bring Constantine or one of his bodyguards, too, and there may be a pack of newshounds on my trail."

"Yes, *please* make sure you have a bodyguard at all times. You don't need to come over, though, because I'm not sick. I refuse to be, because Al and I are going to a play tonight." She picked up a bonbon.

Al shook his head. "You've been overdoing the chocolate lately."

"Right." Lavonia sighed and put the candy down again. "I've heard there's a new costume designer at the theater, and the costumes are scrumptious."

"Who gives a damn about costumes?" Lutsky stood, looming over Marguerite. "I need information. Did you have sex with Dufray or didn't you?"

Marguerite felt her face go red as a poinsettia. People at the nearby tables stared. Mustering her calm, she said quietly, "That's none of your business."

"It damned well is my business," Lutsky bellowed, and now every head in the room turned. "If you fucked Dufray, I need to know!"

Reuben appeared at her side. "Need help?"

"No." *Not unless you can wipe the memories of everyone in the entire room.* "For God's sake, Roy," she hissed.

"You owe me!" Lutsky roared. "Damn it all, Marguerite. You *promised!*"

"I never promised any such thing!" she cried. "I never, *ever* kiss and tell."

"Why, you little bitch—"

Reuben cut Lutsky off midsentence, carried him outside, and dumped him in the parking lot. The bodyguard came back indoors, paid for the lattes, and returned to Marguerite. Meanwhile, everybody in the entire restaurant was staring at her, including Lavonia, who was trying to hide a smile; Janie, who was clutching one of Reuben's business cards; and Al, who somehow managed to look both affronted and amused.

"Ready to go?" Reuben said.

"Yes, please," Marguerite said. "Are there any reporters in here?"

"Not that I've noticed," Reuben said.

"Thank God for that." Marguerite turned to go, but Lavonia put a hand on her arm.

"I didn't want to like Constantine," she said softly, "but I admit to being impressed. Whoever chased you last night . . ." She sucked in a breath. "I wouldn't want to be him."

"Shit, no," Reuben said. "Dead man walking."

Al rolled his eyes. He didn't have much going on in his aura—he was generally a calm sort of person who prided himself on scientific detachment—but irritation flashed out. "I don't know how you humanities types stand it."

"Stand what?" asked Marguerite.

"Endless clichés," Al said. "Chemistry is so much tidier, and, wonder of wonders, it's useful, too." He held out the bag, which still contained a number of bonbons. "Take these, Marguerite. We've had enough, and you need all the chocolate you can get."

She thanked him and dropped the bag into her backpack. They left and a few minutes later parked in the Humanities Building parking lot. Marguerite led her bodyguard upstairs to her office. Any minute now, he would ask for an explanation of that little contretemps with Lutsky.

Except that he didn't. Relieved, Marguerite didn't offer one because anything that didn't involve mentioning auras would be a lie. Why couldn't life just be open and simple, no games, no secrets, no lies?

"What was such a turnoff about Jonetta?" she asked, while she went through her bookshelves for all the Old Irish she could find.

"Apart from being a crazy-ass bitch who attacked his fans?" Reuben said, his eyes on the display of his cell. Judging by the zaps and zings, he was playing a video game.

"Not really?" Marguerite said.

"Oh, yeah." He paused the game. "Never seen a woman so jealous, with no reason at all. I'd swear on my mama's grave he never loved her, but—"

"He never loved Jonetta? Then why did he marry her?" Marguerite moved to her desk and started rummaging through papers.

Reuben hunched a shoulder. "Never any telling why Constantine does what he does. Sure, she was hot, but he doesn't give a shit about hot. Some of his best friends are vampire chicks, and he doesn't touch them. In all the time

I've known him, he never had more than one woman at a time—not that any of them lasted long—but he could have had dozens if he'd wanted. Jonetta got bent out of shape if he so much as hugged one of the groupies or made nice with some random fan-girl. I saw her go at one chick, claws and all, but Constantine got in the way, and after that he wouldn't let her backstage. If you ask me, that was the beginning of the end." He scratched his chin. "Well, it was doomed from the start, but next she did her best to make him jealous. Dumb woman, trying to play games with the man." He gave Marguerite a look, and the scary side of Reuben leaked past his placid aura.

Jeez. "You don't need to warn me." She stopped herself from hotly denying having any relationship at all with the rock star. Obviously, they had something going on, and she had no idea who knew what. "I hate playing games. I like things to be simple and straightforward." Fat chance of that, as long as she associated with Constantine. Which wouldn't be for much longer, after which she'd go back to her orderly, private life. But if that was the case, why had she been close to tears this morning when he'd left?

Something about him made her feel safe, had made her feel that way right from the start, even when he wasn't acting safe at all. And . . . he hadn't been too freaked out about her aura reading. Oh, and there were those kisses, too. Reuben sent some text messages and answered a call or two, and Marguerite focused on her work. He surfed the web while she searched her drawers for a folder of notes. He played more video games while she downloaded and printed several articles to read in front of the television, since it seemed unlikely she would be making love with Constantine Dufray.

Nothing Reuben had told her explained why he would be afraid of having sex. Of marriage, maybe, but . . .

"When she tried to make him jealous, what did he do?"

He looked up from his cell. "Nothing at first, but in the end he ditched her." Whizz. "That's when she started bad-mouthing him." Bang. Zing.

"And his reputation made a lot of what she said believable." Quickly, she added, "To the superstitious, anyway." *And to those who really knew him?* She didn't say that out loud, but—

"He didn't beat her." Reuben paused the video game. "Didn't send her nightmares. Had no reason to, even if he was like that, which he's not. He protects people who can't protect themselves, and he only hurts people to save others, not for vengeance. Knows exactly what he's doing, the man does." There was dogged hero worship in his voice.

And uncertainty in his aura. Lawless sensed it, too, and whimpered and prodded his thigh with a paw. "He's getting bored," Marguerite said. "I guess you are, too. I won't be much longer."

Reuben's agitated aura went limp with relief. He stuck his cell in his pocket and took Lawless into the hallway to play fetch with a rolled-up magazine.

"All done," she said at last. "I need to return this book to the Psych Department, and then we can go."

Reuben silently followed her upstairs to the next floor and along the corridor into the wing that held both the Psych and Sociology Departments. Lawless galloped ahead of them into the Psychology Reading Room and ran smack-dab into Zeb at the far end of the room carrying a tattered manila folder with papers sticking out every which way.

A color printout fell to the floor. Zeb fended Lawless off and gaped at Marguerite, aghast. "Oh, shit! Thank God it's only you." He dove for the paper and jammed it into the folder. His eyes widened at the sight of Reuben. "Who's he?"

"Constantine assigned me a bodyguard," Marguerite said. "I almost got killed last night."

Anguish—not surprise—twisted Zeb's face and aura. "What happened?"

"I got chased through the streets on my bike by someone in a black van. Luckily, I got away."

"Why would anyone want to kill you? It must have been an accident." The dog shoved his nose under Zeb's hand, and he almost dropped the folder. "Stop that, Lawless," he said, pushing him away.

"An accident?" Marguerite knew an urge to clobber someone.

"A mistake, I mean. A bodyguard is a great idea." He scowled at Reuben. "Don't let her out of your sight."

Unbelievable. "For cripes sake, Zeb! If you would just tell us what you know, maybe I wouldn't need a bodyguard."

Zeb gave a hopeless little shrug. "I can't do that. It's nothing to do with you or Constantine. It'll be over soon. Just stay safe a bit longer. Please." He scratched Lawless behind one floppy ear.

"It does have something to do with Constantine," she said. "I told you about the reporter who showed up on the mound. His name is Nathan. He didn't just happen to show up. He was sent there by an informant. Someone's been feeding Nathan all kinds of potentially damaging information, such as suggesting Constantine made Pauline kill herself."

Zeb shrugged indifferently, but his aura said otherwise. He subdued it quickly and said, "People are always saying Constantine killed someone or other. Some of it's probably true." Pause. "But not Pauline. She was harmless. He wouldn't kill her."

"It seems that *someone* did," Marguerite said. "Someone who also has something against Constantine." Pause. "I'm not saying it's only about Constantine, but he's definitely part of the picture."

"That doesn't make any sense," Zeb said again. The instability in his usually tidy aura showed that his confusion was genuine. Lawless shoved his cheek against Zeb's hand, and another printout slipped partway out of the folder, and then another. "Stop it, Lawless! I've got to run. Marguerite, don't tell anyone you saw me here, or I'm totally screwed."

Marguerite's eyes darted over the sheets of paper about to spill onto the floor. "What do you have there?"

"Don't ask me that." Ghastly bursts of misery reamed his aura. Dank green shame clouded it. Marguerite grabbed a page and pulled it out.

Torture porn? She shuddered. Pauline's abusive husband had been into this sort of garbage. He'd even tortured Pauline a couple of times, and it had taken her years to recover from the emotional trauma. "Have you gone completely nuts?" demanded Marguerite. "Where did you get this? My God, what would your father say?" Oh, shit. Now she sounded like Lavonia, but Zeb should be interested in normal sex with girls his own age, not this sort of trash. She'd never seen him so distraught, or his aura so drained.

"Don't tell him," he said. "Please don't. I can't let him see me with this stuff."

God, no. "I won't tell him." *You have to tell him,* admonished a voice inside her. *He's the boy's father.*

No, this couldn't be what it appeared. She simply refused to believe it of Zeb. Such . . . such filthy tastes didn't match his aura at all.

Still, she needed some answers right now. She tore up the offending picture but clutched the bits in her hand. "Come to my office."

"Why?" Zeb was calmer now, beginning to be mulish.

"Because I intend to discuss this with you in private. I have enough problems with the media without someone finding out I concealed this from your father. Who, by the way, is across the street having brunch."

"I know," Zeb said. "That's why I have to get out of here and off campus in a hurry. I'm supposed to be running errands for him." He glanced at the doorway. Reuben grinned a warning. Zeb blew out a breath and turned back to Marguerite. "I'll leave by the entrance at the back of the building so he won't see me."

"I'm not letting you go anywhere with this trash." She set the book she was returning on a table, grabbed the folder, and headed past Reuben into the hall. The bodyguard herded Zeb and Lawless out as well. "And you are damn well going to explain it to me."

"What are you going to do with it?" Zeb said.

"Put it through the shredder, of course."

There was a brief silence. His aura cleared measurably. "That's a good idea. I didn't think of that."

Marguerite mulled this over until they got into her office. Reuben leaned his broad shoulders against the door and stood there looking gorgeous and deadly.

She fed the first few pages into the shredder. "You *want* to destroy this stuff?"

"Of course." Zeb's aura had recovered some of its usual poise. "That's why I was taking it out of the building. Here, let me do it."

"You didn't print it here? Or bring it in?"

"Of course not." The shredder jammed.

"It only takes five pages at a time," Marguerite said, and Reuben placidly took charge of the paper, separating it into piles of five sheets and passing them to Zeb bunch by bunch.

"Of course I didn't print it," Zeb repeated. "What sort of lowlife do you think I am?"

"I don't think you're a lowlife at all, Zeb. I both like and respect you, but I lose patience when my life is threatened and you are acting all suspicious. If it isn't yours, where did you get it from?"

His mouth worked. She waited. Reuben sent a text message and received an answer, but his bored expression didn't change. He must be used to this kind of scene. "It doesn't matter," Zeb said.

"Of course it matters." She ran through the Psych area in her mind. He'd been in the far end of the reading room. Who had offices down there? It couldn't be Eaton Wilson again, because his was at the other end of the hall.

"Door on the right at the end was a bit ajar," Reuben said helpfully, passing Zeb another five sheets.

"Lutsky's? Oh, come on. Don't tell me he's into this—"

"Shit?" provided Reuben.

"Exactly," she said. "I guess anything's possible, but—" She would have known if Lutsky was into torture. He had such an obvious sort of aura.

"The Pontificator?" Reuben guffawed. "Naw." He raised an incredulous blond brow at Zeb. "Really?"

"Not that I know of," Zeb said. "That's why I was taking it out of his office. So nobody would find it there."

"It was planted there?" Marguerite asked.

Zeb nodded. Lawless rubbed his cheek against Zeb's arm and wagged his tail.

"You were protecting Dr. Lutsky? I thought you hated him."

"Yeah, but that doesn't mean he should be outed as a perv if he isn't one."

That was more like the Zeb she knew. She let out a long breath of relief. "Up on the mound," she said. "You were protecting Dr. Wilson."

"How do you know?" Zeb sighed. "Yeah. He's a doofus, but he's not a perv either."

"And someone else, too, the person who made the mask."

Briefly, confusion clouded Zeb's aura; then he said, "No, only Dr. Wilson, because he made the beads, but I was hoping no one would figure that out. The rest of the mask doesn't matter. My mom and I made it for a Mardi Gras parade years ago, but it's been stored with the university costumes and float materials. Tons of people have access to that storage."

She digested that. "This porn is another of the practical jokes you were talking about last night, isn't it?"

"Yep," Zeb said. "Look, I really gotta go." He shot a glance at Reuben, shrugged, and with an air of resignation began to fold his aura around himself.

"Where were you last night?" she said. "Eaton Wilson's van was stolen, and it's still missing."

"It'll be found within a day or two. In the meantime, I disabled it," Zeb said, calmer and more focused as each second passed. "It won't be a problem anymore." His aura muffled itself like a blanket. She could scarcely detect it now. He was trying to protect himself . . . from what?

Reuben? Did he think she really meant to let Reuben beat him up? Maybe he thought Constantine had ordered it, but he wasn't about to give in to threats. A little prickle of pride stirred within her.

Courageous or not, he had to be made to see reason. "That was no practical joke, Zeb."

"I realize that, but there's no reason to kill you. Like I said, it was a mistake. Not part of the plan."

Marguerite said slowly. "Then what was he planning? Why steal the van?"

Zeb spread his hands. "I don't know. Something else to make Eaton look bad, I guess."

Over by the door, Reuben stood solid and immovable as a tree. His aura showed no sign of impending violence, but of course Zeb couldn't see that.

"He couldn't have expected me to follow him on my bike," Marguerite said. "I think . . . I think he came to search my house again. He probably thought I was still out with Tony, or even that I was spending the night with him. Tony has such a rep as a player that it wouldn't be surprising. Whoever it was came back afterward and checked out the house, but as far as I could tell, he hadn't taken anything."

"I don't know what he was looking for." His aura folded close, his vibes still and ready. "Makes no sense."

"Maybe it will, if I have a little more info. Why can't you tell me, Zeb? Who are you protecting Eaton and Lutsky from?" It was a pointless question. The blanket of his aura had turned to granite. He would go down fighting rather than say. "We can't let this go on. I don't know who else is in danger, but you can't protect the whole world."

"I'll take care of it. I'll find a way."

"Why not tell Constantine? We were up half the night talking about this. He's prepared to handle it. That's what a vigilante does."

"Don't you think I know that?" Zeb spoke through clenched teeth, and that carefully constructed wall of determination wavered and shook. He still had his voice under control, but she knew—just *knew*—he was close to tears. Contemplating a beating from Reuben didn't break his aura, but this did.

Her heart wrenched. "Zeb, we want to help you, not hurt you."

The words came out on a howl of pain. "What does it matter if I get hurt? I'll think about going to Constantine. I *have* been thinking about it."

"You have?"

"Of course! I'm not stupid. It's just that—" A whisper of anguish, and the granite slammed shut. "I can't. Not yet."

CHAPTER THIRTEEN

Ordinarily, Constantine would have enjoyed his conversation with the writer from *Rolling Stone*, but today he couldn't think of anything but how he was going to handle Marguerite. He had to believe his guide, believe in himself, get up the guts, and make love to her.

When his cell phone chimed—*Reuben*—he put up an apologetic hand and read the text, which, when translated from Reuben's shorthand, said, *Pontificator says your chick owes him.*

Owes him what? Constantine replied.

The shorthand translated into *Info re fucking you.*

What in hell? This seemed so bizarre that he asked Reuben to type it longhand. Same damn thing.

She denied it. Reuben went on. *I threw him out of restaurant.*

Reuben wouldn't have mentioned this if he didn't think it mattered. So far, he'd been loyal and persistent and always did as he was told, which in this case included reporting whatever struck him as unusual about anything and everything.

He stood, walking away from the writer, and dialed Reuben's number. "Can we talk?

"Have to be later, dude."

This was only to be expected; Reuben was sticking to Marguerite until relieved of that responsibility. "You think she was lying?" Why else would he text about it?

"Could be," Reuben said. "Hard to say."

"Thanks, bro." He hung up, pondering. Lutsky was so desperate for information about Constantine that he might be willing to take it secondhand—although the sex angle was a new one. Lutsky was a lunatic, though, not worth a moment's thought.

As for Marguerite, she hadn't come on to him—in fact, she'd done her best not to.

It made no sense, but he didn't have time for it now. He shrugged internally and returned to the interview.

A while later, Reuben texted again, saying they had run into Zeb and asking whether he should use force to bring him in.

No, he texted back. Marguerite would never forgive him if he or any of his people harmed Zeb. He texted Lep to be sure Zeb was shadowed at all times and went back to the guy from *Rolling Stone.*

~

"Let's go," Marguerite said to Reuben. "I have to talk to Constantine about all this." She handed him a box of books and papers.

"Sure," Reuben said, and opened the office door.

She gave Zeb a quick squeeze. "I'll tell him what you said. Come downstairs with us so I can give you an excuse for being here in case we come across your dad. How did you get into the building? You're not supposed to have a key."

Zeb rolled his eyes, and she didn't push it, wondering how many other buildings—and vehicles—he could open at will. When she tried to return the money he'd given her last night, he told her to keep it for now. "My old man's pissed off enough as is. He might take it and put it in a savings account for me or something equally stupid. At least I can count on you to give it to me when I want it."

"Definitely," Marguerite said. By the time he took off through the parking lot at a run, the granite had softened a little.

No paparazzi hovered outside the building. She drove into downtown Bayou Gavotte. Reuben texted Constantine and guided her past a cop directing traffic to the restricted parking behind the Impractical Cat. Constantine lived in an apartment at the top of the building, two stories above the restaurant.

Reuben's phone chimed. "Constantine says to bring the mask."

"Sure," she said, opening the trunk for Reuben to take it. She put Lawless on a leash, grabbed some reading material and her backpack, and followed the bodyguard into the restaurant through a private door behind the kitchen. Waitresses bustled by, carrying pitchers of tea and plates heaped with sweet potato fries. Marguerite's stomach gurgled. "They serve fried oysters here."

"Sure do," Reuben said. "Have some. Share them with Constantine. Maybe they'll work their magic."

She laughed, but she'd been worrying about Zeb, so aphrodisiacs were the last thing on her mind. Reuben poured

Marguerite a glass of tea and put in an order for oysters and sweet potato fries to be sent up to the roof garden.

"Is Constantine still being interviewed?" she asked dubiously.

Reuben shrugged. "You want to stay down here and face the stampede instead?" He motioned with his chin toward the swinging doors to the dining room.

She went across the kitchen and peered through. *Oh, shit.* She backed away. Her voice wobbled. "How does he stand it?"

"He likes it," Reuben said with a proud grin. "Bunch of piranhas. They can't get to the man, but they'd be happy to eat you up instead. Coming upstairs? The dog can come, too."

She hesitated. "Maybe I could just stay down here and—"

A waitress hustled through the doors, and a reporter plunged after her. "Miss McHugh? Is it true you're going to star in a porno flick with Constantine Dufray?"

Calmly, Reuben set down the mask. His fist connected with the reporter's nose. He kicked open the swinging doors and threw him into the dining room. A horde of reporters pinned Marguerite with avid eyes. She shut out their auras before she passed out. The doors swung closed.

"Only one of them upstairs," Reuben said. She slumped but followed him up a winding staircase, letting the eager Lawless off his leash. The dog bounded through the door at the top, tail wagging. They entered a vestibule of sorts. To one side an archway led to a living room; that must be Constantine's apartment. They crossed the vestibule and went outdoors to a wide, flat roof, where a profusion of potted plants, some of them trees, made a charming garden. A vast awning stretched over a couple of tables and a chaise, and the quiet whir of fans mingled with the trickle of a fountain. Constantine and a middle-aged man lounged at a table with mugs of beer. Constantine cradled a guitar, picking in a desultory way at the strings. Lawless greeted Constantine and then threw himself down, panting, in the shade of one of the trees.

"Be seeing you." Reuben set the mask down and left, shutting the door behind him. Marguerite steeled herself to be polite.

Constantine raised his mug and smiled at her.

Her stomach sighed, uncurling. He knew how to handle the media. She would be all right.

You're so beautiful. Constantine's thought hit her hard and strong. She felt herself flush with pleasure. Had he meant to let that out?

So are you. But she couldn't send her thoughts, so she smiled in return. "Hey."

"Babe," he said and introduced the writer from *Rolling Stone.*

"Nice to meet you," said the writer. "I interviewed your dad once. Great guy."

Marguerite bristled. The first damned sentence out of his mouth! It might sound sincere, but it never ended up being so. "Yes." Control the anger. "He sure was."

"Interesting to talk to," the writer said. "The title of my article was 'Philosopher of Porn.'"

She hadn't seen that one. She'd read a few, but the venom had made her so ill that she'd avoided them from then on.

"'You don't want to just make people hot,' he told me. 'You want them to feel the glory of sex. To see passion as the physical expression of love.' Those were his exact words."

Marguerite nodded but said nothing.

"He said that's why his movies appealed to women," the writer said.

"He was a wonderful father." She let out a breath she hadn't meant to hold. Judging by a machine on the table, they were being recorded, but this guy's vibe wasn't too bad, and with Constantine as her bulwark, she felt almost safe. Constantine put out a hand, and she took it, allowing him to pull her close. As if she'd been doing this forever, she bent and dropped a kiss on his mouth.

They'd parted on uncomfortable terms this morning, and yet this felt astonishingly right. Painfully so, since it was going nowhere.

No, damn it. She was going to find out why he was afraid, and she was going to *do* something about it once she'd had a chance to tell him about Zeb and the torture porn. But for now she had to be cool and play the game.

"Don't let me interrupt," she said, pulling out a paper on sound shifts. "I've got course prep to do." Her heart was practically dancing, which was weirder than weird considering the company and the urgency of the situation. "And if that gets boring, I'll read this fascinating biography I picked up in the store the other day." She opened her backpack and waved the book about Constantine, who grabbed it and chucked it off the roof.

"Hey!" Marguerite cried, and Constantine stood up and kissed her properly.

That felt right, too. Dear God. She so wanted to make love to this man.

Constantine showed the writer the mask and described the setup on the mound, laughing it off. A monumental platter of oysters and fries came up on a dumbwaiter, accompanied by lemons, ketchup, and Tabasco. They all shared and joked about aphrodisiacs and thirteen-inch penises, and Constantine and the guy from *Rolling Stone* chatted about anything and everything while Marguerite fed a flock of pigeons bits of fried batter.

Constantine glowed. If she hadn't been able to read auras, she would think he was just a regular guy who'd had a rough childhood. Who'd happened to become a rock star and was having a good time hanging out with an old acquaintance. He was doing his best to ignore the turmoil underneath, but it kept nagging at him, in sharp little jabs of uneasiness that gave Marguerite a headache, which must be nothing compared to what it did to him . . . and yet he just kept on glowing.

Soon, though, she'd had more of pretending than she could take, so she moved to a wide, striped chaise by a potted palm to read about Old Irish and sound shifts. But she ended up pretending about that, too, because she couldn't stop thinking about Zeb and torture porn and why an awful marriage would scare a virile man away from sex.

The afternoon wore on, and she got a little reading done, but even the fans couldn't do much with the thick, sultry air. She was dozing off for the second time when the writer asked Constantine about the incidents several months earlier when his concerts had erupted into riots and people had been killed. The hiss from Constantine's aura jolted her wide awake.

"We'll stick to impromptu concerts for now," Constantine said calmly through the turmoil. Those riots had been months ago, but at the mention of them, his aura twisted and seethed, a cacophony of clashing colors. "There was only one minor kerfuffle the other night. Some guy was high and started freaking out, but we had people stationed throughout the crowd. They escorted him off the field and took care of him until he came down." He shrugged. "A two-minute interruption's a big improvement on dead people and no shows at all."

Marguerite said, "There was an interruption?" and then wished she hadn't, because now they were both staring at her, and she couldn't blurt out the blinding truth that had just hit her—and Constantine as well, judging by his aura. His bland expression was a front.

"Oops," she said, thinking fast. "I confess. I broke the park rules and went into the woods to pee. Yeah, I know there were port-a-potties, but like most women, I can't stand using them."

The guys were still staring, the reporter amused, Constantine with the touch of a frown.

"Looks like I chose the perfect moment for a potty break," she said and went back to Old Irish.

"I could use one of those," the writer said a moment later. The second he disappeared inside the building, Constantine clicked off the recorder and sent a text message. His eyes bored into her. "You didn't really go in the woods to pee."

"No, but I had to say something besides what I was really thinking. That disturbance must have happened at about the time I lost consciousness."

A dark excitement permeated his aura. He stood, buzzing with energy. His cell rang. "Reuben, the dude who created the ruckus at the concert the other night. Do we know who he was?" He was watching Marguerite while he spoke, giving her a long, assessing look that sent a shimmy down her spine. "Can we find him? Thanks, man." He ended the call, his aura spitting like it had on the mound the other day. He prowled over to her, projecting a vision of a lean, hungry cat.

The hunger was intensely sexual, all directed at her. She dragged herself into focus. "If the disturbance was created deliberately to divert attention from me being carried away, wouldn't it mean two people were involved?"

"That's what we're going to find out." He lowered himself to the chaise, placing an arm on each side of her, boxing her in. Almost like a threat, the darkness in his aura swelled and surrounded her. He leaned in and kissed her.

Oh. She sank into the kiss, ran her fingers up into his hair and held him there, her whole body blossoming under him. Why was he kissing her like this? It was supposed to be over. If he was just going to abandon her again when it got exciting . . . But she couldn't make herself stop and warn him when he was opening her so skillfully, when her breasts ached and her body's demands overrode all else. She was breathless and moaning by the time he broke the kiss. "When's he going to go?" she whispered.

"Not soon enough for me." His voice was rough and full of intent. What had happened since this morning?

The writer reappeared, and Constantine kissed her again and settled back with more beer and his guitar. Marguerite watched him through narrowed eyes, trying to figure him out, but he was the same as always, layers of arousal, pain, excitement, and beneath it all there still lurked a knot of suspicion and fear. She gave up and had another go at Old Irish. She shouldn't have agreed to this topic for a seminar, but she'd asked the students for ideas, and this was what they'd voted for.

She dreamed the delicate touch of feathers, the strength of wings sheltering her as she slept. No, sheltering both her and Constantine, for they were tangled together in sleep. Then she thought she was awake, but the wings remained— great, soft wings that lay across them like a coverlet of love. Evidently, she was still in the dream. She opened her eyes anyway. Constantine was stretched next to her on the chaise; she had draped her arm across his chest. The heat of the day was like a drug, pulling her back under; the palm tree waved gently and ineffectually in the breeze from the fan. No wings. She closed her eyes again.

Wings.

She opened her eyes and sat up. The guy from *Rolling Stone* was gone, the sun getting low in the sky. "My God, how bizarre."

"Mmph?" Constantine yawned.

"Did you just send me a dream?" she asked.

"Don't think so," he said drowsily. "What was it about?"

"We were covered by a huge pair of wings. When my eyes were closed, I felt wings on top of us, but when I opened them, there was nothing there."

Constantine sat up. "No, I didn't send that." He pulled her back down on the chaise and covered her, long and heavy and hot. Into her ear, he said, "This is the kind of dream I'll send you," and instantly her mind swarmed with visions of them naked and entwined, writhing in hot, slippery, unbridled sex.

"Good," she breathed. "But I want the real thing." She melted under him, her legs spreading of their own volition, twining around his to keep him there. Through his jeans, she felt his penis swell. He ran a hand into her hair and lowered his mouth to hers. His tongue probed, invading her, possessive and undeniable. Desire seared her. Scorched her. She arched into him, thrust herself against his erection, twisting and moaning.

"Sure you can take it?" The sultry growl of his voice had her in flames.

"No one-touch orgasms, damn you," she panted, squirming, running her hand between them to cup his erection and squeeze it through his jeans. "I want you inside me when I come."

∼

The whap-whap of a helicopter drowned her out, and she shoved at him with panicked, jerky movements. "Shit," Constantine muttered, rolling off her. She snapped her legs together, flushed, gorgeous, and freaked out.

Fuck! "They can't see us under here," he shouted.

"Right," she yelled back. "I panicked." When the copter was gone, she wrapped her arms around herself as if she were freezing even though it was sweltering out here. "Oh,

God, they would have loved seeing me panic. They would have made me a laughingstock. I don't know how you stand it."

He stood and picked up his guitar. "You know what they say—bad publicity is better than none." He tapped the guitar gently. "And the security blanket helps." Too bad he hadn't figured out a way to have sex and play guitar at the same time.

Visibly, she stiffened her spine. "Well, I'll just have to get used to it."

"You will?"

"I don't have a choice. Some friend I would be if I ran at the first sign of trouble."

The first sign? There'd been nothing but trouble since they'd met.

"I'm thirsty," she said. "Can you order me some tea?"

"No need." He set down the guitar, went into his apartment, and poured her an iced tea, complete with a lemon wedge and a sprig of mint. When he returned, she was straightening her T-shirt. He set the tea on the table and turned up the fan, watching hungrily as she smoothed her shorts, running her hands over her hips, tugging at the fabric covering her shapely butt. Strands of damp honey-blond hair clung to her cheeks. She smelled of sweat and woman, and she wanted him inside her when she came. The brain below his waist did a high five with the bird who guided his spirit. Stuck between these two bozos, Constantine took up his guitar and sat at the table, doing his damnedest to stay cynical. He pondered what Reuben had told him about her owing Lutsky. Would she really report back to that lunatic? More important, did Constantine care if she did?

Usually, he wouldn't. There was so much crap about him out there that something like this didn't matter. And yet, when it came to Marguerite . . . it did.

That's love, whispered his guide. Maybe it was right, maybe he was falling in love, but it didn't feel as good as it was supposed to.

She took a chair opposite him, dropped the lemon wedge into the tea, and took a long swallow. "We need to decide what to do about Zeb. Did Reuben tell you about the torture porn and what Zeb said?"

"Sure, but I need to hear it from you, too." He tried to keep any hint of suspicion from his voice, then remembered there was no point. She probably saw it anyway. "You're the one who reads auras."

She nodded glumly. "It wasn't much use in this instance. Someone tried to destroy Dr. Lutsky's reputation by planting torture porn in his office, and Zeb knew about it and retrieved it before anyone found out. Lutsky's enough of a nut job that he doesn't need any help looking idiotic, but the porn would make him look like a pervert, too. Zeb says that's why he's protecting him in spite of the fact that he hates him, which supports my conviction that Zeb means well." She picked up the sprig of mint, twirling it back and forth. "It's just that none of this makes any sense. The logical suspect would be one of Roy's colleagues in Psych, but we know it's not Eaton Wilson, and in any case, why would some random Psych prof try to destroy you or kill me?" She snipped one mint leaf off with a fingernail and ate it.

"Especially since whoever it is supposedly likes you," Constantine said.

She shuddered. "Zeb says he's thinking of coming to see you, but I'm afraid by the time he makes up his mind, it will be too late. Someone might get killed, or what if whoever's playing these so-called tricks figures out what Zeb's doing and comes after him?" She groaned. "I don't understand why he's protecting the perpetrator as well as the victims."

"Interesting, isn't it?" Constantine said. "Are there consequences to him if this all comes out? Is he afraid of the perpetrator? Or does he care about him, too? Seems to be a mighty complicated kid. Anything else to tell me about this morning?"

"No," she said absently. "Until the last few days, I would have described Zeb as . . . hidden? Not exactly reserved, because he's not shy or socially inept, but he doesn't let people know what's going on inside." She took another swig of tea. "Even I got only glimpses when I first knew him. But unlike you, he doesn't cover up with a persona, unless surly teenager qualifies as one."

"But surly teenager doesn't seem to jive with desperate protector, does it?" Which meant it might well be a persona. "I got the same message from Zeb this morning by way of Zelda, one of the girls he hangs with. She's been pestering him to talk to me, not because she knows about any of this but because she thinks he's suicidal." He picked a melancholy ballad. "I pretended to consider killing myself several months ago, and Zelda is convinced I meant it then but somehow healed myself."

"I remember that," Marguerite said. "It was right after a riot at one of your concerts where some people were killed. The whole of Bayou Gavotte was in an uproar. Media everywhere, crowds in the streets. I was so worried about you."

246

"You were worried about me," he repeated, stilling the strings.

"Of course! A lot of your fans were. Didn't you aim a rifle at a helicopter and then a gun at your head?"

"A broken rifle and an unloaded gun. Just a little joke between me and the media." Back to the ballad.

She huffed again. "They were saying horrible things about you, but it wasn't your fault all those people died. They must have been on drugs. In fact, they were, weren't they?"

"Some of them, but that's normal for concerts. And don't tell me riots happen, too. I know that, but this was far worse than the usual. I was in a foul mood that night, and the playlist was a violent one. What if I was telepathing my thoughts without meaning to, sending death and destruction messages without even realizing it?"

"Oh, come *on*." She plucked another mint leaf. "That's a theory the media cooked up." She took little nips off the leaf and chewed them. "You don't seriously believe it, do you? Is that why you haven't performed publicly all these months?"

He shrugged. "No one wanted me at a paying venue. Seemed a good time to take a break."

"Don't lie to me," she said, eating one more mint leaf and dropping the rest on the table. "You do believe it." She sipped, eyeing him over her tea. "Sort of."

"Sort of," he repeated. "Yeah, you could say that. I didn't mean any harm to my fans, so why would my thoughts have such a negative effect?" Might as well tell her everything. Even if she went and told Lutsky, it wouldn't be any worse than what Jonetta and the media had said. "On the other hand, I know exactly what I did to—"

CHAPTER FOURTEEN

A monstrous bird dived under the canopy and slammed into Constantine, knocking him out of his chair. He fell in a flurry of flailing arms and wings, and the guitar smashed into the fan with multiple twangs and a harsh splintering of wood. Marguerite leapt up, toppling her own chair, her heart thudding crazily against her chest.

Constantine scrambled up, roaring out a string of curses. He shook his fist at the bird. "Fucking turkey! I get your point. Did you have to destroy my guitar to make it?"

It *was* a turkey. A wild one, like the kind Marguerite occasionally surprised in the woods. This bird didn't seem the least bit discomposed. Its wattles quivering, it eyed Constantine malevolently and flapped up onto the parapet. It launched itself across the alley to another roof and then to a dead pecan tree.

Marguerite turned to Constantine, gaping. He was scowling at the turkey, his eyes narrowed so much that they twitched. He indicated the huge bird with a sweep of the hand. "Meet my sp—"

A jay flew straight into his face, screeching, and zoomed away. He cursed again, picked up the guitar, stroked the ruined wood, and set it on the chaise. He turned off the fan. "Let's go inside."

"Good idea," Marguerite said faintly. "Oh, you're bleeding!"

Constantine wiped a hand across his brow, catching the trickle of blood. "Of course," he said, glowering at his hand. "If I'm injured, you'll have to tend to me." He ripped off his T-shirt, revealing an expanse of gorgeous copper skin. He pounded his chest, shouting to the sky, "Why didn't you peck me here, so she'd have to undress me to play nurse?" He tossed the T-shirt off the roof.

Okay now, this was really weird, but if he was addressing one of the assault birds, it didn't reply. Thank God for that.

"Why not peck me below the belt, so she'll have to take off my jeans?" he said, suiting action to words, stripping down to his tighty-whities, except they weren't white but pale gray.

Hmm. He had quite an impressive package under there. He hooked his thumbs in the waistband.

She got her voice again. "Don't take that off out here, you crazy man!"

He ignored her, still addressing the sky. "Huh? See what you did?" No birds dive-bombed in response. "She thinks I'm crazy. No, let's face it—she knows I'm crazy. Any more bright ideas tonight?" He stripped off his underwear and his erection sprang free.

"What a relief," Marguerite said. "Even after all those oysters, it's a reasonable size."

Constantine didn't seem to notice. "Well?" he shouted. "What's next?"

Marguerite grabbed her backpack and his hand. "What's next is that somebody might show up with a helicopter again, and we wouldn't want to dispel the thirteen-inch myth." She tugged, but he didn't move. What was he waiting for?

A dove flew over them and pooped on Constantine's hair. His aura sent out purple zaps every which way. The dove alighted on a nearby wire and cooed, although it sounded a lot like laughter. Marguerite gave a horrible giggle, tugging at Constantine again, and this time he obliged. She got him through the door and then peeked out again. The dove flew away.

"At least no birds will attack you, or—or poop on you in here," Marguerite said, giggling again in spite of herself.

"No guarantee of that," Constantine growled. Footsteps thumped on the stairs. Constantine cursed and went through the vestibule into the living room, and a moment later Lep burst from the stairwell.

"Don't ask me," Marguerite said, as they watched the rock star's bare butt recede down a hallway. "He got knocked over by a wild turkey and pecked by a jay, and then took off all his clothes." She bit her tongue and didn't mention the poop.

Lep's cynical brown eyes assessed her. She assessed him right back: plenty of doubt and suspicion. He was nowhere near as cordial as this morning, but he didn't seem worried either. As head of the Bayou Gavotte underworld, he was definitely dangerous, but did his attitude mean that he knew what was going on or that he just didn't care? No, he cared about Constantine—a lot. "Go for it, girl," he said. "Fuck his brains out." He turned and disappeared down the stairs.

Marguerite shut the door and made her way through the living room, which was spotlessly clean and sparsely furnished with a sofa and coffee table, on which sat a lap-top. She dropped her backpack by the sofa. A number of guitars sat tidily on their stands, and the cords on the re-cording equipment in one corner were tucked away out of sight. Ahead of her in the hallway, Constantine dabbed at his forehead with a towel.

"Just because Lep says something, it doesn't mean you have to—ouch! Shit!" He dropped the towel, clutching his head with both hands, and kept going.

She hurried after him. "What's wrong?"

"Nothing," he snarled, and a cat with a struggling bird in its mouth streamed through her head. "Are you game for shower sex?"

She pulled her T-shirt over her head and tossed it. "Um . . . sure, I guess."

"You *guess?*" He whirled, projecting a fire-breathing dragon, and paused for a long look at her breasts. They swelled within the confines of her bra, the nipples hard and tingling.

"I've never been all that keen on shower sex." She un-hooked the bra and let it fall.

His eyes darkened; his smile sent curls of arousal to her belly. "Apparently I like it a lot. Why else would I have bird shit in my hair?" This made no sense, but he brushed a thumb across one of her nipples, sending all rational thought scurrying.

Except one. "Do you have a condom?"

He led her through a bedroom, where he grabbed a condom from a dresser drawer, and into a spacious bath-room, bright and sparkling clean, the shower tiled with a garden of tangled vines and hanging flowers, red, sensual

... wicked. He turned on the shower and faced her. God, he was good to look at, even with blood oozing onto his forehead and bird poop slowly slipping down his hair. His aura reached for her, snakelike, hissing about past treachery and lies, perilous desire . . .

She thrust away the frightening images. "I've never been keen on any kind of sex, if you want the truth," she babbled nervously. Those were just his random thoughts leaking through to her; there was no real reason to be afraid. "It didn't seem worth the bother. I had planned to—"

He stopped her with his mouth. It was a ruthless, take-no-prisoners kiss, and she leaned into it, slinging her arms around his neck, heedless of poop and plans and visions of snakes. She mashed herself against him, every inch seeking contact, skin to tingling, slippery skin.

He broke the kiss. "With me it will be . . ." He stuck his fingers into her waistband and pulled her toward the shower. His aura twisted. "Memorable." He let her go and stepped under the water.

"Memorable is good," she said, ignoring the twist of her own heart at the thought that this would soon be a memory. Little whips of anger suffused his aura. They frightened her, but she was shaking with need, the need she'd always scoffed at in romance novels as something that didn't exist. Maybe it was just a want, but she *wanted* this more than anything, *ever.* She fumbled with the button of her shorts, yanked the zipper down, shoved them over her hips, and kicked them aside.

And then suddenly he wasn't *with* her anymore. His head was thrown back, his eyes closed as the water ran over him and his roiling, pent-up anger. A lion roared anguish and threat and thunder through Marguerite's mind. She didn't understand, but she refused to let him back out again. She stepped into the shower, took hold of his penis, and dragged her hand slowly up that hot, waiting shaft. He hissed. She caressed him again, running her thumb over the head.

Constantine sucked in a long, harsh breath and rolled her panties down. Her clit pulsed expectantly. Light as feathers, his fingers slid down the crack of her butt to her waiting core. God, she was wet, *so* slick and ready, and he kissed her again, plundering her mouth with his tongue, while below he caressed and opened her with mind-blowing gentleness. She mewed with delight and ran her arms around his neck and rubbed her bare leg up against his, wanting to climb him like a tree.

He ripped open the condom and sheathed himself, then cupped her ass and lifted her, poising her over his shaft. She smiled down at him, and his lips quirked just a little, sending a shiver of love twirling through her in response. So beautiful he was, eyes closed now, wet lashes against his copper cheeks. She took his penis in one hand and rubbed the head through her slick folds and across her clit, once and then again. He let out a groan and held her still, utterly silent except for his harsh breathing. She positioned him at her vagina. "It's been a long time since I've had sex, I'm going to be tight, go slowly . . ."

The coils of a serpent surrounded her; its head probed at her entrance. "Tight is good." He pushed and withdrew, probed again, deeper, deeper, sending little tongue-licks of flame through her belly. Slowly, slowly, he lowered her until he was inside her to the hilt. His aura let go of the remnants of anger and pain and flared with pleasure.

"Your colors are so beautiful," she breathed, almost on a sob.

He braced her against the cool tiles and began to move. Golden trills of excitement, throbs of crimson lust, purple sensual twists . . . *his* pleasure flowed into her with every stroke. She dug her fingers into his back and clung to him, reveling in the squish and squeak of her breasts against his chest, the water sneaking past her nipples, his hands, one under her ass, the other cupping a thigh, the slow, teasing thrusts and the answering clench of her sex around him. Higher and higher she climbed, the golden darkness swirling up to flush out all thought, to sweep her into a pulse and throb that went on and on and on, until he came hard and harder, and then held her still against the shower wall.

When he let her down, she slumped against the tiles to let her shaking legs recover. He said nothing, merely ditching the condom and reaching for the shampoo. She watched, sated and yet not, while he shampooed and rinsed his hair. She savored his powerful arms and thighs, the copper-brown muscles of his chest and abs, the penis nestled now in its bed of dark hair.

She wanted to do him again.

"Memorable for sure," she muttered. "But addictive is a better word for it."

His aura twisted, flamed. "Don't even—" He grunted, squeezing out his long hair. "Fucking bird won't let me get a word in edgewise anymore."

"What bird? What were you going to say?"

"Some bird, any bird, anything that would stop you from fucking me over and over again." He reached out of the shower for a towel and handed it to her, then got one for himself.

"If there's something I should know, you need to tell me, bird or no bird." She dried herself and turbaned the towel around her head. "Well?"

"Apparently, I'm not allowed to say it yet."

"Who's not allowing you? Don't say a bird. That doesn't make sense."

"Me, then," he said, shrugging again. "I guess. I never have been able to figure it out."

What had she said to start this crazy conversation? Her cell phone rang. She padded naked into the living room for her backpack and dug it out. *Lavonia.* She flipped it open.

"Marguerite." Lavonia sounded absolutely awful. "Please be careful. I'm so scared for you."

Marguerite stood and moved to the far side of the room for some privacy. "What's up?"

"My horrible dreams." Lavonia's voice was thick with tears. "I had another one this afternoon. Everybody's dead in it—you and Janie and Zeb—and I'm blind, and there's nothing I can do to stop it."

Janie? What did she have to do with all this?

Nothing, Marguerite admonished herself. She was becoming as superstitious about dreams as Lavonia. "Stop what? I thought you said we were dead."

Lavonia sobbed at the other end. "Don't joke, Marguerite. I'm so scared it's a prophetic dream and I'm supposed to *do* something, but I don't know what!"

"It's not a prophetic dream," Marguerite said. "It's your imagination running wild."

"I know," whispered Lavonia. "But I don't feel right. Not at all."

"You and I both know feelings can't be counted on. It could be something as simple as PMS. You know what that does to the female brain."

"I'm not PMS-ing," Lavonia retorted, more like her usual self. "It's not that time of the month."

"That doesn't mean your hormones aren't out of whack. Have a good strong cup of coffee to perk you up, go eat a fabulous supper, and have a great time at the theater."

"That's what Al said." She heaved a huge sigh. "And I agree with him that you need to stay away from that rock star. He's not safe."

"Since when?" Marguerite demanded. "This morning you said you liked him."

"That's why he's dangerous. He overrides a woman's common sense. You need to go someplace where he's not so you can think straight again."

With difficulty, Marguerite refrained from pointing out that Lavonia was the one whose thinking had gone distinctly wonky. Marguerite was doing just fine, considering she was dealing with attack birds and a lunatic lover.

Oh, *God,* what a lover. Why was he so conflicted? Why shouldn't they make love again and again?

"Can't you go someplace else for a few nights?" Lavonia pleaded. "Get away from here until this all blows over?"

Not a chance. She had better things to do tonight, such as trying Constantine out in a bed. She was utterly ravenous for more. She'd never been like this before. It might not last, but it was way too good to waste.

"I can't go anywhere. I have work tomorrow," Marguerite said, and then said it a couple more times before finally hanging up. She took off the turbaned towel. "My friend Lavonia thinks I'm in danger associating with you. She wants me to leave town."

Constantine sat naked and cross-legged on the carpet, combing out his long hair.

"Some part of you agrees with her, the same part that's been keeping me at arm's length," Marguerite went on. "On the other hand, your bird, whatever that is, or some part of you that identifies with the bird, wants me to stay and sleep with you again."

He watched her from under hooded eyes, and her nipples hardened instantly. "And again and again," he said.

"I want to do that, too," she said. "But apparently some part of you doesn't think it's such a good idea, the same part that avoided it in the first place."

"Don't try to psychoanalyze me, babe. It's a real turnoff. Let's just do it."

She wrapped the towel around herself and dug in her purse for a hair pick. "Your weird, secretive approach to things is a turnoff, too. If you can go around acting like a nutcase, I can ask questions and try to figure out why."

He cast his eyes heavenward, as if looking for inspiration. Or asking permission from some bird.

"I don't care what the bird says," she said, tugging the pick through her tangles. "If it wants me to sleep with you, it has to let you talk to me."

He laughed. "Good luck ordering the bird around. Stop attacking your hair, girl." He stood—a fluid, graceful cat-serpent-river—and took the pick. Gently, he worked through the snarls. How relaxing to be ministered to like this. She closed her eyes and sighed, and desire crept silently into her belly.

No. No way would she let him seduce her into abandoning her questions. "I glanced through that book about you. I've read articles, too. There's never much on your early years, except that you lived with your mother on the Navajo reservation. You gloss over it as if nothing happened, but you were eight years old when you left there. Your life didn't start in New Orleans. It started out west. Why don't you talk about it?"

"It's not a pretty story," he said. "What I recall of it is mighty unpleasant."

"You don't try to suppress all the other unpleasant stories about you. Why this one?"

"It's over and done with, and it doesn't matter anymore."

"It does," Marguerite said. "It made you who you are."

That struck a chord; his aura flared. "It's not just my story. It reflects badly on my mother and on the Navajo people, too. I've already done enough harm. I don't want to do any more."

Memories of what she'd read about the Navajos flooded her mind. "You carry a lot of violence and anger. I bet you could use a healing ceremony."

Now his aura was majorly annoyed. He moved behind her, combing the hair at the back. "Not going to happen, babe. I don't belong there anymore. I have to find my own way."

"You'll feel much better if you get it off your chest. Anything you clutch to yourself like that literally weighs you down." She huffed. "It's in your aura—guilt and shame and misery all wadded up together."

He rolled his eyes but moved to her other side as if he hadn't been trying to hide anything at all. As if he was cool with being so vulnerable, which he wasn't.

"You know I have this gift." She hated this. "Just believe me, damn it. You'll feel much better if you let some of it go."

A struggle went on in his aura. Her own chest tightened in response, but she sat quiescent while he finished with her hair. Finally, he said, "I'll tell you about my wife, but if you really want to have sex with me again, we should do it first."

He eyed her from beneath heavy lids again, sending her tantalizing images of what they would do together, visualized the blood pounding languidly through her body, pulsing in her pussy, moisture gushing to welcome him.

She blushed but scowled. "Stop that."

"Are you going to fuck me or not?" He winced and telepathed: *Would you prefer romance? Touch me, sweetheart.*

She closed in on him, took his penis in her hand, ran her fingers lazily up and down. He shuddered. "I don't expect you to fall madly in love with me," she said, letting him go again, "but I also don't want to feel lousy about myself afterward."

"Talking about my wife will make you feel lousy for sure, without the benefit of any good physical stuff. It may turn you off for good, and I'd like to get laid again first." *Sorry about the lack of finesse.* He went to the window that looked out over the rooftops of Bayou Gavotte. Denser clouds were building overhead; soon a shower would break the tense Louisiana heat. "Something bad is going to happen tonight."

Marguerite came up beside him, put her arms around him, and stretched up until her lips brushed his. "Not between you and me."

~

Zeb downed four iced coffees in a row, staying awake to reassure Zelda that he wasn't planning to kill himself. It wasn't doing any good. She knew something was wrong, and she wouldn't let go. Sweet, persistent little bitch. He wanted a lifetime of friendship with her, but how likely was that?

He stood, yawning. "Give it up, Zelda. I'm not suicidal, but I might become that way if I don't get some sleep. I'll walk you to your place, and then I'm going home to crash." He said the last sentence loud enough for the cop a few tables over to hear him.

The cop, who looked wet behind the ears, was a friend of Zelda's mom. She'd greeted him and they'd exchanged some small talk, and then he'd got a free coffee and pastry and taken a little table in the corner.

Usually cops took a short coffee break and then left again. This dude had been sitting in the corner doing Sudoku puzzles for half an hour. Maybe lack of sleep was making Zeb paranoid, but he didn't think so. He was pretty sure people had been watching him ever since this morning at Hellebore U. First a guy he thought was one of Constantine's roadies; then an old lady who'd sat beside him on a park bench followed slowly behind him until he'd begun to run. When he'd turned to glance back at her, she was on a cell phone. After that, one of the waiters from the Impractical Cat, a big, tough-looking dude, seemed always to be close by, even when Zeb had gone to the supermarket to get sugar and chocolate for his dad. Fortunately, Dad hadn't been home when he'd dropped them off, so he'd escaped . . . and now he was being watched by this cop.

Sure, the cop's too-casual glances their way might be meant for Zelda, or maybe he thought he was playing knight in shining armor, protecting the cute little vampire from statutory rape. *Sorry, man, I'm way too stable for that.* Zeb had wondered all day if he should go ahead and screw Juma as a sort of last meal, just in case, but . . . no. If he was going to do Juma, he'd do her right.

Zelda's cell phone chimed, and she held up a hand. She read the text. "Can you walk me to the Cat instead? I'm meeting Juma for peach cobbler and ice cream."

"Sure, why not?" He hadn't been able to make a decision anyway, so why not tempt fate?

"Maybe you can talk to Constantine if he's there."

"Maybe so," Zeb said. More and more, this truly was a temptation: to lay his burdens on an experienced pair of shoulders, especially since the possessor of the shoulders had absolutely no emotional investment in Zeb's dilemma.

"Really? Yay!" Zelda trotted along beside him, talking nonstop about how fabulous and what a great friend Constantine was.

A patrol car turned out of the coffee shop parking lot even as he and Zelda headed down the main drag toward the Impractical Cat. Aw, fuck. Constantine would probably just shunt him over to the police. Maybe he already had done so—otherwise why was he being shadowed by a cop now rather than some bodyguard-in-training?

He still hadn't made up his mind by the time he opened the door of the restaurant and ushered the still chattering Zelda through. "We'll go straight to Lep's office and—"

"Fuck," Zeb said under his breath, pulling Zelda behind a row of booths in the direction of the kitchen. "My father's here with his girlfriend."

"So?"

So he couldn't stomach pretending with his father anymore. "I said I would be home tonight working on French verbs."

"But what about talking to Constantine? If I ask, he'll let us sneak upstairs. Your dad won't know."

Zeb glanced back; the cop was coming through the front door. "Later, girl." He kissed Zelda swiftly on the cheek, ducked through the swinging doors, crossed the kitchen, and went out the back. A surprised shout followed him, but he skirted the dumpster, vaulted the back fence, and took off into the neighborhoods beyond.

He couldn't go home. The cops would look for him there, and he needed to be out and available, just in case. He kept moving, but once the adrenaline rush of escape drained away, exhaustion took over. He had to sleep *now*. Anywhere—a garage, an alley, a shed . . . a car.

He should have four hours free before he had to be on watch. Once again, he put himself into the hands of fate. He made it through two more blocks without passing out and crawled wearily over the fence into the parking lot where Eaton Wilson's black Ford van was still parked between two Hellebore University vans. If the cops found it—found him—so be it. Zeb climbed inside, flopped onto the bench at the back, and slept.

~

Constantine pulled Marguerite hard against him, destroying what resistance remained to her in a blast of desire. Within seconds, they were on the bed, naked and entwined. They kissed and kissed, exploring each other in luxurious abandon. His hot hands roamed her and his erection brushed her belly. She'd never felt like this with a man before—so desperate with want and need and love.

No, not love. She'd meant what she said. She didn't expect him to fall in love with her. She didn't know what she wanted anyway, and his past had bent him so badly that he might not even be capable of love.

She didn't want to think about all this, and then she couldn't think anyway because another blast of images overwhelmed her. It was crazy: images of being undressed, slowly and tantalizingly, when she was actually naked. Visions of copper-brown hands cupping her breasts, while in reality one played in the crack of her butt and the other toyed with her clit. His mouth on her breast, his penis in her hand, while her mind saw him entering her, filling her, fucking her hard. Her vaginal walls clenched and clenched. She wanted him in there, in there *now*, before she exploded. "Oh, *God*," she said. "It's going to be over too soon. Don't you ever do this slowly?"

"Next time," he said, ripping open another condom and sheathing himself. He loomed over her, took her in a long, deep kiss, and pushed himself inside.

She groaned, spasming again. She wrapped her legs around him, thrills rocketing through her with every stroke, and again she was helpless in the grip of the heat between them. "I don't want to come so soon."

"We'll do it again, *really* slowly." Visions of languid, lazy sex rolled into her mind, driving her to bliss as he pounded into her, his head thrown back, his features alight. Her heart burst with sheer, cataclysmic delight.

Afterward, they lay silently until he slipped out; then he rolled off her, chucked the condom, and gathered her into his arms, pulling the sheet over them. This felt like love, so sweet and *together.*

Had it been like this with his wife? She didn't want to ask. She didn't want to break this blissful mood. She closed her eyes and held him.

She dozed, waking to darkness and the enticing smell of food. From the next room came the sound of his guitar. She dressed, combed her hair, and went to join him. He waved toward a platter of muffaletta sandwiches. His aura was suffused with uneasiness, which might be about discussing his wife, as he'd promised.

She should give him a little time. Her stomach grumbled. She took a sandwich and bit into it.

She had almost finished the sandwich when he said, "Whoever killed her saved me the hassle of a divorce," he said. "We shouldn't have gotten married in the first place. She might still be alive if we hadn't. I didn't love her—never did—but I didn't want her dead."

She swallowed the last bite and wiped her mouth with a napkin from a pile on the table. "Then why did you marry her?"

"Pigheadedness. I knew better, or in hindsight it seems that way. The bird warned me, but I didn't act on what it said or what I knew." He laughed.

"What?"

"I was imagining what it would have been like if I'd tried to talk to Jonetta about my spirit guide."

Now it all made much more sense. "The bird you keep talking about is a spirit guide?"

His fingers stilled on the guitar. "You could call it that. I've had it since I was a kid, and without it, I would have been dead long since—that or a murderer without even the excuse of being a vigilante. If you think I'm twisted now, you should have seen me then. Power and hatred are a lousy combination, and the bird guided me through a lot of crap. Even knowing that, I got sick of being told what to do and not to do, and too much of it making only partial sense, and none of my questions having real answers." He closed his eyes. "You grow up and realize that answers are elusive and that it all depends, but I wasn't there yet. It never approved of my beating up and killing people, but it nursed me through it all. Then I married Jonetta, and it abandoned me."

~

He was babbling. He opened his eyes. Blinded by the concern in hers, he shut them again. He'd begun to think of her as he did of Lep—a trusted friend—and then, while she was asleep, Lep had directed him to Nathan's latest blog—an interview with Professor Lutsky that more than confirmed this morning's little scene in the restaurant. That had upset him more than it should, but she hadn't known him before yesterday. Why shouldn't she agree to check him out for a researcher friend?

Then, on a whim—or perhaps he should see it as a compulsion—he'd gone through her backpack. What he'd found there had, quite frankly, confused him. He supposed he would have to confront her about it . . . but the real problem was that he didn't *want* to believe anything against her. He hadn't thought much farther than getting back in the saddle, but instead of a couple of quick fucks, he'd been making love to her. She didn't expect him to fall in love with her, but what if he already had? Love and trust were supposed to go together . . . and he was mighty naive if he believed that.

The bird said nothing, which could mean anything. As usual, it all depended. On something or other.

Fuck.

He set the guitar between his knees, and she took his hand. He welcomed her touch. He couldn't help it. "But it came back again," she said.

Constantine gave a mirthless laugh. "Back to the rescue." He sucked in a deep breath. He had to get his head together enough to explain. He twined his fingers through hers. It felt so damned good. And safe. Since when did he want to be safe? She could blab all this to Lutsky and the media for all he cared. No one could distinguish the truth from lies anyway. "Jonetta and I married for promotional purposes." That pretty much said it all.

"Sounds like a weird reason to get married," Marguerite said. He tried to read 'and stupid' into her tone of voice, but she was a lot more polite than the bird.

"Big rock star, hot new actress, lots of publicity. We had it all planned—a hasty marriage and then a spectacular divorce, and if we disagreed somewhere along the line, there was a watertight prenup, so neither of us could screw the other over financially."

"What happened?"

"She fell in love with me." Again he found himself comparing Jonetta with Marguerite, who never in a million years would go for such an arrangement. "Our agreement was clear. It was a fake, from start to finish, no love involved, sex if she wanted it. Not that I objected to screwing her, but I didn't care one way or the other. But before long, she became obsessed with me. She wasn't the first one; there was a vampire way back when, when I was just a kid . . ." Hurriedly, he pulled out of that pathway. Marguerite didn't need to hear about his first kill. Which just went to show that he wasn't thinking clearly. *No one* needed to hear about it, especially someone who might well blab it to the whole world. "I don't know why I'm digging up that crap. Women tend to fall for me, but if I ignore them, they usually go away. I was stuck married to this one. She desperately wanted me to fall in love with her, while I frankly and openly didn't give a damn. I got annoyed and then bored with her, and replaced, uh, what little relationship we had with orgasms."

"Huh?" Marguerite choked on a half-laugh.

"Not too clever of me, because she got addicted. For a while she just craved more and more quick and easy orgasms, but soon they weren't good enough. She had to have me inside her while I gave her the orgasm fix. I didn't want to be inside her. By then, I didn't want to touch her or even see her. But I felt it was partly my fault, and she'd gotten into drugs instead, but that didn't do the trick, and she was so damn desperate . . ."

He took a deep breath and plunged. "That's when I started hurting her."

CHAPTER FIFTEEN

H urting her," repeated Marguerite numbly.
"When we had sex," he said. "I should have refused
her point blank, but by the time I figured that out, it was too
late."

Ah. Jonetta's claim about nightmarish sex with Constantine had been the simple truth. "You hurt her with your
mind."

"What else?"

What else, indeed? His mind was an instrument of torture. "But you didn't mean to. Stop beating yourself up, for
God's sake!"

"What choice do I have?" he snapped. "When you're
stuck with a mind like mine, you have to know how to control it." His aura flared and swayed. He wrapped it around
himself. Hugging himself. Then embarrassment flooded his
aura and he let go. He took refuge in the guitar, and for a
while just played and played, one riff after another parallel-
ing the changes in his mood. "She said it hurt. I didn't know
what she was talking about, so I tried slowing down, being
gentler. Not that I was being rough, exactly, but I wanted to
get it over with."

No wonder he hadn't wanted to talk about this before
having sex.

"That was only the beginning. No matter what I tried, it got worse every time. She'd start shrieking and punch me. I'd pull out, and she'd get even madder and hit me some more. I guess the need outweighed the pain, but the next time we tried it, she ran away screaming."

"You didn't mean to hurt her," Marguerite said.

"I don't suppose she meant to beat on me either. She was acting in frustration and self-defense." Pause. "I refused to touch her after that, so she waited till I was asleep and came at me with a cleaver."

Marguerite sucked in a horrified breath.

"My spirit guide must have realized I was finally ready to listen. It woke me up just in time. I took my guitar and moved here. She spouted all kinds of shit about me, and I countered by giving the fans one-touch orgasms. Then somebody fed her that cocktail of drugs that killed her."

"But you were hours away at the time, so they couldn't pin it on you," Marguerite said.

"Luckily, because the concert that night was another impromptu deal. A friend called from Mississippi and I up and went, just for the hell of it. Maybe the bird whispered in my ear, and I did what I was told for once." He rolled his shoulders. "After she was killed, I tried taking up with a woman a time or two, but I couldn't stomach it. What if they got addicted, too? What if I got angry again and hurt them without meaning to? Every time I even thought about having sex, I felt the rage building inside me . . . so I gave up." He paused. "Until you came along."

She didn't say anything. What was she supposed to say? That she wouldn't come at him with a cleaver?

"So now you know." He fiddled with the tuning pegs unnecessarily. The guitar was perfectly in tune, but his aura was a mess.

"Um, yeah." She sat up. "Well, the sex has been great so far."

"I guess that's what the bird was after." Notes trickled from his fingers. "Show her it can be okay before you freak her out with the past."

"I'm not freaked out. I'm not afraid of your mind—I guess because I can usually see what's going on."

He eyed her sideways. He was going to have to confront her . . . but first, he wanted her one more time. "Does that mean you want to make love again?"

"Already?" She smiled and leaned in to kiss his cheek. "If we go slowly."

"I'm out of condoms, but there are some in my truck." He put down the guitar and Lawless leapt up, eager to go along. "Come on, boy. We'll be right back."

Constantine went down the stairs and out by way of the kitchen. He let Lawless out through the gate and went into the garage to get the condoms. He stowed several in his pocket and went to get the dog. He took a deep breath of the damp night air, wishing it could clear his mind. Everything seemed off-kilter, and instead of helping him think straight, screwing Marguerite had fractured him all the more.

His spirit guide was uneasy, too, although not about Marguerite; it seemed unable to express what was wrong, an unusual state of affairs. The patio was empty now, but there were people around, so he hung back, serenaded by trilling insects, cloaked by the friendly darkness. Shortly before Marguerite woke, Lep had called about Zeb's arrival and abrupt departure out the kitchen door. According to Zelda, he was headed home to avoid his dad's wrath, but one of Lep's people reported he'd never shown up there. Why had he lied to Zelda? Where had he gone?

A man's laughter cracked the night. Constantine froze against the wall. His gut squirmed and heaved. Fear uncoiled inside him.

What in hell? He'd confronted perverts and killers and dealt with them fine, but his whole being cowered at the sound of that voice. He crept to the corner of the patio wall and stopped.

The high-pitched squeal of a frightened dog split the night. People's voices: "What happened?" "Nobody was near him!" Lawless shot around the end of the patio wall and cringed at Constantine's feet, whimpering. *Quiet,* he told the dog. *Stay.* He visualized himself as a bush and inched forward.

People walked to and fro in the parking lot, couples, a boisterous family, a lone woman . . . The laugh broke out again, like a lash on broken skin. Constantine struggled to focus. Might be the guy in a shirt and jeans striding toward the corner of the building . . .

"You go, girl!" said the voice. "It's bonbons for you!"

Memory slammed into Constantine. He fell to his knees beside the wall, black terror tossing him like a sandstorm, depriving him of breath, choking him to death. He cried out for his guide. Insects sang. Car doors opened and shut, and random voices, normal voices, drifted through the humid air. A couple crossed the parking lot, murmuring to one another. More doors, then a car driving away.

Constantine finally got his breath, gasping until he heaved and retched into the dirt. An owl fluttered onto the wall above, and Constantine crumpled at the base, a helpless child again.

An Enemy's voice, an Enemy's laugh . . . But this Enemy, the one who had started him on his twisted, hateful path, was supposed to be dead. He'd been killed in a drug deal gone bad, long, long ago.

No, evidently not.

Chills shook him, fear for everyone he cared about, but the persistent flapping of the owl, coupled with Lawless's frantic licking, got him going again. He staggered through the gate to the patio and unlocked the door with shaking hands. Lawless slipped through, and Constantine followed, pulling the door shut behind them.

What in hell was he going to do about Marguerite?

~

Marguerite waited impatiently for Constantine to return. The uneasiness hadn't dissipated during their conversation, but arousal had overlaid it at the end. He wanted her again—she was certain of that. Good, because she wanted him, too.

Shortly after he left, Marguerite heard a frightened squeal that might have been Lawless, but when she opened the door to check, the only sounds were vehicles and voices in the parking lot and on the street. She went back indoors and indulged in a few of the chocolates Al Bonnard had passed out that morning. She was licking the gooey filling off her fingers when her cell phone rang.

"Are you still with Constantine?" It was Lavonia. She sounded ghastly.

"Yes, I am, and why are you calling me again? You sound even worse than before."

"I'm sick to my stomach, so Al's taking me home. I'll be fine, but I'm scared for you, Marguerite. I don't think you should go home, though. You're too vulnerable there. There've been reporters hovering there on and off all day, by what I hear."

"That's why Constantine insists I need a bodyguard."

"In Bayou Gavotte, sure, but not elsewhere. He can't force you to stay. Say you're going to New Orleans to stay with a friend."

This again? "I told you before, I have work next week."

But Lavonia yammered on: school didn't start till Tuesday, Marguerite's first class was on Wednesday, and she'd sleep so much better knowing Marguerite was safe. Her voice raised in pitch to almost a shout. "Tell him you have an appointment. Make an excuse and go!"

Marguerite stifled her growing annoyance; sometimes it was easier giving Lavonia what she wanted. "Actually, I don't need an excuse. There's an exhibit in the French Quarter that I'd hoped to see, and I need to do some shopping there, too. I should drive into town tonight so I can get an early start tomorrow."

Relief suffused Lavonia's voice. "Thank you! I feel better already. See you in a couple of days." Finally, she hung up.

Marguerite turned. Constantine stood in the doorway, his aura gray as death. Lawless hovered beside him, his tail completely still.

"What's wrong?" Marguerite said.

"Nothing." Constantine's voice was flat and cold. "You're leaving."

Slowly, Marguerite lowered her cell phone. His aura was so tight it made her shiver. What had happened? "Do you want me to go?"

"You just told your friend you're going to New Orleans." He motioned to the dog, and it lay on the floor by the door, watching them.

"Because she wouldn't let up until I did. Lavonia's been having awful dreams about everybody being dead, and what with the dreams I had, she's all freaked out and wants me to get away from Bayou Gavotte for a few days."

"Who being dead?"

"Me and Zeb. Janie, too." Why were his eyes so empty, his aura shunning her, shutting her out? This wasn't the same man in whose arms she had slept only a short time ago. It wasn't even the uneasy man who'd left to get condoms. "I need to go home and get some clean clothes."

"And then go to New Orleans."

"I might just do that, if you don't want me here," she said, the annoyance she'd felt at Lavonia morphing into anger now. "I thought you were going to get condoms, though."

"I'll screw you once more if you want." His aura was scaring the shit out of her.

"Once more. You're saying . . . you'll do me a huge favor and screw me once more and that's all? If I *want?* Because your aura is telling me you don't."

"I changed my mind."

How dare he? Through her mounting rage, she tried to read him. *Fear.* "You think I'll get addicted to you, like Jonetta?"

"Score one for Marguerite," he said, but a trickle of relief in his aura told her it wasn't that simple.

"I won't get addicted," she scoffed. "I thought there was a chance I might fall in love with you." His aura shot sparks. "Don't freak out. I've changed my mind, too. Apart from the stunning sex, you're just too fucking weird." She didn't usually come out with the f-word. She must be more upset than she realized.

"I'm not weird, I'm crazy," he said. "I talk to birds, real or imaginary. They get all up in my business and tell me what to do."

"I can handle crazy," she said. "It's not being believed that I have a hard time with. I thought you understood about my so-called gift." Why was she surprised? Nobody ever did. "I thought you didn't mind it. I thought you'd gotten over your stupid suspicions about me, but I see by your aura that you haven't. I'm a trustworthy person, and I hate not being trusted."

"I'm not big on trust, babe, and you seem to lie pretty easily—not only about me up on the mound but to your friend just now."

"Strictly speaking, it wasn't a lie, since I merely implied that I would go to New Orleans."

"Uh-huh. You also lied about not knowing Zeb."

She got a grip on herself. "No, I just didn't admit to knowing him, and it was to protect him."

"Plausible, but it doesn't inspire me with confidence in you."

She huffed. "You don't inspire confidence either." At the moment, he was inspiring the urge to kill. She grabbed her backpack and felt in the back for another couple of bonbons. *Ahh. Chocolate.*

Much better.

He sat on the couch. "I don't want to inspire confidence. You do. You also lied to me about what happened with Zeb and Lutsky this morning. Did you think Reuben wouldn't tell me everything? Not that he needed to, as it turns out." He opened the laptop and the screen came to life. "I guess you haven't seen this."

So much for the feel-good rush of chocolate. A chill settled into her gut as she perched herself at the edge of the couch.

It was another story by Nathan Bone. He'd interviewed Roy Lutsky, who said Marguerite was a gifted psychic who'd promised to help him with his research by getting close to Constantine Dufray and analyzing his character by psychic means. In particular, she was to seduce him, have sex with him as often as possible, and give detailed reports of her experiences.

"What the hell?" Marguerite leapt up, clenching her fists. "Oh, how dare he! That is the last time I will ever, ever promise to help Roy with anything!"

"So you admit it?" Constantine's voice was casual, even amused.

"There's nothing to admit." She glared at him. "You believe this bullshit, don't you? For your information, all I promised Roy, at least a year ago, was to tell him what your aura was like, both from a distance at concerts and close up if I ever had a chance to meet you. He knows about the auras because my father told him. He worked summers for my dad when he was in college."

"Uh-huh." Constantine stretched his powerful legs and sat back. "Whatever you say, babe. Now, there's also the unpleasant little fact that you purposely destroyed evidence this morning. Fortunately, Reuben's not as empty-headed as he pretends to be. He pocketed a few pages under cover of the noise of the shredder."

She felt her face fall. She hadn't thought of it like that. "I—" Damn. "I didn't think of it as destroying evidence. I was just so appalled that . . ."

"Sorry, babe." He picked up her backpack and held it up, as if that was supposed to mean something. "That won't cut it, since we know you'd seen it before." He reached inside the backpack and pulled out a manila envelope.

She grabbed the envelope. "You searched my backpack while I was asleep?"

"I do what I have to." His expression was smug, his aura stronger now, dark and determined. Beneath it, she thought she glimpsed pain, but she didn't give a damn. He deserved it.

She grabbed the backpack, too, and set it beside her. "You're such a jerk. Pauline left this envelope on my bed the night she died. She'd printed out some papers on language and cognition for me." Marguerite reached in and pulled out the stapled articles.

Between them were several pages of the same awful porn. They appeared to have been crumpled up and later flattened out. "You found these in here?"

"You're not fooling anyone, babe."

"Stop calling me 'babe.' I didn't put them here," she gritted out. "I didn't even look in the envelope until now. I got home that night, shoved it in my backpack for future reading, and got a call in the wee hours about Pauline's body."

"Sure. Whatever you say."

"Which means either Pauline must have put them there before she went out and died or the murderer did."

His aura flickered with interest, but he merely said, "You don't give up, do you?"

"Or *you* put them there," she flashed.

He laughed, his aura showing such genuine surprise that she had to believe him. "Why would I do that?"

"Because you're an asshole." She stuffed the articles and porn back in the envelope, put it in the backpack, and zipped it up. Oh, God in heaven, this *hurt.* He didn't want to believe her. He didn't *want* to trust her. He never had.

"I *am* trustworthy. I have a *gift,* and it's *special,* whether you or anyone else believes it or not."

He shrugged.

The rage simmering inside her surged up, hot, volcanic, and unstoppable. She grabbed the sandwich tray with shaking hands, shrieked at the top of her lungs, and threw it across his pristine room. Crusts scattered, plates shattered, and tea sloshed all over one of his guitars.

Lawless scrambled up, whimpering, and skittered out the door. Misery washed over Marguerite. "Believe what you want. It's your loss, not mine. Come on, Lawless." She hefted her backpack over her shoulder and left.

∾

Go with her, he told the dog, and Lawless went.

Constantine texted Lep downstairs to have her followed. He needed her out of the way, as far away as possible, as soon as possible. She had to believe he didn't give a damn, because if the Enemy thought he cared about her, there was no telling what he might do. It was dumb luck that he'd had something with which to drive her away. For her own safety, she had to hate him. She had to want to stay away.

She was telling the truth, the bird said forlornly, and Constantine found himself agreeing. Not that believing her did much good, because she would never take him back after this. He hadn't expected her to react quite so violently—she didn't seem the tantrum type—but perhaps it was all for the best that he now knew.

Keeping to the shadows, he went downstairs in Marguerite's wake. His people had kept the back area free of reporters, but judging by the rage in her every movement, she would have mowed down anyone who dared to get in her way. She didn't turn once, just marched out the back without a word and went straight to her car. She drove off, and silently, Reuben got into his Cadillac and followed her.

~

Zeb surged out of a coma-like sleep with a gasp. His heart banging, he held himself still and listened. Silence all around, but something must have made him shoot awake like that. Maybe the cops had found the van, in which case he was toast. With a sensation close to relief, he raised himself and peeked out the window.

The white van next to him now had a metal sign on it covering the university logo, but in the dim light he couldn't make out what it said. What was going on? He'd thought nothing was planned for tonight, at least not until the small hours. Had he slept that long? It felt like he'd had five minutes max. He crept to the front seat at the other side of the van and waited, wishing he hadn't disabled the vehicle, but at least the disconnected battery meant no telltale light would come on when he got out. The instant the white van's engine rumbled into life, he slipped out, pushed the door gently shut, and sneaked around the back, considering his options. The white van was backing up toward him, its rack for abandoned bikes gleaming in the first few drops of rain.

He didn't want to deal with this, whatever it was, but if he called the cops, if he went to Constantine, would anyone believe him?

The van stopped, the gears clunked out of reverse, and the vehicle moved forward. Zeb ducked behind the row of parked vehicles and sprinted parallel to the white van in the direction of the gate. The van came to a halt at the gate, Zeb crouched behind a bush, and the skies let loose. The driver got out to open the gate, cursing. As he got back inside the vehicle, Zeb made a mad dash through the rain, crouched low, shoving the terror of being caught back down his craw. He would do what he had to, whatever that proved to be. The driver drove through, got out, still cursing, closed the gate again, and hurried back inside the van.

Zeb took hold of the bike rack and swung onto it as the van moved slowly forward. He held his breath, praying hard, but the van kept moving and turned into the road.

The rain settled to a steady downpour. The metal of the rack bit into Zeb's hands as he clung on. Up until yesterday, he'd thought he could handle things himself. He'd only had to counteract sick practical jokes. What if Marguerite was right and Pauline had been murdered . . . But, if so, how? And why?

He'd waited too long, trying to understand, to adjust, to be the thoughtful, considerate, forgiving kind of person his mom had wanted him to be. The van rolled steadily toward downtown, then slammed to a halt at a red light. Zeb's head smacked the spare tire, the rack ripped his hands, and he fell onto the road. Heart lurching, he dragged himself up. He clenched his fists, gearing for battle, but the light changed and the van moved away.

He sprinted after it, keeping to the side of the road. He was a long-distance runner, never a great sprinter, but rage and desperation thrust him forward, past one street and around the corner of the next.

Two blocks further, the van turned into an all-night gas station downtown and pulled up at a pump. Zeb slid into the shadows at the roadside, panting, allowing himself some slack, letting the rain wash and soothe the bloody rips in his fingers. Still a chance. He crept along on the wet grass next to the sidewalk. Streetlights glistened on the wet pavement, and he hurried by, keeping just out of their reach.

Next door to the brightly lit gas station an abandoned house slanted slowly toward demolition, bordered by a scraggly hedge. Zeb sank down behind the bushes and breathed and watched the van, trying to come up with a plan. Who could the bastard be after this time? Where could he be going? Not after Marguerite; God, he hoped not. She was with Constantine, so she would be okay, and she wouldn't go running out at night alone anymore. He tried to think, to come up with a plan. Maybe he shouldn't have chickened out at the Impractical Cat, but with his father right there, he just couldn't take the chance. What were the odds that Constantine or anyone else would believe him? Because of his employment record and a couple of blood tests, people thought he was a druggie with a violent temper who couldn't even hold down a job.

The rain kept falling on the bushes and trickling down his back. He couldn't even send up a silent prayer to his mother, asking for help. He had made her promises, and it looked like he was going to have to break them. She had always told him he could only do his best, but what did that amount to? How did someone like Constantine steel himself to harm—or even kill—someone he knew or maybe even cared about?

The van door slammed shut, and Zeb scrambled forward, keeping low and directly behind the van. He wrapped his hands in the bottom of his T-shirt, gripped the rack, and positioned his feet on the bumper just as the van slid forward.

They puttered through town in the steady rain, and Zeb crouched grimly against the rack. Past one street, two, five; even with the T-shirt as a cushion, his hands were killing him. Another block, and the van slowed, turned, pulled into the gravel parking area next to the small park in the middle of town. No one was in sight, and few lights showed in the houses flanking the park. Why had he stopped here? Zeb unclenched his hands and stepped lightly down, scuttling to the right into the yard of a dingy brick apartment building occupied mostly by dopeheads. He crouched in the muddy shadows beside the marijuana-scented porch, and watched and waited and tried not to hope.

CHAPTER SIXTEEN

Marguerite wasn't in any shape to drive. She'd never been so enraged in her life.

And upset with herself for distressing poor innocent Lawless. "I'm sorry, boy," she said, reaching over to caress him. "I'm not mad at you."

He licked her hand, and she almost burst into tears. Then she noticed Reuben behind her, and the rage surged once more. She struggled, got herself focused, and made it through downtown Bayou Gavotte without running over any slow-moving pedestrians.

It began to rain, and at the last minute, she drove past her own street. She had to calm down before going home. She had to decide what to say if any reporters were there, and she had to get past them—in and out—without showing how much she was hurting inside. She doubted Reuben would let her be stomped to death by a horde of reporters, but if she claimed she was still going out with Constantine, he would report it as another lie—and yet she refused to demean herself by publicly dissing Constantine either.

After fifteen minutes of driving in circles, she went home, drained but in control. There were five unfamiliar cars parked near her house. She pulled up in the driveway. Jabez was on the porch, sipping iced coffee with a couple of women in suits. Three men leapt from their vehicles and came over to hers before she'd even had a chance to open the door.

Jabez and Reuben were on them. "No comment, no comment, no comment," they said, shoving them all aside, ushering her through the rain to her front door.

Oho. Not giving her a chance to diss their beloved leader, huh? "Actually, I do have a comment," she said sweetly, smiling at the women in suits. "Constantine is absolutely *amazing*, and some of the stuff you hear about him is true." She paused. "And some of it's not." She went indoors. So there, she thought bitterly. Let them chew on that one. Maybe she wasn't as hopeless at dealing with the media as she thought.

Reuben followed her. "Are you still guarding me?" she demanded, doing her damnedest not to be pissed off at him. He'd only been doing his job when he'd tattled on her.

"Just following you, ma'am," he replied. That "ma'am" had an ominous feel to it.

She took a small overnight bag from the hall closet and packed enough for a couple of days, including food and a leash for Lawless. She changed into clean clothes. Now all she needed was her sketch pad. She still hadn't decided where to go tonight. Tomorrow she would go with Lawless to the levee in New Orleans, sit under a tree, and have a lazy time drawing the boats and the passersby. Her mouth was already watering for coffee and beignets.

Where was her sketch pad? She'd left it on the coffee table the previous night. She was sure of that. She didn't remember seeing it this morning, but she hadn't been looking for it. She'd hardly been in this room at all. She went through the entire house, and then did it all over again, bitching under her breath. "Where the hell is it?"

Reuben was hanging by the living room window, picking his teeth. "Looking for something?"

"My sketch pad." She opened the front door, beckoned Jabez inside, and asked if he'd seen or moved it.

Total indifference. "No, ma'am." He went back outdoors.

"I need to speak to Constantine," she told Reuben.

"Don't suppose he wants you back there, ma'am," Reuben said, very cool, very sure, striking a chilly misery into her heart. They had a routine for dealing with cast-off sexual conquests.

Assholes, that's what they all were. "I didn't say I wanted to *see* him," she said. "I want to know if he moved my sketch pad or saw it or anything."

Reuben appeared to consider, heaved a jaded sigh, and sent a text message. Marguerite gritted her teeth and waited. She was close to exploding by the time the exchange of messages ended. Reuben said, "No."

"No, what?"

"Didn't see it, didn't touch it."

Oh, shit. It had been there when she'd left to go out with Tony. There when she'd returned, because she remembered closing it to cover the sketch of her sex dream but leaving it on the coffee table. Someone had searched her house between then and when she'd returned with Constantine in the small hours, and her sketch pad was what they'd taken.

"I need to talk to Constantine," she said again.

"Sorry, ma'am," Reuben said. "No can do. He wasn't any too pleased I texted him. Said I should know better."

"Fine," she said. "I'll handle it myself." She picked up her overnight bag, but Reuben took it and silently carried it out to the car. She slung her backpack over her shoulder, locked the door behind her, and was ushered to her car by Constantine's minions.

She found Gideon's card in her wallet and gave him a call. "I'm sorry to bother you at home, but I need to speak to you. Something went missing from my house last night that I think you should know about."

"Does Constantine know about all this?"

Marguerite took a breath to get her voice under control. "He won't talk to me."

"Aw, shit. What's eating the dude?"

"I don't know and don't care. If you decide my information has any significance, feel free to let him know."

Big sigh. "Sure. Come on over to my place," he said and gave directions. She drove a ways out of town along the river on Highway 43 and turned into a long driveway bounded by well-tended shrubs. At the end of the drive stood a sea-green Victorian house lit up by outdoor lights, with a riot of flowers on either side of the stairs and in pots on the veranda. A big mutt with blond curls raised its head from the porch, sniffed the air, and barked once. A woman about Marguerite's age with auburn hair in an untidy ponytail came around the side of the house with a wheelbarrow full of weeds and clippings, but she set it down and took off her gardening gloves when Marguerite pulled up and got out.

"You must be Marguerite. I'm Ophelia. Ever since the baby was born, I have to fit in the gardening whenever I can. Fortunately, I have good night vision, but it's going to start raining again any second." She stuck out a hand. She had a cheerful aura and a dazzling smile, which quickly turned to a scowl when the red Cadillac drew up. "Reuben, what are you doing here?"

"Following Ms. Marguerite," the bodyguard said. "Constantine's orders." The dog on the porch stretched and came down the stairs.

"Following her? Why?" She glanced at Marguerite and rolled her eyes. "Because he said so, I suppose. Well, *I* say you can leave." The tips of a pair of fangs peeked out from beneath her upper lip but disappeared immediately, and an embarrassed flush crossed her face.

Either Reuben didn't notice or he already knew. "Sorry, Ophelia. No can do."

"I will not have Constantine persecuting people on my property," the vampire said, and Marguerite began to relax. The blond dog panted cheerfully at the sight of Lawless through the car window. "You can let your dog out. We have three dogs here for him to play with." Marguerite opened the door, and Lawless bounded out to join Ophelia's dog in the standard sniffing routines.

Reuben's eyes flickered uneasily. "Please don't tell Vi. I don't mean to disrespect you, but I'm between a rock and a hard place here."

"Constantine being the rock, as in 'dumb as,'" Ophelia said. "He makes me so mad sometimes." She took a breath, her aura busy. "Tell you what. If he won't let you leave, wait at the side of the road. It's a public place and none of my business who parks there."

"That works," Reuben said, cheering up. He backed his car out of the driveway.

"So much for him." Ophelia grinned. "Vi's my sister, and the possibility that she might stop sleeping with him is too much for him to take." Her eyes widened. "Oh, honey, are you all right?"

"No," Marguerite said and burst into tears.

～

"What the fuck happened?" Lep said.

Constantine hadn't moved since returning to the rooftop apartment. Still sprawled on the sofa, he turned his head just enough to see his friend in the doorway. "She had a tantrum."

"Sure, but why haven't you cleaned up?"

Constantine hunched a shoulder.

"This isn't like you, bro." He paused. "Looks like you had a lucky escape, though."

"Maybe."

"I mean it, man. You don't need another Jonetta."

"She's not like Jonetta."

"No?" Lep retrieved the tray from where it had landed on top of an amp and began picking up what remained of the plates. "Could have fooled me."

Constantine sat up. "Hey! That's my mess to clean up."

"Then you should have done it by now, shouldn't you?" Lep tossed the remains of the sandwiches onto the roof, where some bird or other would enjoy them. "I have news for you, none of it good. I talked to the dude who created the disturbance at the concert. Swore he hadn't planned it. He'd had one beer before the concert, and that was it. Apologized like crazy, said he didn't know what got into him.

Said he's been upset about stuff lately, but it wasn't like him to go ballistic. I think he was telling the truth."

Constantine hunched a shoulder again. "It was just an idea."

"Another thing—Janie who works in the fan club's been seen with Nathan once too often. She had dinner with him tonight. Think we should fire her?"

"Whatever." Constantine stood.

"You might want to stay sitting down," Lep said. "You haven't heard the worst yet."

"There's worse?"

"I got an email from Nathan," Lep said. "Not that I tend to believe what he says, but this had the ring of truth to it, and it was easily verified."

Constantine wiped the guitar dry. It might be salvageable, but he wasn't sure he cared. "Just tell me."

"The cop who beat me up in Baton Rouge," Lep said. "He was Marguerite's uncle."

"Her uncle."

"By marriage," Lep said, "which is probably why it took Nathan a while to find out. Marguerite's mother and his widow are sisters."

The last tiny spark of hope inside Constantine went abruptly out. He felt the bird ruffling its feathers, but it remained silent. Constantine got down on his hands and knees and mopped up the rest of the tea Marguerite had spilled, while Lep put the tray on the dumbwaiter and came back to gather the scattered CDs. Constantine swept the floor and put the broom and dustpan away.

There's a valid explanation, the bird said at last.

Maybe, maybe not, but that didn't change a thing. He needed to do anything but think—about this or anything else. He picked up another guitar. "Jam with me tonight, bro?"

～

Zeb crouched in the mud, anxious and shivering, until finally a fair-haired guy in a pale T-shirt and jeans hustled around the corner from the main drag. He slowed, peering into the empty park, then turned on a flashlight and poked around in a trash can. The van window came down, and the driver softly hailed him. The fair-haired dude went over to the van; the driver unfolded a large sheet of white paper in his gloved hands and shone a flashlight on it for the newcomer, who grinned and nodded and, after a few seconds' conversation, went around to the passenger door. The newcomer looked vaguely familiar; Zeb had seen him somewhere before, but—

No time to think about it. Zeb scuttled across the road and lifted himself onto the bike rack as the passenger slammed the door shut. Better prepared this time, he'd removed his T-shirt, using several layers of the fabric to cushion his hands from the metal rack. The van headed back across town, past the neighborhoods where Zeb and Eaton and Marguerite lived, past the university, out toward the Indian mounds. Zeb clung while the van rattled and bounced. Even with the T-shirt to protect him, every jolt hurt his hands, and his fingers ached from holding so tight. Where could they be headed? Maybe he was risking discovery for nothing. The bastard couldn't do anything with a stranger around.

The van bounded up past the mounds and kept on going, past the first picnic grounds, past the second, and pulled up at the third. The rain fell steadily, making plenty of noise, but still Zeb stepped down gently, at the same time as the driver and his passenger. His heart beat so hard he felt sick.

The driver clicked on a flashlight, shone it in front of the vehicle, and found the path he was looking for. "Come on."

Zeb crept sideways into the bushes to wait until they had gone a little way and then followed. He stretched his cramped fingers, biting his lip against the pain.

"Is it down here?" The new man was eager and excited, too loud for the rainy night.

"Hold this for me, will you?" The driver passed the flashlight to his passenger. His gloved hand pulled a hunting knife from a sheath on his belt, held it up in the light, admired its glint.

"Where—where are we going?" asked the other man, louder and uneasy now, but he didn't have time for more.

"To the River Styx." He stabbed his passenger casually, up under his ribs, and caught the flashlight as it fell. The man slumped to the ground, twitching, and Zeb, shaking in the shadows, barely managed to stifle a sob.

He had the proof he was waiting for. He knew what he needed to do, but he couldn't move. Could only crouch there, muffling his breathing, trying to slow the thudding of his heart. He didn't have a weapon, but even if he did, would he have the guts?

He didn't think so.

The murderer waited calmly until the man was still, rolled him onto his side, pulled the knife out, and without even wiping it, restored it to its sheath. He clicked off the light and returned to the van. Jesus, was he going to leave the guy lying in the dirt? Well, why not? Unbelievably, it seemed he really had killed poor old Pauline, and he'd left her at the side of the road and then run over her for good measure. But no, he was leaning into the front seat, doing something . . . He emerged folding a sheet of paper, and then folded it even smaller until it fit tightly in a back pocket of his victim's jeans. With a grunt he picked the guy up and threw him over his shoulder.

Zeb pulled on his T-shirt and followed the killer down the path through the woods, his faculties strangely focused and clear. Obviously, the body was to be dumped in the river. It might drift for miles and miles, or get caught on a branch or a rock close by. Probably there was no saving the poor bastard now, but Zeb had to make sure. And whether the guy was dead or alive, he had to find out what had been planted in that pocket. He must not hesitate, and more important, he must not get caught.

He slid along the edge of the path in almost total darkness, keeping well behind. The killer made plenty of noise up ahead, stepping on twigs and crunching leaves as if nothing mattered. A grunt sounded, followed by a splash, and Zeb retreated hurriedly into the trees. He did not shake, he scarcely breathed, and the murderer sauntered by, shining the light ahead of him, scraping his boots on the gravel as he passed. Why not? No one would ever suspect him or examine his boots. He shone his flashlight casually around, then up toward the sky, and with a smile contemplated the raindrops in the shaft of light.

He got into the van and drove away, and Zeb picked through the trees to the water. The body flickered and rolled downriver, almost at the bend, the guy's pale T-shirt ballooning above the water. Zeb plunged in and let the current take him.

～

For a few brief seconds, Marguerite wallowed in Ophelia's sympathetic hug. Then she wiped her eyes, blew her nose, and went onto the back porch to talk to Gideon, who was painting an old wooden chair a vibrant orange, attended by a couple of lazing German shepherds. He waved her to a deck chair.

When she explained about the missing sketch pad with the sketch of her dream, Gideon's mouth twitched. "Interesting, but I'm not sure how it fits in."

"Neither am I." The dog with the blond curls bounded up the steps, followed closely by Lawless. The German shepherds roused enough to sniff the newcomer and then flopped to the deck again. "I tried to get Reuben to tell Constantine, but he refused. He says Constantine doesn't want to talk to me."

Gideon rolled his eyes. "Constantine called a bit ago, asking me to put all available resources into locating Zeb Bonnard and bringing him to the Impractical Cat."

Marguerite stood. "Don't! Constantine will beat him up to get information."

Gideon shook his head. "I don't claim to understand what goes on inside Constantine's mind, but he wouldn't ask me to bring him someone he was planning to beat up."

She swallowed. That made sense, not that she would trust Constantine an inch after this.

"Matter of fact, he told me the kid needs protection."

Marguerite would have preferred to find fault with everything Constantine did, but instead she nodded reluctantly. "Yes. He does."

"Unfortunately, after taking turns with Constantine's people to keep an eye on him all day, we lost him. Any idea where he might have gone, apart from home?"

She shook her head. Now that Gideon knew about Zeb, she had no reason on earth not to tell him everything. "What's really bothering me is the torture porn."

Gideon's paintbrush stopped dead. "Say what?"

She sat down again and told him all about it, both the incident with Zeb and later with Constantine and the backpack, and showed him the porn. "Constantine's convinced I already knew about this garbage. He said I was destroying evidence on purpose. He thinks I'm—I don't know what he thinks. I tried to explain, but he wouldn't listen." Her lip quivered. She took a deep breath. "Anyway, what's really significant is that Pauline's husband tied her up and tortured her a couple of times before she finally got away from him. This kind of picture would have brought it all back. It would have terrified her."

"Terrified her into killing herself?"

"Sure, if she saw it as a threat! She'd had nightmares for years and suffered from crippling depression, and she was doing better, but this might have caused a huge setback." She felt tears prickle again and bit her lip. "Why didn't she tell me or someone else she knew? And if she'd already decided to kill herself, why would she put the porn in an envelope she knew I would open up? I wondered if the murderer had done it, but that doesn't make sense either, if he wanted her death to look like an overdose."

Gideon studied the printouts for a long moment and set them down. He dipped his brush into the orange paint and laid it on with smooth strokes. "You say you picked up the envelope and put it in your backpack *before* her body was found?" Marguerite nodded. "Did anyone else have an opportunity to add something to the envelope?"

"I carry my backpack with me all the time, so that wouldn't be easy. Who am I supposed to suspect? Constantine? Not such a bad idea. Tit for tat, the jerk." She was practically spitting with rage again, but that was better than crying. "Sorry. I'm usually pretty much in control, but I've never been so mad in my life as I was at Constantine, and just thinking about it makes me want to throw things again." She took another deep breath. "Tony Karaplis? He's a close friend. He wouldn't do something like that. Neither would my friend Lavonia." She crossed her arms, sat back in the chair, and fumed.

Gideon's restful aura matched the easy strokes of the brush. He sure got the prize for calm. After a while, he asked, "Was the backpack at your place when the intruder came?"

She pondered. "No, it was in my car both times. I left it there during the concert, and I forgot to take it indoors the next evening after I went clubbing. Constantine left my car by the side of the road when he came to find me, and Jabez brought it over to Janie's place, and the car was empty and unlocked for a while, but it was in such a random spot that

. . . It's really not likely someone found it and planted the porn."

"So let's assume Pauline left those pictures as a message to you. The question is, what kind of message?"

She felt herself pale. "A warning?"

"Could be." Imperturbable as ever, he finished the chair and wiped the remaining paint on a newspaper, then capped the can. "Maybe so you would understand why she killed herself. On the other hand, maybe she saw letting you know as her only hope of seeing justice served and whoever threatened her caught and punished."

"And prevented from hurting anyone else," Marguerite agreed softly. "But the porn doesn't prove anything. She took her own meds, and there was no sign of a struggle . . ."

"Maybe it does prove something, and we just haven't figured out what. Let's go indoors for some good light."

They spread the pictures on a desk, and Gideon took out a magnifying glass. "You see those little blue dots an inch apart in a vertical line on the same place on every page? Even when there are colors covering them, you can sometimes see them with the magnifying glass."

"Printer cartridge leak," Marguerite said.

"Yep," Gideon grinned. "I wonder if the ones Reuben took to Constantine are the same."

"You think these pics are what the intruder really wanted both times?"

"Seems like the sketch pad was just a bonus," Gideon said. "How many people knew about the sketch?"

"Only a few—Tony Karaplis and my girlfriend Lavonia. But if the porn was all he wanted, why didn't he search right after he killed Pauline?" She answered her own question.

"Maybe he thought a break-in would call attention to the fact that it wasn't a suicide. Or maybe he didn't care at first whether it was found, because he hadn't noticed that the printer cartridge had a leak." Pause. "But once he knew, why not just change the cartridge so no one would know he printed them?"

"Maybe something else is out there, something that was printed on the same machine and could be traced to him."

"Or to Roy Lutsky, so he planted porn in Roy's office."

"Constantine will talk to me." Gideon got out his cell phone and made a call. Marguerite huddled into her chair and waited. Ophelia appeared in the doorway, carrying a cute baby girl with bright blue eyes and her father's dark hair.

"Hey, man," Gideon said. "I need to see those porn printouts Reuben brought you this morning." More waiting, and Gideon huffed. "Damn. I wanted to hold that over your head. What do you think?" More silence at this end, and suddenly Ophelia's fangs popped out. "Uh-oh," Gideon said but listened for a few seconds more. "Will do. Gotta go." He ended the call and said, "Calm down, Ophelia. This isn't your problem. Marguerite, he'd already noticed the blue dots and suggested we ask you who might share a printer with Dr. Lutsky. Think about it and let me know." He ambled away to clean up the paintbrush.

Ophelia led Marguerite into the kitchen. "What Constantine really said, in the most sarcastic way possible, was that since you seem so closely connected with everybody in this case, including the murderer, Gideon should interrogate you properly."

"Thanks for eavesdropping for me," Marguerite said. Vampire hearing came in handy at times, even if it was to learn horrible news. She took a grubby tissue from her pocket and blew her nose. Then the baby smiled at her, and she couldn't hold back the tears.

"Actually, it's a good sign," Ophelia said, handing her a full box of tissues. "He wouldn't bother being sarcastic if he wasn't on the defensive. He then did a 180-degree turn and told Gideon to warn you not to trust anybody, especially people you know."

"So why didn't Gideon warn me?"

"Because he thinks that in your current mood, you're more likely to do the opposite of what Constantine says."

"I may be furious at him, but I'm not an idiot."

"They're guys," Ophelia said. "We have to humor them." She settled Marguerite at the kitchen table with a cup of jasmine tea, sat across from her, and put her baby to the breast. "It's not my favorite brew, but my sister swears by it for the crossed in love. Or sex. Which is it?"

"I hardly know him," Marguerite said, "so I don't see how it can be love. And although the sex was exciting, and I wanted to do it again . . ." *And I could feel his pleasure, and it was so beautiful.* She grimaced. "I guess, when all's said and done, it was just sex." She took a sip of tea so she wouldn't start crying *again.*

Ophelia shifted the nursing baby more comfortably on her arm and said nothing.

"At least I remembered to ask him to use a condom," Marguerite said glumly.

"That says a lot for your presence of mind," Ophelia said. "He didn't just steamroll you into it."

Quite the contrary, but she wasn't about to get into the whole bizarre scenario with the birds. "I've never really been interested in sex. Growing up with all that porn around me made it seem sort of blah, and the actual experience wasn't that much better, so I'd given up on it." She tried to smile. "I guess you wouldn't understand, being a vampire."

"I can't relate to it being blah, but I gave up on it for a while because I kept ending up with jerks and crazies. I was a mess by the time Gideon came along."

"He seems like such a stable, easygoing guy," Marguerite said politely, although there was no seeming about it; Gideon's aura confirmed it. The house wasn't cold like Lavonia's, but she cupped her hands around the warm mug as if it could chase away the chill in her heart. "Until I met Constantine, my plan was to wait until I fell in love before having sex again."

"Ah."

"I figured if the sex wasn't interesting, at least love would be there to give it purpose, whether affection and connection or children or whatever." Oh, crap, she was crying again. She reached for another tissue.

"Maybe you're in love with Constantine, and you don't know it," Ophelia said. "Or you aren't ready to admit it. Or maybe you only wish you were in love with him. Or wish you weren't."

"All of the above," Marguerite said. "I've never been so confused in my life."

Ophelia's smile was all sympathy. "You're overwrought and in no shape to judge. You've gone through a lot of weird stuff in the last few days. Given a little time, you'll sort it out."

"Maybe I don't need to, seeing as I'm not associating with him anymore." Marguerite blew her nose again. "At least now my days of media persecution are limited." As the light at the end of the tunnel, this didn't seem nearly as bright as she would have expected.

Ophelia grinned sympathetically. "You have to understand that . . . well, Constantine is hopeless at relationships."

"No, duh."

"Even as a friend he keeps his distance." She took a sip of her own tea. "But he's completely solid and loyal, and ruthless when it comes to protecting people he cares about." She cocked her head to one side. "Even those he doesn't care about. He's obsessed with protecting the weak and helpless, and he hates himself when something goes wrong."

"Like those concerts where people were killed. He feels responsible."

Ophelia's brows rose, and her aura confirmed her surprise. "He told you that?"

"Sort of." She wasn't about to get into details, no matter how sympathetic the listener. Ophelia's aura was busy now, as it had been outdoors when she was deciding what to do about Reuben. Marguerite shook her head. "We shouldn't discuss him further. I don't want to jeopardize your friendship with him." Her voice trembled toward the end of the sentence. "Thanks for the tea, but I should go now."

Sympathy bloomed in Ophelia's aura. "I know you're feeling rotten, but this isn't the right moment to give up. I'll tell you what I know about him, and then you can decide whether he's worth working on." The baby let go of the breast. Ophelia lifted her, and she promptly belched and gave another of those goofy baby smiles. "We don't believe in giving up easily, do we, precious?"

Marguerite frowned. "Maybe he'd rather you didn't talk to me about him."

Ophelia snorted. "Oh, no, honey. In the first place, there are so many rumors cooking about the man that a little truth now and then will be lost in the soup, and in the second place, I promise you he wants me to talk to you."

"Did he tell you that?" Marguerite wanted to slap herself for sounding so hopeful.

"No, but you're the only woman he's slept with in I don't know how long. He must like you a lot, and he doesn't take to people easily, so that's really saying something. And if he's been trying to talk about stuff that matters, it's saying even more."

"Maybe he used to like me, but he's decided he can't trust me, and now he won't even talk to me. But what hurts most," Marguerite added, stirred to anger again, "is that I thought I'd finally found someone who believed me. Someone who wouldn't shun me or freak out or . . ." She sucked in a deep breath.

Ophelia's brows drew together. "Freak out about what?"

Marguerite swallowed some tea. "Oh, what the hell." If anyone understood keeping secrets, it was a vampire. "It's because I see auras," she said. "Don't tell anyone."

"I won't." Ophelia put the baby on the other breast. "So?"

"I can tell a lot about what people are feeling by what's going on in their auras." Ophelia didn't flinch at that, so she added, "I don't usually tell people because it causes more trouble than it's worth. I explained it to Constantine, and he said it was cool, but I could see he didn't like it much, and . . ."

She explained about Roy Lutsky and the incident in the restaurant.

Ophelia gave a whoop of laughter, the startled baby released the nipple and let out a wail, and breast milk sprayed across the table. Still chuckling, Ophelia calmed the baby and finally got her back on the breast.

Marguerite took a napkin and wiped the table. "Reuben told Constantine, but Constantine didn't tell me he knew until after we made love. He twisted everything I've done to protect him, like telling that reporter we were having tantric sex, saying it proves I'm a liar and therefore untrustworthy, when the last thing I would *ever* do is tell Lutsky *anything* about having sex with Constantine. I mean, you're a vampire and a close friend of his, and all I told you was that it was exciting. Would I be likely to give intimate details to a nut job like Lutsky?"

"Constantine expects people to kiss and tell. The biographies about him are full of it, and you must have heard what Jonetta said about him."

Dismay washed over Marguerite. Her childish response to Constantine must have reminded him a lot of Jonetta, reinforcing his decision to get rid of her. "I got so upset that I completely lost it. I screamed and threw a tray with plates and iced tea across the room."

Ophelia shrugged. "It happens." She flushed, both face and aura. "Even with easygoing guys."

"Not to me! I don't know what got into me, but I hope I didn't ruin anything. There was iced tea dripping down one of his guitars."

"Serves him right," Ophelia said. "When did Constantine talk to you about the concerts? Before or after Reuben told him about Professor Lutsky?"

"After."

"Which means he still wanted to trust you, even after he knew. Trusting you made him vulnerable, though, which scared him." She nodded sagely. "He's sure he can't maintain a relationship, so he destroyed it before it destroyed him."

This sounded a lot like psychobabble to Marguerite, but she refrained from saying so. "Do you know anything about his childhood?"

"Not much," Ophelia said. "He doesn't talk about it, but something happened to Constantine when he was very young, before he came to New Orleans. Tony Karaplis has known him since he was eight or nine, and he's always been like this. He doesn't trust anybody, not really. He's pretty close to Tony, and he relies on Lep more than anyone, but deep down he's afraid of something. Betrayal, maybe? Or abandonment? I don't know what it is, but it's shaped his character. If you care about him, you'll just have to live with that. There may always be a degree of separation, no matter what." Pause. "Not that there isn't always one, because a couple is still made up of two people, but it may be greater than you'd like. But you don't seem like the clingy type."

"I'm not." But she needed to be trusted. She needed to be *believed.* She shook her head again. "After what happened today, it's hard to imagine being with him again."

The baby had fallen asleep at Ophelia's breast. She smiled lovingly down at it. "And here I was hoping you two would make some gorgeous babies together."

"I'm not making a baby with any man who's lovey-dovey one minute and cold as ice the next." Marguerite's brain was beginning to clear. "You may be right about his fear of relationships, but that's not what was going on today. We were having fun. He wanted to have sex again and went downstairs for condoms. He was gone for quite a while—way longer than it should have taken—and he came back looking completely wrung out." A spark of hope fluttered into life. What if something had happened while he was gone? "All the arousal in his aura had vanished. The warmth and enjoyment were gone, too. His aura was flat and harsh, and the colors were ugly, and then he fed me all that crap."

Ophelia frowned, her aura perplexed. "You can really see all that?"

"Yes, I can. You have every right to be suspicious," she said belligerently.

"Am I suspicious?" Ophelia looked down at herself as if she expected to see tendrils of mistrust growing from her belly. She laughed. "One of these days, you'll have to tell me all about myself, but if I'm suspicious now, it's not of you. I have plenty of weird abilities of my own." Her aura was busy again. "It's of this whole situation. Something must have happened while he was gone that made him change his mind."

"That's just what I was wondering!" The spark of hope became a tiny, wavering candle. Marguerite thought back, remembering the faint sound of Lawless freaking out, but that had been over almost immediately, and they hadn't returned for a good while after that. "Once he'd started dissing me, and I was getting good and irate, his aura relaxed. He seemed sort of smug."

Ophelia's fangs slotted down, then disappeared again. "Sorry. Just getting mad on your behalf."

"Smug's not the right word. Satisfied, maybe." No, that wasn't it either. "Relieved!"

"Well, duh," Ophelia said. "What could be more obvious? Something happened to upset and really, really worry him. He wanted you out of the way, no longer associated with him, and therefore safe. He got rid of you to protect you. That explains why, after trying to maintain the distance by pretending to Gideon that he really suspected you of something, he couldn't stop himself from also asking him to warn you."

"Maybe," Marguerite said, wanting and yet not wanting to hope, exhausted in spite of napping half the day. She rubbed her eyes. If she didn't leave soon, she would fall asleep on the drive to New Orleans.

"There's no maybe about it. Gideon!" She left the room, and Marguerite laid her head on the table and closed her eyes.

Ophelia came back several minutes later. "Proof!"

Marguerite roused at this.

"Reuben's gone," Ophelia said. "He was supposed to make sure you went to New Orleans, and when you didn't, he reported that you were here, at which point Constantine said he could go. Constantine doesn't want you staying home alone, but he's fine if you're here. He does care about you."

"He cares about everyone who's endangered," Marguerite said, ruthlessly snuffing the candle. "He doesn't want to be responsible for my death, but the fact remains that he won't even speak to me."

Ophelia flapped a hand. "I'm going to give him a good talking to."

"Please don't, or at least not on my account. He didn't love his wife, but he cut her a lot more slack than he cut me."

"He spoke to you about Jonetta?"

Marguerite nodded wearily.

"Even more proof! He never tells anybody about her. He wouldn't even talk to me. He must be absolutely crazy about you!"

The candle within burst into glorious life. She tried to snuff it again and failed. She was in terrible shape if she still wanted a guy who'd treated her like dirt. Why couldn't he have just told her what was wrong?

"Once this is over, we'll sort him out. In the meantime, you're staying here. Policeman's orders. You're unfit to drive tonight."

Marguerite let herself be shown to the spare bedroom. She showered and crawled thankfully into bed.

CHAPTER SEVENTEEN

The body drifted up against a snag a mile or so down-river, a ghastly pale face with blank staring eyes and gaping mouth. Zeb swallowed and forced the vomit back down his throat. He retrieved the folded paper and stuffed it in his own back pocket, then kicked the body off the snag and sent it away again downstream. He followed it for what seemed like hours, guiding it past dozens more snags before letting it go, hoping it would get washed a mile or two further before another dead tree across the river held it. He waded and swam and waded again across to the other bank, and slogged upriver in the shallower water. It didn't seem likely the cops would canvas the entire river for footprints; anyway, his shoes were new and could belong to anyone who ran.

On the way down the river, he had figured out where to go. Zelda's Aunt Ophelia, who was a landscaper, lived some-where along the river, but she also owned some property on the water a short way upriver from her house. There was a big new greenhouse and an old trailer. Zelda had taken him there once to take pictures of the bat houses along the bank, when he'd needed visual aids for a public speaking class at school.

By the time he spied the bat houses on their poles, the first desultory birdsong before dawn had already begun. He pulled himself out of the water by the roots of a cypress, thankful for more drenching rain. With luck, what footprints he left would be washed away, and Ophelia wouldn't visit her greenhouse. The pathway he'd followed with Zelda was somewhat overgrown now but still passable. It was beginning to be light; he threw off the exhaustion that threatened him and hurried, smudging his footprints as he went just in case. It seemed longer than before, but eventually the greenhouse loomed, and then he was at the trailer. To one side there were woods, and to the other a couple of houses, but no lights showed yet in the windows. He found the key to the back door in the same metal box under the stairs where Zelda had left it. He fumbled in the gloom with the lock, opened the door, and went inside. He didn't dare use the lights for fear the neighbors would notice, but it didn't matter. He was safe for now.

The moment he relaxed, he was sick as hell. He groped his way to the bathroom, fell to his knees before the toilet, and it all came up. Not that there was much in there, but he retched and retched anyway. Finally, he got to his feet and flushed. He took the folded paper out of his pocket and set it aside to read when he had some light. He peeled off his clothes and propped himself in the shower. By some miracle, the water was hot. Maybe Ophelia showered here from time to time when working in the greenhouse, but whatever the reason for this blessing, Zeb gave thanks. He stood under the water for ages, trying to think what to do next.

By the time he got out of the shower, it was daylight. He dried himself with a towel from the rack, rinsed his clothes and shoes, and hung them over the shower rail.

Dizzy with fatigue, he took the paper to a window. The thick paper had weathered the soaking well, and so had the charcoal sketch on it. He had no difficulty recognizing Constantine and Marguerite—and not only that, Marguerite's drawing style. Tired as he was, he still snickered at the ridiculous length of the penis. He laid the sketch on the towel to dry and looked for someplace to crash. All he needed was a few hours' sleep, and his brain would start working again, and he'd figure out what to do.

Astonishingly, he found a bed in the room at the end of the trailer. Maybe all this unexpected comfort was an omen; on the other hand, maybe he was making himself a sitting duck. At this point, he just didn't care. He sagged onto the thin cotton bedspread and fell immediately into an exhausted sleep.

∾

Constantine finally packed it in an hour or two after dawn. Agony had its uses; working together, he and Lep had come up with some truly excellent songs during the night. He should probably feel more of a sense of accomplishment, but numbness would have to do. Lep yawned and headed down to the kitchen for something to eat, and Constantine retired to the bed, which smelled of sex and Marguerite. He shut his eyes and willed himself to sleep.

His cell phone woke him. He turned away and put a pillow over his head, but it rang again a few minutes later. Groaning, he reached for it. *Gideon.*

The cop didn't waste time on preliminaries. "Do you have an alibi for last night and this morning?"

Huh? "What's up?"

"From the time Marguerite left you till, say, eight A.M.?"

"Lep was with me," Constantine said. "He came up shortly after she left, and we jammed all night."

"Thank God for that," Gideon said. "Someone stabbed Nathan Bone and threw him in the river during the night."

"Jesus Christ." Then: "Is Marguerite all right?"

"When I left home, she was asleep in my spare bedroom," Gideon said. "I'll tell her you asked."

"Don't! She's better off hating me. She's got to stay away from me. I cannot risk having her death on my account, too."

"She doesn't hate you," Gideon said. "I'd say this was another attempt to implicate you, but how could he have known whether you would be alone?"

How indeed?

"Nathan said on his blog yesterday that you had threatened him," Gideon said.

"No, I warned him that his anonymous informant might be dangerous." Constantine sighed. "He had no idea who he was playing with."

Gideon's voice sharpened. "And you do?"

"Yes and no," Constantine said. "I think I know who did it, but I don't know his name."

"Say *what?*"

"I'm doing my best to remember, but it's from a long time ago. When you're done with the cop stuff, come and see me."

Constantine lay back. Time to dredge up the childhood memories he'd been keeping at bay all his life.

∾

Marguerite tossed and turned for hours, finally falling asleep as the birds began to sing before dawn. She roused briefly at the sound of a phone ringing and later to the baby's cries, but she didn't wake properly till past noon. She showered and dressed, and found Ophelia at the kitchen table drawing a garden plan, complete with meandering pathways and a bridge.

"For a customer?" Marguerite said.

"I hope so," Ophelia said. "They may not go for it. It's going to be pricey." She gave Marguerite a look. "Pour yourself a coffee. There's news."

Judging by the expression on Ophelia's face, not to mention her uneasy aura, it wasn't good. "What?"

"Somebody stabbed that reporter, Nathan Bone, and threw him in the river last night."

"Oh my god. Poor Nathan." Pause. "Is Constantine all right?" Her heart battered her chest. "They're not going to pin this on him, are they?"

"The media will do their best, but he was with Lep all night," Ophelia said. "Unless there's some real evidence against him, he'll be okay."

Marguerite poured a coffee and dropped into a seat at the table. "Nathan was pretty horrible, but he didn't deserve this. Does Gideon have any idea who did it?"

"Not as far as I know, but there's a kid called Zeb who's mixed up in all this, and he's gone missing."

"No." Marguerite shook her head. "Zeb didn't do this. He's a good kid."

"Gideon said the police and the underworld were taking turns keeping him under surveillance, but he slipped his leash last night and never came home. This morning his father called every one of Zeb's friends he could think of, got nowhere, and reported him missing." She rubbed out a cypress tree and drew it again. "Seems like an overreaction to me. Maybe the kid was partying someplace all night and fell asleep there. On the other hand, my niece is one of his friends, and she's worried he's suicidal."

"Al—that's his dad—usually has a cool head, but he's been worried about Zeb lately, too. So have I, but regardless, he's not capable of killing somebody."

Ophelia's aura fluttered strangely. Without looking up from drawing a semicircle of shrubs on the garden plan, she said, "Everyone's capable of it."

Marguerite watched the flutter resolve itself and fade from the vampire's aura. Interesting, but none of her business. "In self-defense, maybe, or to save someone else, but this sounds like cold-blooded murder. Anyway, what motive would he have? I'm a more likely candidate than he is."

"Luckily, you were here all night," Ophelia said. "Do you have any idea where he might have gone?"

"None," Marguerite said. "He could be holed up almost anyplace. His friends wouldn't rat on him, and I think he has some keys that he shouldn't." He probably had a key to her place, come to think of it, because he'd taken care of Lawless once when she and Pauline had both been out of town. But he hadn't been the one to do the break-ins. He had no reason, and he wouldn't hurt Lawless. "I have to go to the office for a while. Can I leave my dog here? I'm not allowed to bring him into university buildings on weekdays."

"No problem. Gideon said don't be surprised if someone seems to be shadowing you. The media are back in hordes, and the underworld people have their hands full, but they'll keep an eye on you if they can."

"How am I supposed to know whether the person shadowing me is friend or foe?" Marguerite said.

Ophelia snorted. "Beats me." Painstakingly, she filled in a pathway with flagstones.

"Or whether they suspect me of collusion with the murderer?"

Compassion suffused the vampire's aura, and she glanced up briefly. "It sucks, doesn't it? Believe me, I can relate. Gideon suspected me of murder once." Her eyes were back on the drawing. "I don't think he seriously suspects you, but there's obviously some connection between you and the murderer. Maybe they think by keeping an eye on you, they'll find him. Anyway, Gideon says stick to public places and don't trust anyone."

Feeling more alone than ever, Marguerite finished her coffee and left.

～

"That's his T-shirt," said a female voice. "He must be here someplace." It was Zelda. "Please be okay. Please don't be dead."

Fuck. Not again.

"Here he is," said Juma. "Zeb, what the hell are you doing here?"

"As long as he's alive, it doesn't matter," Zelda said. "Jeez! He's butt naked!"

"Guys with butts like that," Juma said, "*should* be naked."

"For all the female world to gaze upon," Zelda agreed, and then her tone shifted. "Zeb, are you all right? We've been so worried!"

Zeb groaned, groped for the bedspread, and wrapped it around himself. He tried to open his eyes, and the events of last night crashed into him. He sat up, clutching the bedspread, and forced his eyelids unstuck. "Yeah. Sure." He ran his hands through his hair. "I'm fine. What time is it?"

"It's almost seven P.M.," Zelda said.

Christ. He'd slept the whole day away. He should have been up and heading into town hours ago.

"You don't look fine," Juma said. "That's blood on the bedspread. You're bleeding!"

One of the rips on his palm had opened again. "Yeah, I cut myself last night."

"Everybody's searching for you," Zelda said. "Your dad's been calling everywhere. He even went to the cops. We tried all the usual places, and then I thought of here as a last resort, although I couldn't imagine why you'd—"

Panic roiled up. "My dad's not here, is he?"

"No, but I'm going to call him right now." Zelda whipped out her phone.

Zeb leapt off the bed and grabbed it. "No!"

Both girls gaped at him, although it was hard to say whether they were more focused on his privates or his behavior. He glared at Juma. "Don't you dare call him either. Or text him."

"No problem, dude." She put up her hands as if he'd pointed a gun at her, and he felt himself flush. "You know me better than that."

"Let me get dressed." He stalked off down the hall, still gripping Zelda's phone. If he hadn't been so freaked, he would feel ridiculous.

Zelda was close behind, doubtless butt-watching to her vampire heart's content. "If my mother thought I was missing, I'd call her first thing. She drives me crazy, but I couldn't *stand* having her worried about me."

"My mother is dead, and my father's just pretending to care." He had to pee. "Do you mind?" He glared at her and went ahead, and she had the grace to roll her eyes and leave the bathroom. He splashed his face and rinsed his mouth, then pulled on his still-damp underwear and stuck his head into the hall. At least he was thinking straight now. "I need to talk to Constantine."

Zelda and Juma exchanged glances.

"What's wrong?" Zeb took his shorts off the shower rail. "Yesterday, you were ecstatic when I said I'd talk to him."

"Yesterday, you ran away," Zelda retorted.

"It's life or death now." It had been life or death yesterday, too, if only he'd known. He pulled on his shorts. "Did you come here by car? Is Constantine at the Impractical Cat?"

"Yes, but it's surrounded by news people and fans," Juma said. "This reporter dude was stabbed to death and dumped in the river last night, and some people are trying to blame it on Constantine."

"A *reporter?*" Zeb zipped his fly. Now he knew why the dude had looked familiar; he was the one who'd taken pictures of Marguerite at the Merkin. "That makes no sense."

"Unfortunately, it does," Juma said. "The reporter's been printing awful stuff about him, and about his new girlfriend, too."

"He didn't do it," Zeb said flatly.

"We know that!" Zelda said. "Constantine would never do such a clumsy job. If he had killed the guy, the body would never have been found. Not that I approve of murder, mind you."

"Sometimes it's necessary," Zeb said, flat and sure.

Zelda stilled. "You're reminding me of Constantine again." Even Juma's cynical eyes widened a little.

"I wish," Zeb said. But he didn't have Constantine's savvy or guts, and meanwhile the old man might be dreaming up new ways to wreak havoc. He reached for his T-shirt.

"What's this?" Juma picked up the drawing Zeb had laid on the towel hours and hours earlier. How could he have slept so long? "Whoa. This is a drawing of Constantine and some girl."

Zeb pulled on his T-shirt. Planting the sketch on the reporter seemed like an attempt to implicate Constantine, but why? The bastard's twisted mind might be bursting with reasons to harm Lutsky, or even Eaton Wilson or Pauline. But why would he care one way or another about Constantine?

"That's one bizarro penis." Zelda made a face. "She seems to be enjoying it, but it looks like some weird sort of bondage to me."

"It's clearly symbolic," Juma said loftily. "Where'd it come from, Zeb?"

"It doesn't matter." He put his sneakers on without bothering with his still-soggy socks and reached for the paper.

Juma backed away, holding it over her head. "Tell us."

"Give it to me. This isn't a game."

"Then don't keep us in the dark," Zelda said. "We're only trying to help."

"If you really mean that, do what I ask. Take me to the Cat and get me in to see Constantine." But Juma danced away, so he grabbed her wrist and squeezed.

She yelped and dropped the paper. "You jerk!" she said. "That hurt! Forget the ride. Forget the sex thing, too. You're not my kind of guy."

He folded the paper carefully and returned it to his pocket. "Juma, this is a life-or-death situation. Whether or not you want to have sex with me doesn't matter."

"I think we should do what Zeb says," Zelda said. "I think if we don't, we'll regret it. Anyway, he's stronger than both of us. He could overpower you, get the car keys, and just leave. If he did, would you call the cops on him? Because I wouldn't."

"No," Juma said in a pissy voice, "but shouldn't we know what we're getting into?"

"I'll tell you on the way into town," Zeb said, moving down the narrow hallway to the kitchen. He peered out the front window of the trailer: no one in sight. He'd have to risk being seen by the neighbors. "But you have to promise to believe me."

They exchanged glances again. "Sure," they said in unison. That didn't give him a lot of confidence, but at least he now had a ride.

He got into the backseat. "Is that iced coffee? Great." He took Juma's cup and drank the contents in one ecstatic swallow. "Jeez, I'm hungry. Take me to the first fast-food place you see."

Juma started the car, turned onto the road, and said, "About the paper. Tell us."

"The murderer planted it in the pocket of the dead reporter," Zeb said. He slouched low in the backseat, ready to sink out of sight if necessary. "He's trying to frame Constantine."

Zelda frowned. "How do you know?"

"I witnessed the murder," he said.

They both turned. Zelda went white behind her freckles, Juma stark against her raven hair.

"Wow," Juma said, facing the road again. "I apologize, dude."

"Who did it?" Zelda demanded. "My Aunt Ophelia is married to a cop, and he's a really great guy, and he and Constantine are friends. We could—"

"No. My dad's already been to the cops, so they'll be on his side," Zeb said. "I have to speak to Constantine. I should have gone to him ages ago. I would have, if I'd known . . ." Maybe he had known, deep down, what the old man was capable of. Maybe he'd just refused to see it. To see what the old man had done before and would do again.

Finally, Zeb let the knowledge he'd been holding at bay for months take root in his mind. He let himself *think* it. *Accept* it.

My father is insane. He will never get better.

And the truth he'd been dreading for the last few days:

My father is a murderer.

Astonishingly, allowing these thoughts into his mind, letting himself admit them, gave him a huge rush of relief.

"Once I've talked to Constantine," Zeb said, "he can decide what to do about the cops."

"Okay," Zelda said stoutly. "Constantine it is."

"Who did it, Zeb?" Juma asked.

"You have to promise to believe me," he said again. "You have to promise you'll still help me even if you don't. And you have to promise to buy me a burger, because I don't have a penny on me."

"We will," Zelda said. "You're our friend forever. You know that."

Zeb took a deep breath and told them.

~

Constantine propped himself on a stool and strummed a few chords. "Let me tell you a tale."

"Jesus," Lep said, slouching on the couch and closing his eyes.

Gideon stood by the window, looking down at the crowds outside the Impractical Cat. The sun was going down. "This is a fucking murder case," he growled. "I need to get back out there and *do* something."

"Such as what?" Lep said. "Kowtow to the chief?"

"Pretty much," Gideon said disgustedly. "He wants to know which upstanding citizen I'm going to pick on this time." He glowered at Constantine and lowered himself to the couch. "You realize, don't you, that you can't just off the guy once you find him? We need solid proof, preferably a confession, or this will never go away."

Constantine nodded; no use explaining to Gideon that catching and killing the Enemy would be almost impossible.

You're not five years old anymore, the bird said. At the moment it was occupying a red-tailed hawk.

He sure felt like a five-year-old, after spending the day trying to recall the terror that had shaped his life.

I approve of this killing. The guide often took over a hawk, but for once it sounded like a true bird of prey. *One hundred percent.*

"Uh, thanks," Constantine said out loud and realized the others were staring, Lep in reluctant understanding, Gideon plain harassed.

Take advantage of his weakness, the hawk said. *Drive him out from cover. Go in for the kill.* Constantine strummed a few chords and began to play.

"Once upon a time there was a land of desert and holy mountains, with a sky of a zillion stars. In the shadow of those mountains and under those stars, there lived a Navajo girl who had a thing for white boys." Disgust laced his voice. "Dumb, but no dumber than all the white girls who want to play with Indians." He plucked a few melancholy sequences, then stilled the strings. "I wish this didn't have to come out. My mother's shame is not my story, not something I have the right to tell." He sent his two friends some images: a hogan against a mountain, some sheep and a scruffy dog, and a pretty young Navajo girl, all under a star-encrusted sky.

Accompanying himself again, he went on. "Against the wishes of everyone who cared about her, she married a guy from New Orleans, name of Dufray. Now, Dufray was a druggie, entirely under the thumb of his so-called friend and supplier, a dude known as Bon-Bon because of all the pretty little pills he made and sold." His fingers slid down the strings in a discordant ripple, and he sent his listeners memories of a bleak highway against a dusty backdrop, with plastic milk cartons and other trash littering the roadside, and a convenience store that sold cigarettes individually. "Bon-Bon was a good-looking guy." Or so he'd been told; all he remembered was a beard and dark, cruel eyes. "The Indian girl ended up in his bed instead of her husband's. Her father, who was a shaman of sorts, knew his daughter's lover was an evil man and said so, but she was totally enamored and refused to leave him. She had two sons by Bon-Bon. She called the first one Constantine and the second one Benny."

Lep roused himself enough to open his eyes. "Dufray wasn't really your old man? You never told me that before. Never told me about this Bon-Bon dude either."

Constantine hunched a shoulder. "I never told anyone." For several minutes he messed with an unhappy riff, over and over again, remembering with pain, sending out images of his laughing little brother and his straight-backed old grandfather. "Dufray died when one of Bon-Bon's drug experiments went wrong. Constantine was a strange little boy, and when very young he showed signs of unusual abilities. He could plant thoughts in people's minds and make people see things that weren't really there. Constantine's grandfather, who was wise in the ways of magic, recognized what was happening. He explained to Constantine that while he should cultivate these abilities, he must keep them strictly secret, as the Navajo people would call him a skin-walker and try to kill him." He paused to pick out a spooky melody. "Lep's used to this woo-woo stuff, but it took him a while."

"Can't say I like it much myself," Gideon muttered.

A memory surfaced in Constantine of Marguerite taking mention of the spirit guide in stride. Ruthlessly, he quashed it.

"What in hell is a skinwalker?" Gideon asked.

"A Navajo witch," Constantine said. He tried to channel Marguerite's detached assessment of the paraphernalia on the mound. Not easy when explaining something that had impacted his whole, damned life. "In magical terms, some-one who cultivates and uses supernatural powers for evil. In social terms, someone who sacrifices family and clan for wealth."

"What a load of bull," Gideon said, and Constantine gave him a nod of thanks. Where this issue was concerned, he was grateful for any positive input.

He trickled out a slow, somber melody and centered himself again. "Constantine learned very quickly to keep a secret, but his mother couldn't stop herself from boasting to her lover about their son's abilities. Bon-Bon grew obsessed with the idea of such powerful magic. He wanted those abili-ties for himself. He questioned Constantine over and over, insisting that he teach him how to do magic, too. At five years old, Constantine couldn't have taught it even if he'd wanted to, which he didn't. The more Bon-Bon pushed, the more defiantly Constantine refused. His refusals upset his mother and enraged Bon-Bon. One day, Benny was sick, and his mother had to take him to the health service. The grandfather was away, so she left Constantine with Bon-Bon, promising to return the next day."

Terror avalanched into his mind and out into the room. "Fuck," Gideon said, putting his hands to his temples, and Lep drew a sharp breath.

Not. Enough. Control. "Sorry," Constantine said, sucking the fear back inside, forcing it through the guitar strings instead. A tangle of discordant notes came out. "I'll spare you a description of Bon-Bon's methods of coercion, but they included torture and hallucinogenic drugs. By the time Constantine escaped into the hills, where his grandfather found him, he was a very screwed-up kid."

Lep cursed, and Gideon gaped at him, and Constantine didn't try to laugh it off, didn't try to play, merely clutched the guitar for dear life, and sent images of an eagle, its wings sheltering the terrified boy. Rats appeared, marauders with sharp teeth, gnawing at the ropes that bound the boy, and then he was free. Let his audience make what they wanted of that. As far as Constantine remembered, it was literally true.

"The grandfather threatened to shoot Bon-Bon dead if he came near his daughter or her sons again, and he succeeded in driving him off the reservation. Bon-Bon swore to return and get his own back, but word by way of the gossip-vine said he was killed not long afterward in a drug deal gone bad. All was well for another couple of years, except that the new, not-really-improved Constantine wouldn't put up with crap from anybody. He made a point of scaring the shit out of anyone who got in his way, and even those who didn't, and pretty soon there were whispers about witchcraft in the family. To make a long story short, one day a sniper killed Benny and the grandfather but missed Constantine."

Gideon sucked in a breath. Lep bowed his head.

"Which proved the witchcraft theory, since Navajo witches gain their status by killing a close relative—preferably a sibling."

"That's crap, and you know it," Lep said.

"I'm still responsible for their deaths," Constantine said. "They wouldn't have died if it wasn't for me." He ignored Lep's huff and Gideon's frown. "The next day, Constantine and his mother left the res forever, left the desert and the mountains and the sky of a zillion stars." He played the melancholy tune of one of his old songs. "Since Dufray was his official father, she decided to go to New Orleans and contact his family there so the boy would have some relatives. Family mattered a lot to her, and there was no one else. The boy grew up in the music scene, toying with jazz and the blues, and then segued easily into his first hit. He became rich and powerful, in the way of Navajo witches, and lived happily ever after."

Bitterness welled up in him, rage, regret, and shame, and he gave thanks that Marguerite wasn't here, for she would see it all. "Until now, because it turns out Bon-Bon isn't dead after all. He must have paid someone to spread the word that he'd been killed . . . And now, he's here to get his revenge." He'd probably been around for ages. Years and years . . .

"And you know this how?" Gideon said, and Constantine gave thanks again because Marguerite would have tried to comfort him, told him it wasn't his fault, that he wasn't a skinwalker, that he hadn't meant to do harm. Lep was all business, and Gideon didn't care about anything but closing his murder case.

"I heard him in the parking lot last night. He was on the phone. I heard him laugh. I'd know that laugh anywhere. I still dream about it sometimes."

Gideon shook his head. "That's not evidence, man."

"It is for me," Constantine said. "But there's more. He was talking to some woman, and he said, 'It's bonbons for you!' Same thing he used to say to my mom. He had a thing for chocolates with cherry filling . . ." An idea toppled into his mind. "Lep, can you get in touch with the dude who made the disturbance again? See if anybody gave him some candy. Friend or stranger, doesn't matter."

Lep disappeared down the stairs, and Gideon said, "What's Bon-Bon's real name?"

"That's the problem. I've been trying to remember, but I'm not sure I ever knew."

"Humph," Gideon said. "You realize, don't you, that the candy may explain a lot. Your wife's murder, for one thing."

"Marguerite being drugged." Anger spiraled up at the thought of Bon-Bon anywhere near her, but Constantine tamped it down. He couldn't afford to care.

"The riots at all those concerts," Gideon said.

Hope, almost blinding in its power, washed through Constantine. Maybe he hadn't killed those fans after all.

But spiked candies didn't explain Jonetta's rages or the pain he'd caused her. She'd been paranoid about gaining weight, so she'd rarely touched sweets, and she'd had the same volatility everywhere, not just in Bayou Gavotte. Still, knowing he usually had control over his mind was far, far better than fearing he had none at all.

"Assuming there's some chemical that would get people worked up," he said, "but then gets metabolized pretty quickly . . ." He thought of Marguerite's mood swing just last night. She'd eaten a chocolate bonbon right in front of him, and there'd been other wrappers on the table. He leapt up and went for the trash. He found them near the top, put them on a paper towel, and gave them to Gideon. "Marguerite was eating chocolates wrapped in these just before she had her tantrum last night."

Gideon considered. "Seems the dude knew plenty about drugs way back when. He's had time to figure out a lot more by now, even dream up some new stuff, maybe under the cover of legal activity. A chemist, perhaps."

"Bon-Bon," Constantine said. "Bonnard, as in professor and acting head of Chemistry." Oh, fuck. "He's Zeb's dad."

CHAPTER EIGHTEEN

Marguerite made it to her office at Hellebore University, but she didn't get much done. Everyone seemed to be staring at her—secretaries, profs, students—and mingled with the eager—even greedy—interest in her notoriety were expressions of pity and suspicion. She got security to remove a reporter lounging in the hallway, locked herself in her office, and did some last-minute prep for the coming semester, but the feeling of being abandoned and alone just wouldn't go away.

Maybe she should stop feeling sorry for herself. She called Lavonia. "Feeling better today?"

"Much, much better," Lavonia practically chirped. "Guess what? Al stayed *all night* and took care of me. Wasn't that sweet of him? He never, ever spends the night. I guess we've reached a new level in our relationship. Isn't that great?"

"Uh, sure is," Marguerite said. Somehow, she couldn't visualize Al playing nursemaid, but stranger things had happened lately.

"Did you see the exhibit today? Get any shopping done?"

Oh, yeah. New Orleans. Last night seemed like weeks ago. "No, in the end I didn't go. I spent the night with a friend and slept in late."

"Well, it's a good thing you weren't alone at home. Did you hear? Constantine killed a reporter. If you'd been in town, he might have killed you instead."

Oh, for cripes sake. "Lavonia, I thought better of you. You're listening to all that hype again."

"There's more! Zeb has gone missing, and Al's worried out of his mind. And Janie quit her job and left town this morning. She didn't even say where she was going, just up and left." Pause. "Or she *said* she did. It was just an email to her boss and the coven." She gasped. "Oh my god. Maybe she's dead, too, like in my dream, and we don't know it yet!"

"Not likely. *I'm* not dead," Marguerite said, but nevertheless Janie's sudden exit unnerved her. She'd seen Janie with Nathan in the Merkin the other night. It might not be relevant, but she should call Gideon and let him know.

Her train of thought gave way to Lavonia's trembling voice. "Al's afraid Zeb's dead or, worse, that he's been influenced by Constantine and done something terrible. Or maybe he's even in Constantine's employ."

"Oh, come *on*, Lavonia," Marguerite said. "Doing what?"

"Committing murder for him," Lavonia whispered.

It took all of Marguerite's self-control not to hang up on her friend without another word. "Don't be crazy. Zeb wouldn't kill anybody. Talk to you later."

The instant she hung up, she dialed Gideon but got a busy signal. It was getting late, so she zipped her backpack and left, calling Ophelia the instant she was out of the building. "I tried to reach Gideon, but the call didn't go through." She explained about Janie's sudden departure. "I don't know if it's significant."

"That's for him to decide," Ophelia said. "I'll let him know. I'm a lousy cook, but if you can stand a noodle casserole for supper, you're invited. Gideon probably won't be home till all hours."

Marguerite thanked her but declined, saying she had things to do in town. Another lie, she supposed, seeing as she had no idea what to do next. She hadn't mentioned Lavonia's dreams to Ophelia. If the killer *was* targeting her again, she couldn't risk Ophelia and the baby.

Marguerite got into her car and, since she couldn't think of anyplace else to go, drove slowly downtown. News vans, cops, and gawkers filled the main drag near the Impractical Cat, and rowdy crowds prowled the sidewalks. She left her car near the park and walked the few blocks to Tony's Greek and Italian for moussaka—and hopefully a hug from Tony. But he wasn't there, so she toyed with her food, sipped a strong, muddy cup of Greek coffee, and tried to ignore the news playing on a big-screen TV on the wall. It was all about Constantine and Nathan, and all conjecture. Apparently, Constantine was holed up in the apartment at the top of the Cat, refusing to comment.

And then the bombshell hit. The chief of police came on with an announcement: *Anyone knowing the whereabouts of seventeen-year-old Zeb Bonnard should contact the Bayou Gavotte Police Department immediately. He is wanted for questioning in the murder last night of Nathan Bone.*

Marguerite leapt from her chair, rushed to pay for dinner, and hurried onto the street. But after all that haste, she realized she had no idea what to do. She'd known the police were watching Zeb, but he hadn't done anything wrong. He *wouldn't*. And it was one thing for the police to seek him privately and another entirely to blast it over the news as if he were a serial killer.

She made her way slowly down the street to PJ's for a café granita and a date square. The coffee shop was doing a brisk business. She stood in line, ignoring the stares, calmly polite to acquaintances who greeted her. If it weren't for the suspicion in the air, she might be able to get used to the attention.

But she didn't need to, right? She wasn't involved with Constantine anymore. That episode of her life was done and gone. She hadn't even noticed anyone shadowing her. Forlornly, she found a corner table and spent a half hour pretending to do a crossword puzzle in the newspaper while she worried about Zeb and tried to figure out what to do.

When at last business slowed, she went to the counter again for a cup of decaf.

"Much better," said a dry male voice behind her.

She turned. "Hey, Al." She wasn't supposed to trust anyone, but Al Bonnard had an alibi, and he must be freaking out about his son. "What's better?"

"Your choice of diversion." Zeb's father tapped the newspaper she still held. "Better than that trashy book the other day."

She resisted snapping at him. "It might be, if I could focus on anything. I'm so worried about Zeb."

"That boy will be in a heap of trouble when he returns." Marguerite's surprise must have shown, for he raised his brows. "You've been talking to Lavonia, I see. The stomach flu seems to have affected her mind. Zeb is a great disappointment, but I don't suspect him of performing a hired killing for Dufray or anyone else."

That didn't jive with what Lavonia had said, but maybe she really was addled. Or maybe Al was regretting some hasty words. Usually his aura revealed nothing stronger than mild irritation. Now he showed some other emotion that she couldn't quite pin down. His aura reminded her of a leaky bag with goo oozing out the seams.

"He's probably holed up with some friend and planning to pimp at the Threshold at night," Al said. "I suggested that to the police, but they're too busy with this murder case to care."

She gaped. "That's not what I heard. The TV news said the police want him for questioning."

"They want *Zeb?*" he asked, brows raised, but . . . his aura showed no sign of surprise at all.

She was sure hers did. She couldn't stop staring.

"As if I didn't already have enough trouble with the boy, that joke of a chief had to broadcast it to the world." But Al's leaky aura didn't look upset. It looked almost . . . smug.

"How did you know it was the chief who made the announcement?"

He hesitated, while consternation, yellow and muddy, streaked his aura. "Who else? He wants to get elected again, so he has to make it sound like he's doing something."

She paid and left him in line to order, trying to figure him out. She put a generous dollop of milk in her coffee, added cinnamon and nutmeg, and stirred the brew while absently staring at the bulletin board on the wall. People put ads there for roommates, apartments for rent, kittens to good homes . . . She took a lid and put it carefully on the coffee cup.

Kittens to good homes. That was Lavonia's ad, and . . . Marguerite stared. Blue dots, one inch apart, the entire length of the paper. Had she printed them on her own printer? No, Marguerite remembered—she'd done them at Al's place one night.

But Al couldn't be the murderer. He had an alibi for last night, as did Lavonia, and . . .

Marguerite took her coffee, got out her cell phone, and moved hurriedly toward the door.

"Don't make that call." Al spoke very softly, right in her ear.

She turned, gaping at him. The ooze dripped from his aura, thick and slimy, rotten sludge brown.

He murmured, "If you make a fuss, the police will receive proof that Zeb murdered that idiot reporter." His aura flared with evil intent. She'd seen an aura like that before—when she'd been chased by the black van.

"But—but Zeb's your son!" she whispered. "You wouldn't turn in your own child."

He snorted. "How innocent you are. Take the ad off the bulletin board." She did, and he folded it and put it in his pocket. "Let's go for a walk, Marguerite." The urbanity of his voice contrasted shockingly with the horror of his aura. "We need to talk."

She had no choice. "Sure," she said. He held the door for her. She wanted to run screaming down the street, but instead she preceded him languidly into the heat of dusk. If only someone were shadowing her! She took a sip of coffee as if nothing was wrong and glanced toward the main drag.

"I guess Dufray can't spare any bodyguards today," Al smirked. "We're going the other way." His hand rested on her spine, moving her not too gently in the direction of the park.

He would turn in his own son? "Zeb didn't murder anyone."

His aura surged again. "Fingerprints and blood on a knife don't lie," he said cheerfully. "He's developed such a reputation for violence, coupled with a few positive drug tests, that no one will have a problem believing he did it."

Al had the knife with which poor Nathan had been stabbed. He'd deliberately used a knife with his son's fingerprints on the handle to commit murder.

She had to do something. She had to get that knife.

"You'll never find it," Al said, as if he'd read her mind. "If anything happens to me, it will be handed over to the cops. I did my best to spare you," he added, once they were strolling along the sidewalk. "If you'd listened to Lavonia and stayed out of town for a day or two, you would have been fine."

"If you don't have anything against me, why did you chase me across town and try to kill me?"

His laughter grated. She'd never noticed before how unpleasant Al's laughter could be. "I couldn't resist," he said. "It didn't have anything to do with you, not really. Lavonia had told me about your dream, and messing with her superstitions is entertaining."

God. Poor Lavonia.

He chuckled. "Admittedly, I got a little carried away."

"Like when you ran over Pauline's body as well as inducing her to kill herself?"

"Figured that out, too? You're way too smart for your own good."

Anguish swept through her. "You killed her because I told Lavonia about my dream that she was going to commit suicide?"

"Hush, Marguerite. You don't want me to get carried away again, do you?"

No, but he would anyway. His aura was itching to let go. "Why?" she cried. "What did Pauline do to deserve that?"

"She was weak," he said, as if that explained everything. "This world is full of weaklings. My wife was one. I thought a vampire would be strong and ruthless, but all she wanted in life was to help other weaklings. Once I got rid of her, I had hopes of Zeb, but he's turned out to be a wimp—and a goody-goody, too."

Realizations jostled one another in Marguerite's mind. Al had killed his *wife*? How? Hadn't she been in a car accident? Lutsky'd been driving, and . . . She shook her head. She had to focus on the here and now. Al had another grisly dream, this time Lavonia's, to turn into prophesy—herself, Janie, and Zeb, all dead. She had to find a way to prevent it.

If Zeb and Janie weren't already dead. She might be the only one left.

"As for Dufray . . ." Al's voice was suffused with disgust.

"What does Constantine have to do with this?"

"Besides being a weakling?" He laughed again. "You'll see. You want to help Zeb, don't you? You want to save him."

"Of course I do!" She wanted to spit.

"I might consider sparing him," Al said, "if he were replaced by much bigger prey."

Not that she believed a word of that, but . . . "Such as who?"

"Dufray, of course."

"Why? What has Constantine ever done to you?"

His face twisted. His aura bloomed with bitterness and hatred. "Nothing but ruin my life."

What? How? But she couldn't get the words out. She could only gape.

"You're going to call him for me. Arrange a meeting."

She stopped right there. "No. I can't trade Constantine for Zeb."

Al laughed. "In love with the bastard, are you?"

She felt herself reddening in the semidarkness. Maybe, maybe not, but she wasn't about to get into that with Al. "It's nothing to do with love. We parted on very unpleasant terms last night. His bodyguards treated me like a pariah. They followed me home to make sure I didn't come back."

"That rankles, does it?"

"It was horrible, but just because he's a jerk doesn't mean I can trade him for another human being."

"Why not? Time for a little revenge, Marguerite." He nudged her onward. "Wouldn't it be fun to take him down a peg or two?"

No! But Al would never understand that. "I want to put the past behind me, but I can't deliver him up to you to be murdered. At least Zeb has a chance if he's picked up by the cops."

"Who said I want to murder Dufray? Even if I did, I wouldn't do it now. I'm enjoying the results of my handiwork too much. He's in such deep shit, and all because of me." He grasped her elbow and got her moving again. "He owes me, and the only way I'll ever get what I need is by forcing his hand."

"What does he owe you? Money?"

"You have disappointingly little imagination, Marguerite. You'll find out when we meet up with him. Oh, yes, you'll be there, too. I need all the ammunition I can get."

"And if I refuse?"

"I think you know the answer to that," Al said softly. "Who knows? Maybe you can wheedle Dufray into bargaining for both you and Zeb." He chuckled, and Marguerite could only describe it as gleeful. "Or maybe not."

~

Now that Zeb had someone to talk to, it all came pouring out. Well, not all. He told them the bonbons his dad handed out sometimes contained drugs, but he wasn't about to whine about having to watch what he ate or drank for fear he'd suddenly find himself hallucinating or so speeded up he felt his heart might explode. He wasn't about to tell them about how he'd learned to figure out what set his dad off and what didn't, even if it made no sense, and to live in the Zone so his dad would think he was cool with going along with whatever role he'd been assigned. "Not long before she died, my mom told me Dad was unstable and carrying around a lot of anger. She was trying to work him through it. She asked me to be considerate and understanding."

"And you tried," Zelda said, her voice brimming with compassion. "Even more so after she died."

Zeb nodded. "It wasn't so bad at first. Supposedly he was helping me get over losing my mom by playing practical jokes on Lutsky because her death was his fault and by messing with Eaton Wilson because he wouldn't shut up about how great my mom was and how perfect she expected me to be."

Maybe his mom's death had turned his dad from unstable to crazy, but it had taken Zeb a long time to figure that out. And even longer to accept it. "Lately the jokes turned nasty. He got Lutsky's password and wrote obscene emails to Constantine's fan club, and he slipped hate propaganda into the middle of Eaton Wilson's class handouts. I had to spy on him constantly to try to counteract the next awful thing he'd think of. Then he drugged Marguerite—she's the girl in the drawing—and left her on the mound with all that junk, and the next night he chased her across town, trying to kill her. Zelda, can I have your coffee, too?" Without waiting for an answer, he guzzled it all down.

The girls were taking it pretty well, considering. While they drove into town, Zelda surfed the Internet on her cell. "Unbelievable. The police chief wants you for questioning!" She glared at him, fangs bared. It was beginning to get dark, and they glowed a little. "Don't you dare change your mind again. We will not give you up to the cops. I can sneak you into the Cat, no problem."

"What I want to know is, who made the cops think you have anything at all to do with the murder?" In the rear-view mirror, Juma's eyes narrowed almost to slits. "I always thought your dad was a bit of a slime." She pulled into the Burger King drive-through.

Zeb slid onto the floor at the back. "You did?"

"Yeah, the cool, sophisticated prof thingy was obviously a role, but I never imagined anything like this." She bought him a burger and fries, and he sat up enough to eat them.

By the time he finished, they were approaching downtown. "You might want to stay out of sight again," she said.

Zeb slid lower. "I think he had something to do with Pauline's death, too. She was Marguerite's roommate. And I should have known better than to believe he got tickets to Constantine's concerts because he wanted to humor me. I feel like such an idiot for not figuring it out sooner. I'm pretty sure he handed out spiked candy and got people riled up, and that's what started the riots where those people were killed."

"Your dad's a serial killer," Juma said. "You realize that? Whoa! There he is."

Zeb huddled on the floor. "Where?"

"Just leaving PJ's with some woman. Stay cool. He's not even looking our way. There, we passed him."

Zeb shot up to look out the window. "He's with Marguerite! Stop the car."

"Why?" Juma pulled over.

"She thinks he's a friend! He could be planning anything. He already tried to kill her once." He dug in his pocket for the folded drawing and handed it to Zelda. "This changes everything. I need you to take this to Constantine. Tell him everything I told you. Tell him I had to go after my dad and Marguerite."

～

Cold fear invaded Constantine's gut and settled there. "What's the latest on Marguerite?"

"Last I heard, she was at Tony's," Gideon said, "which is pure luck. She won't come to any harm there."

Constantine's phone rang. Every time it rang, his heart leapt a little with hope and then dropped again. Marguerite wasn't going to call him. She might not even answer if he called, but he had no choice. He had to warn her to stay where she was. With Tony, she would be safe.

It was Leopard. "Zelda's down here," he said. "She insists on seeing you and only you. I told her you didn't have time for kid stuff, but she's showing fang, bro. She worked her way through the rowdy crowd outside, scared the shit out of several people, and had to fight off a couple of horny customers before she made it to my office."

Jesus. "Send her up."

"We're on our way," Lep said. "I got ahold of that dude from the concert. Not candy, but cookies. Peanut butter macadamia nut. Who'd refuse one of those? Some chick was handing them out, but she was eating them, too."

"Maybe only one or two were doctored. He only needed one person to cause a disturbance. What did she look like? Was she white? Black? How old?"

"White chick, pretty, brown hair, he thinks. It was kind of dark in the crowd, but he figured he'd recognize her if he saw her again."

Constantine exchanged glances with Gideon. It was a long shot, but . . . "Have someone show him a picture of Janie from the fan club."

A minute later, Zelda came bursting through the door, followed by Lep and Juma. Zelda's fangs were still full down. She was way too young to be such a stunner. "What is it, Zelda girl?"

She was out of breath and looked both scared and enraged, but she sucked her fangs into their slots before pulling a folded paper out of her pocket. "Zeb said to give this to you."

Constantine opened the paper: Marguerite's sketch. This was the dream he'd sent her? He would have laughed if he didn't feel like crying instead. He passed the paper to Gideon. "Where did he get it from?"

"It was planted on the body of that reporter who was murdered." Zelda glared, daring him not to believe her. Juma's silent body language said much the same, but that was her habitual stance against the world.

"And Zeb knows this how?" he asked.

"He witnessed the murder. It was his father who did it, and he was trying to frame you."

"Right," Constantine said. "He's tried to frame me for a number of crimes. He must be frustrated at his lack of success."

Her fangs slotted back down. "You already *knew*? Do you have any *idea* what Zeb's been through?"

"Unfortunately, yes. I have nothing but admiration for Zeb."

Zelda advanced on him, her small fists clenched. "Then why didn't you *do* something about it? Why didn't you *help* him? I kept calling you, and you did *nothing!*"

Gideon folded the paper and stuck it in his breast pocket. "Calm down, Zelda."

She rounded on Gideon. "How can I possibly calm down? The cops are after him. *You're* after him. How *could* you?"

"That wasn't me, but my boss trying to cover his ass," Gideon said. "And Constantine only figured all this out a couple of minutes ago. Where's Zeb now?"

"He's trying to protect Marguerite," Juma said. "We saw her leaving PJ's with his father, heading in the direction of the park. He followed them to make sure she's safe."

"He's afraid his dad will kill Marguerite, too," Zelda added.

Bloodlust, the kind Constantine seldom felt these days, the kind he thought he was done with, thrust into his gorge. "He won't until he's used her as bait. It's me he really wants. Lep, see if we have anyone in the vicinity of the park, and put everyone on alert."

"But why?" Zelda cried. "What does he have against you?"

"He's my father, too," Constantine said. "Does Zeb have a cell phone on him?"

"No," Juma said. "His dad confiscated it." Pause. "Professor Bonnard is your *father*?"

"Whoa, that must be why Zeb reminds me of Constantine," Zelda said. "So Zeb's your brother!"

His little brother. His chance of redemption.

"How can he be your father, too?" Zelda asked.

Constantine tuned out as Gideon briefed the girls on his history. Zeb had done his best, but he probably loved his old man. Hoped he would change, be all right in the end.

Constantine had no such illusions, and no qualms about committing murder. A mourning dove landed on the windowsill and paced back and forth. *Kill. Kill. Kill.*

CHAPTER NINETEEN

Zeb couldn't risk following them directly until full darkness, so he sidled along in the bushes, took the first right and kicked up to a run, making a left at the end of the block. At the next intersection he waited, and just when he began to fear he'd miscalculated and lost them, Dad and Marguerite sauntered across the street a block away. Once they were out of sight, he took off again, looping around to the same street by the park where he'd hovered only the night before. Marguerite's car was down this end of the block near a van and a couple of other cars.

Maybe the old man was just walking her to her car, but Zeb didn't think so. He'd have to play it by ear. If Marguerite got into her car and drove off, perfect. If not . . . He lingered behind the pittosporum hedge that bordered the park, folded his aura tightly against himself, and waited for them to turn the corner.

Marguerite stopped to sip her coffee. Dad nudged her forward again. She elbowed him. Zeb sucked in a breath. Did she have no idea what the man could do? Maybe she knew she was a goner, so she didn't care anymore. She didn't look scared, though—just majorly pissed off.

They were arguing by the time they approached the vehicles. "I'm a terrible actress. He'll know I'm lying."

"For your sake, I hope he won't."

"He doesn't want to talk to me. He may not answer his phone."

"He'd better."

"The lines may even be jammed, what with the whole world trying to contact him."

"Not by his private number," Dad said. "He keeps one line open for people that matter."

"How do you know?"

"I've made it my business to know," Dad said.

"I have no reason to suppose I matter anymore, if I ever did." Marguerite was practically spitting.

"If you don't matter to him, you don't matter to me either," Dad said. He placed a hand on the back of her neck, and Zeb braced himself. His old man was strong; he could kill her with the twist of a wrist. Zeb couldn't risk interfering unless she made a run for it, in which case he'd tackle the old man. But the park was deserted; she wouldn't run if no help was in sight.

Suddenly, he had an idea. He opened his aura and spread it wide, wide. If she looked at the hedge, she'd see his aura sticking out at the end and above it, too. She might even recognize it as his and know he was there for her.

"As long as he cares whether or not you're alive, you're of use to me," said his dad. "Bear that in mind, and don't try to warn him, or you'll be sorry." He steered her past the vehicles and into the park in the direction of the hedge.

Zeb froze, hardly daring to breathe. Marguerite's eyes flickered. She came to a halt and got out her phone.

"What a pity you lost your head over that dirtbag rock star," Dad said. "Don't lose it again now. Make that call and pray he answers."

∿

Finally, for the first time since his childhood, Constantine and his guide were entirely in accord. Zeb needed to live. So did Marguerite. Bonnard had to die. Whether or not Gideon got the proof he needed, there was no other way.

"I understand now," Zelda said. "Zeb isn't suicidal. He talked about dying because he's afraid his dad will kill him."

Constantine's cell rang. *Honey and Eyes.*

His blood ran hot, then cold. He had to maintain his cool and play it right.

He let it ring until it went to message, then waited a good two minutes, his blood congealing to ice, before he said, "That was Marguerite. If she doesn't call again, I'll call her back. I need absolute silence, even if I say something that pisses you off." He grimaced at Zelda. "If you can't control your fangs, consider it a good sign."

The phone rang again, and this time he answered. "What do you want now?"

Both Zelda and Juma stiffened at this.

Play along with me, he telepathed, focusing hard on Marguerite. *Don't be afraid. Everything will be fine.*

There was a pause, then Marguerite's trembling, furious voice. "I want nothing from you, Constantine. This call wasn't my idea."

He forced a laugh. "So whose was it?" Judging by the echo, he was on speakerphone at the other end. The dove had gone to roost, but a nighthawk called outside, and a great horned owl was perched outside the window.

"Zeb is with me," she said. "He says he's sorry he didn't come clean with you earlier. He says he knows something about the murder last night. He wants to talk to you, but with no one else around."

The truth or a lie? Had Zeb fucked up already and they were both at Bon-Bon's mercy? "If he knows something," Constantine stalled, "he should call the cops."

"He can't do that. Aren't you listening to the news? The cops are after him. They won't believe him."

"And he thinks I will?" Silence at the other end. "He's taking a big chance, babe. If he tells me the truth and I don't want what he says spread around, I might have to kill him. If he's lying, I might get pissed off and kill him. You know I don't like liars." He paused, eyeing the owl through the window. "I have a feeling you're lying to me right now, babe."

"Don't call me *babe*! You don't have any feelings at all, you two-timing jerk."

Whatever reasons she might find to hate him, two-timing wasn't one of them. She must have heard what he'd tele-pathed. *Good girl.*

Constantine managed a whoop of laughter. "I'm a rock star, babe. What do you expect?"

Zelda's fangs slotted down, and Juma's eyes narrowed. Gideon gave him a thumbs-up. Juma rolled her eyes, and Zelda reddened and sucked her fangs back inside her gums. "I'm sorry," she whispered. "I know you would never, ever be a two-timer."

"I expect *nothing* from you," Marguerite ranted.

"Wise of you, babe," Constantine said and directed his focus to his spirit guide. *Where?* he asked the bird. *We get it right the first time, or we're screwed.* "Put the kid on the phone. I'll talk to him right now."

More silence; no, there was the sound of a passing car in the background. They must be outdoors. Lep left the room in a hurry. A second later Constantine saw him on the roof making a call.

You're doing great, he telepathed to Marguerite. *I'll come get you. I promise.* He had never, ever cared so much about a message reaching its destination. *Just keep playing along.*

"He says no." Marguerite sounded breathless. Afraid. Didn't she believe him? "He says he can't take the risk that you're recording him."

"Bring him to the Cat, then. I'll have him escorted in."

"Right past the cops? That's impossible."

Where? Constantine asked his spirit guide again. *This could well be Dufray's last stand. Let's choose someplace memorable, in case we screw up.*

The mounds.

He and the bird seemed unusually in sync today. He telepathed it as a suggestion, focusing on Marguerite but letting a little slip sideways. Would Bon-Bon recognize a thought that wasn't his own? He'd never shown an aptitude for anything but cruelty way back when.

"How about out at the Indian mounds?" she said, and the owl gave a self-satisfied little flutter. Constantine didn't answer, letting the silence drag out.

"It's going to rain, so they'll be deserted," she added.

Still he said nothing.

Marguerite's voice broke. "Constantine, *please*. You're his only chance."

"*His only chance*," Constantine mimicked in a falsetto. "You're such a drama queen, Marguerite. Don't expect me to believe that obnoxious kid said anything as girly as that."

"I hate you," Marguerite sobbed, and Zelda's fangs snapped back down.

"You and countless other people," Constantine said. *I'll save you*, he telepathed desperately. *I swear I will*. The horned owl broke into his maudlin promises. *On the mound. Under the tree. Nine o'clock tonight*. It flew away and disappeared against the purple evening sky.

"Tell the kid I'll be on Papa Mound at nine P.M.," Constantine said. "I'll be by the big live oak."

"Nine!" Marguerite wailed. "That's an hour away."

An hour in which anything might happen to her. *Are you fucking sure?* he asked the bird. *If either of them dies, I'll spend the rest of my life massacring you and your kind*.

A nightjar laughed, and a barn owl screamed with mirth. *Nine o'clock*, came a distant call, and Constantine sighed long and loud. "I can't just walk out, or the paparazzi and the cops will be right behind me. It'll take a while to get away unseen. Take it or leave it." He gritted his teeth and ended the call.

~

"Bastard," Zeb's dad said. "You're not such a bad liar, Marguerite. I'll give you a B-plus."

Zeb clenched his fists. She'd done a great job, seeing as she was being threatened by a murderer, but he hoped like hell Constantine hadn't believed her.

"Turn your phone off," Bonnard said. She did. "Now throw it in the trash can." She tossed the phone, and he guided her toward the cars. "Let's go kill . . . some time." He laughed. "We'll get something to eat."

"All right," Marguerite said in a tight, furious voice. She unzipped the outside pocket of her backpack and took out her keys.

"Not in your car," he said, pushing her forward. "In the van."

Zeb hadn't seen this particular van before—dark green and quite new—but he recognized the magnetic signs on the side, purportedly belonging to the Watershed Management Department. His dad had used them before.

"You don't have to shove me," Marguerite said, wrenching away, stumbling and dropping her backpack and keys. "If you want to avoid attention, be civil."

"I like attention," he said. "I deserve it. Get moving."

She picked up the backpack and stomped toward the passenger side of the van. He opened the door for her and shut her in, then went around to his side.

"I should have gotten Master Teacher," he said as he opened the other door. Why didn't she just get out and run toward the main drag? Why had she even made that phone call? Zeb was pretty sure she'd noticed his aura. Didn't she know he would help?

The old man must be holding something over her head—something big and really, really scary. But she'd dropped her keys and left them there, a clear invitation to follow. Or, more likely, to go for help. He would do both.

"Acting head of Chemistry. What a load of bull. They should make me head and be done with it. I'd be Dean of Science by now if the idiots at NSF didn't keep turning down my grant applications." His dad got into the van. "I'm the most brilliant chemist of the twenty-first century."

Yada yada yada. Zeb had heard all this over and over again.

The engine of the van came on, but over its rumble the old man kept ranting. "My drugs are works of pure genius, and those are only the ones people know about. I deserve the Nobel Pr—" He slammed the door shut, backed into the road, and drove toward the corner where Zeb crouched. Zeb ducked around the end of the hedge just as the van passed it and waited, heart hammering, as the van approached the corner. The van picked up speed and drove away. It passed the next intersection and disappeared.

Zeb sprinted for Marguerite's cell phone and keys. He punched in Zelda's number with one hand and started the car with the other. He backed out and drove toward the corner, lights off, while the phone rang and rang. *Please answer. Please.*

She picked up just as he reached the corner. He edged forward, craning his neck. The van was already a couple of blocks away. He turned the corner but kept his lights off. From the phone came a hesitant, "Hello?"

"Zelda, it's Zeb. Did you reach Constantine? That phone call he just received from Marguerite was crap. My old man made her say that."

"We figured," Zelda said and gave a little yelp.

Constantine's voice came on. "Is she all right? Where is she?"

"She went with him in a green van," Zeb said. "I couldn't get the tag number without being seen." He described the signs on the sides. "He told her they were going to get something to eat."

"He's taking her to *dinner*?"

"Why not? He doesn't know anybody suspects him. There's no evidence against him. There never is, but I think he has killed a whole bunch of people."

"Not much doubt about that," Constantine said. "Did she seem scared?"

Zeb thought about it. "Maybe, but mostly she acted pissed off. Maybe she doesn't think he's going to hurt her, or at least not yet. He said she's useful to him as long as you care about her, and since you answered her call, I guess he assumes you do. But he made her throw her phone away, so he won't be having her call you again. I'm afraid he'll drug her or even kill her. I wish I'd told her everything. He makes all these weird drugs in his lab, and—"

Constantine interrupted. "Which direction did they go?"

Zeb pulled himself together and turned on his headlights. "They're headed north on Oak. I'm going to follow them in Marguerite's car, but I have to stay way back in case my old man realizes he's being followed."

"I'll get someone else onto them ASAP. In the meantime, I'm counting on you, bro."

Constantine was counting on him.

"I apologize for my earlier behavior," Constantine said. "I shouldn't have threatened you."

"I should have trusted you," Zeb said. "I just didn't—I didn't realize, and I didn't think he'd—"

"You did what you could. Are they still in sight?"

Zeb centered himself again. "I just turned onto Oak. They're about three blocks ahead, near Sacred Heart School. But don't send the cops after them. He must be holding something over her head, something big."

"Could be," Constantine said.

Constantine didn't sound convinced. "I know Marguerite," Zeb said. "She wouldn't lie like that without a really good reason. She did everything he said, and she didn't run away when she had the chance."

"I won't send the cops," Constantine said. "I'm going to keep that appointment at nine o'clock."

"But he might kill you," Zeb said.

"He can try," said Constantine Dufray.

~

The instant he hung up, Constantine called Jabez and explained the situation and the meeting at nine o'clock. "We don't know why Marguerite didn't try to run when she had the chance. The bastard must be holding something over her head."

"You want me to find out what it is?" Jabez asked.

"No, I'll do that. All I need you to do is make sure the girl stays safe."

"Will do," Jabez said.

Fine, but Constantine had to make sure the bodyguard understood the priorities. "I need the guy alive, but nothing matters more than the girl."

"Right," Jabez said.

It still wasn't enough. Did he really understand? Constantine had to just say it. "I love this girl, bro."

"I got that," Jabez said. "I'll keep her safe."

∼

Al left the green van at the local mall and switched to a white one sporting Park Service signs, so they fit right in when they parked behind the mound museum. Al took the driver's seat again but made Marguerite sit on the floor so she wouldn't be visible from outside. She hadn't dared to look behind on the drive over, nor could she risk glancing hopefully into the woods.

Constantine had telepathed reassuring messages, had urged her to play along. She had to play it cool and do what she was told . . . but why nine o'clock? What if Al went completely off his rocker before then?

Maybe that aura she'd seen in the park had been Zeb's; maybe he'd retrieved her car keys and phone; maybe he'd contacted Constantine and told him what his dad was really like. All she could do was hope.

Al had visited a drive-through for slaw dogs and several orders of oily fries. Maybe the prospect of revenge—and probably more murder—gave him an appetite.

"Constantine's an idiot. I've been messing with him for years, and he never figured it out." Obviously, Al intended to kill her. Otherwise he wouldn't be confessing about his whole, twisted life. He laughed around a fry. "That's one of the advantages of being dead."

Marguerite didn't have any appetite, but Al seemed inclined to take it personally if she didn't eat. She'd managed to force down one slaw dog. She sprinkled more salt and vinegar on her little pile of fries. "Huh?"

"I've been dead for years." Al sucked down some Coke. "Threw a little money at one of those drunken Indians and had him spread the word that I got killed in a drug deal gone bad. Then I gave him a hit of something that didn't mix with alcohol, and boom—no chance he'll ever change his mind and tell the truth."

By now, she'd figured out Al liked being told how bad he was. "That's terrible."

"Uh-huh." He crammed down a bunch more fries. "Then I bought a rifle, got in some practice, and shot Constantine's grandfather and little brother."

"You—you—oh, how *horrible!*" she squeaked.

Al grinned and squirted a bunch more ketchup on his fries. "I didn't have anything against the kid, mind you—unlike Constantine, he did what he was told—but the grandfather was an interfering old bastard, so I had to get rid of him. The kid happened to be in the path of one of the bullets. Just as well, though. Judging by Constantine and Zeb, he would have been a disappointment, too."

Finally, she found words. "You're Constantine's *father?*"

"Yep." Al offered no explanation, but judging by his aura, he wanted her to ask for it. He was feeding on attention as much as on fries.

"Then why is his last name Dufray?"

"His mom was married to Dufray. He was my first kill, purely by accident, believe it or not. A couple of pills I gave him didn't mix. But he was a wuss, so nobody missed him.

She hopped from his bed to mine the first day she saw me, the little slut." He must have noticed a spark of anger in Marguerite's eye, because he laughed again. "She was a hot babe, but dumb like most women, Lavonia included. I don't know why I put up with her. Yes, I do. She has great tits, and she loves fucking, although she's not into spanking, like Janie."

Janie, who had left town in a rush this morning.

He snorted. "Janie's smarter than I thought but not smart enough to escape me. You want me to give her a little extra punishment, just from you, before I get rid of her?"

Marguerite managed to stammer out, "Why? What has she ever done to me?"

"Well, for one thing she gave Nathan Bone that story about Lutsky yesterday. For another, she set up an appointment last night where I met up with Nathan and gave him your sketch, not that she had any idea what I wanted it for."

"Oh." After Al's ghastly disclosures, Janie's malice seemed like child's play. "She was bound to do something obnoxious because Constantine liked me better. It doesn't matter."

"Come on, Marguerite," he said. "Surely you want a little revenge."

Marguerite shook her head, and Al rolled his eyes. "If I decide to spare you, I'll get you pregnant. You'll have to get off your high horse, though, and stop pretending to be perfect. I thought Zeb's mom would be ideal, since she was a vampire, but she turned out to be a do-gooder."

She must have looked appalled, for he laughed. "Don't you find me attractive?"

"Everybody thinks you're attractive," Marguerite said bitterly.

"How do you feel about sex?"

Disgust roiled up, but she couldn't afford weakness right now. She ate a fry and analyzed his aura. He wasn't particularly turned on, or at least not sexually. Why ask her that, then? Just to freak her out? Maybe Constantine had inherited his aura control from Al, although the way they dealt with it was opposite—Constantine preferred to play outward, to conjure visions and send them with his telepathic mind, while Al pulled his aura tight and smooth, concentrating on concealment. He'd done it unbelievably well. She'd never guessed. Never even suspected Al might not be who he seemed. He'd been hiding his true self all along, but not anymore, or at least not with her now. Maybe he found it relaxing to let go. Did he have any idea what he was doing and what she could see? Zeb hadn't understood his own aura control until she'd explained it to him.

"Well?" Al leered in the darkness. "Do you like sex?"

"Not particularly," Marguerite said. "All that hoopla about my dad's porn films was a real turnoff."

"Not even with Dufray?"

"Don't talk to me about that jerk," Marguerite said, chomping on another couple of fries.

"No one-touch orgasms?" Al's expression was intent, in sync with the excitement in his aura. Evidently, his professed scorn of Constantine had all been an act.

"He really is telepathic, you know." Al sounded like an eager little kid. "Most of that stuff in the trashy books is true. He can send thoughts and images to people's minds. But I guess you know that."

She shrugged. Constantine had telepathically suggested that they meet at the mounds, but if Al realized, he might change his mind. "Supposedly he sent me a sex dream, but so what?"

"Oh, come on, Marguerite. You've done a great job of putting on an act, but you want revenge as much as I do."

Huh? "I'm pissed off at him, sure, but so what? I'll get over it."

He rolled his eyes. "Just can't give up on being a goody-goody, can you? I was surprised you didn't take the opportunity I handed you on a platter up on the mound. You could have ruined him then and there."

"I don't want to ruin anybody," she said.

Al huffed. "Maybe you wanted a more thorough revenge. Seduce him, make him fall for you, then dump him like the dirt he is. Big mistake, Marguerite. He dumped you instead, and nobody cares."

She said nothing. Constantine might or might not care about her, but he wouldn't just let this lunatic murder her.

"Do you think he'll save you? You can always hope, but when I tell him your big secret, he might just kill you himself. Unless I kill him first and save you."

"I don't know what you're talking about. He already believes the worst of me."

"That's what you think. I'm going to have the time of my life, taunting Constantine with how blind he's been about both of us."

She gave up on trying to figure him out. He opened a metal canister and held it out to her with a smarmy grin. "Have a bonbon?"

She almost took one, then snatched her hand back. "No!"

"These aren't drugged," he coaxed. In the gloom, his grin was even creepier. "They're my private stash."

"Thanks anyway." She took a swig of her coffee; he hadn't touched that. Realizations crowded her mind. All those candies he carried around and handed out . . . She recalled Lutsky's blowup in the restaurant. Her own fit of rage with Constantine. Lavonia's convenient illness last night and her belief Al had been there the entire time; she'd probably been out cold for hours and not realized it. Zeb's inability to hold down a job . . . The people who'd gone ballistic at concerts . . . and, *oh my God*, Constantine's wife.

Where had it all begun? "Why do *you* want revenge?"

"Because the little bastard wouldn't show me how he does it. Telepathy's not magic. It's just technique. His grandfather could do some of it, too, but he wouldn't help me out either." Al tossed their trash out the window. "People who don't help me end up dead."

CHAPTER TWENTY

Zeb shadowed them through the woods on one flank, Jabez on the other. The big black bodyguard, who had come to take over surveillance of Dad and Marguerite, had told Zeb to go home.

"I can't do that," Zeb said. "Marguerite needs me here."

"I'll take care of her," Jabez said. "I can get close enough to protect her without being seen. You can't."

"She still needs me," Zeb said. Could she see auras at night? If he could just get her to see it, she would recognize his aura. She would know he was there.

"To do what?" Jabez said. "Go home."

To give her hope, but Marguerite's secret was not his to give away, so all he said was "Or else what?"

Jabez only laughed and vanished into the forest, but Zeb refused to let the man affect him. He might not be as efficient or ruthless as the bodyguard, but even if he didn't get much chance to reveal his presence to Marguerite, he wouldn't do anything so craven as to leave. This was *his* problem. He'd had enough of hiding, enough of running away.

He was nearing the edge of the woods not far from Papa Mound when Marguerite's shrill "What?" floated back in the muggy air.

Zeb moved slowly forward, straining to hear. His dad murmured something, and Marguerite snapped, "Why?" Again, he couldn't hear his dad, but a minute closer, it became obvious: Marguerite was taking off her clothes.

Zeb's aura flared out all on its own. Crap. He wanted to reassure her, and she was faced his way, so she might have seen his reaction. He tried to pull in his aura, to tamp the arousal. She looked mighty good in her underwear, and now she was reaching around to unhook her bra.

"Why?" she said again, more softly.

"So you won't chicken out at the last moment," Dad said. "And if you do, you'll be very, very visible with all that lovely white skin in these dark, spooky woods."

"You're such a freak, Al. What will you do if I run away? Shoot me?" She took off her bra, and Zeb's aura flared again.

Whatever. He wondered if she could catch Jabez's aura, too, and if it frightened her.

She wasn't acting frightened. She shucked her panties. "Is that what you've got in that duffel bag, Al—a gun? Or is it another knife? Whose fingerprints are on it this time?"

So that's what he was holding over her head. It might be bullshit—but it might just as easily be true. Zeb backed diagonally out of the woods onto the path. He got out his cell phone and made a call.

∼

Bring the copper mask, the spirit guide said.

Without questioning why, Constantine obeyed and left by the roof garden. He jumped down to the next roof, climbed to another, traversed a few more, and eventually lowered himself quietly to the ground in an alley almost a block away. The dense night air clung to his skin, but clouds were building in the west. Distant thunder rumbled; soon they would have more rain.

If only he could just work up a violent rage, kill the Enemy, and be done with it. Instead, once he'd ensured Marguerite's safety, he was going to have to confront him. Stave him off. Find out as much as he could and waste some time while Gideon did an illegal search of Bonnard's house for something to justify a warrant. Then Constantine would have to find a way to kill the bastard without making it look like murder.

He hated to admit it, even to himself, but he was afraid.

Oh, no, you don't, the bird said. *Kill.*

It wasn't the killing that scared him. He didn't like killing, but sometimes it had to be done. The bird agreed. *Expose his weakness, drive him out of cover, go in for the kill.*

He ran through the humid night toward the Indian mounds. He was definitely afraid for both Marguerite and Zeb, but that wasn't it either. He was relying on Jabez to keep Marguerite alive and unharmed until he arrived. If Jabez didn't succeed, no one could. He doubted Zeb would obey Jabez's orders to go home. He sure wouldn't, in Zeb's place. Not that Constantine doubted Zeb's ability to handle himself, but he was yet another unknown in a mess of unknowns.

He circled the same parking lot where he'd kissed Marguerite the other day. Ahead on noiseless wings, the great horned owl disappeared into the path through the woods. Constantine followed, shedding his own weaknesses one by one, but fear of his lifelong Enemy hovered like a ghostly Cheshire cat, grinning and taunting him, disappearing and then reappearing someplace else. In spite of this, he didn't think it was Bonnard's malevolence that was eating at him either. His reaction yesterday had been one of shock; today he knew what he faced. He was a grown man now.

Not only that, Zeb had survived the man for seventeen years. He would have to ask Zeb how he'd done it when this was over. He longed to get to know his little brother . . .

You're not allowed to have longings. Everyone's counting on you.

Yeah, and it sucked. He conjured a vision of a stag, the mask its antlers, and left the woods, crossing to Mama Mound. At the top of the mound, he imagined himself a pine tree and took a look around. Funny how he'd convinced everyone of his invincibility. What a crock.

The owl dove past his face, claws scraping his cheek, narrowly missing his eye. *If you don't get this right,* the bird said viciously, *I'll spend the rest of my days systematically pecking your kind.*

Constantine wiped the blood from his cheek, letting out a puff of laughter even so. At least someone meant business, even if it was only a bird. He cast a long slow glance over Papa Mound: no one. *Yet,* agreed the owl. His cell phone vibrated. Jabez.

"You're not going to like this," the bodyguard said.

"Just tell me."

"First thing, the kid wouldn't leave. Said Marguerite needed him there."

"Figures."

"He's good, though. Not as good as me, but for an amateur, he's very, very smooth."

"Good to know. Keep any eye on him."

"Second thing—Bonnard made her take her clothes off."

Anger boiled up, but he forced it out in a long, slow breath. If she'd been in danger of rape, Jabez would have said so. "Does she seem frightened?"

"If she is, she's hiding it well. Asked him if he had a gun in his duffel bag to shoot her with if she ran away or if he'd just frame someone again with fingerprints on a knife."

"Shit," Constantine said. "Maybe that's what he's holding over her head."

"Could be," Jabez said. "Maybe the kid thinks so, too, because he backed way off into the woods. I couldn't see what he was doing, but he came back after a minute or two, so I bet he made a call."

"Let Gideon know, and tell Lep to make sure those girls aren't being roped into something dangerous."

"Will do," Jabez said. "There's more." His tone boded ill.

"Jesus, bro. If it's that bad, get it over with."

"She asked why she needed to get undressed, and he said he doesn't want her chickening out at the last moment."

Chickening out . . . about doing what?

"He said she wants revenge as much as he does, and she'll thank him when it's done."

His unruly heart sank. That's what was eating at him. He didn't blame her if she'd loved her uncle and wanted payback, but it did away with any hope of a reconciliation. "Thanks, bro. Where are they now?"

"Exiting the woods from the south. Sorry, man. I thought she might be the one for you."

"So did I." He ended the call, conjured a vision of a stag again, and fled to the top of Papa Mound.

∾

Marguerite toiled naked up the side of Papa Mound, more furious by the second. Being naked made her feel vulnerable, and vulnerability made her scared, and fear enraged her. Al refused to let her take the stairs, so she stumbled through clumps of grass and weeds, with Al taunting about how slow she was. Grass burrs attacked the soles of her feet, and she had to keep pausing to pick them off. If she blundered into a nest of fire ants in the dark, he'd think it was the best possible joke.

Help was close but not forthcoming. It wasn't quite as easy to see auras at night, but sexual arousal showed up vividly regardless. As she undressed, she'd caught flickers of lust from both Zeb and someone else—someone with more control over his desires but less over his aura. She supposed they couldn't help noticing a naked woman, but why couldn't they have rescued her? Constantine must have *some* sort of plan, but she was losing her cool—and losing it fast.

A flash of lightning lit up the sky ahead, followed by a rumble of thunder. The wind picked up, and she shivered. A tentative raindrop landed on her nose.

Several steps from the top of the mound, she heard Al unzipping his bag behind her. She began to turn, but he said, "Stop," and took her by the arm.

She obeyed, but she'd caught the flash of an aura not far behind them—the same one she'd seen in the woods earlier. "Is it nine o'clock yet?"

"Just about." Something fell over her head, choking her. She grabbed at it, gasping, almost falling backward. She clawed it away from her throat. A noose!

"Stay still, and it won't get any tighter," Al said. "Keep struggling, and I'll tie your hands."

She froze, terror washing through her in waves and waves. Why didn't the man who was following them come and help her? "What the hell is this for?" she squeaked. "I did everything you said."

"Yeah, you've been a good little girl, if a mite sassy," he murmured close, way too close, and bit hard on her ear. She muffled a cry and stayed perfectly still. "This is so Dufray knows I'm serious. If anybody else sees us—hey, this is Bayou Gavotte, world capital of kinky sex, and you're the daughter of Porno McHugh. No one will be surprised. Let's go."

He tugged on the rope, and she hurried next to him, clutching the noose at her throat. They reached the flat top of the mound. Lightning flashed again, illuminating the broad, empty surface. Where was Constantine? They walked slowly across the lawn, and for the first time, tension reamed Al's aura. From the tree up ahead came the plaintive call of a nightjar. A huge horned owl swooped down and landed on one of its massive limbs. Where was Constantine's aura? He must be here. He *must*.

"Where the fuck is he?" muttered Al. "Did you say something that warned him? If he doesn't show, I swear I'll string you up here and now."

"Not necessary." A stag with a huge rack of antlers materialized from under the tree and bounded gracefully toward them.

"Stop right there, Dufray," Al said. "No games."

The vision disintegrated into long, powerful legs and the copper mask, its beads clacking against one another, feathers quivering in the wind. Constantine tossed the mask aside and halted only a few yards away, hair loose on his shoulders, naked but for a loincloth. His body appeared relaxed, but his aura shivered with intent.

"No?" His teeth gleamed white in the darkness. "You look like you're ready for some fun. Planning to play ride the pony?"

Marguerite shuddered, and Constantine's voice slipped into her mind: *Stay calm.* But his aura was cold and hard as a diamond, as sharp and unyielding as steel, his emotions buried so deeply as to be invisible.

"You know why I'm here," Al said.

"To be reunited with your long-lost son." He laughed, a wicked jeer that didn't even twitch his aura. "I'd say it's great to see you again, Bon-Bon, but I don't like telling lies." Pause. "Don't like liars much either. Where's Zeb? Was that another of your lies, Marguerite?" *Just play along.*

"Yes," she croaked. "But Al forced me to tell it. He forced me to call."

Al's laugh rasped in the humid night. "Out of the kindness of my heart. They say confession is good for the soul, and Marguerite has something to confess. She's been planning on telling you for years and years now. She came to Bayou Gavotte to tell you, but she's been waiting for the right time and place."

Constantine cocked his head to one side, his voice amused, his aura telling her—nothing. "Go ahead, then. Confess away."

"I don't know what he's talking about," she said. "I don't have anything to conf—" Al tugged on the rope, and she gagged.

"Get it over with," Al snarled. "Tell him who you really are." He tugged again.

She choked out the words. "Please! I don't know what you mean!" Constantine might have been made of wood for all the interest he showed.

Al grabbed her arm and yanked her close. "Tell. Him."

Constantine yawned. "You don't need to pretend, Marguerite. I already know about your uncle."

"My—my uncle?" Her brain whirled, tilted. Settled. *Oh.* "The cop in Baton Rouge?"

"Duh," Constantine said. "Before Nathan died, he passed that juicy bit of news to Lep."

"But I'm not—that's not—" She stopped. Al chuckled, but Constantine's vibe was more bored than ever.

Stay calm, he telepathed. Out loud, he said, "I'll miss Nathan. Did he dig that up himself, or did he get it from you, Bon-Bon?"

Al laughed. "Nathan was such a trusting soul, and not very bright. He never figured out who I was."

"But it's not true," Marguerite said. "Yes, he was my uncle, but he was—" She stopped again. "I don't want revenge. I—"Al snickered beside her, and Constantine's aura remained cold and closed. Once again, he didn't believe her. Tears scorched her eyes and burned her throat.

"You were saying?" he asked politely, but his aura shut her out, making it clear that he didn't really want to know. On the live oak tree, the owl hovered, still and silent, its talons sharp and cruel on the bough. Was that his guide, the same guide whose feathers had caressed her and Constantine while they slept?

Fear and despair washed through her. If Constantine didn't care enough to do something soon, she was going to die naked with a rope around her neck.

But she would keep one small shred of dignity. "Forget it. I've had it with not being believed." She'd spent her whole life not being believed, even when it mattered most. "I thought you were different, but for all your talk about lies, you can't even recognize the truth."

Al snorted. "That was a pretty good speech, but it's not enough. He might save your ass if your explanation sounds plausible enough."

"He's right," Constantine said. "It's worth a try." *I'm going to save you.*

"It's not a plausible explanation," she raged. "It's the truth, and you don't deserve it."

~

"Uh-huh," Constantine said, and the bird agreed. Emotion slammed against the floodgates of his mind. Desperately, he held them shut.

She let out a long, low keening sound of rage, or terror, or grief. He'd buried all emotion in order to face his father. Judging by Marguerite's reaction, he'd succeeded too well.

Hadn't she heard his reassurances? Did she really think he would take his own petty revenge and let Bonnard kill her? *Marguerite, I will save you, I swear.*

The horned owl loomed menacingly on a bough above. *Get on with it. There's not much time.*

Constantine began tossing out images of the kind that had excited Bon-Bon so many years ago. He threw out a coyote and telepathed to Marguerite: *Hold onto the rope.* She clutched the noose at her throat. He conjured a cougar. Tentatively, the rain began to fall.

Constantine eyed his father, whose grip on the rope was still too tight. "Now that Marguerite's confession is over with, what do you want, old man? Are you enjoying the magic show?" He sent up a vision of a writhing snake. Up, and up, and up.

"I'm not interested in childish games," Bonnard said, but judging from the way his eyes followed the illusion, he sure was. Always had been.

Now, the horned owl said, spreading its wings. The hair on the back of Constantine's neck stood up. *Here's your chance.*

Constantine scattered the illusion. "We can do some weather magic if you like."

One, two . . . The owl dove from the tree, skimming the surface of the mound.

Constantine opened his hand and threw a vision of dancing light toward the huge oak behind him. It exploded in time with the thunder, a dazzle of fireworks high over their heads, as true lightning struck the tree with a horrendous crack. Constantine shot forward. He separated Bonnard from the rope, kicked him in the nuts, and sent him screaming to the ground.

Not the weakness I was thinking of. The bird sounded amused but pleased.

Constantine thrust Marguerite behind him. He tucked his emotions in tight. "Take off the noose."

She struggled with the rope. "He says he has proof that Zeb killed Nathan." She got the noose over her head. Her voice sounded rough and unused. "He says the police will get it if anything happens to him." She held out the rope. "I think it's a knife with Zeb's prints."

"Thank you." Briefly, his eyes met hers and held, and a crack opened in his emotional shield. It was too late, but he had to tell her anyway. *I love you. I'm sorry.* Hurriedly, he sealed the crack again and said aloud, "Take the rope with you and go away."

He didn't wait to see whether she obeyed. Jabez and Zeb were both close by, so she wasn't in danger of anything but embarrassment.

Or of watching an execution take place.

From overhead, the owl called again for haste. *You are what you are. Do you think she doesn't know?* Wind ripped the surface of the mound. Fat drops of rain spattered the lawn. Constantine picked up the mask, shaking off the water. "Now it's just you and me, Bon-Bon. What do you want?"

Bonnard got painfully to his feet. "I should charge you with assault." His voice shook; he paused and got it under control. "I wasn't going to hurt Marguerite. I'm a respectable citizen with only a few kinks. Entirely normal by Bayou Gavotte standards."

The time is ripe, the owl insisted.

Constantine had to finish this first. "I repeat: what do you want?"

"An exchange," Bonnard said. "Something I want for something you need."

"And that would be . . . ?"

"Your little brother," Bonnard said. "More than anything in the world, you want your little brother back."

"The brother I loved is dead," Constantine said coldly. "He can never be replaced. If you're referring to Zeb, why would I care about him one way or the other?"

"Because you want redemption." He said the word as if it were poison. "You think if you take care of Zeb, you'll be forgiven for the death of your other brother."

The floodgates of Constantine's emotions shook under the strain. How did the bastard know?

Bonnard put up a hand. "Oh, I'm not saying you fired the shot, but you killed him as surely as if you'd done the deed yourself. He needed to die so you could become a skinwalker."

"That's ridiculous!" Marguerite croaked from close by.

Skinwalker walker walker . . . The word echoed off countless surfaces in Constantine's mind, over and over, as it had done for years, always in his father's terrifying voice. The gates burst, but he wasn't a child anymore. He projected a ravening wolf, teeth and jaws, slavering fangs, advancing upon his nemesis.

Bonnard put up the other hand, backing away. "Tsk, Marguerite. You need to read up on Navajo lore. To become a skinwalker, one must sacrifice a family member—usually a sibling."

"There's no such thing as a skinwalker," Marguerite cried. "It's just superstition."

Constantine shot a glance at her; she'd hardly retreated at all. "Go *away*, Marguerite."

"Deny it all you like," Bonnard said, "but it was inevitable, whether you wanted it or not. You were born to be a skinwalker, and what you were given proves it—the fame, the fortune, the power." His voice quivered on that last word. He was as power hungry now as he'd been way back when.

The great horned owl was back on the tree, hovering silently above them at the tip of an enormous bough. *Circle in. Dive for the kill.*

Not with her here, Constantine retorted

Bonnard sneered. "You'll never be a good guy, Dufray, but if having a little brother makes you feel like one, you're welcome to him. He can move in with you. Be your little buddy."

"In exchange for what?"

"We finish what we started years ago. You teach me skinwalker magic. Everything you know."

"What?" Marguerite shrieked. "Don't you dare!"

"Beat it, girl!" Constantine yelled back.

She's not going to leave, the bird said. *And she's not the only one listening.*

And just like that, it all fell into place. He knew what to do. He faced his father. "What about the evidence Marguerite just mentioned?"

"Marguerite will say anything to get back in your bed. If I had any such evidence, would I admit to it? I'm a responsible citizen. I would never risk being an accessory to murder."

"No, you'd commit it yourself," Marguerite hollered. She'd retreated toward the edge of the plateau.

Constantine telepathed to her: *Keep talking, keep fighting me.* He focused on his father. "No deal without the evidence, Bon-Bon. I want my brother free and clear." *Say it all out loud. Everything he's done.*

"He'll never give him to you," Marguerite scoffed. "He wants control. He kills anyone who crosses him. He killed your grandfather and your innocent little brother."

Rage and relief spiraled together. "That clears the Navajo people."

Bon-Bon made a derisive snort.

"He killed your wife," Marguerite said. "He killed my roommate. He killed your fans."

"What a load of bull," Bon-Bon said, his mocking laughter echoing through the night.

Who else? Constantine telepathed.

Move in for the kill, the owl said. Its curved beak glinted in another flash of light. Constantine turned the mask in his hands, around and around. Raindrops shivered across the copper in the rising wind.

"He killed Dufray, your mother's husband," Marguerite proclaimed, arms upraised, a naked, avenging goddess with hazel eyes and honey-blond hair. "He killed the Indian he'd bribed to spread the word he was dead. He killed Nathan, and he was going to kill me."

"Anyone else?" Constantine asked, dancing now. Bonnard's eyes flicked back and forth between him and Marguerite.

"He killed Zeb's mother," Marguerite said. "He drugged Roy Lutsky, causing the accident that took her life."

The hair on Constantine's arms stood up. The beads rattled; the feathers shook. "You hear that list, Bon-Bon? No self-respecting skinwalker would bargain with such a freak."

"Then you won't get your brother at all, Dufray." Bonnard picked up his duffel bag. "He has no guts. He'll be stuck with me, at my beck and call, for ever and ever, amen." Electricity built in the sky, yearned toward the ground.

Constantine raised the mask. The bird spread its wings. *Now!*

"Like hell I will!" Zeb lunged over the crest of the mound. "You killed my mother. I'm going to kill *you!*"

Bonnard whirled, snarling.

"Stay back!" Constantine, too, lunged at Bonnard, but the bird got there first, a missile of wings and claws, driving them apart as the lightning struck.

CHAPTER TWENTY-ONE

Marguerite flew across the grass and knelt beside Constantine. She saw no aura at all. She ran her fingers over his face, bent her ear to his chest.

His heart beat back at her, strong and firm. *Oh God, thank God.* She kissed his forehead, his cheeks, his lips. He muttered, stretched and groaned, his aura pulsed into life, and he seemed almost to wake but then subsided. She lifted his head, pushing his wet, tangled hair back from his face. All the confusion that had crowded her at Ophelia's house had resolved into a single truth. "I love you," she said. "How could you believe I ever wanted to harm you? I've loved you for years." But he didn't hear her. Tears burned behind her eyes. "Thank you for saving my life."

She shivered in the windblown rain. They had to get out of the weather, get dry and safe. She heard distant shouts; maybe help was on the way.

Something was burning. She got up and glanced around. Zeb was nowhere to be seen. Al Bonnard lay flat on his back not far away. What if he, too, were alive? She crept reluctantly toward the motionless body, needing to know for sure. Then she realized where the burning smell came from. She gagged and swallowed it down, recoiling from the stench.

The tree creaked ominously above her head. A bat swooped from among the branches. The tree creaked again, louder . . .

Marguerite ran back to Constantine and grabbed his shoulders. "Help! Zeb! Anyone!" She wasn't strong enough to both lift and carry. She took ahold of his feet and tugged him away from the tree. "Wake up, damn it!" she sobbed, and heaved and dragged and heaved again.

A bough cracked, more bats dove; she hauled Constantine's helpless weight another yard and another. Suddenly Zeb was there, heaving Constantine's shoulders off the ground. Together they stumbled away from the tree. A massive branch of the oak crashed down, its base thudding across Al's body and its outermost branches quivering inches from where they stood.

They lowered Constantine to the ground, and Marguerite keeled onto her knees, her arms and shoulders shaking. Zeb limped away, toward the edge of the mound. She sat on the wet grass and lifted Constantine's head onto her lap, sheltering his face from the rain. He breathed, in and out, and so did she. At least they were both alive. The wind sighed softly over the grass.

Zeb appeared again, cradling something in his arms. "The lightning killed the owl. Is—is Constantine all right?"

"He's still unconscious," Marguerite said. "Are you okay?"

"I got thrown halfway down the hill, but I'm all right." Warily, he glanced around.

Her eyes went involuntarily in the direction of the huge oak bough. "Your father's under there."

"Is he dead? What's that smell?"

She tried to form the words. It turned out to be unnecessary.

"He got fried? And then crushed like a roach?" Zeb's voice shook a little. "Good. He got what he deserved." He laid the owl gently on the grass next to Constantine and shucked his T-shirt. He held it out. "Put this on. I asked my girlfriends to bring you some dry clothes, but right now they're calling Gideon O'Toole and helping Jabez fend off the reporters."

The media was here?

Oh, what the hell. After tonight, she could deal with anything, but at least she wouldn't have to face them naked. "Thanks," she said, moving Constantine's head gently off her lap.

Constantine groaned and opened his eyes. "Zeb okay?"

"Thank God you're awake." She stood, pulling the wet T-shirt over her head.

"I'm fine," Zeb said, adding a fervent, "Thank you."

"Bonnard dead?"

"Yes, he's dead," Marguerite said. The T-shirt stuck stubbornly to her skin, but it almost covered her butt.

"Thank you," Zeb said again.

"Mission 'complished." Constantine's voice was mildly slurred. "Damned bird. Still not sure what its plan was."

Oh, dear. "Constantine, your bird is dead, too," said Marguerite, pointing out the limp, scorched remains of the owl.

Constantine rolled slowly to the side and ran a gentle finger over the wing feathers, plastered together in the rain and wind. "A willing sacrifice. Damn, that can't be what it meant to do." A nightjar called plaintively from nearby, and a screech owl cried. "Maybe one day I'll get it right." He sighed and sat up, turning wearily to Zeb. "Where do you think he would have put that knife?"

"I'll find it," Zeb said. "I know all his hiding places. He was bullshitting you if he said it would be sent to the cops. He would never take that kind of risk." His eyes went to the massive limb under which his father lay. "I can't believe I'm finally free."

"I can't believe I have a little brother." Constantine stood, his aura shaky.

"I—I couldn't do it myself," Zeb said. "Mom said he had all this anger, and I should be kind and considerate, and then she was gone, and it got worse and worse, but I—"

Awkwardly, Constantine put an arm around Zeb and pulled him close. "Hey, there," he said. "It's over now."

Zeb shook violently, and his aura wept.

"Your mom couldn't have had a more loving son," Constantine said. "And I couldn't ask for a better brother."

Marguerite turned away, a huge lump in her throat. The skies let loose, and she walked to the edge of the mound, blending her tears with the rain.

~

Constantine went down one end of the mound to deal with Gideon and the media, while Zeb escorted Marguerite down the other and through the woods. She'd never seen Zeb's aura so relaxed and confident. They retrieved her wet clothes and shoes and rendezvoused with his girlfriends in the parking lot. Zeb and the girls went away to search for the missing knife, while Marguerite drove to Lavonia's.

For once, Lavonia had very little to say. After exclaiming at the news of Al's death, she listened in devastated silence to Marguerite's catalogue of Al's crimes. Afterward, she ran to the bathroom, was violently sick, and then huddled on the couch, wrapped in the lavender throw. "He was sleeping with Janie, too, wasn't he?"

"It looks that way," Marguerite said. "From what Zeb tells me, it was an on-and-off thing. Al had sex with her whenever he needed something, such as free concert tickets. He also gave her cookies to hand out at the concert the other night, but it's unclear whether she knew what she was doing, since only a few of them were likely laced with drugs. We think she freaked out and left town when she heard Nathan Bone was dead. She was involved in setting up a meeting between him and Al, so I guess she put two and two together and feared for her own life."

"Good riddance. She was causing issues within the coven, so we're better off without her." Lavonia lapsed into silence again. Marguerite made herbal tea and tried a couple of times to get her friend talking, or at least back to bed, but Lavonia just said, "You should go. I need to deal with this alone."

"Sure, but . . . are you all right?"

"Of course not," Lavonia snapped. "I've been sleeping with a serial killer! And now I'm—" Her aura flared hysterically, and she broke off, flapping a hand out from under the lavender throw. Determination smoothed her aura, but a chaos of other emotions seethed beneath it. She took a deep breath. "I'm wallowing in my anger. I want to be alone so I don't have to hold it in." She stood, speaking through clenched teeth. "I mean it. Go." But at the door, she softened. "Poor Zeb. How is he?"

"Relieved, I think." Taking concern for Zeb as a sign that Lavonia was already working her way up and out, Marguerite left. To her surprise, Reuben in his red Cadillac was parked behind her car.

"Escort duty," he said. "Powwow at the Cat."

But by the time they got to the Impractical Cat, Gideon and the police chief were on their way out. The lab in Al Bonnard's spare bedroom had yielded enough evidence, including spiked candies, to back up the sworn statements of Zeb, Marguerite, Jabez, and Constantine. The knife, which Zeb found below the bottom tray of a toolbox, proved to have plenty of blood on it but no prints at all. The police chief was inclined to arrest Zeb anyway, but a short, private talk with Lep—coupled, Marguerite thought, with a fierce little smile from Zelda—persuaded him to permanently change his mind.

Zeb and Constantine went to breakfast together the next day to discuss Zeb's immediate future. He departed with a girlfriend on each arm. Which left Marguerite alone with Constantine. He picked up a guitar and sat at one end of the couch, tuning the strings.

She tried to read him. Something was bothering him, but for once she couldn't figure him out—or maybe, after not pegging Al for a murderous lunatic, she'd lost her confidence. Up on the mound, she thought he'd telepathed that he loved her, but in all the chaos she might have been mistaken. Perhaps the uneasiness meant he still didn't believe or trust her. Most likely he never would. "I guess I should go," she said, rising from the couch.

"Zeb tells me you saved my life," Constantine said, his voice as awkward as his aura.

"Um, yeah, with his help," she said. "And you saved mine, so I guess we're even."

"No, we're not." Constantine picked a few melancholy notes. "Look, Marguerite, I'm sorry if you couldn't read me up there on the mound, but I had to corral my emotions. I didn't know whether I could handle Bonnard if I let anything affect me, and that included you."

"I understand," she said, twisting her hands together. "It's all right. I really should go." She eyed Lawless, who was curled up on a chair, looking very settled for the night.

"If that's what you want, I'll have Reuben take you home and keep the hounds off you." Sadness washed through his aura and echoed through the guitar strings. "But I was hoping we might start over. Start afresh."

"I don't see how that's possible," she said, struggling nevertheless with a surge of hope.

He rubbed his face. "I know. I was terrified when I first realized Bon-Bon was alive. All I could think of was that he would destroy anyone or anything I cared about. Short of kidnapping you, the only way to keep you safe was to drive you away. I guess I can't apologize enough to make it better, huh?"

That explained his discomfort. "I don't need an apology," she said. "I need to be trusted. I need to be believed."

"I do believe you," he said. So, at last, did his aura—shining through clear as clear. Her heart leapt with the joy of it.

"I know I have to become more trusting," he said. "As Ophelia puts it, love doesn't include emotional insurance."

"No," Marguerite said ruefully, "it sure doesn't."

"Now that Bonnard's dead and I know I'm not losing control of my mind, I'm ready to give it a try," Constantine said. "Actually, I'd say I'm desperate to give it a try." His lips twisted. "With you, if you'll let me."

She bit her lip, gazing up at him. "If I know I'm going to be believed, I won't have so much to hide." She wanted to throw herself into his arms and start anew right then and there, but the specter of Uncle Dan hung between them. "About my uncle—"

"You don't have to explain. He was a racist cop, but for all I know, he was a beloved uncle, too. It's none of my business. I know *you* mean well."

And she saw he meant every word of it. "You say that, but unless I tell you what happened, you'll always wonder." She crossed to the window.

He came up beside her, large and male and beautiful, his arm close but not quite brushing hers. She'd been right, that first day, to feel safe with him. "Then tell me," he said.

She took a deep breath. "My uncle was a sexual predator. From a very young age, I knew there was something wrong with him—I could see it in his aura. When I was eight years old, his attitude toward me changed. I knew he meant to do something scary, but I did my best to ignore it until one day he tried to get me alone. I refused. I told him I knew exactly what he was thinking, and that I would scream my head off and tell the whole world if he so much as touched me. That shocked the hell out of him. He played all innocent but backed off in a hurry.

"My little sister was born not long after that, and several years later, after my father died, my mom decided to move to Baton Rouge to be close to my aunt. I freaked out, because my sister can't read auras, and she's a shy little thing, and she would have been too scared to stop him. I warned my mom, but she always hated my aura-reading. She got offended, my sister got upset because she liked Uncle Dan, and my aunt wouldn't speak to me. I didn't know what to do. He'd never actually done anything to me. If I'd accused him, a suit for slander would have been the least of my problems. He might have had me harassed, even beaten. I was gearing up to go to a lawyer for advice when you threatened him. It was like a miracle. He went insane right before our eyes, and within a short time he killed himself.

"Al was right when he said I came here because of you, but it wasn't for revenge. It was to figure out if you really had sent those nightmares and, if I could find a way to say it, to thank you for saving my sister, and probably me as well."

Constantine blew out a long breath.

"I've loved you ever since, and I don't believe you're a skinwalker," Marguerite said. His aura shivered. Evidently, this had eaten at him for years, and maybe it always would. "But if you are one, you're the good kind."

The corners of his lips quirked up. "That's a new twist on the skinwalker legend. I'll try to be." He held out his hands and offered her his heart. "I love you, Marguerite. Can we start over?"

"Yes, please," she said, and stepped straight into his arms.

They held one another for a long while, talking about Constantine's childhood and how best to provide for Zeb. Later, in bed, their lovemaking was slow and sweet.

Afterward, the night's events played themselves through Marguerite's mind once again. "What about the owl? We should give it an honorable burial."

"Tomorrow," Constantine said, "on the mound where it died."

"That sounds perfect." She paused, suddenly sad. "Is your spirit guide dead, too? I mean, it's a spirit, so it can't really be dead, but is it gone?"

Constantine's mouth curled. "Are you kidding? It sacrificed one of its kind to save my life. I'll never hear the end of it."

"Oh, good." With a long, happy sigh, Marguerite snuggled down beside her lover and closed her eyes. A pair of powerful, protective wings settled over them as she drifted into sleep.

~

Constantine Dufray tightened his arm around Marguerite. *Thank you,* he told his spirit guide. *She truly is a treasure from the heavens.*

An unidentifiable tropical bird with brilliant feathers strutted through Constantine's mind and then was gone. The bird hadn't been able to resist that dig, but it wasn't in an I-told-you-so mood. It settled its feathers more comfortably over them. *Always and forever,* it said.

As usual, its cryptic utterance might have more than one meaning. Constantine had no control over the guide, but he intended to do his damnedest to keep Marguerite. Three days ago, he wouldn't have believed the woman existed who would sleep so easily and naturally in his arms, who would so readily accept the shelter of those wings. And, wonder of wonders, she read his every emotion. God, what freedom that gave him. No games, no pretense—he could just be himself.

He *did* have control of his emotions—he knew that now. He was still a vigilante—he had a mission to keep Bayou Gavotte safe—but he wouldn't harm his innocent fans. He laughed to himself. Most likely his new songs would have less violence and more peace and love, which didn't seem like such a crock anymore.

It's not easy to commit murder by lightning, he told the bird, *but we were almost in sync.*

We were perfectly *in sync,* the bird said. *That back-and-forth was part of getting it right. It always has been.*

Unbelievable.

We've come a long way, the bird said.

We? Purely out of habit, Constantine sent it a snarl. They'd so rarely gotten along smoothly, and now the damned guide wanted him to believe it was all part of the plan . . .

Oh, what the hell.

A very long way, he agreed.

ABOUT THE AUTHOR

Barbara Monajem spent most of her childhood on the west coast of Canada, a place she continues to feel deeply connected to, even as she's wandered and lived all over the world. After a year living in Oxford, England, which gave her an early taste for historical fiction, she spent many years in Montreal. She now lives in Georgia. She has a deep affection for New Orleans, which provided the inspiration for Bayou Gavotte, where her paranormal romances take place. In addition to her three paranormal romances, she is the author of seven Regency romance novellas and has won numerous awards for her work including the Maggie Award (Georgia Romance Writers), the Daphne du Maurier Award (Kiss of Death Chapter), and an EPIC e-Book Award.